The Old Country

The Old Country

SAM NORTH

SIMON &
SCHUSTER

London · New York · Sydney · Toronto

A CBS COMPANY

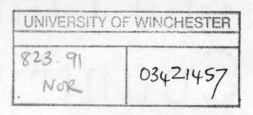
First published in Great Britain by Simon & Schuster UK Ltd, 2007
A CBS COMPANY

1 3 5 7 9 10 8 6 4 2

Simon & Schuster UK Ltd
Africa House
64–78 Kingsway
London WC2B 6AH

Simon & Schuster Australia
Sydney

A CIP catalogue record for this book is available from the British Library

ISB-13: 978-0-7432-7546-0
ISBN: 10: 0-7432-7546-2

Typeset in Bembo by M Rules
Printed and bound in Great Britain by
William Clowes Ltd, Beccles, Suffolk

For Jane Turnbull

Acknowledgements

I'd like to thank the following for their editorial help: Jane Turnbull, Rochelle Venables, Tom Williams, Jenny Bush, Matthew Hamilton.

Part One

Michael rose from his bed. A rug was strategically positioned so his feet wouldn't have to touch the bare floor. It was always colder in here than outside, summer or winter, yet he survived. One foot was put in front of the other. The heart still beat, even though anguish assailed it. And God bless his new hip – not a moment of pain from that direction.

How far down in the world he'd come, he thought. From the grandeur of Sitten Hall it had been a giddy drop, to here – a small, square livestock barn converted into a dwelling. Five years ago calves had given birth downstairs, while upstairs there'd been nothing but nests of spiders and out-of-date hay and straw, and it wasn't much different now: he felt like a beast, moving about inside these rough, damp walls.

He was grateful for it, though. The rent was zero, nothing. In lieu, he looked after old Mrs Mclean a bit. She liked to have someone about the place to walk her dog and feed it when she was away, listen to her reminiscing from time to time, help her move bits and pieces of furniture. He was a caretaker; that was his title now, which rather gave the lie to the junk mail he received addressed to 'Sir Michael Gough' or 'Lord Woodford'. The shame was that he couldn't do more for her. Sometimes she approached him with a screwdriver or a hammer and nail and a tale of some broken fitting or other but they both ended up staring at the plug or the lamp or the broken door, and he wouldn't have a clue.

He checked the dial on the electric storage heater. It was full on, as he'd thought. There was no reason for it to be different from the last time he'd looked. The fingertips of his right hand had turned white; the blood couldn't reach all the way. He already had on a thermal vest and pyjamas and now he swapped the pyjamas for two shirts and a jacket and the usual trousers and hundred per cent wool socks. The hair-dryer was plugged in, ready for duty. He switched it on, slipped the roaring nozzle under his vest, front and back, and waited until he could feel the hot air coming out at his neck. He moved it to between layers one and two. Lastly, he poked the nozzle up each sleeve for a good while before switching off and fixing the buttons at collar and cuff, knotting a tie also to help seal in the heat. That was better. These were tricks that anyone living in an enormous, unheated, draughty castle for most of his life would have had to have learned, he supposed.

He made his way to the bathroom, his feet thundering briefly on the section of bare flooring. He was waiting for further donations of old carpet to fill in the remaining gaps. The trick was to find the old Hessian-backed type and then lay it upside down to avoid the garish colours which so blighted the eye. It was more hard-wearing that way up and the Hessian surface was comforting: it reminded him of the changing rooms in his old prep school.

In the bathroom it was a job for a man of his size to squeeze around and face the sink without kicking the lavatory or sitting in the bath. When he managed, he leaned forward and peered into the mirror to check for any unsightly deterioration that might have occurred overnight. His face was heavy, square, a bit jowly, the eyes pale blue and bloodshot. His skin was too blistered, the nose too broken-veined, to escape the accusation – he'd drunk hundreds of gallons of alcohol during his life. The wrinkles were a fraction deeper than yesterday, no doubt. The curly hair was grey and wispy, lacking the springiness of his youth, and there was a pronounced circle of baldness. The moustache was speckled and brittle to the touch. There was nothing to be done about all this. The helpless march of time – sixty-seven years gone!

He leaned closer and spotted a long white hair which reached from the inside of his nostril almost to his lip; it must have grown there quick as a mushroom. He pinched it hard between his fingernails and pulled. His nose smarted. Other than that he was as presentable as any other boozy old gent fallen on hard times, he would guess. Thanks to his tweed jackets and his brogues lasting so well he still had the air of a man who was getting a bit of what he wanted, someone who might expect the world to fall in with his wishes from time to time. Which was an illusion, needless to say.

He pawed aside the curtain which guarded the stairs – every effort against the escape of heat from the living room had to be exerted at all times – and trudged down. At the bottom he fought his way past the second curtain, which was in fact an old bedspread nailed across. He felt the customary good cheer, the lift to his morale, seeing his lovely stuff, his very own possessions, piled to the ceiling on every side, waiting, like him, for the bigger and better home, the place fit for human habitation, which must be a possibility, around the corner, when his premium bond was chosen. Or maybe Patsy would take him back one day.

It was his habit to approach the window and run his finger down the metal strut which the plasterers had used to make the die-straight, upright corner in the wall that abutted the window sill. The dampness of the place meant there was always a seam of rust growing out of the white emulsion, and he could tell how much moisture was creeping into the room, and into his bones, by taking a sample. Today there was a decent residue. Autumn was underway. To head into winter was like diving into cold water.

The toss-pottery of this place! The wood-burning stove was

too small to fit a log in it. There was no damp-proof course. The barn had been built up against a bluff of stone on the uphill side, which meant that every drop of rain that found its way through the inch or two of soil was funnelled right into his wall, whereupon it climbed as high as it could and soaked right through the stone and into the room. And once in here it grew a layer of green mould on anything that happened to be made of leather – his shoes, his belts, the strapwork of his father's army uniform. And then it set out to find him, and attack his knee joint and make the bed sheets cling to his limbs . . . he could go on. Pity the poor person who actually had to live here for any length of time.

With a jolt he realised he himself had lived here for five years. And the two years before that he'd camped at Pinky's. He must get on. Create some luck for himself. Duck and weave.

He noticed he'd left his wallet out. It was on top of the blanket which covered the suitcase containing all his old papers from Sitten Hall, which in turn balanced on top of half a dozen broken dining-table chairs due for mending as soon as he had any money, underneath which was the box which held some of the tools from the old workshop.

He picked up the wallet. It was no good leaving it there. The whole system would come down around his ears if he did that. He went into the kitchen, which was built in the lean-to attached to one end of the barn, and stepped up to the crowded work surface. How did all this stuff get here? Pots and jars and cans . . . they sort of gathered. He pushed the bottles around until he found the right one. The labels being upside down always made him giddy. It was because they came from the pub: the landlord used the empties from the optics to fill with ullage for him, free of charge. It used to be sent back to the brewery to reclaim the tax but now the landlords threw it away, generally speaking, and Nicholas at the Plume of Feathers had agreed to put it to one side. Bless him for that, thought

Michael, as he poured himself a glass. Wait just a bit and a third fermentation worked on the dead yeast and put a bit more condition into it; still a weaker beer than the stuff you might buy from the pump but it was better than nothing. It hinted at the memory of being drunk.

Michael took his glassful and rooted among the cereal boxes, shaking each in turn until he found a morsel still left. It was Sunday, he didn't need to worry about food, but even so he liked to go through the motions. He shook out the tea towel printed with village scenes back in good old Woodford – the Whistle and Feather, cricket on the green, the old cider press – and tucked a corner of it into his collar. It did for a bib. He fixed it with the clothes peg and sat down.

After he'd finished breakfast he wandered through to the living room. He had a couple of hours in which to indulge his lonely pursuits. He uncovered Granny Banana's chair, the only piece of furniture which resisted having other possessions piled on top of it so it squatted, fatly, in a sort of deep, narrow trench. To watch television he sat properly in the seat, while to use the computer, as he was about to now, he perched on the arm and faced up to the old Tandy PC given to him by Natalia, complete with a compliment slip from the hotel she worked at sellotaped to the casing. It whirred into life, always a little cranky, but he knew its quirks and could get to where he wanted. While it ran through its procedures he leaned over the downstairs storage heater which still gave off heat. The wallpaper popped up – a photograph of his daughter Mattie and her son, Michael Junior. His contribution to the Gough heritage! It wasn't as great as it should be, but it made him proud. He went back to the screen, turned the keyboard upside down and shook out the crumbs from last night.

Miraculously he achieved online status first time around and went to check his eBay bids. He was still in front on the secondhand *Plants and Flowers Encyclopaedia*, which meant he'd probably overbid. The 1935 gold fob watch supposedly taken from an Italian soldier in the war, so the vendor had claimed, was way past his pathetically optimistic early offer; twenty-two people had trampled all over him in just one day, which was a bit insulting. Next he visited poshtotty.com to see if Green-eyed Girl was there but he'd confused his world clock. He quickly lost interest and scooted over to Poolsidechat where Biker Nut was always good for a laugh at this time of day.

Before he knew it, the morning had gone. He'd orbited the world twice and adventured with the brave and the bold in cyber space and it was time for Sunday lunch at his brother's house. He checked himself in the mirror in the little porch, half expecting to see that white nose hair grown back already, but no. He took off the tie, though; he didn't want Philip and Natalia to think he attached too much importance to their hospitality. Whereas, the sad fact was, it was his only real social life, and the one proper meal of the week – which was some-times, when they had other guests, dropped off here, a plateful covered in tin foil and driven over and put down for him as if he were a dog. Very welcome it was too. He always wolfed it down.

Before he went he nodded goodbye to his best friends, Computer and Telly. A shiver of guilt ran down his spine at the amount he'd spent online last year. He'd told Natalia he'd needed the money for liniment or prescriptions or birthday presents. Never mind; it wasn't the worst of crimes and he'd managed to stop now.

Escape From The Living Swamp, he thought as his new hip easily negotiated the doorstep and the ramshackle path to the parking area. The Land Rover waited for him. It was an incon-gruous vehicle, transplanted into Mrs Mclean's country garden. In Philip's farmyard it had looked the part; now it was a sorry reminder of how things had changed. He fingered the ignition keys regretfully. The engine was noisy, she always heard it and today, for once, he didn't want to talk to her. He started up and trickled past the main house, eyes glued to the latch on the front door. He saw it lift and the first inch or two of a gap widen; she was coming out. He put his foot down to get out of the gate before she managed actually to appear, and in his rear view mirror he saw her float out and raise an uncertain hand. Lovely as she was, and the widow of a dear old friend, none the less . . . not today, Josephine.

Bath, six miles.

Half an hour later he reached Sweetcombe Road and parked among the Vauxhall Astras and Ford Orions. He paused at the wrought-iron gate fronting number 16 and listened. No screaming – it was safe to enter.

For three years this four-bedroomed semi with garage had had its doors slammed, windows opened and closed, its electric cooker stuffed with meal after meal, carpet squares worn out, beds made and unmade almost continuously, by the unfeasibly young family of his brother Philip, aged sixty-three to his sixty-seven.

He felt a twinge of jealousy. His brother was nearly as old as he was, yet had a wife under forty, and *three* young children. Not to mention a home of his own. Philip had come down in the world also – this place would be valued at a fraction of what the farm had been worth – but none the less, he owned the ground under his feet.

Michael had his own key. It used to be the other way round: Philip had had a key to Sitten Hall in the good old days. Michael called out and went through to the kitchen, the warmest room in the house. Natalia greeted him and quickly shouted at the ceiling, 'Emma, David, Ben, come, your uncle is here.' He sat for a moment and watched her work on the roast potatoes. She wore the green dress with a big rust-coloured cardigan. Her coal-black hair was looped behind her ear and her slippers were trodden down at the heel; they slapped the floor tiles softly. At first the whole family had thought she must be as shy and self-effacing as she appeared, a slender figure who wished to be unobserved and to remain in the background, but they'd found out soon enough: she was forged out of iron, set in concrete foundations, and she caught bullets in her teeth. There was no question, she was in charge of them now. The children were her domain, Philip was her shadow, Michael was beholden to her, the hotel was under her thumb. Who could possibly, in a million years, have guessed that's how it would have turned out?

She put the usual cup of coffee in front of him and asked if he'd remembered his insulin injection. He replied that he had, but the truth was he couldn't have . . . he made a mental note to check.

There was a torrent of noise and the children tore in. Their shiny black hair bounced with health. The big, mournful eyes shared by all three of them were alive with intrigue as they threaded around the furniture chattering about something or other. They had their mother's translucent whiteness of skin. He liked the two boys perfectly well but always sought out his niece Emma, aged seven, not just because she was so pretty to look at but because the occasion of her birth was engraved on his memory and he took an almost parental interest in her. Seven years ago – how time had flown. He winced. And David, six years old. Ben, five. They were ever more vigorously chasing his own generation into their graves. Quite right too.

'Michael, is time,' whispered Natalia, nodding at the kitchen clock.

'So it is.' He rose to his feet, pushed the cup away, still half full. 'See you in a bit.'

He went outside, followed by the children. They liked travelling in the Land Rover, that was the reason for his popularity today. He opened the waist-high metalwork gates; one of them dragged unhelpfully on the ground and it felt like he might break it altogether. He couldn't help comparing them with the gates that had guarded the entrance to Sitten Hall. These . . . were paper thin and light as air. The curls of metal looked cheap and nasty and the black paint peeled from the patches of rust. Whereas, to push through the ones guarding the driveway to the old place, in the days when the Lodge was in use and the 'keeper' lived there, had been like trying to move through a dense thicket of ironwork that towered over your head. When the Lodge had become dilapidated the gates had stood permanently open and some years later they'd been lifted off their hinges, stolen.

He gathered the children and shepherded them across the road, then hoofed them into the back.

It was twenty minutes' drive to Greenaways. The route was familiar; he could measure its every yard. The whole town of Bath moved with increasing speed and liveliness, he thought. The name of the place, with its connotations of bath chairs and spa treatments, spoke of the old and infirm yet everyone seemed unaccountably younger every time he came – and there were more of them, in newer, faster cars than ever before. He was certain the queues at the traffic lights were longer. The reds showed for ever while the greens just blinked on for a few seconds. His foot was more often on the brake than on the accelerator. The young seethed around him. It seemed a non-sense, that the country's population was ageing. So, where were all these old people?

Once at Greenaways he parked and went to make himself known at reception before going back outside to wait. Natalia expected him to watch over her children at all times. He leaned against the Land Rover, his arms aching from the heavy steer-ing. The autumn sun, thin and sharp, warmed him a little. The vehicle jogged his back as the children moved randomly inside like flies in a jar. He could almost run and jump as they

did, with his new hip bedded in. He'd been told, though, that
the replacement would only last for twenty years; he should
take it easy, make it last. He had other medical worries. His
liver was calcified, there was a strange pattern which appeared
in the upper left-hand corner of his eyeline. It was the reason
he had a tendency to steer to the left, in order to look for it. It
was amazing that he was still allowed to drive, what with the
number of dents he'd put into this vehicle. Also, there was a
crop of polyps on his neck and chest which he'd been advised
could be got rid of by tying threads of cotton tightly around
them.

Jiggling the keys, he limped a pace or two to keep his knee
working and to escape the ear-splitting scream coming from
inside the Land Rover.

How much longer?

A minute later the Greenaways front door opened and two
male members of the nursing staff rolled Granny Banana down
the wheelchair ramp and trundled her over. She was ninety-
three, which made him feel young as a baby. She'd scrambled
through world wars one and two, witnessed the infestation of
radio and TV, the telephone, motorcars, air travel, the computer age. She'd seen the decline of the British Empire and the
triumph of Red Rum and here she was, a well-preserved, frail
relic of her era. A charming skeleton.

He received the usual puzzled stare – she didn't know who
he was. He opened the passenger door; that was his job.
'Sunday lunch, Ma!' he called into her ear just to let her know
which way up she was.

Sometimes he wondered how often he and his brother
would meet if it weren't for old Banana cementing them
together. Banana, so called because of the curve of her spine.
Well, it had become even more bent during the last five years.
It was like she'd been left in the sun and had shrunk, the shape
become more accentuated.

The two young men lifted her easily into the Land Rover. She was as thin and crisp and fresh as a bit of dry-cleaning. He went to shut the door but something stopped it. The door thudded and bounced open. God, no – had he caught a stray ankle, dangling down? Thankfully it was only her coat. The second time it shut. He gave an extra push to make sure.

Dear old lady, he thought as they loaded her wheelchair into the back. The children separated like a shoal of fish, squealing and pushing to make room for the cumbersome appliance. The Greenaways staff headed off. There was something complicit, secretive, in the way they went, walking in step, slightly turned towards each other, and he wondered what they knew that he didn't, about his mother. What were they up to? Selling her silver-backed hairbrushes on eBay, probably.

At last he was in the driving seat, all aboard, ready for the off. He started up and, for what seemed like half an hour, executed a six-point turn, heaving on the wheel this way and that. He glanced over at his mother as he dribbled the vehicle down the immaculately tended driveway. She was slumped in the corner. He caught her blinking. She had chicken's eyelids, he thought; they came from the bottom upwards, he was sure. What a marvel of medical science was Granny Banana! She'd died twice already but had been pulled back each time to face the music again. It was why the cost of the health service had shot up, thought Michael. Those who used its precious resources should, by rights, have died on their first go round the system. Every time the National Health saved a life it created another more complicated and expensive piece of work for itself further down the line. It had kept Granny Banana going all right – more of this drug, less of that one, another op – and had given her many more Sunday lunches with her two elderly sons, Philip and Michael, and their families. Hurrah.

There were no cars coming; Michael swung onto the main road. He could handle this sticky-porridge gear shift. He was

cutting the mustard in every way. He'd mastered the new tech-
nologies, he could click wherever and whatever he wanted,
plus there was a crowd of young Goughs, his nephews and
niece, bouncing off the sides and making a racket in the back,
not forgetting his own lovely grown-up daughter and her child,
growing up in Bristol, not far off, while up the other end of the
scale there was his mother here, the old Banana, still breathing – yes, past, present and future going strong, rubbing along
together. Take away their money and their stately, it still wasn't
easy to knock the Gough family off their perch! He was lifted
by a rare sense of pride and wellbeing which made him want to
floor the accelerator and take off. The centrifugal force dragged
at the vehicle's occupants. The children screamed and laughed
and fell in a heap. Michael leaned into the corner and clung to
the wheel, driving this old farm beast. He was optimistic, glee-
ful even, after that imaginary visit just now from his one solitary
grandchild, salvaged from the wreck of Mattie's placenta. They
were all mixed up in a human soup of a family, and there might
be even more: Philip had a young enough wife. So, onwards,
Goughs. Keep going! He curled his fist, ready to punch the air.
Fight back! Climb again!

Except, now, there was a dull report and a sudden breeze as
the passenger door flew open. Out of the corner of his eye he
saw his mother upend and fall out.

In the same instant he stamped – twice, thrice – trying to
find the brake, while uttering a cry of panic and disbelief.
Within thirty yards he'd disentangled his foot from the pedals
and brought the vehicle to a halt, wincing at the screams of
complaint as the Land Rover bucked the children off their
seats. He climbed out, feeling utter dread. Three weak-kneed
steps later he'd rounded the side of the Land Rover. He could
see Granny now – she looked like that same bit of dry-cleaning,
but someone had dropped it in the road. A queue of cars
waited behind her. Someone was getting out to help.

He walked forwards, each footstep full of portent. She lay utterly still, and looked presentable apart from a scuff mark on the shoulder of her coat. He heard the click of the Land Rover's back door and he knew the children were out. Should they see this? No. But they were too quick; he found he couldn't shoo them back. He went to Banana's side. Someone else, a stranger, was asking him something. More people surrounded them. He heard a voice talking into a mobile phone. Granny's mouth was moving; she wanted to say something. Michael knelt close to her but couldn't make it out. If only everyone would leave them alone. He knew that he himself was saying things, waving his arms, but didn't quite know what was what. The situation was running away from him.

Minutes later sirens wailed and became louder before stopping abruptly. The homely shape of an ambulance drew up, and two police cars. Michael and the children were moved to one side so the medics could get to work. Traffic was directed around the incident; Michael himself was asked to move the Land Rover onto the verge. The policeman's voice seemed to come from a long way off. The next he knew, he and the children were in the back of the ambulance. Someone was calling Philip and Natalia on the phone. He repeated the number for them twice. The paramedics were in and out of his vision in a confusion of green uniforms. The space was cramped, they bumped into one another. The one in charge had bushy red hair. They were talking to each other and not to him any more. He could tell from their tone of voice that things weren't going well. There was a hurt look in their eyes.

He found himself leaning over Banana, who had an oxygen mask covering her nose and mouth. Yet underneath, through the plastic, her lips were moving. 'She's trying to say something,' he said. Someone lifted off the mask. Once more he ducked closer to try and catch what it was. The vehicle swayed, pulled at the corners. The siren cut through any hope of hearing her.

His nephews and niece sat on the other bunk, dead quiet as instructed, their eyes glassy with excitement at riding in the ambulance. Caught up in the whirl and fury of the accident, they were fearful. They waited there, leaning against the tilt of the vehicle, smiling dutifully at the kindness of the paramedics. Granny Banana lolled on the bunk, empty of life. Everyone in the vehicle knew. Her heartbeat had stopped, the valves would be empty of blood, immobile. The oxygen wouldn't be carried any more from her lungs to her muscles. Her mouth was dead still, all that swallowing machinery was useless now; it didn't work. Her fluid levels had dropped, her blood had spilt internally, seeped away from the major organs. The kidneys couldn't filter out the dirt and excess water when the blood pressure had dropped too low, and the kidneys themselves had failed from lack of oxygen. Death had occurred. The layers and layers of Granny Banana's muscles would be shrinking, even now.

Sixth of October – mark this day, thought Michael grimly, and the hour: twelve forty-five. Her time of death. Even the National Health Service would have run out of tricks. End of story.

The news travelled fast via telephone. First to hear was Natalia, who presided over a lunch that would never happen. When Michael rang her from the hospital it was like a series of tumblers spun in her head, to unlock certain arrangements and add more tasks to the list. The food mustn't be wasted. The chicken would cool down and go in the fridge. The roast potatoes could be chopped and fried to go with eggs at breakfast time. The broad beans and broccoli were put into the blender to make soup even as the fridge door shut on the potatoes and the phone was in her other hand; she was asking if her shifts at the hotel could be altered to cope with a funeral without it being allowed to eat into her earnings. The funeral itself would have to be the cheapest available.

The next task was to tell her husband.

Philip was in his 'office' – which was in fact the garage – leaning over the sort of bench that did for a table, asleep on his folded arms. He awoke with a start to hear his name spoken in his wife's quiet, shy voice. And she was touching him, which was unusual, rubbing a small circle on his shoulder. She did so many things all at the same time that it often looked like she had three pairs of hands but it was seldom he felt one of them anywhere on his person. 'Philip?' she said.

'Hmm?'

'I'm very sorry, your mother is dead. Michael is ringing just now.'

It took a moment of blank nothingness before Philip could sort out the whole idea. 'What?'

'Your mother is dead,' repeated Natalia, almost in a whisper. 'She fell down. In the road. I am so sorry.' She stayed for a while, digging that hole in his shoulder, while he hummed and hahed and repeated, 'Poor Ma.' He rose to his feet and circled the tools and DIY paraphernalia, leaning on three fingers here, or with an elbow against the wall there. 'You want for a while to be alone?' she said. 'Come and find me when you ever want.' She withdrew as soon as was decent; the door clicked shut.

Philip sat down again and tried to face up to the news. It was unexpected. It must be sad, yet he couldn't feel that. He himself, an old father to young children, was overburdened with life springing up underfoot, even the plants growing in the garden seemed like an unwarranted intrusion. The prospect of anyone dying and tipping the balance the other way was to be welcomed. A small corner of his mind emptied of duty, of care, of memories of his mother, only to be immediately flooded by a million other anxieties. He began to stand up but the board across the old toilet which comprised his office chair tilted and set him off balance. He recovered and stood there. She'd fallen, Banana gone? He listened, in the welcome inertia and silence of this block-built garage, and wondered where the children were, if they knew.

Patsy, Michael's ex-wife, was leaving the house of one of her music pupils in Frome when her mobile trilled and she heard his unmistakable voice. That was more of a shock than anything. Banana dead, yes, all right, she'd died before. But Michael's dear old voice! A powerful nostalgic love was conjured in her breast; it lodged there and she had to lean against her beloved Renault Clio while she tried to hold onto it. She took a breath while she listened to him recount the circumstances of the accident and she took her turn in giving her condolences. She told him he mustn't blame himself. Half a minute later she was driving back home to Sitten Hall, where she still lived in the apartment left to them after they'd gifted the house and grounds to the National Trust. Memories of Granny appeared like clips from home movies of a life long since gone. Granny Banana eating at the table, always the same noise of sugar crunching between her teeth while her slightly overshot lower jaw moved up and down. The box of pills that she'd stirred with her forefinger, chasing the brightly coloured tablets around and muttering under her breath. The nonsensical things she'd say: leaning forward at the family dinner and asking, 'Was it Cheltenham?' when no one had been talking about Cheltenham.

Patsy changed gear, deftly, and found herself going faster, what with the excitement of the old lady's death. It had been Granny Banana who'd first called her The Tall Woman. She'd had so much to do with her, and for so many years, and had held her in such affection always. She couldn't have done better for a mother-in-law.

When she reached the entrance to Sitten Hall – derelict lodge house, oak tree, iron railings, gates missing – she could picture Banana easily, right here, dressed in two coats and a Puffa jacket, lifting her walking stick to wave, the little dog at her ankles . . .

Mattie heard the news from her father while she was sitting on the living room floor of her flat in Bristol. She was tall and big-boned like her mother but from somewhere else she'd got the very strong, black hair. Dimples creased her cheeks like an echo of her smile, and a matching set of little dents also were to be found each side of her nose. Her skin was more of an olive hue than that of her parents but she had her father's blue eyes, without the broken veins. She was alone except for Michael Junior, her seven-year-old son, who played nearby but out of sight, having ignored the plastic figure of Robin Hood which she now twirled idly in her fingers. She could hear the sound of arrows being fired – a 'paaa!' noise, followed by the 'shhh-toof!' of them landing in the enemy's chest and then the 'Ughh' of the man dying. Her son was in his own world, as was so often required of him. She listened as her father told her of Granny Banana's death, and felt the same clench of anxiety as when she read those *Daily Mail* stories, spread across two, three, pages revealing how the gift of life could be taken away quickly and arbitrarily. When she'd finished talking to her father she looked down at her wrist: quite strong-boned, used to hauling recalcitrant ponies to a halt in her childhood, but around it was Granny's bracelet that had been handed down to her on her wedding day. It had been given to Granny Banana by a strange man, and Mattie had always wanted to meet him. She knew only part of the story: as a child this man had been evacuated to Sitten Hall during the war, and Banana had been kind to him. He'd grown up and become rich and he'd remembered her, sent this bracelet which now was Mattie's – she who wasn't the kindest of people after all. But maybe she

would inherit kindness now. Sometime later, she pegged her
dead-straight, jet-black hair behind her ear and told her son
Michael Junior of his great-grandmother's death, and when
Simon came home from the Institute she told him also. The
news flattened their week, knocked everything else out of the
diary. Simon wondered, as he ate his pasta bake, if there was
even a small amount of money coming to them. Mattie said
that the bracelet was everything.

Natalia and Philip's children guiltily enjoyed the excitement
of being brought home in a police car that afternoon. They
were told that allowances must be made for their father – he
was shocked, grieving. But he appeared as usual to make his
Sunday afternoon tour of the house, testing each light switch,
looking up to the ceiling to see if the bulb worked.

The children suspended all games and lounged in the sitting
room, whispering among themselves about what was going to
happen next. They each told the others what they remembered
of the accident. Emma had been the first to arrive at the scene.
She'd run, whereas her brothers had walked, and warily. She'd
caught up with Uncle Michael just as he was bending to touch
Granny Banana on the shoulder. Her eye had been drawn
quickest to the bright red colour: blood was trickling from
Granny's ear. She'd crouched down and told Uncle Michael
not to move the patient – she knew, from playing *Theme
Hospital*, that blood in the ear meant a head injury. She'd even
picked up Granny's wrist and searched for a pulse. Granny
Banana had been her second real-life patient. David had been
the first when he'd shut his finger in the door.

David recounted how he'd seen most of the accident, even
though he'd stopped short of the knot of people surrounding
Granny, after he'd felt the fear in his stomach. He remembered
the sweets Granny Banana always used to give them. He felt
bad about that – only thinking about the sweets. Emma told
him not to worry.

Ben, the youngest, claimed to have done better than David: he'd pushed through all the people surrounding the scene of the accident and had stood at Emma's shoulder and seen everything, even the blood. It wasn't meant to be there; what should have been on the inside of her skin had somehow got to the outside and there she was, lying on her side. It was like the carton of milk that had dropped on the kitchen floor yesterday. Granny had been broken, she'd spilt.

That same evening, Sweetcombe Road was unusually quiet, out of respect it seemed, for the dead woman who'd visited every other Sunday. Not a door or window opened. No music played. There was a blissful absence of hammering from the DIY enthusiasts. There weren't the usual cries of children in the back gardens. Cars moved slowly.

Michael's footsteps broke the silence.

It was strange how a few hours had changed everything, he thought. His right ear was still uncomfortable from pressing the phone receiver against it all afternoon. He'd had to shift boxes and boxes of stuff to uncover the built-in wardrobe and clear enough space around it to open the doors. All that work, just so he could find his one dark suit. A moth had flown out from behind the lapel and he'd chased it with unreasonable anger, swatting at it all the way round the room. He supposed that grief was to blame. The suit, when he'd put it on, was unfamiliar, tight across his shoulders and somehow catching at his knees. Then he'd driven here. Arrangements needed to be discussed.

He noticed the liveried funeral director's car parked outside Philip and Natalia's house. Drew and Sons. He checked the knot of his tie and tried to button his jacket. He decided not to use his own key but to press the bell instead. It was only polite. But even as he reached out, the door opened of its own accord

and there was Mr Drew himself, obviously – a thin, short man
with spectacles who held his chin in the air, accompanied by a
junior maybe, a plump youth who hung back, looking in
exactly the opposite direction, at the ground. Natalia was there
also. She hadn't changed into mourning, Michael noticed. She
was just the same unkempt mother of three stroke hotel man-
ager stroke force of nature as on any Sunday evening, which
showed a certain lack of respect, he thought. There was no sign
of Philip, but that was to be expected. Michael himself understood the attraction of the garage, a corner which no one else
wanted, a domain which his brother might occupy alone.

Michael shifted up a step into the porch, shook Mr Drew's
hand and said hello, but the other chap said goodbye. Michael
was confused – was he going deaf? This was the very man he'd
thought he was coming here to meet. The arrangements?! He
surreptitiously checked his watch and found he wasn't late. He
was five minutes early.

The next thing he knew, the undertakers had gone. The
door closed. He was in the house; they were not. What had
happened to the meeting? He wanted to ask Natalia but this
polite, sympathetic conversation they were having didn't allow
it.

'So sorry Michael,' she was saying.

'Thank you Natalia. Bad day. Yes.'

'We all have to say, just we are sad, I think.'

'I know. You're right. No getting round it.'

He followed her into the sitting room which overlooked
the small square of garden at the back of the house, and in
here – a shock to the system – lay the coffin, on trestles. Was
Granny Banana, the body, inside it . . . already? All systems
stopped. It seemed indecently quick. 'She's here?' He was confused; it even occurred to him that he might have missed out a
day somewhere along the line.

'Yes, is cheaper,' said Natalia, picking up children's toys and folding a towel under her arm, 'to have her here and not at their . . . building. And more nice, I think?'

'Of course . . .' Michael didn't want to appear difficult. The image sprang to mind of nails hammered home, of woodwork only inches from one's nose. For a moment he couldn't carry on the conversation; he tried to swallow but didn't manage that either. It defied belief – she'd been so quickly transformed from his mother, this morning, into a corpse in the living room, this evening. Her death had been expected for so long and there'd been so many false alarms that it had seemed impossible it would ever happen. Yet Granny Banana, his dear old mother, was no longer. This wooden box contained only the idea of her, and the physical remains. A memory came back to him: how she'd sat on the picnic rug, always so neat and organised . . . the slight leftward sway as she tucked her legs under her. She'd liked picnics.

The lid had been nailed down, yes, and the coffin was a big brown lump of furniture like a prop out of a horror film. Natalia was saying something but her accent and this emotional disturbance meant it was difficult to understand. He followed, trying to catch up, but it broke his heart to trip over the sight of the old fan heater which had accompanied his mother everywhere, almost as old as she was, sitting there in the armchair, cord wrapped around it, ready to be put out for the Sunday lunch. It ought to be buried with her. All their conversations had been accompanied by the gentle background sigh of that heater. He would take it with him, give it a home.

When he surfaced from this train of thought, Natalia was looking at him expectantly while pairing up comically tiny pairs of socks. He felt this might be his cue and he asked, 'Why have the undertakers gone? I thought we were going to talk about . . . things.'

'Not a worry, all done,' said Natalia.

'Hmmm? I thought . . .'

'Cremation Tuesday, the morning,' Natalia went on. 'So we keep it here until then. Avoid the charge.'

'Cremation? But in her will . . .'

'Then on Saturday, memorial service,' interrupted Natalia. 'At the hotel. I asked the owners and they were kind, they say yes, for us to do that.'

Michael stared at Natalia – so young, years and years left in her. All her muscles and joints working away, her face smooth and white as a bar of soap. Light of step. Hailing from a country only just returned to Europe, far to the east, somewhere fierce and new-but-old. Poland, if he remembered correctly. That cleaning job at the hotel – she'd taken it by the scruff of the neck and transformed it into a managerial position.

Whereas his mother was a lifeless, dried-out stick who couldn't speak up for herself, shut in a wooden box.

'In her will,' repeated Michael, 'she stipulated that she should be taken back to Sitten Hall.'

'Yes. I talk 'bout what she want with Drew and Sons. The professionals. An' Philip. They say, is impossible.' She gave her slight smile, which Michael was never sure about. She smiled when she refused him another whisky.

'I thought you could be buried anywhere nowadays, if you get permission.'

'We don' have permission, the National Trust has not given.'

'We haven't asked them. Have we?'

'No, but . . .'

'Well, we should, don't you think? She wrote a special instruction for us. Sitten Hall was where she lived. For years and years. She brought up me and Philip there. Sprocket was her favourite dog. Surely it behoves us, as her family, to—'

'But the professionals, you know? They said to me that. She was writing something not allowed in her will.'

'Where is Philip?'

'His office.'

'I see.' Michael felt his ears move up and down as he swallowed. A spate of anger threatened. This was ridiculous. 'Well, can we talk about it?' He watched her pale, smooth face for any sign she might give way.

'I would like to agree, like you.' Her voice was even quieter and more apologetic and she looked as if she was going to disappear with shyness. 'But anyway, is the cost, Michael.'

His shoulders sagged. There it was, the final blow. Money. Michael had none, Philip neither. Only Natalia actually earned any and she had none to spare, not least because she paid off Michael's credit card from time to time. 'The cost . . .' Natalia's words beat around Michael's brow. Guilt surged in his breast. Here he was, the penniless older brother, standing up on his hind legs and bleating about doing this or that while having no resources of his own. He was ashamed. Any pennies he needed had to be tugged from Natalia's pockets; sometimes he'd wished she'd lose her job and become destitute just to escape the prospect of another humiliating call to ask her for help.

'Think about how much,' said Natalia in her funny, self-effacing voice, although, as they'd found out by now, her backbone and her brain cells and her willpower had all been welded together into one child-loving, forward-moving, money-saving, husband-keeping, career-building, human workhorse. 'Transplant all the way back,' she said, 'the miles to Wiltshire. The service there, we have to pay for a room, or something like that. But my hotel have said the function room is without cost. And we can plant a tree. A tree, just like she says, but in the grounds of my hotel. Less money by miles. Close for visits. Is that all right, Michael? I know is not what she wants best, but . . .'

Was there no end to these miniature socks she was plucking out of the bag? He shook his head. 'A funeral is a once-in-a-lifetime thing, for heaven's sake. I'm quite happy to go to the bank and ask for a loan. She must have left some bit of money.'

'She still is under a tree,' answered Natalia very quietly. 'That is what she wanted, just is a different tree. Hmm?'

'A different tree,' murmured Michael. He supposed he should not expect Natalia to understand how much old Quercus meant, why Banana had chosen it.

'The cremation is Tuesday,' whispered Natalia and carried off her socks to wherever they must go.

Michael was left alone. He rested the tips of his fingers on the coffin. He knew how cheap this type of pine was. The handles glittered optimistically but were made of plastic sprayed with gold paint.

There were slips of paper resting there which he picked up. Doctor's certificates. Her name was written down – a pity they hadn't managed to put in Banana. No one would have called her Lady Edith Gough. The unknown hands of the professionals, consigning her to her grave . . . No, not a grave, but the incinerator, like a piece of rubbish.

The disbelief returned. She'd left clear, written instructions! Surely it wasn't too much to ask that some effort be made to fulfil them. No one had even rung the National Trust. And as for the cost, there were ways of doing things cheaply. There was no need for a hearse, they could fold the seats down in the Subaru. He should telephone Drew and Sons right away and tell them that he, Michael, was head of this family, not bloody Natalia, and there was no way he was going to allow Banana to be cremated. Instead they would take her back to Sitten Hall and bury her alongside her favourite terrier Sprocket, under old Quercus, the giant oak that guarded the entrance to their ancestral home.

The next morning was, for Michael, like crossing the Sahara desert: a barren and thirsty place, and hard work. The phone was up to his ear, down again, up to his ear, down. It was still greasy and familiar from the previous afternoon, but there could be no delay.

'Pinky?' He could imagine his friend's plump neck swelling over the clerical collar and the flutter of his hands.

'Michael, how are you bearing up?'

'Fair. But wanting to know, can I count on you to do the funeral?'

'I'd be insulted if you hadn't asked.' The older he got, the more Pinky sounded as if he had to get the sentences out quickly before he collapsed, too breathless, every word a last gasp.

'It will be at Sitten Hall.'

'Naturally. Are we going to tip her into the vault. Is there room? I presume yes.'

'No, remember, the tree, she asked to be buried under Quercus.'

'Ah . . . yes. The tree. The dog. Sprocket, and all that. Well, these days that will be achievable. I presume. Bear in mind Michael, that you take the lovely church out of it, and it loses spiritual gravitas.'

'I know, I agree Pinks, but, it's what she wanted. And perhaps it gains something, I don't know, a kind of outdoorsy charm.'

'You can find *outdoorsy charm* at any common or garden picnic. But not spiritual gravitas. The church is made for these things.'

'Pinky my dear, you don't need to tell me. I love all your costumes.'

'Well. Whatever. Name the day and I'll drop everything. The tree, the dog, whatever. I'll make it count.'

'Not quite sure about the details yet. Can I call you?'

'Old friend, I am yours. Wherever, whenever. As soon as you've got your lines straight and tied off.'

'Pinky, in a while. Thank you for your stalwart support.'

'Back at you, Michael. As ever.'

Michael set the phone back in the cradle, but only for a

moment. When he was sure he could remember the number he picked it up again. The earpiece would make a dent in his head, the amount of time he was spending on these requests.

The other end answered. 'Gina?' he asked. She sounded different.

'Hullo?'

'It's Michael.'

'Michael, I got the news when I saw Patsy yesterday. I was so sorry to hear. Granny Banana was such a special presence. I think of her every time I walk past the wartime exhibit and see that photograph, you know, and that account of her contribution to—'

'Thank you so much, yes, it's a sad time.'

'How are you doing? How can I help?'

'I was after getting the arrangements sorted out.' He gripped the handset more tightly.

'Of course. Tell me what's what.'

'Gina, I'm calling you in your official capacity, asking permission to bury her at Sitten Hall, as per her last will and testament.'

'That's fine, of course it is. This is her final resting place, we've always known that. We can cope, whichever day you choose.'

'Were you aware . . . did you know about the arrangements that we put in place? I mean . . . before we . . . before I left.'

'Yes. That's all fine, Michael. Really.'

He felt a wave of relief. This was easy. Natalia please note, he thought. Everyone was saying yes left right and centre. All it took was a bit of determination. People were good, and kind, they wanted to do the right thing. He was allowed to be a touch annoyed with Natalia. She hadn't made an inch of effort. And yes, there would be an additional cost, but . . . he'd lost track, now, of what Gina was talking about. Her voice was like a fly buzzing in his ear.

'. . . the vault,' she was saying, 'if there is one space left. We will need to arrange to open it up, though, and that might require . . . well, what is it, concrete? Will you need some kind of machinery to get into it?'

A cold sweat broke out on Michael's brow. 'No, not the vault. I know she has her place there, but she wrote in her will what she wanted.'

'Oh, I'm sorry, I didn't know. What did she want?'

'It's a bit different . . .'

'What was it?'

'D'you remember her dog, Sprocket?'

'Yes, I do . . .'

'And you remember where I buried Sprocket, under old Quercus, at the end of the drive? She rather wanted to be buried there, if that's all right.' There was silence at the other end. Michael waited. He could practically hear the wretched Gina woman thinking. Was she worried about having to close off the driveway to visitors? 'Pinky's agreed to conduct the service,' he added hopefully.

'That is the sweetest thing,' said Gina eventually, 'that she wanted to be buried with her dog. How typical of her.'

'To cause a fuss you mean?'

'No, just to . . . oh I don't know, say exactly what she wanted. She was eccentric, of course, we all knew that, but there was always a meaning to what she did, always a kindness, a desire to—'

'So,' interrupted Michael, slightly feverish in his desire to roll straight over the hesitation he could hear in Gina's voice now, 'can I go ahead and arrange transport et cetera? We need to move quite quickly.'

'Michael, I want to say yes, and I hope I can say yes, but I feel duty bound to ask the Trust about this, first.'

'Queen Anne's Gate?'

'The regional office will be able to give me an answer, I

think. Let me phone them, just to make sure, and I'll call you back.'

'Thank you Gina.' He put the phone down, wearily. He wasn't accustomed to this kind of slog. Why was he going to such trouble, he who could hardly be persuaded to go an inch out of his way, for anyone? It was because he was ashamed, he realised. To be so incapable, and for his dead mother to witness it from beyond the grave, was forcing him to swim through treacle, to climb sand-dunes.

The truth was, he didn't have time to wait for Gina to start winding up the Trust's giant cogs. Today was Monday; he had until tomorrow to throw a spanner in the works. He'd better get hold of Drew and put off the cremation otherwise there'd be a fight over possession of the coffin at the very jaws of the furnace, or the bonfire, or whatever they used. He picked up the phone again but then put it back down in order to take a moment and rehearse what he might say. He mumbled out loud like a madman, 'Mr Drew, sorry to put you out, but we, the family, have had a change of heart . . .'

No. It wasn't any good trying to pull the wool over their eyes, pretending there hadn't been a falling out. After all, Natalia must have written out a cheque already. He must tell the truth. 'Mr Drew,' he practised, 'Natalia might be my sister-in-law, but . . .'

He stopped. Perhaps he shouldn't mention Natalia. He and Philip were the blood relatives, Granny's sons no less. He tried again. 'Mr Drew, my brother and I are joint next of kin, but we have had a disagreement with his wife . . .'

Instinctively, Michael knew that he must not do this over the phone. He needed to see the whites of the man's eyes. He should drive into Bath and visit their offices. Granny's fate, it seemed, lay in the hands of Mr Drew. Which was odd. He checked his watch: ten fifteen a.m. 'Not bad eh, Natalia,' he murmured, 'almost . . . managed to sort out the whole thing in an hour. The Goughs can move fast when they want to.' He was gaining ground on Natalia. The old empire spirit had come into sway. Fairness, and industry, and organisation. The bloodline, his genes, stood him in good stead.

By six p.m. on the same day Michael had returned from his meeting with the undertakers having won a stay of execution exactly as he'd hoped. The next annoyance was to have to hurry back, so he could answer the door to Curly, from Cribb's House Clearances.

'It's a bit piled up, but come in and have a look,' said Michael. Curly carried a clipboard and was expansive, avuncular. His generous stomach, buttoned into a checked jacket, stood out as if it were on offer to anyone who might want to take it off him, as a token of his affection. 'Oh, I'm sure we can see what's what,' he said, brought to a halt just inside the door and standing in the few square feet of space left. 'Is it . . . all of it you're looking to get rid of, or . . .'

'I have to raise the money tonight. I must attend this meeting with my sister-in-law, you understand, with the actual cash in my hand.' He clenched a fist dramatically. 'Everything must go.' He edged down the corridor between the piles of stuff, towards the kitchen, in order to allow Curly to step in. 'Time is of the essence.'

'I understand, sir. Then without delay perhaps we ought to start with the most valuable things, in your opinion, and then work our way down the scale, and then we can arrive at an appropriate advance for you.' While he spoke he was already fingering the half dozen walking sticks that leaned into the corner by the door.

'Yes, why not.' Michael strained forwards. 'But not that one!' he exclaimed, pointing at the stick, 'not the one with the silver top. Nor the greyhound, that's ivory, a lovely example. See his pin-prick eyes? That one, yes, we can sell that one. Ah . . .

believe it or not, sorry, that's bakelite, the handle. Very unusual.
I'd like to keep it. If I can. This one can go.'

'So . . . one home-made, hazel walking stick.'

'Yes. Off it goes.'

'I've written it down. But the most valuable things? Jewellery,
heirlooms, any of that kind of thing, high value items? That's how
we'll do it, from the top down, until we're through.'

'Hold on, hold on. Grandpappy made that stick. Can't
really . . . it better be kept, I think.'

'Right.'

'I am sorry. That wasn't a good start.'

'No, you're the boss.'

An hour later, Michael had gone through so much stuff,
and was sweating with discomfort and beginning to ramble. He
didn't seem able to talk in sentences any more. He checked his
watch. Time was running out. He was due to leave for the
meeting with Philip and Natalia.

Curly rescued him. 'You know what, Sir Michael? The trouble we're facing, is that you don't want to sell anything. Isn't
that true?'

'I . . . suppose it is.' Michael sagged.

'Can I make a suggestion?'

'By all means,'

'When do you meet your sister-in-law?'

'I'm due round there in . . . an hour's time. God!'

'And you need the money in your pocket.'

'I do, yes.'

'Then I will give . . . to you . . . *now* . . . the exact amount.
Your undertaker's estimate.' Curly fetched out his money clip
with a practised turn of his hand. 'There's enough bits and
pieces here to tell me I'm all right for that. The silver snuff
boxes for a start. The picture of the pigs. So I give you this –
hard cash – and you take it to the meeting. Then if it goes well
for you, we take all this stuff away, all of it. And I sell it for you

at auction, all above board. And you get sixty per cent, I get forty per cent. But it all goes, we will clear this room, are you with me?' Michael nodded. 'However,' went on Curly, 'if the decision doesn't go your way, and your sister-in-law prevails, you don't need this money so you give it back to me. And you keep all your stuff. Everything. How's that? Fair enough?'

Michael's head was spinning. He breathed heavily for a while, working it out. He looked at the bland, doughy but kind face of Curly. Granny's fate now rested with this man's generous offer. It was strange, piled on top of strange. But – he was getting what he wanted. The money ready to wave at Natalia. He thought he saw his mother, in his mind's eye, wink at him and stick out her tongue, just like when she was playing jazz drums and saw someone she knew in the audience. He made the leap. Felt the horrible drop. 'Yes,' he said. 'Thank you very much. Let's do it.'

'Here's my card. Remember to call me. Otherwise I'll turn up tomorrow and take it all away.'

'OK.'

'Sorry to be strict with you. But it struck me you needed a bit of a . . . a shove. We'd never have got there, otherwise.'

'No no, quite right. Well done. Thank you.'

After he'd gone, Michael strode around, fingering through the notes he'd been given. It was some time since circumstances had pushed him into a corner like this. He wasn't any good at it. This whisperingly quiet, fast-moving willpower of Natalia's – it mowed him down, usually. But perhaps, this time, he stood a chance. He had some money. He might be able to recruit his own brother to the cause. It wasn't impossible, to turn the whole thing around.

'Hullo,' called Michael as he rang the bell and at the same time let himself into 16, Sweetcombe Road. He was exhausted and hungry and had sweated into his clothes and his ears ached from the phone. Only twenty-four hours had passed since he last was here and he'd done so much.

If Natalia could pull rabbits out of hats, then so might he.

Natalia drew out a chair from under the kitchen table for him and he sat in it, heavily, and put down in front of them the dear old dragon bowl, wrapped in a tea cloth.

'What's that?' asked Natalia, drawing the sewing basket towards her. Michael noticed – ah yes, her instinctive desire to win – that she'd put herself opposite him, so he was alone on his side, faced by the two of them.

'It's the dragon bowl,' said Michael, unfolding the tea towel carefully. 'I brought it with me, if you don't mind, because I didn't want Curly to have it.'

'Ah, the dragon bowl,' said Philip fondly.

'Who is Curly?' Natalia frowned and leaned over her child's name-tape, smoothing it into position on the school jumper.

'The house clearance man. I've sold everything. Literally, he is going to empty the place. Thank God, at last, I hear you say. And you're right, it's a good thing. You have told me so often Natalia. But I couldn't see the dragon bowl go. Too many memories.'

He did love it, this last remaining heirloom. For eighty years it had been in his family's keeping. The greens and yellows were still rich and lustrous, the dragon's body coiled in flight, a blaze of fire and smoke coming from its nostrils, its eyes large and round, the pupils vertical crescents of black except for a point of light in each which spoke of its determination to fight and conquer and avenge, and breed more dragons.

'So I was going to ask you,' he went on, 'can I keep it here for a day or two, while his men blunder back and forth, carrying boxes? Don't want it broken.'

'Michael?'

'Hmm?'

'You say, you've sold everything?'

'I know, you always said I should. It was getting on top of me. Literally. One of my little rat runs was blocked up by an avalanche last night. Took me an hour to get to bed. And it means I . . . we . . . all of us! Have enough money, now, to answer dear old Granny Banana. And her needs. Actual cash, the best kind, folding.' He picked up the bowl and leaned back to put it on the sideboard behind him, out of the way. 'Hurrah,' he went on, taking the fat envelope from his pocket, 'all sorted.' He put it down in front of Philip, who must become his new recruit now, surely. What best to say? The right words would do it. An emotional appeal. Family history, tradition . . .

His head was empty; it was like clutching at thin air.

'Michael,' said Natalia softly, 'Michael, listen.'

On Wednesday morning Michael stood, head bowed, in the clean, spacious entrance to Haycombe crematorium. His only achievement, after all that, had been to delay Natalia's plans by one day. Her tactics had been devastatingly simple. It was he himself who'd called Gina and asked permission, but it was she who'd sneaked in and made her own call and quietly hijacked the answer – made it the one *she* wanted to hear, and the one it was easiest for the Trust to give. No.

It was a cremation, then. Events were out of his control. It was infuriating.

Nearby lingered Natalia and Philip and the children – rather artistically arranged against the odd, 1960s wall with coloured glass octagons dotted throughout – as well as his ex-wife number three, Patsy, their daughter Mattie and her husband and their son. Immediate family only. They were held here, like sheep waiting to be dipped, because their allotted slot was for twenty minutes and even as Michael walked with leaden feet

into the chapel the last victims were being ushered out of the
back. It was like a conveyor belt. He wanted to shout out,
'Sorry, Ma!'

Inside, three magnificent windows, floor to ceiling, of clear
glass except for an opaque white crucifix in the middle, took
up the whole of the south-facing wall of the chapel and gave
them a huge, sun-filled view of the ongoing work of Somerset
farmers for miles and miles, and this sudden shot of beauty, like
a syringeful emptied into his arm, increased the poignancy of
the occasion. Despite himself, Michael liked this room.

They all fitted into the one pew. He was grateful for Patsy's
hand tucked behind his elbow. On his other side was his
grandson, Michael Junior, who had inherited some of his
own features, the wrinkled forehead for instance, although
not the surname Gough. He was the only little person carrying the baton for him and Patsy, their only child's only child,
but carrying it he was, and bravely. Beyond him stood Mattie,
his lovely daughter, bold of limb, the sort of girl who crosses
a room in three rolling strides and sits with her ankle on her
knee like a man, but who's built like a proper woman, none
the less, handsome as her mother was but with the additional
attraction of dimples and youth and excitable dark eyes. Then
her husband, Simon. The dreaded Natalia and her three.
Philip.

They were facing what looked like a small proscenium arch
theatre. A pair of blue curtains stood open. On the stage was a
large, solid plinth – the catafalque. It seemed unnaturally tall. It
was going to be a chore to lift her up there, he thought. Music
started – too loud. It was quickly brought down to the right
level. A Mozart Sonata. The bearers from Drew and Sons
walked in, four of them, carrying Banana on their shoulders.
That was why it was so high – shoulder height, of course.
Everything thought out.

How very professional of them to handle her without the

flowers falling off. Except, he realised, watching the coffin tilt, they were probably glued on.

The vicar, or priest or whatever he was, had been provided by the crematorium. Michael hadn't asked for Pinky, afraid of being turned down by Natalia, and now he was glad. Pinky wouldn't have been able to hide his dismay at performing in such a place whereas this man, climbing into the pulpit now, had a kind face and looked comfortable and at ease.

The music was turned down, a touch suddenly. The vicar began. 'We are here, among just the closest members of her family, to close the book as it were, on the life of Lady Edith Bruce Witherington Gough, and if that name isn't a breath of the old empire, I don't know what is. Yet she was humble enough to ask everyone she met to call her by her nickname, Granny Mandana.'

Mandana?? Michael and Philip glanced at each other. The children watched to see what the adults would do.

The vicar explained, 'And that's the name we shall use for this service, because we are among people who loved her dearly, and who knew her by that name.'

Michael rose an inch or two off his seat. His voice sounded too loud. 'Excuse me, it's Banana, not Mandana.' It was his own fault; at the last moment he'd asked the vicar to call her by the name everyone would recognise – the children wouldn't have known who Edith was – and no doubt he'd mumbled, and the vicar had misheard.

'Banana?' asked the vicar.

'Yes. Everyone called her Banana because she was stooped, you know, her back was bent, like a banana.'

The vicar gave a light thud with the heel of his hand on the pulpit. 'I am *so* sorry,' he said firmly.

Michael was moved by such a genuine reaction. 'No, don't be silly, not your fault in the slightest. How could you know. You're doing brilliantly.' He sat down again.

'Well, to continue, Granny . . . *Banana*,' he said emphatically, 'was a wife and mother, a grandmother and a great-grand-mother. She reached the age of ninety-two years old . . .'

'Ninety-*three*,' Michael thought, but it really didn't matter, not with such a genuinely nice man saying it. He let the rest of the speech drift over him. Banana would have been amused at the mistakes, he knew. He remembered her smile, which had become more comical after her false teeth had given up the ghost. He wondered what had happened to her wedding rings. Were they in the box with her? These musings took him through the service. He found he hadn't been listening much but, he thought, all of this was unexpectedly lovely. The view . . .

The children's attention also strayed. Emma tried to imagine what Granny would look like right now. She herself had a money-box in the shape of a coffin; you put the coin on top and pressed a button whereupon a skeleton sat up sharply, long hair flying around its half decomposed face, and its hand swung out, scooped up the coin and dragged it back into the coffin before it lay down again. Granny Banana would look like that.

David, standing next to Emma with head bowed, stared from under his fringe as the music started up again and the blue curtains suddenly started moving all by themselves, until the coffin disappeared. He glanced at Ben whose eyebrows popped up.

Everyone waited in silence, staring at the closed curtains. The music stopped. There was a barely audible '*Phhht*' – similar to the sound of the airbrakes on a lorry. Prayers were said. 'Amen,' they all repeated.

Their twenty minutes were up. The crematorium assistant nodded at Michael, who edged apart from the others, feeling self-conscious. He was escorted one way while everyone else was shown out of the back of the building. Even as he followed his guide through a side door and down the steep concrete stairs, he was aware of another set of mourners gathering. The conveyor belt had moved on.

He was led down to a small basement room. Immediately his eye was caught by the three steel hatches, all in a row, at around waist height. These were the oven doors, no doubt. He was introduced to the operators, Rob and Bob, who wore matching green T-shirts. They had such perfect manners, not grovelling with sympathy but kindly in an ordinary way. He silently applauded them for that. Also there was a schoolgirl, one of their daughters no doubt, who seemed happy, and smiled at him and introduced herself in a confident way. She was obviously a well-adjusted child. The coffin was on a waist-high steel trolley, waiting. The flowers had been removed, he noticed.

'All right then?' asked Michael. He would try his hardest to be a cheerful mourner.

'Very sorry for your loss, sir.'

'Thank you.'

'Are you ready to proceed?'

'Yes, yes, let's do it.'

Rob – or Bob was it? – wheeled the trolley to the door of the middle furnace and winched it down to the correct height. Michael stood with his hand on the coffin. He wanted to find a few last words for her.

Rob pushed a green button and the steel door rolled up smoothly and as it did so a roaring sound filled the room and a hellish red light spilled from the inside of the oven. At the same time they were struck with a blast of tremendous heat. Bob asked him, 'Would you like to—'

'No, no,' he interrupted, raising his voice to meet the roar, 'you do it. Is she feet first? Yes.'

They began to roll her forward, off the trolley and into the furnace. Michael tapped the coffin and called out an apology, 'Sorry old thing . . .'

Flames poured from the end of the coffin and Michael had to step back. It seemed like brave work; the fire was so greedy it could hardly wait, coming out of the furnace to get at her. When she was inside the red button was punched and the steel door rolled back down. The red glare diminished, the roaring lessened, the air cooled, bit by bit. Rob and Bob were saying something.

'. . . won't take that long,' ended Bob.

Michael put his hands in his suit pockets and tried to remember a prayer. Nothing doing. He was overcome with a numb sense of . . . nothing. The sense of a full stop. He should have had the foresight to write something down . . .

He noticed a docket of white paper tucked into a slot on the outside of the oven. He leaned forward and read 'Cremator 3, cremation 11,367 . . . cremated remains of the late Lady Edith Gough.'

After a while he asked, 'Is it all right if I wait, and see her out the other end?'

'Absolutely fine,' said Rob or Bob. 'It will take about an hour, if you want to come back. Or you are very welcome to stay.'

'Are there many, who . . . do what I'm doing?'

'There's quite a few who do this bit. Not so many who wait for the raking out.'

He thanked them and said he'd better talk to his relatives before they went. He was shown out of another door which led to a set of steps and a path along the side of the building. He followed it and found himself in the area where the others were waiting. The flowers had been moved out here. They'd all cried a bit, that was obvious. No doubt he looked blasted, too. 'Saw her go in,' said Michael, and collared Natalia to pour the details into her ear. He asked her if she minded if he waited around for another hour to escort his and Philip's mother out of the infernal machine. Natalia hurried to say yes but she was avoiding his eye, he noticed. Guilt!

They said their goodbyes and everyone else headed off, leaving him with the Land Rover so he could get back on his own.

He sat for a few minutes on a bench that looked out over the huge view. The sky was as blue as you could want. Everything looked beautiful and cared for.

When the next lot of mourners came outside he felt misplaced, infringing on their care, and he followed the side path back to where he'd come from. In the crematorium another coffin was being loaded in. A chair was found for him and he waited placidly. The cheerful schoolgirl lingered close by.

'And so which one of them is your dad?' asked Michael politely, nodding at Rob and Bob.

'Neither of them. I just like coming down here.'

'Oh.'

'I help a lot, you know, make them tea . . . and other things. I just love being here, I don't know why.' There was a tendon strung tightly in her neck and her eyes were glassy, slightly protuberant.

'You like it?' asked Michael, wrong-footed.

'Yes. I spend all my spare time down here.'

Michael had to revise his opinion of her. How odd. She was an enthusiast. A groupie. 'What an extraordinary hobby for a girl to have,' he said.

'I know, I can't help it. I find it so fascinating. They let me do loads of things: press the buttons, rake out the ashes. I was in charge of the music for your mother's.' Michael remembered the rather abrupt turning-down of the volume.

'Do your mum and dad know you come here?' he asked.

'Oh yes, they're fine about it.' She reached into her blazer pocket and took out a mobile phone. 'I'll show you,' she said, and thumbed the keypad. 'Some of them I record, if there's something interesting. This was a really, really big one. Watch.' She offered him the screen to view. The video picture jerked into life: Rob and Bob manhandled the trolley with a truly enormous coffin on it. The steel door lifted, Rob and Bob heaved and hauled and got it in there and the door slid back down. Rob and Bob turned to face the camera and pantomimed wiping their foreheads and rolling their eyes. A tinny, high pitched word came on the sound track, 'Phew!'

'That did look like hard work,' remarked Michael.

'He took over three hours to finish,' she said proudly. She showed him two more. One was a child – heartbreaking. Michael felt tears come to him, and saw the girl, too, was upset. The second was someone famous that they could joke about. 'Going to hell!' said Michael. She nodded enthusiastically. What an extraordinary girl, he thought.

'I've got work experience with Drew and Sons next week,' she said.

'That's good,' replied Michael, 'well done. I can see you're going to be a valuable member of staff.'

'They will even pay me a little bit.'

'Oh.'

'I know, it's really great.'

After a pause he asked, 'Your mum and dad . . . alive and well?'

'Yes! They are fine thank you.' She said knowledgeably, '*Your* mum will take about an hour. Ninety-one year old lady.'

'She was actually ninety-three.'

'Oh.'

'Even quicker, then? Less than an hour?'

She smiled and joked, 'Oh yes. Ninety-three. A lot less than an hour.' He found himself rather liking the girl, the way she just talked to him as if it were a perfectly normal situation.

'We're having new ovens soon.' She nodded at the evidence of construction work. 'Which is why it's a bit at sixes and sevens at the moment.'

'Oh. Good.' He added, 'It's difficult, isn't it,' and he pointed at the two operators who were hauling the next coffin onto the trolley, 'having them called Rob and Bob, such similar names. I'll never remember which is which.'

'I know,' she agreed.

'Perhaps we ought to have the same name for both of them. Call them both Rob'n'Bob.'

'Rob'n'Bob,' she repeated, and smiled.

When the time came, they went around to the other end of the row of ovens and lifted a small hatch. There was the roaring sound, but not as loud. The same hellish light spilled out but he was used to it by now. Along the bottom of the glowing interior the debris of his mother lay neatly arranged – the bare bones, thought Michael. Rob'n'Bob fetched a scoop on the end of a long metal arm and poked it inside and raked everything towards the entrance, where it fell down a chute and into the cooler. The hatch was wound shut again.

There was a further period of waiting and then Michael and the girl sifted through the remains. 'What on earth's that?' asked Michael.

'She had a false hip,' said the girl.

'Yes, she did! Same as me.'

'Come and have a look at this.' She went to a large drum and lifted off the lid. It was full of all manner of metal pins and false joints, all cremated the same deathly grey. His own false hip would end up in this bin, he thought. Another drum contained smaller nails, paper clips, hair grips and suchlike. Michael had wondered at this girl's hobby but now he could see it was a perfectly lovely place to come and spend your spare time. There was a gratifying kindness and good humour here. He might easily come back himself and bring a picnic.

Granny Banana's contribution to the recycling turned out to include a spectacles case and, in the smaller white bucket, several gold teeth smelted into one lump. When she'd finished passing over the magnets she was put in the cremulator, a machine which contained half a dozen perfectly smooth balls of stone which ground up the bones into granules. The printed docket followed her from one machine to another. She ended up in a thick plastic bag, stapled at the top, the docket safely inside, waiting with a dozen others on a shelf, ready for the funeral directors to pick her up.

It was surprising, what a thoroughly good time he'd had, thought Michael. He was sad to leave. Banana would have been fascinated. She'd been in the best possible hands, every step of the way. He felt quite tearful about it. Not that he'd admit any such thing to Natalia. He'd go back and give her all the gory details, watch her sweat. Serve her right.

It was one of the reasons Patsy had immediately liked living on her own: she could always find the car keys. They were, guess what, exactly where they were meant to be – in the little ceramic dish on the hall table. The broken pockets of Michael's jacket no longer had to be searched. There were a host of similar things she'd noticed when he'd left her, seven years previously. She made the bed immediately after she got up so when she came back from the bathroom the room already looked neat and cared for. She put flower planters on the window sills; Michael wasn't there to complain about not being able to lean out. The draining board wasn't cluttered up with his insisting on doing the washing-up badly. The sordid tails of shaving cream were no longer smeared around the edges of the sink.

Nowadays, though, she missed these exact things. She'd like it if someone mussed the bed and left toe-nail clippings on the bedside table. She wanted to have the smell of him about the place, that scent of gun-oil, freshly killed trout, damp tweed and heavily trodden socks that moved around him like a visible cloud. So, as she prepared to go and stay the night with Philip and Natalia on the eve of the memorial service, she found herself blindly hoping that her ex-husband would be there to spend the evening with them. In her mind she rehearsed the sequence of events: the drive to Bath, a small, rich city in a beautiful nook of the Somerset hills. The skirting round the centre and the arrival at Sweetcombe Road. Michael's Land Rover either parked outside, or not. If it weren't there, if she faced a dinner with just Natalia and Philip, then she'd rather turn round and come home. Natalia was a lovely and kind hostess but Patsy disliked staying anywhere overnight and she could easily make the journey to the memorial service tomorrow morning. No, she was doing all this for Michael, she had to admit as she folded a silk blouse into the case. Then it struck her: was it the very reason Natalia had invited her? It would suit both her and Philip to have him out of their hair, safely back home. Especially now that Banana was gone . . .

She was guilty, suddenly, of forgetting about Banana and thinking only of her own love life, as if she were a teenage girl. The occasion was meant to be about remembrance. She set herself to work. Yes, Granny, we remember how you caught your tongue between your teeth when you addressed the golf ball, before steadily but swiftly drawing back the club and smacking it. You made the same face when you lifted your fishing rod, drawing the line off the water with minimum disturbance, looking over your shoulder at the long, graceful figure-of-eight written in the air behind you, that bit of tongue still peeping out from your lips, which only disappeared when the line was cast and had settled, feather-light, on the water. Whereupon you so intently watched your fly, a speck that swam on every ripple and rivulet, all the way down, until it began to drag sideways through the current, and then . . .

We do remember, Banana. So very fondly.

She finished packing and zipped and buckled her case. It sat on the bed which she and Michael had shared for so long. She still kept to her side. The left-hand set of pillows were forever plump and clean. The grease from his hair used to stain his pillow slips. Disgusting old man.

If it were Michael who'd died, she wondered, would she miss him, want him back the way she did now?

Yes.

But if he'd died, if there had been no divorce, she'd have tried harder and longer with the dating agency to find someone else, she thought coldly. Instead he was frustratingly alive and available. If only someone could point him in her direction and bang him on the head with a club and tell him . . . which, maybe, was exactly what Natalia was doing?

Granny Banana's remains were picked up from Haycombe crematorium by Drew and Sons, dropped into an urn, and driven to number 16, Sweetcombe Road. It was Philip who opened the door and accepted the parcel. He carried it through and left it on the kitchen table, unopened. Natalia, when she came back from work, unwrapped the box and lifted it out. It was around eighteen inches high and of a simple Grecian shape, made in terracotta.

The child-minder brought the children back and they noticed the urn while standing round the kitchen table and dropping broken pieces of KitKat into glasses of milk. Natalia explained what it was and lifted the lid to show them the plastic bag inside. The children looked blankly at their mother. After a moment of discomfort they forgot about it and ran through the house and out the back.

Natalia carried the urn through to the living room. She tried it first on the mantelpiece, but it was too big to sit there comfortably. She moved it to the top of the piano, clearing off all the children's books and music paraphernalia. Better, she thought. She gave the piano a quick dusting, centred the urn, and left it.

It didn't take long – only a few dozen paces – for the children to scour the edges of the garden. Ben dropped his sword and started complaining; the others begged him to shut up until he cried and sat down in a funk. They left him behind and walked back into the house where they rested dolefully on the soft chairs in the living room.

There was a big hole, seemingly, where the coffin had been. After a while Ben appeared again and Emma knew enough to give him the plastic gun that she was carrying; maybe that would stop his whinging.

At this point they noticed the silent, enigmatic visitor – the urn. Everyone was spooked, now, to be on their own with it. It was all that was left of Granny, her body, anyway. Where was her spirit? They dared to take off the lid. Maybe it was escaping right now, wafting into the room . . .

They didn't want to be in here, suddenly. They were fascinated but left, casting glances over their shoulders. They huddled outside for a while and darted back in, but ran back out again, screaming and laughing.

The urn stood there.

Michael was the first of the guests to arrive, in the late afternoon. He brought with him his grandchild, Michael Junior, who'd come to stay the night with his cousins, a regular practice.

They lingered for a while in the sitting room. The cousins circled each other warily. They weren't always a success, these stay-overs. Michael was alarmed to see how much his grandson looked like him. He had that vein which throbbed in his neck all the time. His ears moved up and down, and his eyes bulged in the same way when he was angry. The boy's hair was frightening: like barbed wire scrambled on his crown. He was taller than his cousins and his complexion wasn't so good. When he was ready to become a successful, happy drinker of alcohol just like his Grandpappy, no doubt it would be worse, he'd look like rare roast beef, his own complexion. Poor lad!

He warned his grandson that he had a shoelace undone. Michael Junior squatted to tie it, and Natalia's children, his nephews and niece, took advantage and quietly ran upstairs. When Michael Junior looked up, they'd gone.

The two Michaels lingered, uncomfortably on their own in the sitting room. The boy went into a kind of trance, thought Michael. Why didn't he follow them and get stuck in, instead of just waiting down here? It was because he was an only child, he thought. His beloved grandson looked quite ill, or mentally retarded, just standing there, touching the odd bit of furniture, occasionally blinking or swallowing, which made his Adam's apple bob up and down, while the shouts and running feet of the other children echoed through the house, an unreachable happiness.

'Young man?' Michael wanted to help things along. The stay-overs usually happened without the boy's parents and so Michael took on a quasi-parental role.

'Hmmm?' asked Michael Junior.

'Be off with you. Don't worry about me. They'll be waiting.'

'They always run away,' said Michael Junior gloomily.

'Ahhh . . .' Sorriness crowded Michael. 'I see.' It was true, it happened often.

'I'm all right on my own.' His throat worked; Michael saw it and felt his own move in sympathy. 'Well, can't help with that I'm afraid, us grown-ups. We live in a foreign country.'

The silence grew, they'd burst if something wasn't said. Michael just rolled out what was in his head, 'I had a bit of a fight with your great-aunt Natalia, over the funeral.' His grandson, nodded, looked at him. The way his eyes blinked again and – just slightly – rolled in his head, gave him the look of a lizard. Some people would say he was not the most attractive

child, Michael realised, but he loved him to bits. 'Your Granny,'
he went on, 'had written down how she wanted to be buried.
Whereas it's all been done . . . cheaper than that. So I became
cross.'

The boy spoke at last, 'Why don't you do something about
it?'

'Good idea,' he replied automatically. How little children
understood about the constraints of adulthood! Short of hitting
his sister-in-law with a spade and stealing the coffin there hadn't
been any way of 'doing anything about it'. God knows he'd
tried. In the end, of course, he was secretly rather pleased with
the way it had gone. He wanted to tell Michael Junior all about
the ovens, and the schoolgirl, and the bins full of artificial joints
and pins and screws, but it might not be a suitable subject.

It was overpowering, Michael's desire to connect with this
boy. Mattie had suffered from post-natal depression and both he
and Patsy had put in a few hours in the nursery one way or
another. This was his only grandchild and his namesake.
Michael had to watch out not to follow him round. Yet so
often it felt as though they were strangers moving on opposite
sides of the street, in opposite directions.

Upstairs, David and Ben and Emma rifled the dressing-up
box and found costumes. A chase started. Emma hid in the
towel cupboard, where she found Gormenghast baking himself
in the warmth given off by the immersion heater. David and
Ben ran downstairs. Five-year-old Ben scooted into the kitchen
and turned to face up to his elder brother. David threw a cushion and Ben ducked, so the cushion skidded along the work
surface where the dragon bowl waited placidly for Michael to
take it home. It was shunted sideways; there was a crack, and
then silence.

It had broken clean in half, the dragon's flight spoiled, the
coiling, serpentine strength gone. The points of light in its
black pupils showed dismay and pain.

The boys noticed but they didn't want it to matter; a second later they picked up the cushion and carried on fighting. The broken bowl stood disconsolately on the pine surface for ten minutes.

It was Emma, when she came down, who realised they were in trouble. She carefully slid the two halves of the bowl together and adjusted them until the jagged line met. It fitted together perfectly.

'Look,' said David reasonably, 'it's already mended.'

'No it's not. I'm just holding it together. We have to glue it.'

'OK,' Ben nodded, 'let's do it right now.'

Emma separated the two halves; the dragon died again. 'We have to find Superglue.'

They jumped – there was a voice, the clatter of a door opening, and footsteps. Quickly Emma pushed the two broken halves together. The bowl stood perfectly, as if nothing had happened. Shadows caressed her hands; she withdrew them sharply; her breath hissed and a second shiver ran down her spine. She warned the boys, really warned them, with a shake of their shoulders because this was serious, 'Don't tell Mum, or Dad, or anyone.'

Michael remained alone in the sitting room after his grandson had gone; he parked himself in the usual chair and listened idly to the sound of the boys fighting in the kitchen. He felt the potent absence of the coffin, that huge thing now reduced to the little terracotta urn on the piano.

Granny Banana was dead. One minute she'd been in the passenger seat of the old Land Rover; a moment later the door had popped open and she'd tipped out like an actress in a Charlie Chaplin film. He'd piled on the brakes . . .

Where was Philip, he wondered? Natalia had obviously parked him out of the way somewhere. He wanted to go and find him, give him the time of day for once. It was his mother who'd died as well, after all. Not just now though, he thought. He'd sit here a while longer.

A half hour passed; he might have dozed for a while. It crept up to five-thirty p.m. and autumn sunlight feinted in through the glass patio doors in the sitting room where the piano stood, mute, heavy, silent out of respect for the period of mourning in the house. Michael sat in the armchair, still – equally inert.

When the children trotted in, he was about to greet them but stopped because they hadn't noticed him and they had a secretive air. He was curious to see what they were up to.

The sunlight struck Ben's face as he squinted into the glare. He was carrying a jam jar and headed straight for the piano. 'Ben, no,' whispered Emma. 'Not the real ashes. Over here.' Ben swerved and joined the other two as they knelt at the fireplace. All three children scooped up handfuls of ash and filled the jar.

Michael felt uncomfortable now. Surely they'd see him soon? He was quite used to being treated like a piece of furniture, something to be got round, but this was different. Their concentration was so intense that they'd willed him not to exist. It was as if he were invisible. What did they want with the ash?

David wiped his fingers on his shirt and held up the jar. 'Granny Banana,' he said.

'Her burnt body,' agreed Emma.

They were pretending they'd got hold of Granny Banana's ashes, thought Michael. How extraordinary. He held his peace, didn't move an inch. He wanted to see what they'd do next.

'But her ghost is in the room,' added David.

'Is she still dead?' asked Ben.

'Yes.'

'All of her, dead, fits in the jar?'

'Yes. Put the lid on.'

'Shh,' David warned, 'he's coming.'

All three siblings looked at the door for a second or two as if expecting a monster to appear and then walked, and then ran quickly, through the patio door into the garden, taking the jar with them. Grandpa Michael watched from his chair. His curiosity in their game was replaced, slowly, by a feeling of pity – once more his grandson was being left out, he thought.

Meanwhile from an upstairs window Michael Junior watched as his cousins pulled aside a broken section of the garden fence, went through and crouched down on the piece of scrub land between the garden and the road. They were intent on whatever object it was; he couldn't make it out. Beyond, the cars stalked drearily past in lines. He knew they weren't allowed out there; he felt a dull ache of frustration and shame at not being included. The remains of the second biscuit was stuck in his teeth – it was how they'd bribed him to stay put so they could escape, and now he was left looking at their game from a distance like that stupid boy in *The Secret Garden*. He watched as Ben threw an old can and they ran, pointing at the sky as if following a lost kite. They collapsed to the ground and clutched each other. They crawled hand over hand on the ground, then sat in a circle and talked.

Envy ate at him. He tried to imagine what the game was. If he was allowed, he'd play it bigger and better than all of them.

The game, if only he'd known, was all about Granny Banana. They pretended to add water to the ashes and, of course, since a human body was ninety-something per cent water, this brought Granny back to life. She grew out of nothing, in front of their very eyes, like an indoor firework. Except, as the game went on, she came to be represented by the plastic anatomical model that Emma had been given for her birthday, with the ribcage that swung open so you could take out all the internal organs, and the brain half exposed, and the lungs like a bag of little round sponges that you could squeeze and hear the air suck in and out.

The adults in the house, as well, all had their own kind of solitary communion with Banana's earthly remains, at some time or other, late on that Friday afternoon.

Natalia paused briefly and swapped the dust pan and brush to the other hand and touched the hair back from her forehead. She replaced the lid on the urn and whispered, 'Sorry.' She'd never felt right in the company of the old lady, even though she recognised the latter's acceptance and kindness towards her, the outsider in the family. Now, with the benefit of hindsight, she felt it had been wrong to go through with the cremation against her wishes, but there was no way to make up for it; to carry on was all that was left.

Philip leaned against the piano and offered up a brief prayer for her, wherever she was. On the other side. In heaven. Or just nowhere, the land of nothing. A vivid memory of his mother came to mind. He'd been walking past her bedroom one night – was it at Sitten Hall or at the hotel? He had the impression of pink décor and the scent of dried roses. He'd been a grown man himself, in the full thrust of middle age, when his suits were pressed, his shirts ironed, his phones ringing non-stop, running the farm and the financial services company. He'd glanced sideways, and through the 'v' of the door he'd caught a glimpse of her naked, curved back as she'd stepped out of a pair knickers. Her bottom had looked sad and droopy with several broad wrinkles smiling at him, it had seemed. And it was disproportionately large. What did that frail, thin figure need all that bottom for? he remembered thinking. He'd flinched at the sight and quietened his footsteps so he could pass her room without her noticing.

Patsy, when she arrived in time for dinner and to stay the night, found herself briefly on her own in front of the piano. She kissed the tips of her fingers and patted the top of the urn and murmured, 'Hello old thing. Much love.' Her memory was of dear old Banana at Sitten Hall, staggering a bit after a

good party with jolly talk and cocktails and dinner followed by
some unforgiving card games, and then her bothering to trek
all the way to Mattie's bedroom, which at Sitten Hall was an
arduous, long journey, especially in winter, equivalent to
climbing a small mountain and down again, just so that she
might tiptoe, tipsily, into the room, carrying her cloud of gin
vapours with her, and lean over and push a coin under Mattie's
pillow to pay for her trip to the land of sleep, murmuring a
few words and leaving a smudge of lipstick on the little girl's
forehead. She would rejoin society with a chill sweat on her
powdered skin, tugging down her suit jacket and giving a
characteristic twist of her mouth, saying 'Gorgeous grandchild, Patsy, thank you.'

Patsy blinked, turned away. She wondered what people
would remember about her, when the time came.

She could feel Michael's presence in the house, although
she hadn't seen him yet. And she heard his voice coming from
the door that led to the utility area and to the garage, as she
lugged her bag upstairs.

She'd been invited by Natalia to use their bedroom in which
to change because there was a full-length mirror. It was a small
room; the plain wooden bed she recognised from its previous
home at the farm. In here it was too big; there was barely
enough space to walk around its edges. She dumped the bag;
her arm ached. The sound of Michael's voice reached her still,
up here. Its tone was soothing; she recognised it as the one he'd
previously used for his dog, Snooker. He must be talking to his
brother. She held her breath, trying to overhear.

She unzipped the bag and took out the sheet music. Three
pieces – with practice she'd got them almost as good as ever.
She hoped and prayed that she'd be brave enough to play after
dinner. Underneath the sheet music was a black trouser suit and
a white shirt; these she carefully hung on the end of the bed,
hoping the wrinkles would drop out and she wouldn't have to

iron them. Next came the old tweed suit, Michael's favourite. She went to the bathroom and soaked her hands and face in water as hot as she could bear; it brought colour to her skin. For a moment she stood completely still and held her breath; she'd heard her ex-husband's unmistakable tread, always accompanied by heavy breathing, and she thought he might be about to disturb her. She glanced at the door – the little silver bolt was safely across; he couldn't burst in.

The danger passed. She patted dry her face and hands and went back to Natalia's bedroom. She changed out of her travelling clothes and into the tweed suit, then unsquashed her court shoes and watched herself in the mirror as she slipped them on. To go up an inch in height was not a good idea in her own eyes, but she wasn't dressing for herself. She remembered Michael telling her, his whole face wrinkling with mirth, how he'd made such a fool of himself chasing girls so much bigger and taller than him when he was a teenager. He always had to push them over or get them to sit down, just to reach them.

She touched perfume behind her ears and at her wrists. The Tall Woman, she thought ruefully.

The sound of Michael's cough and the flush being pulled in the toilet brought his horrid male *otherness* back to her. Revolting old man. She suffered a quick, involuntary weep and walked to the door to lean on it, so no one came in. She stared down at her shoes. She wanted her wretched husband back, she did. Michael, come home.

There was no lock on the bedroom; she had to stay like this until she recovered. Shame coloured her; she held one hand to her throat, staring at the piano music on Natalia's bed and listening to his footsteps on the stairs, the volume diminishing . . . They stopped, but he couldn't have reached the bottom. What was he up to, she wondered; would he turn round and come back up?

★

On his way downstairs Michael silently grumbled to himself: he was dreading dinner, he'd have preferred to have gone home and watched television. The hotel and tree scenario tomorrow was a dreadful prospect. All his weakness and poverty would be on display. Sprocket was alone in his grave. Granny Banana would be sprinkled under a different tree in an anonymous hotel garden. His only hope was that it would turn out better than he expected, as the cremation had done. Unlikely, though. He couldn't summon up any more to say about it. The argument was over and now he just wanted to walk clear out the other side of it and get back to his pleasures.

Halfway down the stairs, he had an idea – and stopped dead. If he hadn't been hanging onto the banister he might have fallen. In his mind's eye he saw Ben reaching for the urn on the piano and Emma whispering, 'Ben, no, not the real ashes.' And they'd knelt at the fireplace and filled a jam jar.

But – why not the real ashes? He himself should steal them. It would mean at least a partial fulfilment of her wishes, if he took them back to Sitten Hall. It was so simple a thing. The children had done it, in effect. He should take a leaf out of their book. His grandson's words came back to him, 'Why don't you do something about it?' He would take Granny's ashes out of the urn and put them in his pocket. At a later date he would drive down to Sitten Hall and have his own private ceremony . . .

He swayed with excitement, took one more step down. It was a faultless plan.

No it wasn't. The urn would be empty. When it came to sprinkling the ashes tomorrow there'd be nothing there. He could picture the blank, disbelieving faces of the congregation as the lid was taken off and – a yawning hole opened up. It almost made him blush . . . No.

He went on down.

★

In Natalia's bedroom the newly smartened-up Patsy blew her nose, dried her eyes and did the best she could with powder and lipstick. She hooked pearls around her neck and made herself a promise: if Michael said one nice thing to her, just one nice thing, and they were alone, she'd simply ask him to come home. It would take all her courage, but she must. 'I *promise*,' she murmured, twice over. It might be that the only reason he'd say yes was to come back to the place, to Sitten Hall, rather than for her, but she didn't care. She had enough pride, anyway, all by herself and for herself. It was quite right that he loved the place. She herself didn't like to see him away from Sitten Hall.

The kitchen table was extended to seat four adults and four children. Simon and Mattie were absent, but represented by their son Michael Junior. His solitary overnight visits to his cousins' house being such a regular feature, there was an unspoken theory among the grown-ups that it was something to do with his parents' complicated pursuit of a sibling for him, that he was farmed out on crucial dates. Mattie had moved from being depressed at having a child, to being depressed at not being able to have the next one. Her demons were like spirits standing at the shoulder of her son Michael Junior.

'You *were* playing,' Michael Junior hissed at his cousins. He was furious; the veins stood out in his neck, his brow crinkled and the whole of his hair moved back and forth. 'You were playing Man O' War, I saw you and heard you as well.'

Emma ignored him. She really could punch and kick and pull his head off, when he was doing his only-child behaviour. 'We were not!' It wasn't a lie – they'd been playing, yes, but Man O' War, no. She watched Michael Junior's attempt to swallow her half truth. She wondered at the temper lurking in him. However, there was something – his small ears? – that she was drawn to. Or maybe it was his lovely surname, D'Angibau. Like the sword-fighting man from *Princess Bride*, she thought.

She liked him for the sound of his name? The idea was shocking, but it might be true.

Michael tried his hardest with the pair of roast chickens but the handle on the old carving knife was loose and every time he pressed down the blade spun round, plus the fork seemed a lot harder to pull out than push in, so it was a bloody awful mess on everyone's plate. He might as well have used a hammer and chisel. He was aware he'd been given this job not because he was good at it, not because Philip never attended meal times, but because he was the man with nothing – no house, no wife, no job – so he had been thrown this task as a consolation. But he was grateful to be asked; he wanted to do well by everyone. If only his hands weren't shaking so much. The chickens were slippery as bars of soap and it felt like he had six thumbs as he tried to serve vegetables and pour gravy and hand out full plates . . .

Philip absented himself from meal times because he lost his temper with the children. Natalia had one day thoughtfully handed him a crudely built sandwich and turned him round at the kitchen door, and it had been thus ever since. He wandered the house clutching a tin plate, a silent shadow moving across the open doorways, cramming these brick-like sandwiches into his mouth. After he'd finished, it was the done thing not to show himself until everyone else had left the table. Instead he visited the cupboard under the stairs, which did for a cellar. The few dozen bottles had been put in here by Natalia and he liked to turn their necks and glance at the labels. Each one had an occasion written on it: Emma's wedding. David's graduation. The first grandchild. Then he went to the garage and scratched his head in front of the enormous pile of junk which waited for disposal.

He idled in here now, thinking of his wife. He knew exactly what Natalia would be doing right at that moment: filling up glasses of water for everyone, or dusting sugar on top of the crumble, or slicing raw carrots for Ben to eat, everything done in her usual deadpan way. Her small-footed walk would carry her from task to task without fuss, a study in time and motion.

In the kitchen, meanwhile, Emma, David and Ben squirmed in their chairs. Michael Junior sat quietly. Grandpa Michael stabbed the chickens and thought of Sprocket, Granny's old terrier, the poor creature, who'd so much liked chasing chickens.

'Gravy . . .' David moaned and stared at his plate in disbelief. Who'd put that on there?

'D'you not like it? I'll scrape it off, should I, my darling?' intervened his Aunt Patsy.

Ben echoed his elder brother, 'Gravy?' frowning at his plate. 'Get it off!' He banged his fork on the table, crying, 'Off, off, off . . .'

'Gravy?' Michael Junior tried to join in. 'Yuk.' No one believed him. Patsy answered, 'You like gravy, don't pretend you don't.' Then she checked herself. Let him join in, any way he could, she thought They were all painfully aware of the other children leaving Michael Junior out of things, and it was a real gloom in her heart that she didn't blame them for it; she could see why they did so. Yet, sometimes, wasn't he the life and soul of the party, the best grandchild anyone could wish for? Yes.

Patsy hastily scraped the gravy off David's meat onto a side plate. David was sullen, it was never the same if you did that, there was always a bit of the taste left and it mucked up the whole dish. It looked like someone else had eaten it first and sicked it back up. A splodge of gravy went on Patsy's smart sleeve; she had to squeeze it off.

Michael, from his position carving and serving, cottoned onto his crime and felt a rush of frustration. 'Does no one like gravy?'

'Only I do, and Ben sometimes,' replied Emma.

'Right.'

Everyone carried on.

'Look,' Ben climbed down from his chair – not allowed – and strolled over to the work surface, tapped his gravy-covered fork sharply against the dragon bowl. He looked at David, who flinched and stared, his blue eyes round with shock; sometimes it looked like his eyeballs were going to drop out of his head. Why was Ben drawing attention to the bowl?

Natalia said quietly, 'Ben, sit down please.'

Ben rang another tune on the bowl. 'It's perfectly all right,' he said. 'It's not broken.'

There was silence. Natalia was wary of her younger son's behaviour. There was always some logic to what Ben said even if it wasn't immediately obvious. Why was he saying the dragon bowl wasn't broken, when they could all see it wasn't? She looked at David's face – it was ashen. She felt dread. She remembered how, seven years ago, she had clung onto that bowl, all the way across the field, despite everything.

Ben shrugged and said, 'It's perfectly all right.'

Like a bell tolling solemnly in her head the knowledge reverberated in Natalia: the opposite must be true, the bowl was chipped or broken and this was Ben's way of dealing with it. She must keep quiet and talk to him later on. 'Sit down, Ben,' she said. He climbed back onto his chair to face up to his meal again and replied, 'It's fine.' He drank from his beaker so it hid his face. Emma avoided the gaze of her brother David. Ben walked a trail of gravy across the plate. David's face was a white saucer hanging above his untouched supper; everyone was looking at him, it was unbearable. He was ashamed at Ben's lie. Michael Junior stopped chewing and looked from face to face, wanting to catch up, to understand what was happening.

Emma felt a rush of camaraderie with her brothers. David was begging for help. They must mend the bowl as soon as possible.

After supper she practically trod on David's heels as they left the kitchen; when they were around the corner she pushed him behind the hall table with the dolls' house on it and whispered, 'We have to glue it. Go and get it and bring it upstairs.'

David put his hands together as if in prayer. 'Please. You do it.'

He was too scared, thought Emma. 'We have to fix it right now,' she hissed. 'It was your fault, so you have to go and get it.'

'I can't.'

'Do it.'

'I'll find the Superglue,' pleaded David.

'All right, *I'll* do it then, cowardy custard. See you up in my room.' She went back into the kitchen and sauntered over, lingering close to the bowl. Patsy was talking loudly and cheerfully to Natalia. Emma took an apple but it was taken out of her hand by Natalia, washed, and returned to her. She nibbled at it and tried to work out how to get the bowl out of the room. She draped a tea towel over it, and then watched her mother to see when her back would be turned. She put down the apple and scooped up both halves of the bowl in the tea towel and left, hurrying up the stairs to her room. David was waiting in the corridor, showing her the Superglue. They went to open the door but it was shut fast. David pushed harder; it didn't give.

Ben's voice came from inside, 'Password please.'

David hissed, 'Ben, let us in.' He waited a second and Ben's voice came again, 'What's the password?' These were the same words his Action Man said when you pulled the string in its back.

Emma whispered harshly, 'Ben, stop mucking about.' They could hear voices, footsteps. At any moment a grown-up would come. David put his shoulder against the door and bumped twice, but with no luck. He tried a password they'd used before, 'Chocolate spread', and at the same time gave a shove. Ben's voice came back, 'No.'

'Suicide bomber.' David pushed again.

'No.'

David realised now – and whispered to his sister, '*He* doesn't even know what the password is *himself*, so how—'

'Someone coming,' interrupted Emma. The footsteps were louder and there were voices. Only the corner in the upstairs corridor protected them from view. She settled the bowl firmly under one arm and tried the door. It still wouldn't budge. 'Open up Ben,' she ordered brutally, 'or we'll never let you play with us again.' She kicked the door and pushed with all her strength, which meant the bowl slipped from under her arm and fell to the floor.

There was a muffled thud and a grating sound.

Both she and David dropped to their knees. Emma picked up the towel, feeling its contents looser, more noisy. 'Look what you've done, Ben!' David hissed desperately. 'Let us in!' There was a click and the door unlatched; they slipped through.

Michael was in the sitting room, waiting, encouraging a fourth glass of wine up to his lips. There was going to be a card game, piano playing from Patsy, coffee served – all sorts of delights. But until these things could be organised he was alone, which was odd. In the last few days he'd been so utterly besieged with phone calls and people and questions, with all the nonsense of the cremation, not to mention the police and the doctors at the time of the accident, it had been enough to drive anyone mad. Yet now, unbidden, in the midst of all these people and their goings-on, there was this reminder of his life's customary solitariness.

He could hear Patsy's voice; she was upstairs helping with the children's bedtime. Philip could come out of his office, presumably, now the meal was over. Where was he?

Natalia brought in a tray of cups and saucers and so on. He

drew a breath, but stopped. This wasn't the moment to frighten her with a detailed account of his voyage through the horrors of the crematorium. He would tell her later, when she'd stopped moving, when she was sitting still. He needed her proper attention. At the moment they were like knights jousting – galloping towards each other, lances poised, but passing without striking. He cleared his throat, 'Hmm, thanks, wonderful.' She put down the tray, neatened the chess set and threw him a quick smile. 'I'm pleased that Patsy is going to play for us,' she said as she left the room.

'Me too. Jolly good.'

This sofa was too bulky, he thought, for such a small room. His fingers rested on a bald patch in the cloth. He shouldn't pick at it. The low Japanese-style table which held the coffee things was right up against his shins; Natalia's taste, he would have guessed.

Giddiness started a slow dance in his head – the drink. It gathered pace until his mind was spinning comfortably. He couldn't think of anything else. He stood up to walk it off.

He went and leaned on the piano, deliberately wobbling his false hip to loosen it in its socket. He blinked at the terracotta urn containing the remains of his late mother. 'You all right, Ma, on the other side?' he mumbled. She'd been such fun. The way she'd played drums, jazz style, grinning gleefully, very quickly, when she caught the eye of the trumpeter or the singer, before going back to the serious look, the brushes sliding and tapping on the kit. Her smoking and talking and drinking, and the stories of all the countries they'd visited. The globe had been so much bigger in those days but somehow she'd reached almost every corner of it. The pearls around her neck, the long dresses and suits. The orphanage at Sitten Hall during the war. The glamour of her motorcycle. Her leather hat with the chin strap – where had that gone?

He stood upright, rescued his glass of wine and swigged it. The giddiness had passed, he'd be all right. He gazed at the urn. Reduced to this, she was. Ashes! He saw again the coffin on the catafalque, and the blue curtains drawing across. In his mind's eye the coffin lid sprang open and she sat up. She turned around and looked at him and ticked him off. 'Michael, why did you let them do this to me?' The coffin dropped silently down the shaft; she went to stand up even as she disappeared. At the bottom Rob'n'Bob hauled her out of the hatch but she had one leg over the side, trying to escape from her own cremation. The expression on her face mixed, in his mind, with that time she was stung in the mouth by a bee that had landed on the apple she was eating at a picnic. It was how she'd rolled around, inelegant, in trouble, that had been so shocking. The panic, the appeal in her eyes – help! – similar again to the look he'd seen, years later when she'd grown old, if anyone attempted to put the wrong blanket over her knees or if the fan heater wasn't on stand-by. Rob'n'Bob punched the green button and the door lifted. The roar came, and the heat. As she was pushed in, the flames licked around her body. She hadn't escaped after all. Michael heard her scream, right in the marrow of his bones.

He went and stood at the fireplace, rocking back and forth. Lines were drawn in the ashes where the children had scraped up handfuls to put in their jar. They'd pretended to carry her off, and he'd thought of copying them, doing just the same thing, but for real.

Hold on, he told himself. There was another twist to be made in the plan, which meant it was possible after all. What if he took her ashes, yes, and not only that, but also, replaced them with ashes from the fire? If he did that, the urn would weigh the same. Take off the lid and there would be ashes inside. Scatter them under the tree at the hotel and no one would know the difference.

It was a good job he was holding onto the mantel; the idea seized him and threatened to carry him off.

He went back to the open doorway and listened. He could hear Patsy and Natalia upstairs, with the children. This might be his only chance. It was now or never.

Yet, he couldn't bring himself to do it. This would be stealing, wouldn't it? No, he shouldn't pull the wool over everyone's eyes. It would be terrible if people found out. He sank back, gratefully. It was easier to do nothing.

But the idea wouldn't leave him alone. Would Granny have wanted him to do such a thing, he wondered? He rose and went back to the door and opened it again. He went out, lingered in the hall. Where was everyone? He should check. He strolled back into the kitchen, and then climbed the stairs. He saw a pair of children in the bath. Their soaking wet hair meant he didn't actually recognise them to begin with. David and Ben, white-skinned and dark-haired. Even as he watched, his own grandson Michael Junior came in, undressed hurriedly and climbed into the bath to join his cousins. That was good news. Michael sat down on the closed toilet and watched. The idea of swapping the ashes began to recede.

All three boys ignored him and immediately started on various scenarios for the broken submarine and the dinosaurs. It was going well, his grandson was beginning to move with the others. The bathwater boiled with plots and schemes, pirates and murders, plant-eaters and meat-eaters. The submarine rescued half a dozen knights and soldiers and many died of gruesome illnesses. They accepted Michael Junior; it was as if a switch had been thrown.

Patsy hurried in with a pair of towels.

'What happened to playing cards, you on the piano?' asked Michael hopefully.

'Not long,' said Patsy. 'D'you want to help?'

'No, go on, you do it. You don't see them as much as I do.'

He meandered out. On the upstairs landing he came across
Natalia.

'Michael,' she whispered, pushing one end of the curtain rail
back into the wall from where it had come loose, and at the
same time drawing the curtains. 'I want to say to you sorry.'

He blinked. 'What for?'

'It was a mistake. The cremation. I should not have done
that.' She lifted the lid on the blue laundry basket and dug out
handfuls of children's clothes. 'I was wrong and I want that you
know, I am very sorry.'

'Natalia, my dear . . .' He was startled to see tears in her eyes.

The lid of the laundry basket snapped shut and she tugged
at the airing cupboard door. 'What made me think was, to
put myself in her shoes. If I had said something and everyone
said yes, it will be like that. And then it isn't.' She stooped
and with her spare hand clumsily picked up a pile of folded
sheets and jammed them on the crowded shelf. 'I did the
wrong thing. I did. I see it now. So I want to say sorry to
you.'

'Well,' said Michael, pricked with sympathy for her. 'How
about we take the ashes down to Sitten Hall? That is almost as
good. That would be the perfect thing, for me.'

Natalia had both hands available now for the dirty laundry.
She pressed the airing cupboard door shut with her foot and
managed to wipe her eyes. 'We can't. Everyone is here for
tomorrow. Sixty people. We can't do this to them. But I want
you to know. Just. Because. You know.' She gave her brief
smile and fled.

Michael was dumbstruck by this conversation. It took him a
while to wander on. That was a turn up for the books. The
moral victory was his? It was only a faint consolation, but he
was very pleased. It almost put everything right.

He had a mild revelation, then. This was nothing less
than . . . part of the way Natalia operated. She always used an

apology after she'd got her own way on something, to mend things, to keep her victim's sympathy, to prevent enemies, so she might win more easily next time. It was why she kept winning. It was the tooth in tooth and nail, the hammer in hammer and tongs. He wasn't the victor. They'd just galloped towards each other and she'd knocked him off his horse and he was sitting on his arse in the dust, except he didn't know it. It made him cross, but he was pleased to have been clever enough to see it as it came towards him, struck him.

He passed by the spare room and saw Patsy's bag on the bed. Granny Banana had slept in that room. He was more used to the sight of her hanging onto the bedpost for dear life. He found himself at the top of the stairs again and headed on down. There was some brandy to be had, somewhere. He'd seen Patsy hand it over as a gift.

Philip rummaged through the stuff in the garage, making a pile of things to throw away. This weekend he'd make a long over-due trip to the recycling centre. Not tomorrow – it was the scattering of the ashes. Sunday, then.

His eye was caught by a flicker of movement. What was that? He moved a box. There was a quick scurrying: it was a mouse. It trembled, its nose pointing into the corner, as if it hoped to escape by sheer force of desire. 'Mouse,' he murmured, 'poor thing.'

It turned and limped slowly in the other direction. It was hurt. Gormenghast must have got it and then lost it again. The cat always brought his prey indoors, usually to the bedrooms. Often the first thing he saw when he woke up was a mouse with its head chewed off. He peered more closely and saw that it didn't look quite like a mouse after all. Maybe it was a rat. He examined it closely. Its nose was longer, bigger. He noticed a puncture wound, where the tooth had sunk in. The fur was damaged; there was a point of disturbance in the smooth velvet flank. Philip felt slightly sick.

He watched the rat. It watched him back. He looked as deep as he could into the bright point of its eye. There was something sinister about the oily depth of its fur, its own terror, its panting chest. At any moment it might scuttle, or jump. He imagined the scratch of its claws against his face, its teeth like miniature yellow daggers. He shrank from imagining what it had eaten – rotten food, rubbish, dead things . . .

None the less, he knew the children would enjoy trying to look after it, maybe even saving its life. He cast around for something to put it in and found the box that Emma's trainers had come in, with the word 'Umbro' written on the lid. He moved it closer, aiming to trap the rat. No sound came as it crouched further into its corner.

When he had it in the box, he looked at it closely, noticing the size of its front paws and its tiny, brilliant eyes, like specks of liquorice. Emma especially would get a lot of pleasure and interest out of it. Twice before Gormenghast had presented them with live victims; the first time it had been a blackbird, and then a robin. What had been their names? Antonia and . . .? Eloise. They'd made a comfortable box for both of them, with leaves to keep them cool and breadcrumbs and porridge to eat and holes poked in the cardboard for air to pass through, but neither of them had survived for longer than twenty-four hours.

Philip touched the creature. Inside that puncture wound the damage had been done. Its fur, soft as velvet, slipped easily under his finger when it moved. He replaced the lid and walked it out of the garage.

Michael had downed two brandies in quick succession and the armchair felt like it was floating off the ground. He clung on, his head swimming. Wonderful! He told himself to concentrate on a fixed point to stop it becoming too uncomfortable. He chose the tray of crockery that Natalia had brought in earlier. No coffee yet. No piano, no card game? Hurry up everyone! The milk waited in its little silver jug, the cups were stacked neatly. A matching set, Victorian in style. A blue pattern. Natalia usually gave him a mug, but there were guests. He liked to have a saucer. It made you feel looked after. The sugar jar let the side down – it wasn't part of the set. A big glass thing with an air-tight lid. It gave a rude 'thunk' when you thumbed open the clip. He could see, in his mind's eye, Natalia's fingers doing it . . .

He stared harder, more fixedly, and then stood up with difficulty. The joust between himself and Natalia wasn't over. Why didn't he just do it, steal the ashes? By God, it was his turn to mount up, lower the visor on his helmet, aim his lance and gallop as hard as he could! He staggered slightly on the way to the piano but didn't lose control. He drew the urn towards him and took off the lid. Inside was the thick, translucent plastic bag, neatly stapled at the top. He reached in and felt its cool slipperiness and weight. It was the work of one second to lift it out.

Was someone coming? He dropped it back in and replaced the lid. His brow wrinkled. He listened, and stared at the door. Patsy's voice rang clearly from the stairs, 'Pyjamas on!' She was asking the children to hurry if they wanted to listen to her play the piano before it was bedtime. But was she on her way up, or down? Natalia was in the kitchen – he could hear the banging of pots and pans. No doubt the coffee was about to be brought through and Philip would probably appear soon. It really was now or never. Michael again lifted the bag out of the urn, this time with proper speed and purpose, and slipped it into his pocket. He picked up the urn and veered towards the fireplace. He really was in danger of falling over. Was he very drunk – hallucinating even? He took a moment to listen again for anyone coming and to wonder if he really should do this. It seemed like the empty room and the odd silence demanded it of him, like a hole he was falling into . . . he stooped at the fireplace, took the miniature shovel off its little hook and spooned ash out of the fireplace and into the urn. He was shaking with nerves. He cleaned the outside of the urn, roughly. The next moment he was at the piano, putting it back into position and replacing the lid. There were touches of dust he still needed to brush off.

Then he realised: people would wonder why the plastic bag was missing. They'd all seen it, after all. The ash from the fireplace should be in the plastic bag, inside the urn. He was stuck half way, hadn't finished. He thought he could hear someone in the downstairs toilet. Carry on, he told himself! Ride like hell.

He lifted his mother out of his pocket and tugged at the staple, and then came the question as to where he could put his mother's remains in order to get to the bag – he looked around wildly for some kind of container. One of the coffee cups? Not big enough. His eye lit on the sugar jar. That would do it. He put Banana down and picked up the jar, opened it and tossed the contents into the fireplace. The granules of sugar lay there in a pile. He stirred them into the ash so they wouldn't be seen. He moved swiftly to the next task: it was a strange, absurd thought, but he was pouring his mother into a sugar jar. 'Sorry old thing,' he murmured. The empty plastic bag dangled from his hand. He stopped again to listen . . .

As if on cue there was a child's squawk from upstairs and the rumbling of an adult's voice – Philip's. The downstairs cistern was gurgling, which meant that someone was close by or had been very recently. Michael fumbled to complete the task: he took the urn and stood over the fireplace. He knelt on one knee and spilled the ash out of the urn into the empty plastic bag. He had a stab at closing the staple but failed – he hadn't the strength, had to make do with folding the plastic back down and dropping it back into the urn. He went back to the piano. There was ash all over the place – what on earth should he do with it? He wiped it off with the sleeve of his jacket and put the urn back in position. He could hear the capering of a child's footsteps on the stairs and looked around hurriedly to see if he'd forgotten anything. The urn was too far forwards and the lid wasn't on. The sugar jar was also on the piano, yawning open. He lurched back, rubbing ash from his fingers.

He froze, because whoever it was, was about to come in.

But the footsteps carried on. He peered inside the urn, just to see how the contents met the eye. A touch lighter in colour. Noticeably more powdery, in texture, but with bigger fragments. And the top of the bag was open; the plastic had popped up. He folded it back down but it unfurled again. He pressed it down harder. The plastic obstinately refused; up it came again. If anyone looked inside it would be obvious that the ashes had been tampered with. He'd made a mistake. What on earth could he do? Nothing. Hope for the best. Maybe he could find a stapler somewhere in the house.

There came the sound of Natalia's voice, closer than it should be. He felt dreadful. He was looking at his actions as if from a long way off. It was ridiculous to have behaved like this, like an actor in an amateur play in the village hall. He put the lid on the urn and picked up his mother's remains in the sugar jar, and flipped the top back in position, pressed the wire catch home. She was safe. He glanced back at the piano. Reasonable. Not bad. He'd done it. He put down his mother and took a slug of brandy from his glass, just to settle his nerves. All this was the children's fault. But he wasn't a child. He should – as quickly as possible – put down the brandy and retrace his steps, put things how they'd been before. Hold on, he'd forgotten – without delay he should *hide the sugar jar* . . . he reached out to set

down the brandy and perform this one final task but the click of the door latch stopped him in his tracks; his outstretched hand was useless, holding onto the brandy. The sugar jar stood there while he was numbed with shock. Natalia had the cafetière in her hand. She was in the room. Behind her the boys came running, David, Michael Junior and Ben, all in pyjamas. And then Patsy, carrying sheet music. They were all talking merrily. Michael didn't know what to do. How could he get rid of the brandy glass, pick up the sugar jar and hide it, all unnoticed by this sudden, noisy crowd? His brain fogged over. It was impossible. He was too late. He felt his customary anger at being thwarted for whatever reason. 'Natalia!' He put down the brandy. 'Welcome!' He shot his arm up in the air so it looked like a wave, but that must have looked odd, too anxious, so he thrust out his other hand and pretended to be digging his shirt cuff out from his sleeve.

Natalia brought the cafetière to the tray and set it down. 'Sorry the coffee is late,' she said. 'The children were excited too much.'

'Ah.' His heart sank. He watched as she paired up the cups with the saucers, and poured his little spot of milk from the silver jug, and the coffee. 'Thank you. No sugar.'

'Michael.' She straightened, looked at him strangely. 'You are diabetic. Of course no sugar. This I know by now.'

'Good for you. Course. Sorry.' She stirred in the milk, making just one circle with the spoon, and handed it to him. He smiled at her blandly, trying to remember if *she* took sugar. He'd just have to take a dive and knock it out of her hands. He was fairly sure that Patsy took those sugar substitute things which she kept in the little dispenser in her bag. 'Where's Philip?' he asked unnecessarily. This house was so small and cheaply made, by the standards he'd been used to, formerly. It seemed that you could put your arm up the stairs, along the landing and reach into every corner of every room. If you stood up too sharply your head would go through the ceiling. The doors were light as cardboard.

'He's coming,' she replied. 'He found an injured rat and Emma is—'

She was interrupted by Emma running in, holding a shoe box and crying out, 'Look what we found!'

Everyone gathered round to coo at the injured creature. Michael was grateful for the distraction. Anything rather than have anyone notice what he'd been up to. 'How about the vet?' he asked.

'Vet,' whispered Natalia.

'*Yes*,' said Emma, 'we need the vet!' Michael was pleased, it meant people would be going in all directions. There'd be opportunities for him to escape with dear old Banana. 'After all,' went on Emma, 'we took Gormenghast to the vet when he was hit by a car. And this rat has been hurt by Gormenghast.'

'That's logical,' said Michael.

Natalia sounded calm. 'But Gormenghast survives. Was worth the effort. This rat will die, I think. After twenty-four hours. The most. The shock, what happened? D'you think?'

'Why don't we all go to the vet's?' suggested Michael. 'If that's what's needed. A mass outing.'

'Wait to see if it survives to tomorrow and then we decide,' said Natalia. 'And do you know, this isn't a rat,' she went on, pointing at the box. 'Is a mole.'

Emma's mouth dropped open. 'Ohhh . . . a mole,' she said, slowly, and with her mouth wide open. She picked up the box and ran from the room.

'Let her go,' said Natalia. 'She will come back when she's looked after it.'

The group who'd been gathered around the shoe box broke up and moved away, and one by one the lamps went out – it was Patsy, who'd lit candles and now she walked from switch to switch, darkness and shadows following her, until she'd turned the room into a romantic auditorium. Meanwhile the boys were organised in a line in front of the piano by Natalia. Michael, floating on his cloud of brandy, was easily taken in hand and pointed to a different chair, from where he could see the keyboard. More brandy had been poured for him. The sugar jar was further away now. No one had taken any, thank God. He wasn't going to let it out of his sight. After Patsy had played the piano, there would be time for him to act. This life – nothing but time rolling forwards and . . .

He looked up. His ex-wife-number-three was doing her thing, smiling at the row of children, tucking herself into the keyboard and resting her hands on the notes in readiness. It had been years since he'd heard her play. It was something he'd liked about her right from the beginning, how she could roll the music out so beautifully.

Also, she'd given him a gift earlier on, which was touching. It was a small piece of tapestry and it was draped over the back of what had been Granny Banana's usual chair, a simple 'Banana – In Memoriam' stitched into a moss-green background. The wrapping paper was still scrunched in the seat. Banana's seat. In the old days, before she'd died, it had been usual for her and Michael to have been left alone in here after supper, with Philip in and out as may be, and Natalia always engaged in tasks and chores or children's homework and so on. Now, with Banana gone, he himself was sitting in just the same position, but instead of his old mother opposite there was Patsy's square of tapestry. Patsy hadn't done tap for years. It reminded him of the early days of their marriage. Good times.

Sad times, these.

His wandering gaze took in the iron candlestick on the mantel and the little wooden triptych of family photographs – Banana and her two little sons, himself and Philip, aged eight and four. Further along rested a teddy bear and a miniature silver jug with a broken foot. A photograph of Natalia as a child.

All these items had come from the farm.

The music poured over him; it complemented the nostalgia which grew in his breast. He liked to see the row of boys, and Emma had slipped back in and joined them now, he noticed. All the children fit and breathing and looking up at Patsy, ex-wife-number-three. Even their rows had been fun, looking back. He remembered . . .

But he shouldn't dwell in the past because for the first time in ages he had a task ahead, something he had to finish properly. He had to spirit away the sugar jar. There could be no more mistakes. He shouldn't drink any more brandy.

Even as he thought this, Philip came in and paused, listening, and then unobtrusively took the couple of paces necessary to reach the coffee tray. He picked up the cafetière and poured himself a cup and then hugged the sugar jar close to his chest to unclip the lid.

There was nothing Michael could do. Patsy's piano concert prevented him from saying or doing anything. He was powerless, struck dumb. He could only watch, not knowing whether to laugh or cry, while Patsy played the piano in accompaniment to Philip's loading up two spoons of his own dead mother's mortal remains and dropping them in his coffee, and stirring it. Michael could throw something in the hope the coffee would spill but the loveliness of Patsy's musical interlude forbade it. Philip moved to his seat and for a while the cup waited on his lap. And then he lifted it, puckered his lips and blew gently across the surface of the coffee and took a sip. And then another. He leaned forward and took a third spoon of sugar and stirred it again to try for a bit more sweetness from his own mother's bones! Michael's insides squirmed. Could Philip not see it wasn't sugar? He supposed, in the candlelight, it didn't look that different from that very posh type of Demerara. And Philip was watching Patsy, anyway. But wasn't the taste dreadful? Philip always had sort of eaten anything you put in front of him. Michael had put sheep poo in Philip's water once, when they were children, and he hadn't noticed.

The music slowed to a beautiful, tender crawl. The children watched, spellbound. Natalia quietly sorted through some receipts. Philip stared into space. Michael sipped more brandy, enjoying the absurd, emotional charge of the last few minutes. It was a scandal! He'd like to share it with Patsy; she'd laugh so. But they'd grown too far apart. He couldn't reach her. She was safely, romantically imprisoned in the music she was playing. Shame.

Besides, it was best not to tell a soul, ever. He mustn't be found out. It would be too awful a truth to expose to the harsh glare of publicity.

The music had stopped. There was applause, which Michael led; he kept it going for longer and more loudly. Patsy stood up and took her bow and caught his eye, smiled.

Natalia rounded up the children. It was past their bed times. They called out for more but were reminded that they'd been promised only one piece of music. Philip struggled to his feet to help.

Before long, when the wriggling and the complaining were over, Michael was left alone with Patsy.

'Lovely, Pats,' he said.

'Did you like it?' asked Patsy. 'I've started playing again and I must say I'm finding it . . . good fun.'

'It was a treat.'

They sat for a while. Michael was waiting for her to go, but she remained seated and shuffled the music on the stand. He might have to sit through some more. 'Thank you,' he said.

The shuffling stopped. Silence hung in the air.

'Perhaps I'd better just go and help put everyone to bed,' said Patsy. She stood up as if bitten.

How tall she was, he thought. It was a marvel he'd ever kissed anything that high up. She must always have been lying down.

'I think they've got a bit stuck up there. Can you hear crying? I should go probably. It's only fair when they've got Michael Junior as well.'

'All right. Yes. See you.'

Patsy hurried from the room. Michael was alone again. At last, he could hide the jar.

Emma ran to her bedroom, but when she jumped into bed she felt something odd. It was the broken dragon bowl, she remembered. She couldn't think where else to hide it or what to do so she left it under there for now, but pushed it further down. She wished she could go and check Umbro Mole in his box.

A *mole*, she had her own pet mole. They were mysterious, nocturnal. The only time she'd seen or heard any evidence of one, ever, was when she'd been woken by her mother one moonlit night and they'd watched, entranced, as spoil was pushed out on the lawn – she'd wondered at the thought of that slow, blind animal trundling along its tunnels, working so hard. What strange magic was in the goings-on of creatures!

Dear, sweet Umbro Mole. When she'd taken the box, she'd run outside where it was dark and the chill had gone straight through her pyjamas, but she'd carried on. She'd gone round the back of the house and walked up and down the garden until she found a molehill. She'd quickly lifted three handfuls of loose spoil into the box. It had been cold and damp to the touch. Umbro Mole would feel at home in the dark, with mud all around, just how it liked. Then she'd gone to the garage and found a quiet corner in the bottom of the old chest of drawers at the back, where Gormenghast couldn't reach. Before she'd left him to go back to the others she'd lifted Umbro's little hand, felt a squeeze of wonder at how big and capable-looking it was, and pink – it was exactly like a human hand, even down to the thumb . . .

It was breathing – its flanks moved in and out – so it was alive, still. She'd placed the box carefully with a stone on its lid to keep it safe and shut the drawer and gone back to the others.

Sitting up in bed she crossed her heart and thought of her Granny and now there were tears in her eyes. She clasped her hands together and prayed hard, 'I'm sorry Banana, wherever you are. I wish you were still alive.' She squeezed her eyes shut more tightly. She had an idea: she could write to her. She took the magnetic writing board off her shelf and picked up the plastic writing tool attached to it by a coil. With one shunt back and forth she wiped off the old stuff. On the clean grey square, she wrote in big capital letters, 'Grany. aR yu ther?' She slotted the pen back in its clip and put the machine carefully back on the shelf.

For a while she rested, just breathed, looked at the magnetic writing board. Ghosts were magical, just like the writing board, so maybe Granny could write back. She'd check in the morning.

The door to her bedroom burst open. Michael Junior came in followed by David and Ben, flicking towels. Michael Junior said to her, 'I'm allowed in the game, next time we play, OK?'

Emma saw immediately what had happened. They'd made friends and they'd told him about the game. She had to decide which way to jump. If she allowed the game to continue it was quite likely she'd lose control of it to Michael Junior because he was as old as she was and talked faster. Yet if she refused to let him in she risked being ostracised and they might carry on without her. She looked at all three boys. 'Come on, say yes,' called Ben, 'it will be a lot better.'

'They said I could join in,' said Michael Junior, 'and they told me the game.' Emma drew a breath. 'All right,' she agreed.

Michael Junior gave a whoop and used the easy route up to the top of her desk, which wasn't allowed.

'Michael get down!' Patsy's call interrupted. Natalia hurried in as well; the two women stood shoulder to shoulder. 'Come on, bed time,' Natalia said.

'Sweetie, you're too big now, it's not a very strong desk,' warned Patsy. Michael Junior's face reddened, his brow creased, the vein in his neck stood out, his blood-filled ears bobbed up and down. 'I've only just started in the game!' he shouted. 'The others have been playing all the time and I haven't, not one bit, not since I got here!'

'Come on,' said Natalia calmly. 'You are meant to be getting into bed, not running around.'

'No!' Michael Junior was in tears. He pointed at the others where they waited on Emma's bed. 'They've been playing for ages and *I* . . .' he thumped his chest, '*I* . . .' He stopped, speechless at the injustice.

'They're not playing the game now, no one is.'

'The others were up here before, earlier. You're breaking up our . . . *bloody* game!' Michael Junior's face was strained, he was fit to burst; he glared at them.

Patsy was cross. 'Please don't swear. Game over, Michael. Bed time.'

'ALL RIGHT! Out the way!' Michael called to the others on the bed.

'Don't jump, climb down, otherwise you'll hurt . . .' But Michael Junior did jump across and landed, bang, on the bed. Serve them right.

It backfired. There was something hard underneath the duvet and he was crying over a sharp, bruising pain on the bottom of his foot.

David and Emma looked at each other – the dragon bowl. Emma leaped off the bed and went to the grown-ups. 'I'll get everyone into bed, I promise. In two minutes. Just let me, please!' She started to swing the door shut, and smiled. 'I will!' The grown-ups were laughing at her, but they retreated. She turned quickly back to the bed and threw back the duvet. They didn't even bother to count the number of pieces; the dragon bowl couldn't ever be mended. 'Let's just throw it away, pretend it's lost,' suggested David.

'No, we'll have to tell,' said Emma.

'Million bagsies not me,' said David, 'and it should be Ben, he was the one who originally broke it.'

'Only because you pushed me.'

'I didn't push you.'

'You pushed me with the cushion you threw.'

'Don't be ridiculous Ben.' Emma pulled back the cover. She shivered. 'We have to get into bed. We'll do the goodnight and let's stay awake and meet up again later.'

David and Ben obediently went to their room. Michael Junior went top-to-tail with Emma. They lay in their beds, waiting for their goodnights. Emma could feel the grating pieces of the dragon bowl with her foot.

Michael levered himself forward, preparing for exit. It was tricky getting out of such a deep chair. He pegged both thumbs and forefingers on the arms, wriggled another few inches until he was closer to the edge, pushed hard. Candlelight flickered on his face . . . pain shot into his neck. He couldn't easily do it. He sank back. Gawwd, he thought, thank God Patsy isn't here to see this. Try again.

Unsteadily, he rose to his feet and picked up the sugar jar. Bravo. He gave himself a metaphorical pat on the back.

Patsy did happen to come back in just then, hunting for her glasses, and he knew he was being observed. After all, this was astonishing: he was bothering to assemble things on the tray and take it back to the kitchen, without being asked.

'Wish I had a video camera, Michael.'

'And why is that?' he asked.

'Just to witness you clearing away.'

'I washed up, every night of our marriage.'

'I remember, Michael.' He could hear the humour in her voice. She was taking the Mickey. 'Your washing-up is engraved on my memory,' she went on, 'I shan't ever forget such excitement.' She snapped shut the spectacles case. She was wearing the specs, librarian style. Was she going to read or watch television? He was hoping for the card game but it was too late now.

'Why on earth, I wonder, are you so concerned about that tray, and what's on it?' she asked meaningfully.

He let the sadness of his three failed marriages run right through him; it was like pulling a plug out of the soles of his feet and feeling the level go down, disappear, so he might shrug off her ex-wife style of irony.

'What d'you mean, Pats?'

'Could it be something to do with the sugar jar, Michael?'

He stumbled at that, and looked up at her. Did she know? How? She was amused at something. Her eyebrows were as high as he'd ever seen them. 'I don't know what you're saying.'

'Oh, that's all right then,' she said airily. 'It's just I thought I saw you throwing away all the sugar. Which for a diabetic, is an understandable reaction I suppose. Or was something else going on, Michael? Sorry, I just peeped through the door jamb at you. I wanted to see if the kids were in here.'

'I was . . . interested in the sugar.'

'Interested? I see.'

'It was just a different type of sugar, Pats, that's all there is to it,' he blustered. 'It was stale, and there were horrible . . . things in it so I chucked it away. I'm not about to go into a diabetic frenzy.' He limped from the room, coffee cups rattling, his step very uncertain. And yet part of him wanted to tell Patsy everything, share the whole adventure. How much had she actually seen, he wondered? His mouth had gone utterly dry. His skin crawled, with the feeling of potential discovery and shame.

In the hallway he paused to rest the tray on the table which held the dolls' house and recover his nerve. There was a danger that Patsy would follow, otherwise he'd have taken the sugar jar and put it in his overcoat pocket right now. Except it was too big. He'd carry the whole tray to the kitchen, lift the jar off and take it home . . .

When he reached the kitchen, the room was different. It took him a while to puzzle out what had happened: Philip had obviously taken all the spotlights and aimed them at the end of the kitchen table, where he sat. The tin of fishing tackle was to one side, the lid off. The big messy clump of line, hooks, flies and lures was in front of him and he delicately picked at it, his hair standing all over the place, his spectacles almost hanging off the end of his nose. He was untangling the fishing gear. It meant that the rest of the room was in shadow, which suited Michael's purposes.

He noticed the writing on the lid of the tin − 'Fishing Tackle'. It was written in their own father's hand; Michael had seen it done all those years ago and he'd witnessed the skilful addition of the curlicue underneath, an embellishment in true Spanish style, which gave it such flair. That was a thought: if both their father and their mother were dead, did that make him and Philip orphans?

Natalia was off to one side, her hips and shoulders moving rhythmically. She was up to something, as usual. Michael hovered with his tray, he was about to put it on the table but couldn't resist pausing to look over Philip's shoulder and give him some encouragement. 'Useful task Philip.'

'Got to be done,' murmured Philip.

He put down the tray. Nearly there. Almost mission accomplished. Luck had been on his side, so far.

It was an odd thought, how good luck had latched onto Natalia even more firmly these last few years – job, promotion, children – and you might almost think it was the same luck attaching itself to her as had deserted himself and Philip over the same period. And fate's harpies had put him, Michael, in charge of the Land Rover when the door latch had failed and caused the final, last death of poor old Banana. He put his hand on Philip's shoulder. 'Need a hand? I could start at the other end.'

'It's all right, nearly there.'

'Right y'are. Time for me to go home, then, I think.' He would get his coat, put it on, and then hide the jar under it.

'Michael,' came Natalia's voice, 'you are drinking too much to drive.'

'You're right of course. But I come from a different era, Natalia, when drinking and driving was what one did. Almost *de rigueur*.'

'Don't drive, Michael, it's dangerous.'

'Philip, should I be allowed to drive?' Michael turned to his brother for help.

'Errr,' said Philip, and then, 'Don't ask me.'

He should have known Philip wouldn't join in. It was unfair, he thought, that his younger brother seemed unable to track down his pleasures and get on the outside of them, just when he had a clutch of children and a young wife, everything that should make a man happy, at last handed to him on a plate and . . .

He found himself in the hallway, trying to snap his coat off the hook, which was set too high on the wall for comfort. He managed to get it down, and half shrugged it on, still thinking about Philip. Patsy was standing there in the hallway with him, which was a surprise.

'What you up to?' she asked.

'Off home Pats.'

'You're drunk.'

'I know, I know.'

'Perhaps we can find you a corner to sleep it off for a while. Or, have another coffee.'

'I was just thinking about old Philip,' murmured Michael.

'What about him?'

'So much went wrong for him, if you think about it. Things he'd taken for granted snatched away, sharply. Without ceremony.'

'It's true.' She was helping him with his collar. There was an immediate increase in the feeling of comfort, with her standing so close.

'Imagine, being struck down . . . in so many ways, at the same time.' Michael ticked off his fingers. 'BSE, when was that?'

'2001.'

'The collapse of Equitable Life. He'd assigned all his client base to them. The plunge in internet share prices. He sold out at the bottom of the market.'

'I know, terrible.' She looped her arm through his and they wandered back towards the kitchen.

'Losing the farm, his income – everything,' hissed Michael.

'It was a tough thing.'

'And just at the moment when one child after another poured from his loins, Pats. Imagine. It's why he's a broken man. The way he hides in his so-called office . . . d'you know what I mean? It shouldn't be like that. It's sad for a brother to see.' They'd gone past the kitchen now and were in the porch.

'You've had your own struggles, Michael.'

'True.'

'You said your goodbyes already?'

'No. Yes. No! I haven't.' He stopped. 'Hold on. Very important.'

They were outside, already; he was ahead of himself. He had to go back in to get the jar. Patsy had distracted him.

'Shall I tell you what I remember, every time I look at Philip?' asked Patsy.

'What?' The air was chill, it carried a heavy freight of damp. He pulled his coat tighter, fingering the Land Rover keys in his pocket.

'His side parting. D'you remember, it used to be so sharp and straight, as if it had been cut into his head with an axe, and it was always . . . *there*. You never saw him without it. Whereas now, it's disappeared. I wish he'd buck up, have a shave, you know.'

'Exactly, put on a clean shirt.'

'And a tie.'

'You know, do up his fly buttons,' said Michael ruefully. They leaned against each other, laughing. This was like the old days.

'Pick the spinach off his teeth.'

'Wash his *bottom*.'

They held onto each other tight. Michael felt successful. They'd always enjoyed laughing at his brother.

'Now, have you got your *sugar jar* all right, Michael?' asked Patsy emphatically.

Her words cast an immediate spell. He blinked. She knew every damn thing? She'd seen it all? It took some moments for that to sink in. He was caught by her knowing smile. 'Pats, did you see?'

She nodded. 'I did, Michael.'

'Everything?'

'Yes.'

'Oh. Um.'

'Yes indeed.'

'I am sorry, it's a bit mad, but . . .'

'We have to go in and get it, don't we Michael?'

'We do. So . . .' He turned back indoors; she followed him.

In the kitchen it was as if time had stood still. Philip worked away under his spotlights, teasing out the fishing tackle. Natalia was in the shadows at the edge of the room, busy doing whatever it was.

Patsy wandered in behind him. 'Uggg, it's cold,' she was saying. While the women talked, Michael located the tray on the table, exactly where he'd put it, but the sugar jar wasn't there. For an instant he panicked, but then he saw it, safe and sound, just to one side, on the table. Thank God. He realised he wasn't handling this very well. He felt conspicuous in his overcoat, about to go. It was best to pretend to clear up a bit. He caught Patsy's eye and rattled a cup and saucer as he carried them over to the draining board, all the while talking some fishing nonsense to Philip. He plied back and forth between the tray and the sink a couple of times and then picked up the sugar jar and inserted his body between it and anyone watching, and opened his coat.

It was as far as he got – because he realised the jar was empty. There was nothing in it. Granny Banana had gone.

Ordinary sounds – the even, in-out whistle of Philip's breath as he concentrated on the fishing tackle, the cheerful, low key conversation between Patsy and Natalia, the clinking of bowls and spoons, the forbidden murmuring of the children from upstairs – all seemed extraordinary. Unremarkable sights – the bags of flour and suchlike, the little gaggle of weights, his ex-wife's steady, sympathetic gaze – came to him as if from the other side of some metaphysical membrane. A bubble of unreality enclosed him.

He worked out what must have happened. Granny Banana's ground-up bones had become an unasked for ingredient in Natalia's cake mix.

Sir Michael Bruce Witherington Gough, aka Lord Woodford, aged sixty-seven, educated at Eton and Oxford etc.,

put down the sugar jar and went and looked over Natalia's
shoulder as she made short, sideways steps at the work surface,
concentrating on the job in hand. He and Patsy shared a meaningful look.

After what seemed like an age he trusted his voice not to
break. 'What you up to Nats, hmmm?' His good cheer
sounded hollow.

'Chocolate cake. For tomorrow. The party.'

'Sounds good.' He shouldn't stare at the mixture like a starv-
ing dog.

'You hungry?' asked Natalia.

'No, no.'

He took off his overcoat and folded it over the back of a
chair. 'But perhaps I am a bit over the limit. I ought to hang on
for a bit. Drink some water.'

'Very wise,' said Patsy. There was a huge, desperate kindness
in her tone of voice.

He could cry, he really could. He was there, he'd done it, but
one lapse of concentration, and disaster had struck. He could-
n't think what to do. Patsy might have an idea. That was some
comfort – at least he had an ally. He presumed she was an ally.

'Sit down Michael,' she said, 'and I'll pour you a large glass
of water.'

He did as he was told.

Just as he'd gained control of events, they'd slipped out of his
grip and lay broken in pieces. It was difficult to see how they
might be mended.

A glass of water was put in front of him. He recognised
Patsy's hand, the big strong bones and the large, boldly
coloured rings jostling for attention. The liver spots were new.
'Thank you,' he said, rocking back and forth and trying not to
shout.

Philip clipped the lid back on the tin of fishing tackle and
stood up. 'Finished,' he said. He went to various points around

the table and turned the spotlights back to their usual position. The kitchen took on its former, widespread brightness.

'Natalia,' Patsy piped up, 'why don't you let Michael and I stay up for you, and we'll take the cakes out of the oven. You must be dog tired, looking after all of us.'

'Is OK,' said Natalia automatically.

'But seriously,' insisted Patsy, 'why not? You do so much for us. All the time. Michael and I will take ourselves off to the sitting room and talk about the old days, and he will sober up enough to drive home and I will deal with the cakes. I've got your timer.'

'You sure?' whispered Natalia.

'Very sure.'

'That would be nice.' Natalia lifted the dishwasher door and hung the tea towel back on its hook. 'Thank you.'

They all shared goodnights and Patsy took charge. The oven door shut with a clunk. Natalia and Philip disappeared upstairs.

Michael carried his pint of water and followed Patsy back to the sitting room. They settled in chairs, opposite each other. Patsy positioned the timer on the low Japanese-style table in front of her.

'Oh dear,' he murmured.

'Yes.'

'It's too much. I give up.'

'Hmm. Not a situation we can just leave to sort itself out.'

'No.' He sighed. 'Wonder what Banana would have made of it all.'

'She'd have enjoyed all the fuss, I imagine.' Patsy turned a page of a magazine. A string of pearls was looped around her neck, he noticed. There was a time, in the long distant past, when he'd have known they were worn for him. Dear old thing, she was. Rare feelings of love and trust flew overhead; he enjoyed their brief passage. He clung to the happiness, so precious were moments like these . . . His eyes closed.

When Michael awoke, he was still alone with his ex-wife-number-three sitting opposite, turning the pages of the magazine. Minutes had passed.

She looked up. 'Ah, you're back.'

'Yes. Quick snooze. Sorry.'

'No, it's all right.'

He gazed at the white cliff of hair rising from her forehead. Had he ever invaded, conquered those cliffs, had he been at the very front of her mind? He must have, once, he thought. She wasn't the sort of person to have married except for love. She had loved him. It felt like an achievement. Forget the lack of a first class degree, any career, honours, it didn't matter that he'd earned none of these things. What have you done, St Peter would ask him at the gates of heaven; what, exactly, have you achieved, Michael Gough? Tell you what, he replied, Patsy loved me. The gates swung open.

He caught her looking at him. 'Mmm?'

'I didn't say anything.'

'Oh.'

'Are you all right, Michael? I mean, is your life all right?' She wanted him to answer no. Look at him, fussing with his jacket lapels. If only he'd look her in the eye.

Michael stirred uneasily. 'Life, in general? Um. Yes, thanks. All right.'

'You're just distracted at the moment.'

'Oh. Well, yes, I suppose that's true. Plus, it's not easy to focus on cheerfulness. World in uproar as usual. Granny Banana dead. All the usual nonsense.' He blinked, in trouble again.

'We need to talk about these cakes,' she said in a low voice.

'Yes,' he agreed. 'We have to steal them somehow. Hope you might help me Pats, if you don't think too ill of me.'

'I heard what happened about the funeral. Natalia organising it instead of you. And I can't believe you didn't call me and ask for help. Of course we've been apart for seven years, but if it was just about money, you know . . . I just wish you'd felt you could have called.'

'Oh, well . . . thank you.'

'Did you not think to?'

'No, can't say I did.'

'We were married, Michael, for a long time. Mattie is our daughter, Banana is her grandmother. I would have wanted to see her buried as she'd wished. I would have done everything in my power. I want you to know that.'

'Very good,' said Michael. 'But – too late now. Spilt milk. Thanks anyway.'

'Never mind. We just have to work out what to do next.'

'D'you remember,' he said, changing the subject, 'how she used to go up to Mattie's bedroom and put a coin under her pillow? When she was small?'

'I was thinking about exactly that, earlier this evening.'

'No one to do that now, for the little ones.' Michael wiped the tears out of his eyes. So annoying how drink made you cry, made such a mess of one's composure. Patsy was up to something. She'd unclipped her bag and was rooting in it. She handed him four coins. 'Careful not to wake them,' she said.

He turned the coins in his hand. 'You do it, Pats.'

'No, you're her son and heir.'

He thought about it for a while. 'But you'll *remember* to do it every time, I won't.'

'I'll make sure you remember.'

He nodded. Yes, she would, too.

A minute later he was treading as softly as possible up the stairs. He went to David and Ben's room first and peered into the darkness. Were his nephews asleep? Maybe. He reached up to the top bunk and pushed a coin under David's pillow. He would try and use the same words. 'Your fare. Take you to Dreamland.'

David was half awake, and heard; he gained the comfort of an adult voice. It was soothing after the dramas and grief of this week. He wanted to repair every bad moment, to un-say every ill-tempered word he'd ever said in his whole life. He stirred. His uncle was standing there, a silhouette. 'Hmmm? What?' he asked.

'Shh, it's very late. Nighty-night.'

David fingered his cool sheet and lay as close as possible against the wall.

Michael leaned over the bottom bunk and repeated the same action, the same words. Ben was fast asleep, his limbs thrown out any old how.

Michael moved along the corridor to Emma's room. The glow from the little globe by the bed showed Michael Junior lying one way, Emma the other. These two little darlings had been born one day apart, seven years ago. One his grandson, the other his niece. Michael leaned over and kissed his grandson's forehead, slid the coin under his pillow. 'Your fare, take you to Dreamland.'

He moved round to Emma's side. Gormenghast was in the bed with her; Michael could hear the vibration of his purring and see the dark shadow on the duvet close up against Emma's swatch of hair. She sat up, which gave him a jump. She hissed something at him; he had to ask her to say it again. She told him about the magnetic writing board and climbed out of bed to retrieve it from its hiding place. Maybe Granny might be able to write on the board and answer the question she'd written on it? Michael nodded. 'Well, let's see,' he whispered, 'put it back and maybe you'll get an answer.' He placed it on the floor next to her bed and then he went through the same routine: the coin, the fare for Dreamland.

'What are you doing?' she asked.

'Sending you to sleep, look under your pillow in the morn-

ing,' he said and she smiled, and straight away looked under it
and found the coin. 'Put it back 'til morning,' whispered
Michael. 'It's the fare to take you to Dreamland.' She lay back
down and closed her eyes.

Michael left the room. Upstairs was quiet. The corridor,
which had been a brightly lit rat-run at bed time, was deserted,
softened by the night light, as he went downstairs and returned
to the sitting room.

Patsy wasn't there, so he went to the kitchen. The scent of
new, warm cake filled the room. The timer must have gone off.

Patsy, he saw now, was taking out the second cake and putting it on the cooling rack.

'Is she in both of them, or just one?' he asked in a low voice.

'It was the same mix, so she's probably a little bit in both.'

'Damn. We'll have to take the two of them, then.'

'We can't, Michael, unless we make two more.'

'If we'd had the money to hire a caterer for tomorrow, none
of this would have happened.'

'There must be a caterer, you can't feed sixty people on two
cakes. She will just be adding these to what's there.'

'What shall we do then? We could pretend they dropped on
the floor.'

'I'm not sure I can bear telling her that. *Don't* pick it up
Michael.'

'Why not?'

'It will break, it needs to cool down.'

'No, it will be fine.' He edged the cake off the rack and held
it, soft and moist and hot, in front of him. 'If we just drop
them, right now, and then we can use the dust pan and brush?
Sweep them into a plastic bag?' It was enjoyable to make his
ex-wife laugh. The fact that it had all gone wrong was worth it
for this – for her to be here with him, all the lights switched on
inside. He straddled his legs a bit, held the cake further out,
playing it up for her. 'Ready?' he asked.

'They all right?' said a quiet voice and Natalia slid into the kitchen, wearing pyjamas. Michael almost dropped the cake anyway.

'They're fine,' said Patsy calmly. 'Michael put it down, you might drop it.'

'Quite heavy,' said Michael. 'But perfectly formed.' The shame was almost unbearable; it made him want to throw the cake at Natalia, actually. He carefully put it back on the cooling rack.

'Thanks for doing that, but I was not sleeping so I thought I'd do the icing now.' She sighed. 'So much to do all the time.'

'Yes,' agreed Patsy. 'I'm never sure how you do it, Natalia. I take my hat off to you, I really do.'

Natalia turned to Michael. 'Are you sober enough, Michael?'

'Yes,' Patsy answered for him. 'Come on Michael, let's see you off.'

'Oh. Not sure I am.'

'Yes you are,' insisted Patsy.

'All right then. Suppose so . . .' He completed the usual formalities and he and Patsy found themselves outside again. The same chill autumn night greeted them. She walked him to the Land Rover. They both felt like scolded children. 'What shall we do?' asked Michael. 'It sounded like you had a plan.'

Patsy's arm looped in his as they crossed the road. 'Tomorrow,' she said, 'when we are at the hotel, we'll be able to get hold of them. I promise we will, Michael.'

'All right, I'll believe you. And . . . thanks for your help. All of it . . . only carrying on because you are at my side as it were. Thank you, thank you thank you.'

There was certainly more than one nice thing he'd said to her tonight, thought Patsy, remembering her promise to herself. There was no excuse. The words were at the front of her

mind: Michael come home, I miss you. But she couldn't make
the leap. It was dangerous. Instead she squeezed his arm, hard.

They stopped and faced each other. 'You drunk, Pats?'

'No. You are.' She put her palm to the side of his face.

'A good woman. Here, standing right in front of me.'

'I married you.'

'You did. My big success.'

'That's a nice thing for a woman to hear.'

They gave each other rather an embarrassed hug and said
their good-byes at the door of the Land Rover. He started up,
and left her standing there in the darkness, his ex-wife.

As soon as Emma awoke the next morning she reached for the
magnetic writing board. An answer from Granny Banana had
been left for her while she slept. Written in childlike, wobbly
capital letters (Natalia had used her left hand on purpose) were
the words, 'I am OK.' Emma sat on the edge of the bed and felt
a dreadful, sombre responsibility. She was in contact with the
other side.

David sat quietly in his bunk bed, gaming on Reign Of Fire
with the volume turned off.

In the kitchen Ben lifted a spoonful of Frosted Wheats to his
mouth and chewed. A drop of milk ran down his chin.

Natalia was at the cooker, making eggy bread for Michael
Junior's breakfast; he sat neatly, waiting. When Emma came
down he gave her a sideways look and pitched his eyebrows up
an inch, to say hello. She noticed that he had a napkin on his
lap and his knees were facing the front. He wore a suit and tie
and his hair was brushed. Emma couldn't believe how grown-
up he looked. During the night, in the game, he had been
amazing. She smiled at him and walked closer. He even smelled
nice, quite different from a normal boy. Her two brothers and
her father always smelled revolting. She was enchanted with

how small his ears were, like shells you might find on the beach. If only he wasn't annoying, as a character, she might be able to fall in love with him.

At half past ten Michael turned up and they prepared to leave the house to drive in convoy to the memorial service. The adults, and the children, were fretful. Natalia told Emma to change her top because it was dirty. Emma refused. Natalia tried to lift it over her head. Hatred swelled in Emma; she fought off her mother. Natalia and Philip and the children climbed into the Subaru; Michael and Patsy would follow in the Land Rover.

Natalia made sure of her passengers, tugged the Subaru's gear shift into drive and moved off. Treading on its heels came the Land Rover – Michael caused a blare of horns from oncoming traffic when he turned out at the end of the road. The boot of that Subaru held the cakes; he and Patsy had seen them loaded in.

In the Subaru Emma turned and peered through the headrest. She could see the Land Rover fight its way through traffic to catch them up, driving on the wrong side of the road and swerving in, inches from their rear bumper. 'Uncle Michael is *right behind*,' she said, frowning.

It was a job for the old farm vehicle to keep up; Michael had to barge through a red light but he was determined the Subaru should stay in view. They could see the four children tilt back and forth as the vehicle lurched across town.

David was safe under his sister's arm but he feared for the ashes because his father, in the front, had only one hand loosely holding the urn in his lap; what if it rolled off and fell to the floor? The ashes would spill out. He couldn't bear it; his eyes felt hot from worry. Ben was all right; he'd managed to get away with wearing his army uniform. He liked the inside of the Subaru being so clean. Emma was daydreaming about the reply on the magnetic writing board. She couldn't think of anything else.

Michael and Patsy were worried: they'd lost sight of the Subaru. The town was crowded with Saturday traffic and they strained to see a dozen cars ahead, but inexplicably it had disappeared. It didn't matter too much – Michael knew the way to the hotel – but he wanted to keep the boot in view, to feel that Banana was being properly escorted.

Sure enough, when they turned into the hotel car park there was the Subaru, its doors standing open, the others just climbing out. Michael steered the Land Rover into a spare slot. There were faces he recognised walking past; now he was going to have to remember people's names. Here were Simon and Mattie, strolling affably over, hugging Michael Junior. 'Weather's all right after all,' commented Simon. Patsy joined them. 'Yes indeed. Thank God.' Natalia waited until Philip had shut the door and then turned the key to operate the central locking. With his fingers resting on the boot Michael said, 'What about the cakes, d'you want help carrying them in?'

'I leave them already,' said Natalia. She dropped the car keys in her bag.

'Already what?' asked Michael, 'How d'you mean?'

'The cakes are for the swimming,' she replied. 'The gala. I mean the prizes. Otters, the swimming club. I leave them on the way.'

'What, leave them where?' demanded Michael. He tapped the boot of the Subaru. 'I thought they were . . . in here?'

'Yes, they were. Not now. At the swimming gala. I mean prizegiving. Parents of girls bring first courses, parents of boys bring second courses.' She gave her funny smile.

'Who is doing the cakes for the memorial?' he stupidly asked. 'We need the cakes here, don't we?'

'Is OK,' said Natalia, 'the hotel does the catering, is all being done here, of course. Whole of lunch.'

Michael felt himself turn supernaturally red and he fumbled in his pockets for God knows what. Granny Banana was going to be served up at a swimming gala. This is what it feels like to jump off a cliff, he thought – first the terrible vertigo, the rush of air, finally hitting the bottom, thud . . . death.

A short, middle-aged woman in a stout black suit and shiny shoes approached, her face thoroughly washed and clear of make-up. She came on the children first of all. David liked her immediately; he had good antennae for kindness. She had a twinkly look; when she smiled her eyes squeezed almost shut. She introduced herself as the Celebrant. She had formerly been a teacher at the local comprehensive before changing career, she told them, and now she was a humanist minister. She introduced herself to everyone and commandeered the urn from Simon.

'Humanist?' queried Simon of Mattie as they walked in.

His wife shrugged. 'I think that means you don't have to pay,' she answered cynically.

Michael was distracted by a hundred handshakes and countless hellos as they walked into the hotel. He couldn't focus on people's names, faces. How could he possibly . . . what was he going to do, now? It crossed his mind to ask this Celebrant person if he might be excused but he was swept inside by the mournful, siren call of duty – Granny's memorial, with sixty-odd family and friends arriving. If it had been Pinky holding the service he could have got away with it. Bogged down in polite conversation, he told himself that it was a lost cause. She was gone. It had been his fault.

Inside the hotel, a carpet as soft as a cat's back ran to every corner. Ben immediately headed off and had to be fetched back. They made their way to the function room and joined what seemed, to the children, like thousands of people; it was packed to the edges with legs and shoes and coats and trousers. Some were in smart black suits. Everyone had lit a candle and there was an overwhelming smell of scent. Among the guests were members of the hotel staff who were used to taking orders from Natalia so they were on best behaviour. The children knew André, the underchef from France who often gave them leftover croissants from the kitchen.

Michael took up position in the front row next to his brother Philip. He saw the urn on its presentation table. In a shaking hand he held the order of service printed on a sheet of beige card. This might as well be his own funeral; he wished it were.

The Celebrant took in the audience with her kindly gaze. Everyone knew to fall quiet. 'We are here today to celebrate the life of Granny Banana,' she began. A harp thrummed.

Michael took out his handkerchief, groaned with stress and made a show of blowing his nose even as he barged past Patsy, without explanation. Once he was free of the row of chairs he put his head down and walked out of the room, all eyes watching him.

Everyone looked at each other to see what was going to happen next. Whispers were exchanged. Patsy hurried after Michael, saying that she'd just make sure he was all right. Once outside the hotel she saw his determined, red face behind the wheel of the Land Rover, fighting his way out of the car park. She had to curb the instinct to go after him. It would be more useful if she stayed here. She went back in and conferred in whispers with the Celebrant. Michael was too upset to attend and he'd asked to be left to himself. He wanted just to . . . something. Be on his own. They shouldn't wait, said Patsy.

Michael thumped the steering wheel and cursed the one-way system. Everyone get out of the bloody way! Idiots! Dopey bloody pedestrians! He jerked forwards inch by inch. For the umpteenth time he checked his watch. Twelve-fifteen already. Should he call the police? Hardly.

Twelve-sixteen. It was all he could do to stop himself from ramming the car in front or driving down the pavement. He was ashamed.

The one-way system soaked up another half an hour. And he shouldn't have got lost; heaven knows how many times he'd gone to watch Emma and David – and more recently Ben – trawling up and down in their Otters swimming lessons.

It was nearly one o'clock before he found the Bath Sports and Leisure Centre. He drove around it once, looking for a likely entrance for the gala prizegiving or whatever it might be. He noticed several parents, smoking cigarettes, gathered near the fire door at the back, which was pegged open. He pulled up in a disabled parking space and promptly backed out again; the Land Rover might be clamped and he couldn't let that happen. But there was no other space so he had to just risk it and reverse in. He felt his tow hitch crunch the number plate of the car parked behind. Never mind. He could only pull the front of the vehicle half way in but it was enough. He got out and walked quickly to the fire door.

Inside there was a sea of people, it seemed, all sitting at little tables grouped around a podium with a banner over it proclaiming 'Otters Swimming Club'. He could see forks lifting, knives cutting back and forth, mouths chewing. The prizegiving lunch was underway. A significant number, especially those children not clutching statuettes, were attending a long table loaded with food – the buffet.

A man behind the makeshift desk at the doorway gave Michael a sympathetic smile and asked him something. Michael didn't hear; he was already on his way to the lunch table, trying to see everything at one view. There were piles of white plates interleaved with blue napkins. As he watched, a plate was taken; the napkin fell to the floor. Natalia's words came back to him, 'parents of girls bring first courses, parents of boys bring second courses.' It became clear to him that one end held the first course stuff, so the cakes would be at the pudding end. He could see a hotch-potch of dishes, all types and sizes. He pushed in between a girl with extravagantly long hair and a broad-hipped mum. He leaned over the table, searching. He had to keep his tie from falling into a pavlova constructed like a beautiful Russian castle. There was a flat, dense cheese-cake with a sprig of mint on top, a garish fruit salad, homely apple crumble . . . a cake. He recognised the plate underneath; that was one of them. There was a slice missing. Even as he watched, a plump child's hand began to tear out the next piece. Unthinkingly Michael picked up a serving spoon and smacked it, hard. The hand dropped the cake; he dropped the spoon. He lifted the whole plate away. The child clutched his knuckles and started crying. He was bulging out of his clothes, he had big red cheeks and thin-framed black spectacles, his mouth was open in shock. Probably not a member of Otters – he'd have sunk to the bottom of the pool, thought Michael. He didn't have time to apologise to this seal-shaped boy. 'Hold on!' he said for no good reason. He was too busy searching for the second cake. There was a half-eaten lemon sponge, not a chocolate cake by any stretch of the imagination. He found it, the other dark-coloured one, on one of Natalia's plates – but an even larger chunk was missing. 'Excuse me.' He lifted it off the table. Then he withdrew, stood at a slight distance, a cake in each hand. A pool of silence spread outwards, around him. He knew he was sweating and red in the face; people were looking at him. He was dressed in his black suit and tie as if for an evening concert. 'I'm sorry,' he called out, 'I put Warfarin in them. By accident.'

He looked down at the cakes. Two or three slices were missing from one, and perhaps a bit from the other. Mentally he cursed Natalia – you see where your interfering gets us? He shouldn't worry about it; he could only do his best. 'Sorry mother,' he murmured. He began to filter through, looking for the way out.

The weight of the cakes hurt his wrists. Sweat dripped into his eyes but he couldn't wipe them. Was he talking out loud? He hoped spit wasn't showing at the corners of his mouth.

He hurried towards the door, the hairs rising on the back of his neck. He expected a hand on his shoulder. A prize-winning swimming champion might stop him. How he wished for a helper, fleet of foot, to rush ahead and open the . . . where was the fire exit? He was lost. He was aware of the silence settling over the entire crowd. A middle-aged woman followed him. She said something; he didn't know what. Everyone was watching. The sound of his footfalls became loud. He turned a corner, made his way down this side.

Wrong fire exit. He turned, to find what seemed like a hundred pairs of eyes fixed on him. Never had he been so much looked upon, first at the funeral and now here. He sighted the man at the little table who'd tried to welcome him, over against the opposite wall. He veered in that direction. The silence thickened. The woman who'd followed him called out, 'Excuse me . . .' It was maddening to feel one was holding off the entire world with a pointed stick.

He ignored whatever joke it was made by the man on the door and carried on to reach the outside. The awful, accusing atmosphere of the Sports Hall fell away. He was once more an invisible member of the public, about his business. He walked as quickly as he could. The cakes were a bit damaged and chopped up, but mostly still in hand.

The first part of the memorial service came to an end. There followed a short silence, and another piece of music was plucked from the harp. The Celebrant picked up the urn and, as had been arranged beforehand, offered it first to Ben – who was asked if he'd like to carry it. He knew to say yes. As he did so, flashlights went off and video cameras whirred into focus.

The procession passed through the hotel, but as they went out towards the garden, Natalia stopped Ben and suggested it was David's turn. It wasn't a good idea to have a five-year-old carry the urn down the steps. He refused to give it up; he wanted more photos.

After a brief tussle Natalia knew it was best to avoid a fight and allowed Ben to keep hold of the urn, but as they descended the steps to the garden she kept her hand under his arm. When they reached the bottom, Ben veered off the path and carried the urn across the bowling green at an uncomfortable run, jogging up and down. The grass was shorn so tight it barely existed except as a colour; it was a dead flat, immaculate square of green. The urn was pressed to his chest and carried in a ragged circle; Natalia chased after him. Ben tripped and fell and the urn was on the ground; the cool plastic bag slid out and rested an inch away from his gaze. No harm was done. Nothing was broken. Natalia put the bag in the urn and replaced the lid while Ben clasped it tightly; he was still allowed. He re-joined the procession and they walked to where the tree was going to be planted.

The Celebrant instructed everyone to gather in a semi-circle. The family were ushered to the front and she began, 'Ben, the youngest, will first of all take some of the ashes and cast them into the hole.'

Ben was shoved forwards by his sister. 'Ben,' ordered Emma, 'put the urn down on the ground, no, just here . . .' She had to allow him to do it for himself otherwise there'd be another fight. She gave him the spoon and held the bag for him. He dug into the ashes and tossed the first spoonful into the hole. And the next, and the next.

'Ben,' said Emma eventually, 'you have to leave some for the next person.' Ben went on spooning the ashes. 'I'll leave enough.' His sister was trying to take them away so he had to hurry. He flung a spoonful quickly but it missed and went up in the air. He went to fill the spoon again. 'You've done it perfectly,' said the Celebrant, who had been a teacher after all. She commandeered the spade from the hotel gardener. 'D'you think you can use this grown-up spade and mix it in with the earth?' Ben looked at the spoon and at the spade. He swiftly threw down the spoon and went for the bigger implement; he lifted it with difficulty. Several guests scattered as he swung the spade into the hole in the ground where the ashes now lay, pale grey against the dark brown of the compost and soil mix. He twisted and pushed the handle as hard as he could. He was doing it on his own.

The urn and the spoon were then handed to David, the next oldest. His eyes bulged with shock at the prospect of being put in charge. He clutched the urn tightly and was about to put the spoon in when he had to stop; it was too much. He pushed the urn at his mother. 'Don't want to do it.'

She thrust it back. 'David . . .'

David shook his head. 'No. I can't . . .'

'Would you like me to do it for you?' asked Natalia evenly. David nodded, he couldn't meet his mum's eye. Natalia spooned in the ashes on David's behalf.

'OK,' said the Celebrant, after a while. She turned to Emma and Michael Junior. 'You older ones, your turn now?' Emma went first.

After Michael Junior had upended the bag, the gardener took charge and lifted the young tree – a mountain ash – into position. Several hands held it straight while the gardener backfilled the hole. Many feet tamped down the earth around the tree.

Cakes on plates, thought Michael, just like in Doctor Seuss. Even at a steady walk he was out of breath. Cakes on plates on rakes in lakes. He looked over his shoulder, but there was only

the one woman who still followed, calling to him. He'd lose
her, once he was in the Land Rover.

He put the cakes in the footwell of the passenger side and
went back to climb behind the wheel, still feeling the odd
tightness of his suit around his knees. He swung into the traffic. Where should he go, he wondered? Away from here,
quickly.

Instinctively, like a fox running for his lair, he found himself
driving home. He was going as fast as he could but there was
still some irritating person beeping away behind him. Only
when he trundled past the main house and reached the safety of
his own parking place, in front of his dear little converted barn,
did he stop, thankfully. He sat for a moment, the engine cooling. He needed time to think. He stared at the cakes down
there on the floor on the other side of the gear stick, three slices
missing. 'Sorry Mother,' he murmured.

There was a tap, right next to his ear. Next to him stood old
Mrs Mclean, and at the same time as he was climbing out to
talk to her he glimpsed out of the corner of his eye a strange car
slewed to a halt in front of her house and someone else running
towards him, desperate enough to leave their car door open. It
was that same woman, the one who'd followed him out of the
swimming hall.

He was so distracted that he couldn't make out a word that
Mrs Mclean was saying. 'Hold on, my dear,' he interrupted her,
'sorry about this, but . . .'

The woman who'd pursued him all the way from the
Leisure Centre, no less, hurried over, agitated and out of
breath. Behind her came the fat boy whom he'd smacked over
the knuckles with the serving spoon. These were extreme
lengths to go to to get her son's slice of chocolate cake back;
no wonder the child was overweight. 'Excuse me,' she was
saying and Mrs Mclean swung round to see what was going
on.

'Please,' the woman said. Her son gloomily shadowed her. 'You said *Warfarin*?!'

Michael sensed Mrs Mclean's confusion and wanted to help her with some ordinary niceties of polite conversation. 'This is Mrs Mclean,' he began . . .

The woman's face was too close. 'I need to know if my son has eaten something poisonous and if so, what is it? Does he need to go to *hospital*?' Michael felt a wash of relief; she didn't want the cake back after all. 'Good gracious, no, it wasn't Warfarin . . .'

'You said it was,' she persisted. 'I mean it's extraordinary, to have someone come and . . . actually take their food back, and say that *Warfarin* . . .'

Michael was dismayed that all this was taking place in front of Mrs Mclean, who was being so kind and thoughtful as to just look from one of them to other, making this slight chewing motion with her mouth.

'Was it? Yes or no?' asked the woman shrilly. 'Did you put Warfarin in my son's chocolate cake or not?'

Mrs Mclean looked askance at Michael, disconcerted.

'No, absolutely not,' he said.

'Can you tell us why – why on *earth* – you took the cakes off the table and struck my son very hard with a spoon to prevent him from eating it? Why did you do that?' Michael withered with embarrassment. '*Did* you poison the cakes?' she asked determinedly.

'No,' insisted Michael.

'What was it? I demand to know. It's perfectly reasonable. My son's health is at stake. Why did you go to such lengths to take those two cakes away?!'

Mrs Mclean was waiting for an answer from him as well. 'Er . . .' He stared at the worried mother. Her son rolled from foot to foot beside her.

A possible answer came to mind. 'My wedding ring,' he said

and showed his empty hand, 'accidentally dropped into the cake mix. I wanted it back. Very sorry.'

'Do you *promise*?' asked the woman.

On the way home from the memorial service all the talk was of Michael and his flight. Patsy had said that she'd spoken to him and that he'd gone home. It cast an extra sadness on the event. She was obliged to take a lift back in Mattie and Simon's car.

When the Subaru reached Sweetcombe Road, Emma ran inside as fast as she could, heading straight for the garage. She only had one thought – Umbro Mole. She'd forgotten about him. The magnetic writing board had distracted her and she'd neglected her duty of care! When she opened the drawer the box was still there. Everything be all right, she prayed, begged. She lifted the box out gingerly, placed it on the floor and opened it.

Umbro Mole was still and lifeless; when she picked him up, his body was cold. She stared through her tears at the tiny, humble creature whose rich brown fur already looked a duller shade. She stroked him. There was no doubt. She looked carefully at the black dots of Umbro's not-very-good eyes, two little pin-pricks sitting on either side of his whiskered nose, that seemed to be staring into infinite distance with a kindliness and understanding that broke Emma's heart.

She tilted the little corpse in the palm of her hand until it lay on its other side; there was the puncture wound. That was where the damage had been done. Emma breathed in sharply, sensing the mystery of that. The world of the dead was just the other side of a membrane so wafer thin that she had just reached out and poked her hand through, felt its black emptiness begin to swallow her up.

She carried the poor creature in her cupped hands out of the garage and around to the garden. Under the boughs of the holly tree was the animal graveyard where she'd buried Eloise and Antonia, and here she knelt and dug a grave for Umbro Mole. What treasure should she put in with him? It should be something valuable, that she really minded about. Antonia had been buried with a crystal that she'd found, and Eloise with the Wild Thornberries picture viewer given away in cereal packets.

An idea came to her; she ran back inside, where quite a few people were jamming the hallway. Natalia was defending the house to several relatives who hadn't seen how far down in the world they'd come. Emma dashed upstairs to her room and opened the wardrobe, pulled back the clothes. The broken dragon bowl was there, jumbled up in the tea towel. She unfolded it and looked for fragments of the right size. At school she'd learned that the Ancient Greeks were buried with pottery. She found several pieces about as big as her thumbnail and took them.

When she was slumped to her knees under the holly tree, out of breath, it was only to find that Umbro Mole's grave was empty, he'd disappeared. She was on her feet in a trice and her search quickly widened. Then she saw it – a crow arrogantly pulling at the little corpse on the lawn. A piece of the body, red and elastic, stretched longer from its beak, snapped. The crow gulped, pecked again. For a while Emma's limbs wouldn't move, then she ran indoors. She felt ashamed; she buried the truth right in the middle of her and it sat there, keeping her silent, tongue tied, when she found her brothers and cousin. They made camp in the linen cupboard with a packet of stolen Jammie Dodgers, having found the blue torch which had been missing for so long. They closed the doors and looked at each other's faces by torchlight. She tried to play along, but it seemed that any words she wanted to say clotted at the top of her throat and she couldn't talk. She felt tears coming, couldn't hold them back.

The boys asked what was wrong but she couldn't answer. Ben tried to cheer her up; he put his hand on her arm and said, 'Look.' He popped the torch in his mouth and switched it on. She couldn't even pretend to be impressed.

Michael had a credit card and the Land Rover was in good working order, so without delay he set off for Sitten Hall. He made good progress but every other car zooming past didn't help his morale. The Land Rover was too slow a thing for a dual carriageway.

By degrees, the journey lost its urgency and became mundane – steering wheel, gear knob, indicators, mirror, foot pedals, the road ahead – the whole driving nonsense blurred into an automatic facility. His mind's eye was free to rove back over the past. That bizarre day when he'd finally left Patsy and Sitten Hall behind. The birth of his grandchild while he himself was struggling to get Natalia to hospital . . .

He pictured Michael Junior standing silently in the big sitting room, his Adam's apple bobbing. He saw again his wife playing the piano. Her sinking onto the sofa, and their conversation. He could hear her words almost as if she were sitting next to him now. 'We were married, Michael, for a long time. Mattie is our daughter, Banana is her grand-mother . . .'

If things had gone according to plan they'd have been making this journey together. In his head he spoke to her as if she were sitting alongside him. *To see you again . . . made me realise how much I owe you. All of Mattie's childhood . . . our happi-ness. My whole life . . .*

The lines on the three-lane carriageway began to blur. He

didn't know where he was; he needed a road sign. Sleep threatened. He whistled one of the old songs to help him stay awake.
As he passed the sign to Shaftesbury his right ankle developed
a terrible cramp, his back and arms ached, and he'd become
hypnotised by the blur of tarmac and the monotonous sound of
the engine. He'd driven for more than an hour and needed to
fill up with diesel.

*We did it, Pats. We've got the ashes, we can give ourselves a pat on
the back can't we. Her old companion, Sprocket, last of the terriers, will
share her grave.*

He climbed back into the driving seat. *Did you have fun in our
marriage, Pats? Hope so. I did. Thanks everso.*

All the others had gone; Simon and Mattie and their son
Michael Junior were the last to leave Sweetcombe Road that
afternoon. The bags were in the car, they'd all said their good-
byes and thank yous to Natalia and Philip. The children
mucked about, happily; there had been such a good game with
Michael Junior. Ben put his fists up and, as if he were scared,
Michael Junior turned and ran into the house. Mattie and
Simon yelled at him to come back.

Everyone expected him to appear immediately but the door
stood gaping; he didn't. It was odd. A minute later Simon
went in himself and called again, 'Michael, come on! We're
going.'

Michael Junior, meanwhile, had run up to Emma's room. He
hunted for the broken dragon bowl wrapped in its towel. When
he found it he took it downstairs. Everyone was watching as he
walked over and plonked it in Natalia's hands. 'Sorry, but I
broke this bowl thing. I didn't want to tell you so I took it and
hid it. Sorry.'

Natalia blinked, took the offered package. She was disarmed.
She said to him, 'That is very brave, to own up. Thank you.'

Michael Junior nodded. Emma swooned. Their cousin had taken the blame off her brothers and herself. She *was* in love with him.

Michael pulled out of the service station forecourt. He checked the cakes – yes, looking a touch soft and beaten about, but OK. 'Come on Mother,' he said. 'Chin up. Next stop Wiltshire, Sitten Hall.' Afternoon sunlight freshened the road and lifted his mood. He slid noisily onto the A303.

Once again he settled into the comforting trance induced by motorway driving. Sprocket stayed with him; that dog had been Granny Banana's companion for such a long time. And before Sprocket there'd been similar types of terrier, stretching back into the mists of time. What had been their names? There was one that Mattie had been fond of because it was smaller than their own dogs and looked more like a toy she might play with. Dear old Mattie. He could picture her now, aged around four – they were still living in the main part of Sitten Hall – stamping into the kitchen and shouting at the top of her voice, 'I *hate* them!' Michael had been trying to keep the boiled-eggs-on-Thursday rule going in the absence of staff. He remembered the animal egg-cups – Tiger for Mattie, his own Koala Bear and the Lion for Patsy. The terrier, Sprocket's predecessor, mooching around, getting under his feet, trying to chew his shoelaces, maddening and obstinate, that hair that looked like wire over his eyes.

The egg-timer – how Mattie had loved that thing, constantly turning it to watch the sand flow. But she didn't like the eggs themselves.

He remembered Mattie's four-year-old hand going under the table, and the sound of the terrier licking. He'd kneeled down to call the dog out. It had come quickly, expecting some more food no doubt, so he'd been able to grasp hold of it and lift it. He'd banged his own head. 'FUCK!' he'd shouted. Odd, how impossible it was not to swear loudly and copiously if one hit one's head.

The egg yolk had drooled from Mattie's spoon onto the table. His own egg waited for him while he'd read a comfortably out-of-date newspaper. Father and daughter sitting at the table together, blithely ignoring each other.

Mattie's table manners were often appalling. She'd shoved in a lot of toast at the same time and some of it had stuck in her throat before she'd been exactly ready to swallow, so her mouth had opened; it had been like watching a yawn; like a snake's, her jaw had apparently unhooked and the egg and toast had tumbled out; a torrent of yellow and white breakfast had cascaded down her front and onto the floor. The terrier had darted forward like a mad thing, bashing all the chair legs in his hurry. Mattie had lifted her pyjama top to wipe her mouth at the same time as coughing. And the dog had strolled slowly out from under the table, smiling at him again, waving its little terrier tail, asking for more. When none appeared it had slowly turned around and showed its vulgar rear end as it sniffed its way along the kitchen floor, inch by inch, searching. The terrier's hindquarters, Michael remembered, had had this way of flexing from side to side as if it were building muscles in a gymnasium. It had grazed along, stopped for a moment to lick at a patch where milk had spilled earlier. A great smacking noise came from its mouth. It had glanced over its shoulder at Michael, dolefully, and flexed its bottom in that curious way. Everything had been against Michael at this point. He had no money, no staff, he was losing the ancestral home, his mother was in hospital, the struggle with the dog under the table, fights with Patsy, Mattie wiping her mouth on her pyjamas, the sound of Pasty talking warmly and humorously on the phone to *someone else*. He'd felt so bleak. And he was ashamed to remember that he'd kicked the dog's backside. It had yelped and flown through the air, and on landing had quickly given him one hugely apologetic glance and trotted straight out of the room, eyes down. Mattie had been shocked, angry.

Mattie, who had a dog of her own now.

Years gone past, steps never to be trod again. Ghosts and their footfalls. He was closer to joining the dead himself than he was to the memories of them alive and well. It was enough to bring tears. 'Hold on Sprocket,' he cried, trying to shut from his mind the always-damp hair around the mouth of his mother's most favourite terrier of all. 'Coming.'

Eighty miles had galloped beneath the wheels of the Land Rover. This was his turn-off, Amesbury. How strange and small and left-behind it seemed.

Minutes later he was on the road to Woodford. This entire valley had once belonged to his family. He passed by the derelict east entrance to Sitten Hall, now covered in ivy, long ago sold off with a parcel of land.

And here came the first sight of the sharp right-hander with the old iron railing leaning askew alongside . . . he was only seconds away. He remembered his old Renault 4 – extraordinary how that vehicle had clung to life. He thumped the steering wheel, his nose burned, his eyes watered – there it was, the abandoned lodge, overshadowed by his mother's favourite tree. He slowed, turned under its boughs and into the driveway, 'Quercus! How *are* you?!' His heart ached with old pride. It stood sentinel all alone now at the entrance to Sitten Hall, its partner on the other side having blown down in the great storm of '87.

He pulled over, and parked in its shadow.

Straight away, memories flooded back. He hadn't realised how leaving the place had also meant leaving behind what had happened here. Now, seemingly alerted by the scent if not the actual sight of his old home, his three marriages arrived in quick succession; and his father's death, the negotiation with the Trust over the gifting of the Hall, the struggle against the A303 bypass, Mattie's wedding, his separation from Patsy. These events knitted together in his mind's eye, brightly, as in a kaleidoscope.

'Home, Banana! Hmm?' He glanced down at his old dead mother in the shape of two thoroughly mauled-about chocolate cakes, pushed together on the plates and stuck in the footwell of the Land Rover like . . . yes, like a pair of dark eyes looking up at him. What a ragged, difficult journey this had been.

It crossed his mind to drive on to the top of the incline and see the house itself, but he didn't dare. Gina might spot him, and if she learned what he was up to she'd have to turf him out and that would be ignominious. In any case, he wasn't sure he wanted to see it. From where he stood, there was just a strip of tarmac driveway and a perfectly ordinary swatch of green field on either side, lasting only a hundred yards or so before it made its horizon with the sky. But he knew what was on the other side: a hidden bowl of land, so very gentle in its holding of the mediaeval castle, Sitten Hall, and the river nearby – the whole picture so affecting that once you walked into it you would never want to leave. So he stopped right here, under the tree.

He climbed out, his knees numb and his ears ringing from the hours of noise. He paced back and forth a few times. He tried out a circle with his elbows, did some work on the poor ankle which was suffering from cramp. He took out old Mrs Mclean's spade and slung it over his arm like a shotgun. Aware that this should be done with some sense of occasion, he opened the passenger door of the Land Rover and lifted out his dear old mother, one cake in each hand. He nudged the door shut and set off. He looked like an old groundsman on his way to a picnic tea.

The air was fresh, sweet. He congratulated the valley for that. How the ground rolled away, in this part of Wiltshire. It soothed him. It was as inviting, comfortable and gracious looking as a freshly made bed; he might drop everything and pitch forward with arms outstretched and this landscape would catch him and post him off to some dream place where thoughts and pictures would arrive, unbidden, for his delight, like in a storybook and they would tell him the geography and the history of this place, the how and the when of people's meetings, a story of human sentiment and longing, written on the land. The people who'd lived here, his ancestors, had all passed by in a blur, a blink of an eye, but the miracle was, they had all led directly to him . . . Sir Michael Gough . . . here . . . alive and so on . . . heart beating . . . limbs moving . . . stomach grumbling . . . slight headache . . . in the very first decade of the twenty-first century.

He wondered what landscape the children would hold in their hearts. This was his place, he knew that much, even if it had been taken away from him.

He arrived at the tree. It had been grown inside its own stone wall enclosure, measuring around fifteen paces in diameter, five feet in height and filled with earth. He put the cakes down on top of the wall. Such a beautiful old oak, and, inscrutable, it had suffered so much, over the years. It was only God's plan, he supposed, but how unimaginable was the constant turmoil of who ate what! The tree sucked up moisture and nutrients yet at the same time it was being consumed, outside and in: fungus rotted its core, moths hid in the fissures in its bark waiting for nightfall, beetles dug underneath the bark and tracked through the sapwood, caterpillars lunched on the leaves and red-oak roller weevils rolled them up like so many carpets and laid their eggs in the middle, while galls of numerous shapes and sizes and with glamorous names – red pea, cherry marble, oyster, silk button, spangle, apple – coagulated around the eggs laid in its greenery. Yet, from all appearances, it seemed as placid and fixed as Sitten Hall itself.

The day he'd buried Sprocket – the morning of Mattie's wedding – came back to him and he wandered slowly, poring over the ground to find the exact spot. Rest in peace Sprocket, thought Michael, but I have to interrupt to bring you your old mistress. He knelt and touched the grass. If he remembered rightly it had been on this side, facing the Hall, tight up against the granite surrounding the tree. Here, it must be. He heaved himself to his feet, picked up the spade and began to dig. He wanted to avoid hitting the bones if possible, so he didn't put too much back into it. The earth was thankfully soft. He made a neat pile of the spoil and kept going.

The air began to cool towards evening but he'd become hot and needed to rest. He went once around the tree. The cakes had softened in the sun. He moved them to a shady patch. He was hungry, could have done with something to eat, a sip of water. But – nothing doing. He sat with his back to the wall and let time pass, idly leafing through memories of Sitten Hall. The tree had borne silent, uncritical witness to them all. It had kept its own counsel, carried on with its own thing. It grew ten thousand leaves to shade the lodge-house in summer and in autumn it shot its load spectacularly – year after year came this enormous squandering of its acorns on the road to Woodford. In winter it fell into disuse, threatening the empty, locked-up lodge with the tap-tap-tap of its branches on the roof before starting all over again, girding its loins for another mammoth breeding programme. It was a slower process than the perfunctory coupling of the rabbits, Michael reflected, but not as clumsy as the backside-climbing of rams and bulls, nor as intricate as the dance of mating insects; none the less . . . it was up to the same thing as all of us, he concluded, getting a bit of death and birth and sex, and among the three of them finding a bit of pleasure if you can. Thrice to church – for funerals, christenings and weddings – and always in your own skin.

He climbed to his feet and went back to work.

Some minutes later he glimpsed patches of white showing through the earth. He put down the spade and used his hands instead to scrape away enough to reveal the little skeleton, laid out in exactly the same position as he remembered it all those years ago, on its side. There were still fragments of skin and hair. There was the skull, in which Sprocket's brain had once ticked away, thinking mostly of food, Michael would have guessed. Not much difference between man and dog. He took out the earth with his hands.

When he'd made enough extra space for his mother, he wiped the mud from his fingers and retrieved the cakes from their shady patch. He kneeled at the graveside and lowered them into position next to Sprocket's skeleton. They should be able to look at each other, like a married couple. Come to that, Sprocket had slept on Granny's bed so it was business as usual.

He stood up. Bones of Sprocket, bones of Mother. There: done. Banana's last wish fulfilled.

He started back-filling the hole. The first spadeful of earth landed plump on the cakes, partly covering them. He wished for a hymn and to have Pinky here, the rector of this parish and his childhood friend, in full costume. He wanted to hear some Latin spoken, to have a beautiful church nearby in which a service had just been sung. He wished this were hallowed ground. But if he couldn't have any of that perhaps this was the next best thing. One couldn't hope for a more likely spot to grant peace. A simple immersion in earth, true to God's work.

Throw by throw he replaced the spoil. When he'd trodden it down he stood for a while and tried to think of something decent to say. He'd have liked it to be a prayer. 'See you soon,' he said, which was true enough.

He went back to the Land Rover, grateful for a proper seat.

He didn't want to start the engine. He didn't want to go anywhere, apart from up that slight incline, just to have a peep . . .
Don't, he told himself.

Patsy would be coming back soon. They were meant to
have taken this journey together and he'd imagined her in the
passenger seat much of the way. It seemed right therefore to
wait for her. She might even say yes, she'd have him back. He
sat there for half an hour, reading a fragment of old newspaper
he found in the footwell.

Eventually his curiosity got the better of him. He started the
engine and chugged the few hundred yards to the top of the
rise.

There it was, the first glimpse of Sitten Hall. He stopped the
Land Rover again, and held his breath for a second. On its
gentle mound of earth the moated, four-towered castle looked
as celebratory, as inviting, yes, as a freshly baked cake; he might
pick it up with both hands and break it open and smell the history of his family – and of England – still warm.

Part Two

Sir Michael Gough sank on one knee to peer into the seldom-used cupboard. It was dark and smelled of mildewed wood. Why would they ever have kept a broken hoover, or Patsy's redundant art materials? It was an utter waste of space and whole minutes of his precious *life* had been wasted in moving them from one spot to another several times already. There was that shoe box of old photographs – he'd always meant to sort them out. The giant ceramic lamp without its shade was Patsy's aberration. The split briefcase had, years ago, carried his increasingly worn out hopes for a better deal with the Trust and now lay here empty and disused, which seemed fitting. Mouldering at the back he found what he was looking for: a leather holdall which he'd used for his clothes and so on, in the days when he'd made frequent visits to London. He pushed everything else back and hefted it in his hand; yes, it held firm. He noticed spots of rust on the metal hasps. How time flies, he thought. He could remember buying it brand new.

He went to the bedroom and plonked it on the bed. Mattie had been conceived right here, twenty-seven years ago, although in those days the bed had been in their room downstairs, in the Hall proper. He found himself unable to move; his feet were glued to the carpet by this apparition that visited now: the roll of his wife's back, doughy and white, a gentle, tall woman lying there next to him. The glorious hours of sleep had been like a sea voyage: long, calm hours, time insistently

carrying him forwards to each next day, refreshed and grateful
to put his feet down on solid ground and carry on. The best
times of his marriage had been passed here. Their relationship
had been a luxury in the beginning, the part of life he looked
forward to most, but over the years her disappointment in him
had worn them down to a low-grade state of unhappiness.

His own bed, his own wife . . . he was going to walk away
because he'd lost her.

He pulled open the top drawer: underwear. He fished out
everything that wasn't too worn out. Someone new might
have to look at him, wherever he ended up. A favourite horse-
shoe cufflink winked at him; he chased the other one into a
corner to pick them up. He enjoyed the weight of the gold,
warm and yellow and dense – and how they clinked in his palm
like a game of jacks. He dithered here and there, the tears
coursing down his cheeks. How difficult it would be, not to
come back! The absence of his life here at the Hall would be
like a silence deep inside.

Leave, Michael, while you can still walk and talk. Philip
came to mind, with his young pregnant wife. He swayed
slightly and hung onto the bedstead, the brass knob a greasy
ball in his hand. His own wife, Patsy, replaced his sister-in-law
in his mind's eye: her mouth working, words of disapproval
coming in a torrent. He flinched like a dog that's been beaten.
Next he had her walking around, and when they crossed paths
he shied away. There had been room enough to hide downstairs in the Hall but up here in the flat it had been hopeless,
they could never avoid each other. Then he put her again in
this bed. Next to her he'd lain, frozen stiff, hoping to avoid
punishment. There was no reason to spend the last years of his
life unhappily, yet what was it that faced him, away from here?

Probably, it would be a different shape and form of unhappiness.

But he'd made the decision, hadn't he? In any case, either

path would lead pretty quickly to the grave. How many years did he have left? Not many . . . He groped towards the idea – the fervent wish! – that it might all come good. There was a chance. And certainly this wasn't good for either of them, how it was now.

This was the moment: he stood, bag in hand, about to leave home – and he shouldn't think it was so extraordinary; most people did so in their teens. He never had.

If he asked any of his friends or family to put money on the outcome they'd bet their last guinea he'd return to Sitten Hall within a week, tail between his legs.

He put on a clean shirt and tied his shoelaces tight. He took the black leather holdall and began to wander through the rooms in the apartment gathering those things that he'd need immediately. He took the razor and toothbrush from the bathroom. In the kitchen he unhooked the silver tankard. He'd never been able to stop Mrs Burrell from polishing the inside so to drink from it had always left his mouth coated in a bitter taste. Now she wouldn't get at it. Natalia would follow instructions and leave it alone no doubt. From the hall cupboard he extricated his collection of walking sticks and tied them into a bundle. His fingers looked clumsy and old. How had they got like that without his noticing? Then he thought, why am I bothering with them? They were not an immediate need. He could pick them up later. A framed photograph of Mattie taken when she was twelve went in, wrapped in a shirt. What about all his paperwork . . . he dug out an old split suitcase and went to his desk and with one swipe of his arm scooped everything into it. He pulled out each drawer and emptied those in, too. This would be a perfect opportunity to sort it all out. A pair of Edwardian silver salt and pepper pots were his favourites and wouldn't be missed. His Purdey twelve-bore, in its wooden case. The fishing rods. He'd like to take some of his father's tools but they weren't important enough. He'd have to come

back for quite a bit of stuff, when he'd found somewhere to
live.

In the sitting room, he looked around. He'd passed so many
hours here. The dragon bowl, of course. The warm egg-yolk
glaze on the rim was always so inviting. He cradled it in the
crook of his arm and a stray shaft of sunlight scooped out the
bottom, made it brilliant. He saw the decoration as if for the
first time: three dragons wore scales of green and yellow, intri-
cately laid, like tiles, over the surface of their bodies. They
were coiled in flight over a wild, dense thicket of vegetation set
between scrolled, foliate borders top and bottom. Brilliant jets
of flame and smoke issued from their nostrils. Their eyes were
round and abnormally large. The pupils were slight, upright
crescents of black, which gave them an intense, animal stare,
predatory and determined. In each was a point of light. One
could imagine that in the next moment, if they hadn't been
captured in this decoration, they would have made just one
more lithe twist and taken their prey, or fought to defend their
territory, or copulated fiercely. It had kept by him, this bowl;
out of its comforting depths he'd fed his hunger for treats and
tobacco. The key to its surviving the journey would be good
wrapping.

He touched the top of the television. He'd never lift it.
Needs must; he'd leave it here. ''Bye, old friend,' he murmured. His fingers came away touched with dust. Where
would his next TV be? How big? A digital flatscreen hopefully,
but where would the money be found for such a thing? The
quality of life, the rub of it, as if you could test its fineness like
cloth between thumb and forefinger, was signally not affected
by possessions, this he knew for sure, and yet the lust for the
glory of ownership would always count. Yes, he thought, it was
lust – something sexual – that was the attraction of desirable
things to the human heart. Grand houses, widespread acres,
beautiful clothes: they issued their scent, their mating call was

the sound of the cash register chiming in the background. If you are rich enough, have me.

He sent a silent apology to Raymond Luther, because the few items he was taking with him hardly amounted to the wholesale sacking of Sitten Hall that the head gardener had recommended last year. Ever since turning down any involvement in that little enterprise Michael hadn't been able to meet Raymond's eye with confidence. And there had been a true justice in Raymond's claim against National Trust Enterprises. It would have been a famous burglary, epic in scale, the ten o'clock news a certainty. It should have happened. He imagined − daydreaming − that he and Raymond were arrested, imprisoned and hauled in front of a jury. The twelve good men and true heard the facts and let them off.

Doubts suddenly plagued him. He stared at his armchair, the one his mother had given him. It, also, was too heavy to carry down. How many happy hours he'd passed in its mute, solid, ever-reliable embrace, sitting at his end of the tunnel of TV, beamed in from all corners of the globe: *World's Wildest Police Videos* from Los Angeles, cricket in Australia, game shows from Japan, Formula One in Canada, horse-racing in France, *Crimewatch* − exhilarating. He'd do it all over again if he had the chance, but without the interruptions. He patted the leather upholstery. Pure pleasure it had been, driving this chair. The idea of a new one had no appeal.

That was it. He barked several goodbyes to his past life and left the room. As he shut the door he felt a vacuum yawn behind him; it almost made him fall. He took a deep breath and let go of the door handle. Everything stayed where it was. The ground was under his feet, the walls upright, the roof overhead. The grandmother clock ticked as steadily as before. Time to go.

He went to the phone, picked it up and dialled Philip at the farm. He'd stay there for a few days until Pinky came back from

holiday. The burr-burr was interrupted and a woman's voice
answered – of course, it was Natalia. Philip himself was at
work, trying to save his financial services company from collapse. Michael fumbled, suddenly embarrassed at encountering
this virtually unknown woman on the phone. It had been a
wild, unforeseeable torrent of events that had torn Philip from
his usual moorings: Natalia's pregnancy declared at the same
time as Mattie's, the hurried, registry office wedding, foot-
and-mouth on top of BSE crippling the farm while the
stomachs of the two young women grew at the same rate, the
babies expected on the same day. He, Michael, would simultaneously be an uncle and a grandfather, while Philip was going
to be a father and a bankrupt at the same time, if he didn't
watch out.

'Natalia,' he said into the phone, 'sorry, I just lost myself for
a minute there. Forgot whom I'd called. It's Michael.'

'Hello.' Her voice was quiet, distant. Such a *young* woman in
his brother's bed . . . the same twinge of jealousy struck him for
the umpteenth time. Philip married and about to become a
father? It was so unlikely that it had to be true.

Michael struggled with the dilemma: should he ask her or
talk to Philip first? He blurted out, 'I wonder if I could come
and stay at the farm for a couple of days. Is that all right?'

There was a pause. His heart sank. She was going to say no.
Or maybe he'd spoken too fast and she hadn't understood. The
silence went on for an impossible length of time. He was com-
posing a graceful withdrawal of the request when her shy
answer came, 'Yes, of course. When is it you arrive?' He was
relieved. The plan held fast. Philip's wife . . . *wife?* . . . had
saved him, broken his fall. He'd be eternally grateful. He
searched her tone of voice for any sign of despair at the
prospect of his coming but could only pinpoint surprise. She'd
been startled that he'd asked, he who never went anywhere
other than from armchair to bed to dining table to armchair.

That had been the reason for the momentary silence. Her easy compliance, he thought, betrayed the housekeeper in her; she would always be Philip's servant, the poor girl. He schooled himself to carry on.

'Sorry to land myself on you, it won't be for more than a night or two, just while, er . . . while . . .' He ground to a halt.

'You mean while Mattie has the baby? Yes, please, is close by, both of you must stay.'

Michael felt his nerves shredding. Of course that was a good enough reason; he should just grasp it and go. Not Patsy, he wanted to explain, just me, on my own. But any display of emotion or of urgency would beg questions, and awful sympathy from Natalia. 'Thank you. But I think it will be only me. Do you want to check it's all right with Philip?'

'No, he does not mind. He will be happy you come.'

Michael felt moved. Such kindness – and from a young woman he'd always rather wanted to seduce himself. He really must be in a desperate state, he realised, even to think such nonsense.

For some minutes he stared at the motley collection of belongings in the hallway. Was this all he needed, to carry on? Might as well be tied up in a spotted handkerchief. Funny to think how many had been his possessions, once: everything in Sitten Hall, plus the house itself, a castle no less, hundreds of acres. He'd never earned a penny in his life but had merely watched with growing disbelief and frustration while all that he'd inherited had been taken away from him. His life had been accompanied by the sensation of a draining away, like a sink emptying of water, from overfull to these last few drops. Perhaps it was the story of the whole country: the gathering of great wealth from the Empire, bringing it all back, the great and the good hoarding it, building their statelies, indulging in the Industrial Revolution, inventions upon inventions, piling up wealth, while subsequent generations, he among them –

lazy, unqualified, inactive, eccentric, profligate, spoilt, addled by whisky and TV – had lived off the fat, watched the spoils dissipate and the old country become less grand, but more . . . something. Old.

One trip downstairs took care of the rods and tackle and the gun; he returned for the bag and the suitcase full of papers, and a third time for the dragon bowl and sundries. Long journeys, all of them! He trudged, step by step, upstairs downstairs, neither fish nor fowl now. He wasn't landed gentry so much as . . . upended. He ought to renounce his title. He had neither profession nor trade. He was merely . . . a beast, he thought, as he walked the concourse fronting Sitten Hall, a creature without territory, a bundle of nerves. The castle loomed over him.

It was the last time, he thought, that a Gough's footsteps would ring out on this hallowed ground! He got into the Renault 4 and simply drove away.

Simon sat alongside Mattie's bed in the Bristol Royal Infirmary's labour ward and ate his sandwiches.

She smiled at him. 'Try now.' Mattie was heavier, so her dimples made less of a dent and her black hair was glossier from all the baths she'd taken and all the hormones and vitamins swirling around her system.

Simon swallowed his mouthful and lowered an ear to the mound of her stomach, waiting for any sign of life from his unborn son. His curly hair tickled Mattie's skin. He could hear her digestion gurgling. The strange tubes and chambers in there, pulsing with life and the work of maintaining life – at the end of all that machinery was their baby. They'd decided they would christen him Michael, after his grandfather.

The baby turned; Simon felt a soft warm push as a limb wiped across, momentarily. It was exciting. They had come through all the anxiety of the last six weeks and tomorrow morning they would reach the end of the pregnancy. Success. Their son would be born by elective caesarean. He smiled and squeezed her hand. 'There,' he said and he felt her knuckles, her palm, the pad of flesh at the base of her thumb, the familiar strength of her wrist.

Mattie was OK, now, with seeing the veins under her skin. Before, she'd been squeamish: under the surface ran her blood in its channels, the same blood they'd both prayed, night and day, would not be loosed into the cavity of her womb. If it had done so, the blood loss would have been equivalent to cutting both wrists at once, Dr Macintyre had said. For the six weeks Mattie had been in hospital, she had not even been allowed off the ward. In the fridge waited bags of her blood type in case the sudden dash to surgery was required.

But now their sojourn was over. They'd escaped. She felt proud and pleased and light as air, underneath the natural anxiety over the operation tomorrow. 'Finish your lunch,' she said.

He sat back and took the half-eaten beef-and-mustard sandwich off the bedside unit. 'They can hear, you know. He'll recognise your voice. And mine.'

'Hmm.'

'Some people play classical music to their babies in the womb. Meant to increase their intelligence.'

'Let's hope that intelligence is not a burden our baby is going to have to bear.'

He saw her checking her watch. 'Want to get rid of me?'

'Course not, idiot. Just finding out how much time we've got left.'

They sat in silence. Mattie wished to be invigorating and funny but her sense of anticipation meant she was unable to make small talk. Men would never know the great, lumpen boulder of fear that came with pregnancy: the responsibility of carrying two lives, the baby's and one's own. It was an instinctive, animal passion. She'd read somewhere that new fathers thought they were allowed to die once they had bred, whereas new mothers thought the opposite: they were never allowed to die or even fall ill because a child would always need them.

At two o'clock Simon leaned over and kissed her. 'This evening,' he murmured.

'Yes, for the last time.'

'We're there. We did it.'

She tugged his arm. 'Thanks, for always coming. Six weeks!'

'I always wanted to, every minute.'

After he'd gone Mattie lay there, still as a log. She was impatient. The ache to get up and do something grew fierce at times. She couldn't be stoic about it; she pulled forever harder on the minutes as they passed, one by one, under the big hand of her watch. There were twenty and a half hours left before she held her baby in her arms. She would kiss him and tell him his name, Michael Junior.

She felt bad that Simon's manliness had become diminished. The pregnancy and the need to pay for things – the fact of her body and its condition – had tethered him and had slowly wound in the slack to bring him down to earth. No longer could he volunteer to run the logistics and purchasing for Greenpeace operations. He couldn't give up his job at the Bleuler Institute. She'd noticed a thickening around his hips and his hands were whiter, less used. She must be careful to give back to him that side of himself. If he was less adventurous, less of a man, then she herself might lose the instinct to run with him, fuck him. The chemical foment between lovers could not be started up again once it had died down, in her experience.

It was terrifying how transient her affections were.

The Asian girl, Sara, who occupied the bed next to her, came back from visiting her premature twins in intensive care. She looked drawn and thin as always but she was smiling. They talked for a few minutes. The twins were putting on weight.

Perhaps tomorrow they'd be released. The SCBU were careful
not to make predictions to parents, they gave the picture as it
was at that moment and asked for everyone to take a step at a
time. It was because things might change so quickly.

She'd miss the incredible flow of people through this ward.
She'd met so many women in such different circumstances. It
had been a crash course in what humankind went through,
trying to breed.

She told herself: calm. This was the part in the film when the
hero is surrounded by desert and the sky is blue and empty and
featureless over his head. He's come a long way and is trudging
up the last sand dune. We know, she thought, there's an oasis
that he will see when he reaches the top. His feet are slowing
right down but he will get there, just about, and when he
does . . .

For every yard that he put between himself and the old place a
giant, new landscape opened up ahead of Michael. It was
intensely liberating, even if the generations behind him stared
accusingly. He shrugged off their disapproval as, gleefully, yet
scared as a rabbit, he hunched over the steering wheel and
beat the Renault 4 along the drive, past Quercus, onto the
open road.

Freedom!

His own father would be chief among the disappointed
ancestors. Michael nodded at the memory of his Brylcreemed
forebear. The cool steady gaze issued from the family photograph. 'Sorry Papa,' he said, 'story over. All good things come
to an end. Must dig in now. Adapt to survive. Batten down the
hatches. Watch out!'

Fervent hopes and wishes milled around in his mind. He'd
quite like to fall in love with someone younger and prettier
than Natalia. A fold of ten pound notes in his pocket would be
useful for a drink and a bet. He'd be grateful if a few hundred

acres could be found somewhere for him to wander in, and sunshine. He could wish to be fed twice a day. But for now all he had was a few days at the farm while the babies were born. After that, Pinky was back from holiday and had offered him temporary accommodation. From there he would find something of his own. If the worst came to the worst he could call old Mrs Mclean. She'd always find a corner for him.

It was bliss to have mended the clutch pedal; just two spots of weld were all that it had taken, a banknote changing hands with the blacksmith in the village. What fun to change gear as much as he wanted – second, third, second – but he was going in circles; he'd lost his exit, this roundabout made him giddy. The Renault canted over like a sailboat in a storm. He found the way out, swerved towards the southwest, and the road straightened in front of him. The steering gave a little wriggle of complaint. He felt the usual dissatisfaction with the single lane carriageway on this section of the A303, albeit he'd campaigned against the widening of the same road near Sitten Hall. He resented the queue of traffic building up behind him, waiting to overtake. He hoped they all got a laugh out of his bumper sticker, 'My Other Wife Is A Dog'. Patsy never travelled in this car.

The dragon bowl was his silent companion in the passenger seat. He glanced at it. Wrenched from its comfortable position next to his armchair, uprooted, driven off – well might he feel sympathy for this tiny but important emblem of his past life. He steered with one hand so that with the other he might check inside it for old times' sake. Previously there would have been tobacco, Werther's Originals, maybe chocolate, in the bowl, but there was only a shred or two of stale Golden Virginia now. Patsy would never again try to bribe him with fun-size Kit-Kats. He'd better get used to the idea. He murmured that word out loud, *gone*. He had to pinch himself – Sitten Hall was no more.

It was a relief. He was unburdened to an enormous extent. He felt sorry for his ex-wife eking out her last days there. Visitors seethed over the place like flies on a corpse. The great unwashed, effectively, had got their hands on the place. It had been a kind of inch-by-inch revolution. And they deserved it. How much stronger and more virulent the working classes had become since the war. It had liberated them. They had won their own country. In a way he felt as if he was joining them. He'd be a visitor to Sitten Hall, now. Ordinary Joe Bloggs. Michael Gough. Maybe he would renounce his title. It would be part of his rebirth. He'd escaped, just as the ground was pulled out from under the feet of his own type and class of person. If they didn't adapt they'd end up extinct, he thought. Rather sad.

A half hour later he turned off the A303, heading along the single track lane towards Frome. There was mercifully little traffic and the sun shone. The car was working properly. He felt optimistic. So far, so good. He was a grown-up, he was coping magnificently. It was all a question of logistics: departure, arrival, food and board, fuel for the motor, everything in place, in the proper order. All he had to do was keep going, maintain position.

He turned off at the crossroads. The sun winked at him through the gaps in the trees. The carburettor sucked in petrol greedily, the wheels turned. The road dipped suddenly: this was the last downhill before Philip's farm. He recognised the triangular warning sign advising 'slow'. He was going too fast. There was a fierce right-hander at the bottom, he'd need to be in control. The same old hand-written sign, grown faded over the years, poked out of the hedge: 'Children Playing!' Never in his visits to Philip's farm had Michael seen any children in the road but he supposed they'd be grown up by now. Unless the little darlings had actually been mown down . . . he gripped the wheel more firmly. There was a quantity of dried mud in

the dip: a tractor had been at work during the winter and no
one had cleaned up. Perhaps he should change gear . . .

He'd always been mysteriously good at motors, whether
driving or mending them. Even at school he'd been preoccupied with all types of vehicle. He remembered that at the age
of nine or so he'd driven a pretend tank around the playground. A long time ago, that was. Nineteen forty-nine? His
prep school had been an imposing Victorian building
arranged in an L-shape. Hunger had eaten at his belly; food
was still rationed. He could take his mind off it if he kept
moving. With the war just won, fighting machines of all sorts
were *de rigueur*. His favourite had been the Sherman Mark II.
The memory led him to seek out the Renault 4's dash-
mounted gear lever as he breezed downhill in this narrow,
summery, sunlit lane, and his hand closed on the familiar
elbow of plastic sticking out of the dashboard because, when
he'd been driving the Sherman Mark II, his left arm had been
used to operate the throttle/brakes, an imaginary lever to be
pushed forwards or backwards to go faster or slow down. His
right arm had been the cannon, thrust forward, fist clenched
at the end of it, winched up or down to find range . . . No
one had been as good as he, at that! It had been the noise in
the back of his throat which had been so distinctive, so cred-
ible. Less successful was the idea of thrusting his school blazer
up the back of his short-sleeved jumper to signify a turret
crammed with soldiers. Plainly, it was nothing like, but his
voice had been the envy of other boys as it had ground the
gears, marked the shifts in engine noise with utmost authen-
ticity. He had wound the gun up and down, fired and
reloaded, rolled forwards or backwards . . . There'd been
plenty of other twit-faced toffs at that school.

The corner at the bottom of the hill was coming too fast. He
moved his foot across to the brake pedal and stroked it to steady
the old Renault 4; it was a fragile creature. Lord knew, the

wheels weren't far from coming off entirely like in an old-fashioned cartoon.

Not one corner of the playground, he remembered proudly, had been safe from his Sherman tank all those years ago . . . forward, swivel gun, fire . . . yes, great fun. Often younger boys wished to join in. Sometimes he let them. It had been a success, perhaps the only time in his life that he'd received recognition for a talent that he alone possessed.

Except – he frowned – there had been that accident: he'd been reversing out of a cul-de-sac under heavy fire when he'd squashed the smallest boy in the school, a shrimp called Prime, far from home and invisible, who'd somehow got himself right under Michael's tracks. The tank had swivelled suddenly and Prime had been knocked off his feet. Michael could see his face now, anguished and dropping out of sight.

He hadn't made any effort to pick him up or apologise; that had been a mistake. But as far as he was concerned this was war and innocent people did occasionally get caught up in it. There was no question that he might risk the safety of the tank and its crew.

Even now, today, he was still itchy with embarrassment at the thought of that turret on his back. He must have looked such an idiot.

Prime's scream – how loud, how piercing it had been. He'd rammed the throttle forward and taken off in a new direction, engine grinding. Prime's shrieking and wailing had brought the playground to a halt. Everyone was looking at Michael accusingly.

Meanwhile a lone figure had detached itself from a group of boys, many of whom sported non-regulation shoes. It had been Burns of course, who was a year younger, blessed with rich, dark good looks and the same name as the romantic Scots poet. Burns had followed him and called out, 'Oi, Gough, you twit! What about Prime! Pick him up can't you? Say sorry!'

Michael hadn't stopped or slowed down; on the contrary he'd pushed the throttle forward a notch and broken into a lumbering trot.

The God-like Burns, with heroic blood in his veins, had sneaked up behind him and pulled the blazer clean out from under his school jumper.

Michael had been touchy on the subject of the turret. Some people were teasing him about it, and now Burns had revealed it for what it was: just an ordinary item of school uniform. He'd swung his cannon around; his closed fist pointed at Burns.

Burns had smiled. 'Gough! Put it away.'

Michael's scalp had moved forward, compressing his brow and folding it into a set of wrinkles, and his fist had lashed out – Burns had ducked of course. Michael's eyes peeled open, then blinked to normal, then peeled as far back again, while he'd shouted, 'Give my *bluddddy* turret back, Burns! My soldiers are in there.' A horrible swallowing action disfigured his throat, and his Adam's apple had bobbed up and down like a potato in a barrel of water. Everyone would recognise the symptoms: he was about to go berserk.

Burns had sauntered further away with the blazer and stopped close to the fence. He didn't seem to register the danger he was in. To onlookers it was incredible, but the incredible was to be expected with Burns. He had casually thrown the blazer over the fence.

An eruption was inevitable now. Everyone held their breath, waiting for the fight. Michael had glared around; he'd noticed little Prime hurrying indoors while other boys shuffled into position, the better to watch . . .

He'd hurt Burns during that fight. Another mistake. He wished he hadn't.

Fast forward fifty-one years and the grown-up Michael had overdone it. He'd failed to concentrate. The tyres hit the dried mud and lost grip; he had to straighten, allow a slight drift.

The hedgerow started to flick against the side of the car. He sailed out of the arc of the corner, teeth gritted, but he flinched, and was hauled out of his daydream and into this very present moment because another car was suddenly, mysteriously, *there*, heading straight towards him. He saw the other vehicle's bonnet dip sharply under heavy braking. However, he was still in his Sherman tank, so to speak, and his first instinct was to pull backwards on the throttle as he would have done in the playground, which translated into his uselessly tugging at the dash-mounted gear lever on the old Renault 4. This lost him a whole second. Too late he moved his foot from the accelerator, and then another fatal moment of confusion affected him: for years he'd trained himself *not* to use the clutch pedal because it had always fallen off, but now he couldn't remember which pedal was allowed if any . . . He was sailing towards the other vehicle. He could see the driver and it was a shock because he recognised her. It was Philip's new, pregnant wife, Natalia. He could see her flour-white face, eyes widening as, at last, his foot stamped hard on the brake pedal. She was watching in disbelief. He stood on the pedal; he tried to push it right through the floor. It didn't seem to make as much difference as it should. The heat had taken all the efficiency out of the brakes. A fraction of a second later Natalia's eyebrows popped up and her mouth opened just before he slid into her with a bang. They seemed to be face to face, literally a few inches from each other, at the moment of impact. It was almost vulgar, but only lasted a moment before the airbags blew out and obliterated all sight of her and his own steering wheel came quickly towards him and with a 'thud' he lost consciousness.

At three-thirty p.m. it was Philip who unexpectedly turned up to visit Mattie. He'd never before come alone; previously he'd

always accompanied Natalia. He hurried across the ward, suit
and tie immaculate, energetic and competent as ever, but he
looked different. He was moving with more determination, as
if having to lean into a strong headwind. He was frowning.
Normally he might glance and nod at the other patients, he
would be conscious of others watching him as he ran the
gauntlet between their beds. This time he was fixed on her, he
was anxious.

'I was wondering if you'd seen sight or sound of Nat?' he
asked quickly, after greeting Mattie.

'No. Why?'

'She hasn't turned up, we were meant to have an appointment here, at the ante-natal ward. I thought she might be up
here, seeing you.'

'Hmm. Don't know. I wasn't expecting her.' Mattie and
Natalia had become close because of their shared pregnancies.
They looked like sisters, even, except Mattie's manly stride and
careless good humour didn't match Natalia's diminutive, almost
Chinese steps and her serious, self-effacing manner.

'She's usually punctual. Her phone goes straight to voicemail. It's a worry.'

'There's no answer at home?'

'No. But of course why should there be? George doesn't
answer the phone, he's outdoor staff, and she's meant to be
here, for the appointment.'

'D'you think we should ring the police?'

'I'll give it another quarter of an hour or so, see if she pops
up.' Philip wasn't used to feeling such anxiety on behalf of
another human being. It was exhausting, and meant he was
nigh-on incapable of turning his mind to the many things
which needed his attention.

'She's probably shopping or trying to park.'

Philip had a pain in his chest: it felt like his heart was being
opened with a tyre lever. He gritted his teeth and carried on.

'I wouldn't normally be worried but, you know, I hate to think that she's . . . that she might need help.'

He wanted to get to the other side of this crisis as quickly as he could. He had transformed his financial services business into a wholly owned subsidiary of Equitable Life because it promised security and strength and, of course, it had delivered exactly the opposite: disaster and uncertainty. There were maintenance schedules on the house, farmland and vehicles which had fallen behind due to a temporary cash flow problem. BSE, and now foot-and-mouth, had knocked the farm for six. There were ten yards of disinfectant-soaked carpet laid out in the driveway and for the foreseeable future there'd be zero income. Thank God for the increasingly vertiginous climb in the stock market, which he was taking advantage of. He was certain he shouldn't sell yet; he should buy more. The prospect of the bubble bursting was beginning to frighten people but it was an opportunity for men such as he who weren't sheep, who made the trend rather than followed it. It took courage to go higher. He must raise more money on the farm and buy more Arm Holdings, more Last Minute to cover his losses. They were new, exciting companies and the price would continue to go up. It was one of the symptoms of the new, computerised, global trading network that confidence rose and fell in bigger waves and more quickly. Such a marketplace wasn't for the faint hearted. Money went in and out of people's pockets quicker, more uncertainly, no sooner there than gone. And where there was nothing yesterday, suddenly today there was a huge fortune . . .

Even someone as brave as he was, in this bear pit, felt the panic of rising shares. It was as if invisible monsters scrabbled at his pockets, pulling money out of them and making more of it, conjuring it out of thin air. No one had worked to give it to him; there was no one producing widgets, no company finding oil, no hotel chain gobbling up other hotels. It came suddenly

out of nowhere, just an idea in the electronic ether. The fear
was of being left out. Then came more scrabbling as shares rose
even higher. The monsters grew bigger and more aggressive.
The fact that the money was invisible, didn't exist, made it feel
more mysterious. What was happening? People's confidence in
the new internet stocks, in the very business of shares, any
shares, was soaring.

Yet, after only a few minutes of thinking about money –
about all the things he had to do about money – his mind
returned to Natalia. She was twenty minutes late. It was unlike
her. He pushed aside all thoughts of calling his broker and
dialled her number again. Straight to voicemail. Where was
she?

The anxiety rose in his breast. Natalia was dead. Or stuck
somewhere, giving birth. It was all going wrong. There were
complications. Pictures replaced each other in his head:
Natalia's stomach moving, her jaw moving back and forth in
agony, sweat breaking from her brow. The cord tightened
around the baby's neck, its lips turned blue.

For how much longer could he keep Natalia and her unborn
baby safe, alive, warm, fed? Money – again it turned to that. So
much money had fallen out of the holes in his pockets in recent
years. It was almost too much to bear. His insomnia for
instance – he recognised it as one of the symptoms of the post-
traumatic stress disorder reported by soldiers returning from the
fight to liberate Kuwait. He'd read about it in the *Daily
Telegraph*.

His niece Mattie was looking at him expectantly. He should
say something but couldn't think what. It was like having a
gobstopper stuck in his throat. He made the usual polite noises
and returned to the ante-natal department.

Mattie watched him go. She was glad to be alone again.
The ward sank back to normality. She dispensed with the next
ten minutes, drew them past her, moment by moment, inching

along. It was quiet, steady progress towards tomorrow morning and it was all she wanted. She kept her heartbeat low, her muscles relaxed. She sent soothing messages to Michael Junior inside the womb. The hours ahead were like the last few downhill strides in this long hike she'd been on. The caesarean at ten-thirty a.m. tomorrow was the finish line . . . home, babe in arms. Healthy. Alive.

A feeling of achievement stole over her and she set another target: a half hour without talking to a soul, without worrying, success sliding easily towards her.

After the sudden, harsh noise of the accident there was silence in the lane except for the sound of Natalia's car radio. Bit by bit the birdsong returned, and there was a quick rustle of grass as all creatures returned to normal habits. Whatever grew in the hedgerows kept on growing. Dust stirred up by the skidding tyres crept dryly over the surface of the road, settled on the foliage.

Half a minute later, Michael regained consciousness to find himself in exactly the same position as before: in the Renault, nose to nose with Philip's Rover. The bonnets of both cars were folded up, misshapen. The dashboard and steering wheel seemed closer, the seat more cramped. His head ached fiercely. His knees were sore and the seat belt had bruised his hips, but in all important respects he was OK: his limbs moved, he lived and breathed.

There was, yes, the strange, unworldly sound of a voice talking from the other car's radio, both engines having stopped working. It made the silence deeper and more sinister.

He couldn't see Natalia. She was no longer in the driving seat. It was difficult to twist around; he wanted to unplug his belt but it was already floating and tangled around him. The door refused to open until he put a firm shoulder against it.

The impact must have bent the door pillars out of shape. He climbed out of the car and stood, tweaked by various discomforts. His knees . . . There wasn't time to worry, he had to find out if Natalia was all right. He limped over.

When he reached the Rover's passenger door it was like a joke – the twin airbags had gone soft and hung limply. He pushed at the white balloon, trying to look under it. The radio gave off its steady, unconcerned voice.

There was no one in there. He withdrew, the pain beating in his skull with renewed fierceness, and looked around. Had he been unconscious for ages? Natalia might have walked off to fetch help. The road heading back to the farm was empty. The other direction, from which he'd travelled, also remained obstinately devoid of any sign of life.

The June sun beamed its summer harshness on his crown. He took a step or two and called out, 'Natalia?'

He must *do* something. Not his strong point.

A moment later, he heard her shy, uncomplaining voice, 'Here . . .' He skirted the rear of the Rover to find her sitting in the hedge.

'Natalia? You all right?'

She was leaning forward, both hands were clasped around her knees. 'Natalia? Hmm? Is everything OK?'

'Yes. Fine.'

'I'm so sorry,' continued Michael, rubbing her back. 'The accident was my fault. Unforgivable.'

Natalia's stomach protruded nearly as far as her knees. She moved both hands over it in a circular motion. 'Are you hurt?' asked Michael.

'I'm sure not.'

'Can you stand?'

'Yes, of course.' Natalia took his arm and pulled herself up; he was surprised at the fierceness of her grip. He steadied himself so he wouldn't veer off balance. 'Have you got a phone?' he asked. She shook her head, 'No, sorry,' she whispered, 'is at home, I was only going to fetch petrol.' Michael peered behind her curtain of dark hair. Glimpses of her face told him she was concentrating: it was as if she were in a distant place rather than beside him. He wondered what it was like to have such flawless, white skin. Very odd.

As for Natalia, the sudden rush of adrenalin injected into her system by the accident hadn't diminished. It was as if the moment of panic had taken root in her and remained even now the danger had passed. The age-old life force within her had detected an emergency and was rushing her into labour. She wished above all for this ache to subside. It disturbed her whole system.

Michael was saying something; she couldn't concentrate. It was important he was here — she needed help — but it was as if he were tethered some way off, out of reach.

'I think I have bruised my knees,' said Michael. 'We must get back to civilisation, I think.'

'Maybe . . . can you walk?'

He took a pace or two, then more; he completed a small circle and bent over and rubbed his knees gently. 'Ouch.'

She watched him. 'I will go back to the farm,' she said. 'Is only a few miles.'

'A car will come along soon,' said Michael. 'We should wait here together, I think.'

A minute passed. The two wrecked cars waited, their bumpers locked together. It occurred to Michael that one of them might still work and they could drive out of here. He tried the Renault first but there was no sign of life; all power was lost. He sat in the Rover and it started up, but the immediate hiss of escaping water vapour from the front told him the radiator had been punctured and the engine would seize in moments if he didn't switch off.

They were stuck.

Five minutes passed. He tried not to look at his watch. The time dragged, silently. He thought of Mattie in hospital, and Philip's business troubles with Equitable Life. He remembered Sitten Hall. As from today it was no longer his home. How reduced he was . . . Then he looked at Natalia and wished he could think of something to say.

It was like a gap in the conversation at a dinner party, he thought. Awful. There didn't seem to be a way out. The ache quickened in his head. The heat came down mercilessly, flattened the fields around them and baked the tarmac underfoot so that it gave off mirage-like distortions of air close to the surface.

It was important to do something, break the spell. Michael clapped his hands. He hoped that the action would help bring a word, an idea to mind, something to say. He even opened his mouth, ready. But – nothing.

Natalia could smell petrol. Her baby turned and turned inside the womb, alarmed by the adrenalin in their shared bloodstream. 'Tell me,' Natalia whispered in her own language, 'are you coming?' She moved her hands to a new position, waited . . . 'Now?' she murmured, frowning. Sure enough, the answer came: a rolling action, of knee, foot or elbow, against the membrane. Her belly tightened. An instinct turned in her. Yes.

An image sprang to mind of the photograph taken during her last scan: the baby's mouth open, eyes closed, deep in a pre-conscious sleep. Was it now awake?

She wandered up the road a few yards to the overgrown gateway, which let into the hedge just uphill from the scene of the accident. If she could see a house, closer than the farm, she would try to walk there and ask for help.

Michael remembered his dragon bowl. He limped to the Renault's passenger side. The seat was empty. Then, in the shadowy depths of the footwell he saw it, upside down. Of course, it had been thrown forward by the impact. Gingerly he lifted it out, turned it over. There was no crack, even, that he could see. He checked the rim. It was all right. He ran a finger around the inside. He looked for Natalia: she was leaning over a gate, dead still, as if listening to something.

'Come on dragon bowl,' he murmured. He walked it around, wondering where to put it for safe keeping. After all, he couldn't be sure what would happen to the cars – some other incapable pensioner might come down that hill too fast and ram the Renault from behind, or it might be towed away. He'd have to keep the bowl with him. He found a safe spot in the hedge and planted it there for now.

He looked in both directions, hoping for sight of a car – the glint of sunlight off a moving windscreen – or for the sound of an engine.

He wondered at this strangely empty feeling, as if the entire planet had been abandoned by human kind. The world was waiting for something to happen; everyone else knew what it was but somehow they'd been left out. Armageddon. Life on earth was going to stop.

Suddenly he remembered: it was the European Cup. Thursday, the match against Portugal. Everyone would be indoors watching television. No wonder the almost occult silence, the empty roads. Even the rush of the A397 was absent.

He limped over and shared Natalia's gateway. 'The football is on this afternoon, I just realised. The world and his wife are watching. Not long 'til it's over, though. We'll be all right. Not to worry.'

'What about I walk?' she replied. 'If we can see a house, the nearest one. See?' She pointed.

Michael looked across the fields. A roof was visible through the trees. It looked perfect; doubtless it was stuffed with telephones. They should make their way there and ask for help.

'Will you be all right? It's only a couple of fields I suppose.'

That sensation crossed Natalia's stomach – the belt tightened again.

Too tight.

She didn't betray her discomfort. She simply waited until the belt loosened again. She heard Michael's voice, 'Hmm, Natalia? I'll come with you. We'll go together.'

'Hold on,' she said. She went back and switched off the radio in her car and shut the doors – tidying up. They'd made a mess in the road and she wasn't going to leave it like that. Michael went and found the dragon bowl and secured it under one arm. He limped back up to the gateway, Natalia helping him. It was amazing the effect it had, her hand on his elbow, just that slight pressure making it easier. They left the mangled vehicles behind them.

On the other side of the gate youthful stinging nettles were beginning their copious, hard-working expansion. A middle strut was broken. The catch refused to budge, even when Natalia tried to lift it into a more helpful proximity to the post; grass and earth growing over the bottom held it in an iron grip. The gate obviously hadn't been opened in years.

Natalia climbed first; Michael watched. Her belly was plump on top of the gate, like a bag that he could take by the handles and carry for her. In that bag – the mad thought occurred to him – was a nephew or a niece, for him. 'I'll look after you,' he said. 'We'll be all right.'

Just as he believed he'd escaped everything – wife and home – he was in charge of a young, pregnant woman.

When she was safely on the other side Natalia took the dragon bowl from Michael. 'Very valuable,' he insisted, and she dutifully found a safe spot for it. Next, it was his turn.

Michael pulled himself up on the second bar and then waited. His balance wasn't so good and his knee was hurting. Natalia didn't hurry him; he was grateful for that.

She was quite shocked: his face was dramatically brightened

by sunlight and therefore suddenly appeared truly blasted by drink and age, the moustache and eyebrows springing out in every direction.

Slowly he lifted that bad knee and rested it on top of the gate. She had both hands ready to catch him. 'Careful,' she said.

'Softlee softlee catchee monkey,' said Michael. 'I'll rest here for a second. Don't want to fall off.'

While they waited, a first, proper contraction swept in and took possession of Natalia. The exact middle of her was the centre of the discomfort and it gripped harder, made it worse. Not a sound escaped her lips. If Michael had been observing closely he might have seen her sway and bite her lip for a second, nothing more.

'All right?' she asked. 'Can you put your leg over, now?'

'Ohhh . . . Ahhh!!' said Michael. He'd knocked the bruised part of that knee against the gate – not wise.

'That's good. Nearly here,' she encouraged him. Her contraction edged away slowly, like a receding tide. He was saying something but she didn't quite understand.

Michael adjusted his position on top of the gate. 'Bravo,' he said, 'I'm doing well.' It would make an absurd picture, him clinging onto the gate like this, having so much trouble. It was the knee's fault. Otherwise he'd have hopped over, hardly touching. He leaned slightly forward, gripping tightly, to execute the last stage. His shoe bumped against the woodwork, found a good purchase.

'Nettles,' Natalia pointed.

'Hmmm?'

'Careful the nettles will not get you,' she explained. Michael looked down and saw what she meant. 'Ah, thank you, yes, spotted.' He registered the unfamiliar planes of her face, her colouring, her black-as-coal eyes. Lucky old Philip, he thought. Maybe there was another one of these available somewhere for himself.

He swung the other leg over and climbed off the gate, but the ground was unexpectedly rough and his toe caught in a hummock; he found himself pitching forward. It meant he had to plant both hands in the nettles. He felt their feathery, multiple touches. The stinging was immediate on his wrists and on the palms of his hands. 'Bloody hell,' he swore. It felt as if boiling water had been poured over his arms. 'Christ,' he said, as his skin went hot with the poison and he swayed back and forth. His breath hissed. Natalia was pulling up dock leaves. 'Shall we carry on?' she asked, as she rubbed the leaves vigorously on his stings.

'Which way?' asked Michael. He couldn't see any house or roof any more, just a small, rough pasture and a tree-lined hedge and another field beyond that.

'This. Here.' She pointed.

'Where's the dragon bowl?' he countered. Natalia fetched it and started to walk, cradling it in her arms.

Michael followed her. He was a bit amazed at everything – the stings, Sitten Hall, Patsy, the car crash, Natalia and Philip. What on earth was he doing here?

At four-thirty it was Granny Banana's turn to visit Mattie. She walked carefully with her stick on one side and her driver ready on the other. It took them some time. Mattie waved and smiled several times. When they arrived, the driver made sure of a chair for Banana and then withdrew tactfully. For a while they talked about Granny's walking again, and how Sharland House had been so wicked in prescribing such a heavy dose of tranquillisers as they had. She described her new home, Greenaways. It was so much better and kinder. And it was such a pleasure to walk again. It made her feel like a grown-up, she said. And then she was quick to ask about Mattie, and to lean forwards further in her chair and listen to the latest goings-on in the ward, and Mattie's fears about tomorrow.

Clasped round Mattie's wrist lay the silver-and-copper band which Granny had given her. They'd asked her to remove it for surgery but she'd clung to her argument that it harboured all the kindness and good luck there was in the world and that it must never leave her. They'd agreed she could keep it on as long as they covered it with surgical tape. Mattie tapped it and smiled.

Banana held her hand. 'So pleased you wear it. Utterly good thing Mattie, that it's found a new home. One that appreciates it, you know? The main thing with jewellery, of course, is that its owner gives to it a . . . special value. I did, with this bracelet, for years and years and years, and it is such an oddly powerful pleasure for me that you do, too.' She gave Mattie's hand a weak shake. 'Makes you wonder, my goodness, who's going to have it next, whom will you give it to?'

'Tell me the story, how you got it,' said Mattie.

'Oh, I must have told you before.'

'No, never.'

Granny kept hold of Mattie's hand and took them both back to years ago, to miles away, deep into her memory of the river bank at Sitten Hall, not the Avon itself but a tributary. Rivulets tumbled over one another in this shallow stretch, their foaming white backs rising continually like a shoal of fish. It was March 1941. Michael was only a year old and Philip hadn't been born yet. Thirty-seven evacuee children had been billeted at Sitten Hall by the Waifs and Strays Society and one of them was missing; and Granny Banana – a young woman, before she ever earned the nickname Banana – was looking for him. As she walked she told herself not to hurry. The task was to scan both banks of the river and find him.

The water wasn't deep enough for a ten-year-old child easily to drown, she didn't think. The dusk settled; another inch of daylight failed. She called again, 'Aaron!' Past experience told her he wouldn't keep running, he'd be holed up somewhere.

Each time he ran away he thought he was going to keep going all the way back to London but he always grew frightened at the anonymous power of natural features – a turbulent river, a too-steep hillside. She walked on, calling him every minute or so. The enormous importance of world events, their urgency, impressed itself on her: Plymouth had been blitzed the day before and she'd heard on the radiogram the call for vehicles. It had been declared an evacuee area. More children cut loose . . . She hastened her steps; hunger gnawed at her middle. 'Aaaaaronn!' She wondered if Harriet was still looking as well, or whether she'd gone back. The others would need to be fed.

She continued upstream. The valley narrowed. A deep, black pool, a circle at the foot of a waterfall, stared at her with its one steady eye. She looked around the edges, hoping not to see him floating face down . . . thankfully, no. She pressed on.

Half a mile further on she reached the border of the parkland and the trees crowded to the walled boundary. She went through the gate and followed the path. Under the trees the light had disintegrated further: it was almost dark. She found a pair of boots – positioned neatly side by side – and recognised them. Why would he have taken them off? To cross the river? If so, surely they'd have been closer to the bank. She headed downhill until she reached the edge of the more vigorous stream as it wore out the head of this valley. She had seen a sheep drowned here once. The darkness prompted her to believe such a nightmare might happen to Aaron. No, she'd hear him soon, his plaintive voice calling for help, and he'd be found crouched in some sheltered spot, spooked. He would only come out from a hiding place if he could hold someone's hand. And then there would be his silent walk back to Sitten Hall. She'd hold on, talk for both of them.

She hopped across the stream – curiously it seemed smaller, quicker than it should, but she blamed the darkness. She

climbed the other side of the valley, calling his name. She was
heading for the army training camp where the soldiers practised
survival skills. More than once Aaron had been found in the
rough-hewn shelters and dug-outs constructed there.

However, the curve of the land began to fall in a different
direction from the one she would have predicted. The darkness
cloaked her senses and, try as she might, she couldn't recognise
where she was. There should have been a stretch of pines but
she walked underneath beechwood. The ground obstinately
continued to rise.

When she came across a wire fence she knew she'd lost her
way. She grew frightened. She stopped and listened, but the
silence of night had descended. Underfoot, the sponge of leaf
mould and earth gave her the feeling of floating on air. She
called for Aaron — and this time the timbre of her voice
changed, sounding like a cry for help, herself. She cursed her
terrible sense of direction. Panic shivered through her, an electric shock that ran through every nerve in her body.

She decided she must return to Sitten Hall and find more
help. If she headed downhill she'd hit the stream; and if she
followed the stream she'd find the Avon, and if she followed
the Avon she'd reach Sitten Hall. It could only be a few miles'
distance. Even in the dark she'd be able to follow this plan. She
started out. Her body was strong; she had on a good pair of
boots. It wasn't cold, she would be all right. Logic told her that
if a small boy could spend whole nights at a time out in the
woods and survive then certainly so could she. Men and
women the world over were facing unimaginable dangers and
tests of their resolve; she herself must face this small trial. Yet
the darkness eclipsed all logic. Its magic power invaded her,
despite the comparable lack of danger. She used Aaron's
word — yes, she'd become spooked. She came across a broad
track, running along the bottom of the valley, which was
bounded on the downhill side by an earthen bank. She could

hear the stream on the other side. She climbed up and peered down through the gloom: the stream was running from left to right. It was obvious that the track followed the course of the river; she'd be safe walking along it. From her vantage point on the bank she shouted as loud as she could, 'Aaron, I am lost myself and heading back to the Hall. Try and make yourself known. Can you hear me?' She paused, listening for a reply, but heard only the gurgling of the water and the soft movement of night air. Her fearfulness made her cross, impatient. 'I am as frightened as *you* are,' she shouted, trying to make her voice carry in all directions. 'I will come back with torches and with some people to help me. Can you hear?' She waited.

Again, nothing. She climbed down off the bank and began walking along the track. She cried a little. This wretched boy! He took so much time from the other children, yet she knew that behind all his difficulties lay the fact that he had had so much taken away from him. Both parents. A life. Safety. It was no wonder he wouldn't eat at table but instead took all his food and hid it in his room. He fought over the clothes they distributed – nonsensical rows with children bigger and older than him over a pair of secondhand shoes which would never fit him anyway. The other children gave way to him; they knew he had no fear and no boundaries. They hated him for it, quite properly. Yet she felt in her bones that his behaviour would not be mended by sanctions or punishments or any appeal to a moral code. Only if people gave to him freely, and gave enough for long enough, would it turn around. As she walked she rehearsed the little talk she'd give, yes, to the other children along these lines. She'd explain Aaron's background and she'd ask them – beg them – to join her on a mission. They were going to mend this child. When they felt like hitting him, instead give him something. Anything. Give him their favourite thing! Do it mysteriously, without explaining it.

She herself was going to give him extra helpings from her own ration book, favouring him over her own son even. They would give him the best clothes they could find. Could they do that? She ended by saying that if any one of them was in difficulties, she'd do the utmost in her power to mend them too . . .

Her tears at being lost in the dark segued into tears for Aaron — a lost boy!

In front of her was a line across the track: she strained to see what it was. Step by step it grew until she recognised it as a jump made for ponies. Whoever had built it had taken advantage of the bank to rest a pole on it; the other end was jammed into the side of the hill. She knew where she was, now — she'd stood at the other end of this little mile-long course of jumps often enough, waiting for the children, or a riderless pony, to come back. Somehow she was on a completely different tributary from the one she'd thought she was on. Relief flooded her . . . She'd found her way.

They'd gone back and found Aaron, all right — that and many other times.

Aaron had survived the war and gone to America. Slowly but surely he'd made a fortune and in the early '70s he'd sent Granny Banana the silver-and-copper wristband. Twenty-seven years later, in 1999, Granny had given it to Mattie on her wedding day and Mattie had worn it every moment since. It would accompany her into the operating theatre tomorrow.

Mattie and Granny Banana talked on. They veered close to discussing plans for the christening but it wasn't allowed — bad luck to talk of such a thing before they had both Natalia's and Mattie's babies safe and sound in their arms.

Instead, Mattie was left to imagine one of her favourite scenes: she and Natalia at Sitten Hall, Natalia's arm linked through hers. Both of them were wearing cool white dresses, standing on a swathe of green lawn in brilliant sunshine. They both had their dark hair worn long, untied. And in the arms that weren't linked together, they held their first-borns, newly christened. Michael Junior and . . . someone.

The photographer looked up from his camera and exclaimed, 'Lovely.'

Michael and Natalia walked up a slight incline, Natalia keeping her hand on the small of Michael's back to help him along. A mass of insects hazed drunkenly a few inches above the ground as if they were spores of the earth, drifting upwards, drawn by convection, the heat . . .

A sun-baked, nettle-burned sweat had broken out over Michael's hands and wrists. He touched around his cuffs: the skin felt lumpy, tight and hot.

'We will make it, we are OK,' said Natalia encouragingly. 'Keep going.'

Michael nodded. He was looking down, to make sure he stepped between the cow faeces littering the grass. He didn't want to spoil his brogues. 'How far to the house?' he asked.

'Just maybe is one more field. You will see the roof again in a minute I hope,' replied Natalia.

They made steady progress. A dozen bullocks were taking the shade under the trees over by the bank, looking at them curiously. Perhaps it was because of his bruised knee, but he felt vulnerable. 'Don't like the look of those,' he said.

'Don't worry,' she said quietly. 'They are young. Like teenagers. They might come. They might look. But we are not troubled.'

'Hmmm.' Michael shouldered his responsibilities. He must protect Natalia.

They made their way. More minutes passed.

Natalia felt another contraction arrive. She held her breath, kept quiet as a mouse, shook her head, walked a bit quicker.

Her jaw trembled. She fought against the instinct to stop and throw herself on her hands and knees. There was no question now – this baby was on the way.

They tracked across the field. Step by step they drew closer. The bullocks stood up to take a look – except one, which remained sitting down, noticed Michael. He wondered why. It was ill, maybe. Meanwhile the rest began sauntering in their direction. There was a yobbish, uncontrolled atmosphere about them. He stopped, and felt Natalia's hand rub his back. 'Is really all right,' she said, 'even when they start and run. They will not be coming near.' She tucked the dragon bowl more firmly under her arm and pushed Michael onwards. 'Is the cow with the baby that is a worry. These ones might run a lot of times but they won't be harming us.'

Michael was pleased to see there wasn't a proper fence as such, merely a bank topped by stunted trees which they could easily scramble over.

The nearest bullock tossed its nose in the air and broke into a canter, straight at them. Michael stopped. 'Is normal,' said Natalia. 'You want to carry on?' The bullock veered away, skittered behind them. The others, in a pack, decided to follow and now ten bullocks thundered towards them. Michael was frightened; he waved his arms and shouted, 'Gerroff you . . .!' It struck him he'd have been good in the war, after all. He could face up to danger all right. 'Bugger off!' he called. 'Go away!' The bullocks streamed past on either side, kicking up their heels. Natalia drew him on. 'Bloody . . . beasts!' said Michael.

Natalia quickened her pace; if the contractions were coming this quickly, she must hurry and reach safety. Ahead of them the other bullock remained sitting down. Except it was a cow, Natalia realised. A warning bell rang.

Now that they'd arrived at the tumbled-down bank Michael could see there was an electric fence strung along it. This was good news. As soon as they were the other side they wouldn't be bothered any more by the bullocks. He glanced behind him. There was turmoil in the gateway: they rolled around and then took off in a new direction, thankfully not towards them. Michael could tell that he and Natalia were the centre of their interest. All this mayhem and stampeding was because of the human trespassers in their field.

A moment later he and Natalia reached the electric fence. It had two strands, the first running at nearly waist height and the lower one at below knee level. They could hear its ominous ticking every couple of seconds. He and Natalia faced up to it.

'Will you be able to step over?' she asked.

Michael came closer. 'Absolutely. Maybe push it down a bit,' he said. 'With something. Whatever.'

'Or under if you like.' Natalia found a safe spot for the dragon bowl and put it down so she could scout for a stick. She found a suitably dry one, around two feet long.

'Ladies first,' he said gallantly and took the stick off her, rested it gingerly on the top wire as an experiment, ready for the jolt. 'I can either push the top wire down, or hold the bottom one up, whichever you prefer,' he said, hoping the electric current wouldn't travel through wood. 'Click,' went the fence. A small pulse went up his thumb. It was bearable. 'Over or under?' he asked.

Natalia imagined stepping over the wire: the possibility sprang to mind that she might overbalance. Or Michael could make a mistake and let the wire snap upwards . . . anything was preferable to that. She sank on one knee as if about to be knighted, holding her belly protectively. 'Under,' she said.

'OK then.' Michael scooped up the bottom wire and lifted it as far as it would go. To his right, he met the eye of the cow that was sedately lying down, but which had stopped chewing the cud and was looking at what was happening with increased interest. Behind them the bullocks rampaged from one corner of the field to the other. They were showing off. He had to admit it was unsettling to hear their hooves beating up the ground. 'Hurry up!' he called. There was more than enough room for Natalia to pass underneath yet she was not moving much, beyond swaying slightly. 'Off you go.' Natalia grimaced and tipped forwards on her hands and knees and began to crawl. Michael hoisted the wire higher and watched her shoulders go safely through.

Natalia could smell the fresh, salady smell of the grass with the danker, faerie scent of the earth underneath. The ground was dry, rock hard. The next contraction had floated in, worse this time. She just had time to check her watch before she forgot everything around her: the fence, the ground, Michael, the bullocks . . . all disappeared. She could think only of keeping quiet. She went into it – yes, that was what it was like, being overtaken by the sea, the waves to be faced up to, beaten, only for the next one to be higher. She stopped, sank lower, on her elbows, and rocked from side to side. It grew worse.

The cow struggled to its feet.

Michael was poised; he pulled the wire higher, off Natalia's back. 'Forwards, go on!' he called. He kept one eye on the cow which had for no good reason decided to become alarmed. Then he heard a feeble bleat to his left. He looked: curled up in a shady spot, its head wobbling uncertainly, was a new-born calf.

The cow put its head down, glared at them.

At his feet Natalia had stopped for some reason. He felt a rising panic; sweat poured from him. 'Hurry up Natalia!' He gave her bottom a push with his foot – it was more of a kick, in fact. He had the difficult job of keeping the electric fence up. She didn't move. 'Natalia, go on!' She didn't respond. He found himself talking instead to the cow in a very sane voice,

'Don't you dare.' The cow swung its head sideways sharply to see him more clearly; he stared into its cross, wide eye. It cuffed the ground, once, twice.

He kicked Natalia's backside. 'Go on Natalia.' The cow danced sideways, shuffled two paces backwards, lowered its head. 'No!' Michael commanded. His wrist ached. He couldn't hold up this stick for ever. At the same time came the thunder of the bullocks' hooves behind him, and because he'd been distracted the electric fence wire dropped off the end of the stick.

Natalia was jolted by a nerve-wracking 'thud' which sprang every few seconds from the small of her back and travelled through every nerve in her body right to the ends of her very *teeth*. Logical thought was not possible when her brain emptied every time the shock hit her. It struck thrice before her head cleared and she realised it wasn't the contraction. As if bitten she scrambled clear of the electric fence. Tears coursed down her cheeks. The pain of her contraction still visited.

The cow trotted moodily towards its calf, alternately snuffling at it and then swooping around to check Michael who was scrambling and trampling and clawing his way through the electric fence any way he could, dishevelled and frightened. The cow also received a bolt of electricity across its brow as it walked back towards him and stirred its head in the fence. It shuffled back, stunned, noisy, and hurried to its calf. It briskly plodded in circles, licking the calf and swinging around to look at them.

Michael had to sit down; his back was playing up. Natalia wanted to get him over to the other side of the bank. The cow was still alarmingly close. Only the frail tendrils of the electric fence protected them. She went and hooked an arm under his and tried to lift him. 'Michael?'

'Wait, wait!' He shifted position. The nerve threatened to snag. 'Bit uncomfortable,' he said.

Some minutes passed.

'Come on Michael, we need to move.'

'I should just rest for a bit.'

'We must go.'

'Hold on.'

'Can you walk?'

'Wait, just need a breather . . .'

The crisis was over, after all. They were safe and sound. All was well. The sun stared down with its yellow eye. Other creatures were about their business, undisturbed. The county of Somerset was like a rug of great beauty, made out of a smaller, denser pattern than Wiltshire. It might be all right to die here, he thought, with the sun on his face. Yes, a death scene would be like this: a sudden step sideways, an unravelling. Quietly, out here in the field. Yet he wanted to see Mattie's baby, his grandson. And Natalia's of course, his niece or nephew. He shifted slightly. It was uncomfortable. Maybe he was going to end up in the orthopaedic ward with a seized back. He had a vision of his mother's face. Banana stooped over him; he could reach out and touch her. There she was, blocking out the sun, a bit unsteady on her feet, the walking stick poking out at an angle. She raised an imaginary glass and toasted him. 'Can you stand up?' He literally heard her voice.

'Can you stand up?' asked Natalia.

'Yes, in a mo.' He breathed for a while.

'Where did it hurt?' she asked anxiously.

'No, it's fine . . .' He tilted forwards, testing to find where the nerve gave its warning. Her arm was around his shoulders. The warm fecund smell of cow muck rose in a cloud around his nose and mouth. He really was in a filthy mess, stuff all over his shoes, but no matter.

Natalia helped him up and he shuffled over the broken-down bank and into the next field.

'That all right?' she asked.

It wasn't dead right. The last thing he wanted was back trouble. 'It would be best if I sat down for a minute or two,' he said.

'OK.'

Like a couple of ramblers with all the time in the world they sat side by side on this other side of the bank, Michael unnaturally still and tilting well forwards, Natalia holding her belly. They looked over a sweep of pasture which was closed off from stock. The grass was sweet and long, a dark green crop which you could almost sense growing. Natalia was still an impenetrable mystery, thought Michael. He'd like to ask her about her past, where she came from, what she'd left behind.

He winced. The middle vertebrae – old enemies. He'd have to take care. He really didn't want a trapped nerve.

Natalia stood, carried her belly for a few paces. 'This way?' she asked Michael.

'No no, further round. That way.' Michael pointed.

'OK,' she agreed.

She helped him up, her arm around his waist, and listened to his painful exclamations. She set them going in the direction that she knew was right. The picture came back to her: Michael entangled in the fence, the cow moving towards him with a frisky, kind of insane, energy. 'All right?' she asked.

'Yes,' he puffed, 'I think so. But it's this direction. More uphill.'

'You said this way, when I asked you before.'

'Did I?'

'Yes, you pointed at that.'

'OK, this way, then.' A pretty young woman's arm around him did help add some glamour to the situation, he thought. 'You walk?' asked Natalia. 'Or I get help for you.'

'I can walk, yes, yes,' said Michael impatiently.

'OK?' asked Natalia again.

'The loveliest thing is to have your help. Thank you.' As he started off Michael looked at the ground in front of him, an overview of a small patch; his feet featured prominently as they moved into it: one, then the next, then the first one again . . .

Presumably, he thought, birds looked down on the earth like this while in flight, except from much higher. They didn't just see a square yard, but a whole hillside. He imagined soaring hundreds of feet up – he'd always wanted to fly.

Natalia couldn't help letting go a small groan. She had to stop, lean over on her knees, pant a bit.

Which bird would he choose to be? wondered Michael. Pigeons were the idiotic teenagers of the British woodland, but it was incredible how they could navigate at speed through trees. They always looked like they were in such a hurry. Crows, on the other hand, appeared to have time to think about everything in obsessive detail. They were the intellectuals. A buzzard, if close to the ground, seemed ponderous, vulnerable; only at height, when it soared, did it start to come into its element. He would be a kestrel – lighter and faster than the barely viable old buzzard. The excitement of that superb eyesight. The folding up of your wings so that you might drop like a stone, locked onto prey . . .

Natalia held her breath, panted a bit more. She checked her watch. It had been nine minutes since the last contraction.

'You all right?' asked Michael.

'Yes,' came the whispered answer, a bit later. 'Sorry.'

'Something in your shoe?'

She nodded.

'Found it?' he added, after a moment. 'Hateful when that happens. Can be the tiniest speck but it feels like a boulder.' He waited for what seemed like an age.

'All right now,' she said.

Michael's thoughts meandered on. The truth of it was, he wasn't much like a kestrel or any other kind of bird of prey. He was more of a badger or a donkey. Preyed on, rather than predator. And there never had been much flight in him. If he'd had

to escape from trouble a lumpy trot was all that could be
expected. The bird's eye view of the hillside turned back into
a few square feet of earth, with his slow, smelly old man's feet
moving back and forth in it. He wasn't much good on this
rough terrain. An armchair and a television set was more his
habitat.

He realised he was curiously empty-handed – he'd forgotten
the dragon bowl. He stopped dead in his tracks. 'God! The
bowl.' He looked at Natalia.

'Hold on, I get it,' she volunteered and turned round,
headed back the way they'd come.

'Hurry up!' Michael called, and waited patiently. For a
while she was out of sight; he could hear nothing. He almost
expected the bellow of an outraged cow and Natalia's scream,
together with the fizzing of an electric fence, but nothing
doing – only more sun, the twittering of birds excited to be in
England in June. Michael could hear his own breath, also.
The heat, as well, had a kind of sound; maybe it was of air
rising, of insects, of every living thing soaking up warmth, but
it was definitely, together, audible. Yes, he'd enjoy just sitting
with the sun on his face. He remembered how often in the
summer he'd take a chair, any old chair, out to the side lawn of
Sitten Hall and point it at the sun and bask. Usually he'd sort
of half read a newspaper or a book but essentially it had just
been the soaking up of the sun's rays, dreaming of past summers, especially boyhood summers. The flash of a kingfisher
beating its way up the river. An ants' nest, crawling with soldiers and scouts – it had been fascinating to look at their
continual, automatic work, the heap they'd made, underneath
which was a complete city perfect in design and function. He
remembered one morning approaching the river, a guilty secret
weighing on his conscience: he'd left a line in overnight,
merely tying the nylon fishing line to a stout gorse bush and
going home – which was the opposite of sportsmanship. The

next morning, the sun on his face just like now, he'd crept back to that same gorse bush, seeking the invisible, clear line. When he'd found it, it had been with relief because it was slack, which meant he hadn't caught anything. He could feel the cruelty of it now; if he had caught something, the poor creature would have been thrashing around for hours. He'd never do such a thing again, he'd told himself. He'd picked up the line and begun to draw it in. Immediately a fierce yank had signalled not only had he caught something, but this wasn't a normal fish. Some creature of the night, it fought with eviscerating, continual, muscular effort. He was frightened and immediately dropped the line as if electrocuted. He watched it straining, angling back and forth as whatever monster it was pulled up and down stream in an effort to escape. Naturally, he'd been unable to do anything about it. There was no way he was going to pick it up again. Eventually he went to get help. Shamefaced, he'd told their young tutor, Crispin, who came down and picked it up. Michael watched as it cut into his hands. He'd kept pulling; it took all his might.

When Crispin had at last hauled it in, there had been an eel writhing on the end, thrashing around in the grass at their feet. Crispin had tried to pick it up. It easily twisted out of his grip. It had an oily strength and blind determination that Michael had never come across before in any creature. He was too scared to go close, even.

Crispin had killed it quickly. He'd unfolded his penknife and chopped its head off. It took several attempts. Michael had watched, aghast. With each cut that he witnessed, Michael became kinder, more empathetic, and when it was over he swore never to kill another living creature again, if he could help it.

Later, they'd discovered the true extent of Michael's crime: the eel hadn't eaten the worm, it had eaten a trout that had eaten the worm. The trout had a bellyful of eggs, ready to lay. Worm killed by fish killed by eel killed by Michael . . .

The eggs foamed from the trout's gut. The struggle of life against death had been as lithe and as powerful as the eel's fight. But, thanks to Michael, death had won, all the way up the line . . .

Yet the crisis hadn't disturbed the peace and the tranquillity of their surroundings; nature had blithely carried on. It was as if the emergency existed underneath, on a separate level.

It had taken days for his ten-year-old self to surface back to sunlight, the birdsong, the work of ants. Perhaps he never had been as carefree again. Yet the war, just at his back as it had felt like, had thrown up worse horrors for each and every person to witness, suffer.

A minute later, Natalia brought back the dragon bowl, undamaged. 'Good old dragon bowl,' he said, 'well done for coming through thick and thin.'

At four p.m. Patsy appeared at Mattie's bedside carrying flowers, moving quicker than usual and looking frayed around the edges. Her hem was crooked. A strand of hair hung loose from the swept back wave that rose from her forehead.

'What's up?' asked Mattie.

'Well, you're the thing that's up, we're one night away from the birth of your first child, our first grandchild.'

'Ma, you're doing your speeding thing, I can tell, which means something's happened.'

'What speeding thing?'

'You might as well tell me straight away. I don't want to go into one of those long conversations where you pretend everything's all right.'

'Am I that obvious?'

'Yes.'

'Oh dear.'

'What is it then?'

'Your father and Natalia have had a car accident.'

'They . . . what? How come they were in the same car?'

'No, they were in separate cars that ran into each other. And they've gone missing, slightly.'

'You're joking.'

'The cars were found in the lane near the farm. They'd had a little bump. Knock for knock I expect. There was no blood, the farmer said. No sign of either of them. Both cars out of action. So, someone's picked them up and given them a lift somewhere, but we don't quite know where.'

'I don't believe it.'

'It's absolutely typical of your father. Confusion and nothing quite working and everyone else having to scurry around and clear up after him.'

'Oh Ma, don't.'

'Sorry.'

'Have you tried Natalia's mobile?'

'Of course. Straight to voicemail.'

'How long ago did this happen?'

'No one quite knows. Obviously I was expecting to see your father tomorrow morning one way or another. He was on his way here, no doubt, but his car was full of suitcases and fishing rods and so on, which I think means he was taking me up on my offer and leaving home. So the trial separation is on; I think that's what that means.'

'Oh Ma, I'm sorry.'

'Don't be. He was going to stay at the farm, if I had to guess, although Philip knew nothing about it. Typical that he left it right 'til the absolute deadline.'

'Trial separation? I can't believe it. For God's sake! You've been divorced for years and years. Does he do everything the wrong way round?'

'I know, it's funny isn't it? Ridiculous man. Where does he think he's going to go? You know what it is, don't you?'

'What?'

'It's Natalia. He's seen Philip with a young woman and he's jealous. He thinks he can get a young woman. But who's going to pick him up off the floor? No one. Mark my words, that's what it is. D'you remember at that dinner, just before your wedding, when he asked Philip if he might phone her? "Extra chores," was the term he used, I believe, and I bet I know what extra chores he had in mind for her. D'you remember?'

'Yes . . .'

'Well, then. That's my theory. Late life crisis. And don't forget either that Michael's first wife was stolen from Philip. When it came to Natalia, Philip saw his older brother looming over him again, and that's why he made his move, there and then. Fascinating isn't it. Men are such animals.'

'Women are, too.'

'Yes, I suppose we are,' Patsy sighed.

'So where are Michael and Natalia now? Maybe they were hurt . . . and taken somewhere?'

'No, that's one thing I am sure of. If they were hurt then the ambulance would have been called and we'd know about it. I think they're perfectly all right and they've got a lift with somebody and they just . . . well, I think it's a bit thoughtless of them not to call.'

Mattie picked up the framed photograph which had stood on her bedside unit for weeks. It showed herself and Natalia standing sideways on to the camera, in the tiny garden of their flat in Bristol. It was a fine spring day and they'd both been wearing floating cotton dresses. Their bumps stuck out proudly. At the time they'd both been seven months gone. The start of Mattie's hospitalisation had been a week away; her pregnancy had been effortless so far. Natalia was several inches shorter than Mattie, her skin was paler, but their hair was the same rich black, which made them look like sisters. Mattie felt they *were* sisters, in a way. It was because she was an only child, she guessed, that she'd latched onto Natalia in a big way. She wondered if the other woman realised how important she was to Mattie's scheme of things. The unborn children would be christened together, that was the plan. The two women would have flat stomachs, their slim looks returned to them. Their babies would play together.

'What could it be, what's happened?'

'I don't know darling.'

'George is at the farm?'

'Yes. I suppose he's used to pigs and cows giving birth. He has some experience.'

'God, don't say it. Imagine. George with his ropes and his buckets of warm soapy water, trudging towards a screaming Natalia.'

'And Philip. D'you know . . . are we allowed to think,' went on Patsy, fussing with the flowers on the side table, 'that he's going a bit bonkers? Can we say that?'

'In what way, how d'you mean?'

'He never quite answers the question you ask him. For example, when he phoned to tell me about the accident, I asked him cheerily, how's things Philip, and his answer was to jump in and ask me a question of his own, if I'd heard from Natalia. Fair enough, but it's not too much to ask that he should answer civilly, it's like everything is just slightly . . . wrong notes being struck all the time. And it's not as if it just happens once. It's all the time. I mean, when I started talking about Natalia being perfectly all right one hoped, he ignored my efforts completely and moved onto the subject which he wanted to talk about, Equitable Life or some such. I'm sure he never used to be like that. He was definitely Mr Sensible, but now he's Mr Distracted.'

'Perhaps he's disoriented by the accident.'

'No, it was happening before the accident. I don't like to be uncharitable but it makes me slightly . . . *dread* talking to him, which is a shame.'

'How old is he?'

'He's not sixty yet. Not old enough to become difficult.'

'Hmm.'

'D'you think it's because of Natalia? I mean, not her deliberately causing it, but a young woman suddenly thrown on his plate, on his bed rather, to – er – deal with, d'you think?'

'It should have made him happy.'

'Yes, but maybe *too* happy?'

'You mean exhausted.' Mattie smiled.

'Yes!' Patsy laughed. 'Godddd! The mind boggles! Philip and Natalia.'

'Heart attack soon, then,' added Mattie.

'And now a tiny baby,' protested Patsy. 'What's that going to do to him, if his head is already spinning?' They enjoyed a quiet moment thinking of Philip with a baby son. It was an impossible thought; the picture couldn't be made. 'No one would have dreamed all this would happen,' said Mattie. 'Do you think Natalia married Philip for his money?'

'No. There was a little . . . look, you know, going back and forth between them, for ages. She told me. Not a grand passion, but she married to make a life for herself with a man whom she'd taken a liking to. It's a good enough basis for a marriage, by anyone's standards, it really is.'

'That's true.'

Patsy's hands tied and untied. 'All this . . . blue!' she said.

'Blue? Eh? What?'

'To see you surrounded by all this stuff' – she waved – 'coloured blue. The walls, the corridor, the floor, that machine, this machine, look, your blankets. It's your *least* favourite colour. I just want to redecorate.'

'Oh, Ma,' said Mattie. 'I'd help you.'

'Honestly. If I'd had a paint-brush. Or I could have gone to John Lewis and bought some different blankets. I feel your pain, I really do. Too late now though. You're out of here. Well done. Me too.' She rooted in her bag for her car keys. 'And I thought . . . or rather, what d'you think . . . that I shouldn't come in, this evening. If we find your father, he might drop by. Simon's lot are coming. I think that's enough. I know . . . well, if I were you I'd want just to have Simon with me. Your last night and so on as . . . *not* parents. Is that right? I mean I can come, if you wish, of course I always love to. But I don't want all of us to gang up on you.'

'Please come for a short while. And then perhaps Simon and I can be left on our own for the last hour or so.'

'That's a good idea, darling. I'll make sure everyone's out of your hair by eight and that will give you and Simon together until nine.'

'OK. That's great. Thanks a lot, Ma.'

'I'm excited, Mattie. Tomorrow little Michael Junior will arrive. And what will you be like, as a family?'

'Don't have a clue. Will we be happy? Lucky? Don't know.'

'And that's all right, darling, because you will find out. The main thing I remember, when I became *your* mum, is that up until then I'd spent all my time trying to get a grip on life, find a handle if you like, by which I could, you know, get a sort of jolly firm hold of it so I could do with it what I wanted; and when you were born suddenly life got a handle on *me*, in no uncertain manner, and it was going to do things to me whether I liked it or not, and that was the scary part. Does that make sense?'

'Yes, Ma, it does.'

'And your little baby, when he appears tomorrow, will certainly bring you happiness but also despair. But only sometimes.'

'I'll be all right.'

'Of course you will be. You'll be a good mum. Goodbye then, my darling.' Patsy leaned over and kissed her daughter's forehead. 'I'm so proud of you. Your father and I are looking forward to being grandparents. Stay safely tucked up.'

'I will.'

'I'll call you when we find Mattie. Sorry, what am I saying? I mean Natalia. And your wretched father. I think I might be divorced.'

'I'm so sorry.'

'Don't be.'

'Or a widow, if he's fallen over in a ditch.'

'Don't!'

'No doubt there'll be some perfectly rational explanation.'

'Yes . . .'

Once they'd made their way through the stand of beech and oak, Natalia and Michael saw it: a medium-sized Georgian country house built in golden Bath stone, of the type that many of Michael's schoolfriends had lived in. He was used to visiting such places and trying not to show even the slightest grain of superiority, but the boot was on the other foot now. He'd inherited a stately that could swallow ten of these yet, in his current circumstances, he'd give his eye teeth for just such a comfortable gaff to run to. The Georgians had been clever at designing the perfect small country house. They had the whiff of the faerie about them, but then stretched that little bit taller to give a romantic, graceful form, appropriate for ordinary human habitation.

'There we go,' said Michael. 'Saved by the bell.' He could see a croquet lawn and a border of roses. A large conservatory had weathered in, attached to one end of the house, while from the other side a separate coach house or some such peeped out, built in identical stone. Probably garages now, thought Michael, which explained why there were no vehicles parked on the gravelled forecourt.

He and Natalia started out across the stretch of field that separated the wood from the half-mile long, winding driveway that led to the house. Michael kept an eye out for any sign of the person or persons who lived here, but the garden and surrounding grounds remained empty of life. Hopefully there would be someone inside. If only he had x-ray vision and could bore into the house, go through all the rooms, find out who was there . . .

It was sweet with new grass underfoot as they made their way. Michael remembered one of the walking sticks, the silver-topped cane, which would look rather dashing, accompanying him; it was back at the Hall. It seemed like a long time ago that he'd driven out of the entrance gate for the last time but it was only a few hours. He and Patsy would meet at the hospital tomorrow without doubt and he wondered what they'd say to each other.

They reached a round concrete tank set into the ground. It was presumably something to do with the water supply to the house. Natalia let go of Michael and veered off, leaned against it.

'What's up?' Michael had come to rely on her help.

Natalia found a clean patch of ground and sat down. The grass was prickly under the heel of her hand and her belly was an uncomfortable block, hard and unforgiving, in front of her. She could no longer disguise the contractions. She put her hand on her belly and said to Michael, on an outward gasp, 'Baby arrives.'

'Hmmm?' He didn't think she should exaggerate; there was no need to get worked up. It made for a strange sight: a young woman gracefully and quietly sitting on the grass while an older gentleman, dishevelled and with cowpat on his best shoes and in danger of a trapped nerve in his back, stood nearby, tilting over at such an angle as made it appear he was looking for something in the grass. It was like a photo-shoot for a 1920s Absurdist magazine. He looked at Natalia, the curtain of hair obscuring her face, noticing the barely audible keening sounds she was making.

Maybe she wasn't exaggerating. Baby arrives – could she really be going into labour? He took a closer look and noticed her compressed lips, her closed eyes . . . If she was, then it was a bona fide emergency. He was nonplussed. Surely Natalia wasn't going to give birth? It would be like stepping through the looking glass; they'd be in a different world. All bets would be off, anything could happen. Fauns or dragons or rabbits holding tea parties. This was the English countryside, he thought.

Natalia threw herself back against the concrete bunker and screamed, her arms flailing for support in mid-contraction. She clung to it for dear life. All Michael's doubts fled. This was happening.

Natalia felt the sweat break out on her forehead as she journeyed through the contraction. When the pain had eased and she was recovering, she felt a tickling on her fingers. Just under the concrete lid of the water pump housing, in a sheltered indentation only a few millimetres wide, a web cocoon began to seethe with life. Two hundred tiny spiders issued from eggs, fought their way out and began an immediate hunt for food. Many of them would quickly be eaten by birds. She glimpsed a dozen of them running in and out of her fingers. The pain ebbed further out and she set her hand against the concrete surface so they might run off, and she wished them luck.

So many of them, such a race against time to grow and find their spot . . .

That contraction had been much worse. Was the child going to be born in a field, before they even reached the house? She looked at her watch. It had been eight minutes since the last one. She wondered how far dilated she was. She had felt as though she was being eaten by a shark, but she'd get through it as long as she didn't become exhausted. She might lose her dignity; perhaps her elderly brother-in-law was going to be the midwife; it didn't matter. All she wanted was to reach the other side of this birth and hold her baby, safe and well. She begged the hours ahead – as few as possible – to deliver her child. The only fear was of some medical complication. The cord might be around its neck. It might not be facing the right way . . . all Natalia could do was shut off such thoughts and pray to whatever gods were near.

The pain had gone, but lurked in her middle ready to return. She watched the spiders dash madly over the surface of the concrete bunker. She ought to get going. She must stand up, walk.

'OK? Hanging on in there?' asked Michael. All thoughts of it being a pleasant thing, to be in the utter stillness and quiet of a summer afternoon in an English west-country pasture, had gone. It felt dangerous.

She held her tummy. 'Very very sore. Is coming.'

'Is it . . . are you sure?'

'Yes. I must be in hospital. Sorry, the shouting.'

'My dear, make as much noise as you like.' This was a call to arms. She needed his help; there was no one else. 'Let's go,' he said. 'Time waits for no man.'

It was his turn to help her now, with an arm around her shoulders. They pressed on towards the driveway. The ribbon of tarmac swooped for a quarter of a mile or more and they intercepted it about half way along. They stumbled over the first cattle grid and marched past another group of cows.

At the second cattle grid came another contraction. The pain was disfiguring: her mouth pulled back, lines were written on her brow and between her eyebrows. She leaned over, staggered, crouched on all fours. The tendons in her neck strained. It was another life-and-death crisis, just under the surface of a summer's day, thought Michael, which scared him. It was up to him, that death should not even get a look-in, today! He felt a powerful affection for Natalia; he wanted to protect her as much as if she were his own daughter, or his own wife. 'You all right, you done, can we press on? Nearly there.'

'Yes, coming.'

He perched against an old tree root while she recovered. He didn't need to say anything. She'd become a sort of creature. They'd reached that kind of intimacy. His eyes were on her. She turned to look at him. His eyebrows popped up and his ears moved. 'Hmm?' he said, to escape the shame of being caught staring.

'Sorry,' she said again.

'Nonsense. You fit to carry on? Look, the house is right there. Just a few hundred yards and we can call an ambulance.'

'Yes.' She too felt how unlikely this situation was. A real English Lord was her midwife, in the middle of the countryside in faraway England. Michael held her elbow and pushed forwards. They crossed the final cattle grid and entered the grounds of The Old Rectory, as he now saw it was called from the name carved into a slice of oak nailed to the gate. Her keening, and a new noise, a sort of hissing of the breath between her teeth, told him this situation was becoming desperate. He begged for whoever lived here to be at home. The garage doors stood open and there was no car visible, which might be a bad sign. If no one was here he'd have no alternative but to break in and use their phone. Natalia's distress had deepened and it had brought from him a deeply felt response. It was no longer surprising that he had his arm around her, and that hers was around him. There'd be no question of trying to make it somewhere else. She was on her last legs.

They hurried on, he more or less upright and she tilted forward, like the Don and Sancho. He urged her, 'Come on Natalia old thing, you're doing fine, we're on the same side, you are having your baby, and we will all smile and laugh, won't we, when this is done. And we will all be at the christening, in a month or two's time, gathered around the font, and afterwards we will sip champagne and eat cake, and we'll tell the story, won't we, the incredible story, of what you did, how your baby was born, hmmm? That's it, one foot in front of the other, you're doing utterly good things, hmm? I'm here, I've got you.' She was sort of spinning in his hands as he said this.

When they arrived at the gravelled forecourt of the picturesque English house the door mercifully swung open and a figure stepped out, arms outstretched in welcome, as if they were expected. Michael's panic eased. A saviour had been found. He was no longer alone. One phone call and Natalia would be transported to the maternity ward, perhaps even by helicopter. He'd often seen the air ambulance in action on television. He himself would be allowed to travel with her. At the hospital he'd lie on one of those tables with a hole in it, attended by an attractive student masseuse.

At the same time Michael felt Natalia's hand clutching his arm. 'Hnnhh,' she said. '*Mad.*'

Michael, also, had noticed the strange, stiff-legged gait of their host as he walked towards them, and the wideness of his smile.

'Is mad,' repeated Natalia. 'We go.' She turned against him; he had to shift his position to cope. An undignified grunt escaped from him. 'Wait,' he said. The figure was close enough now for Michael to see that Natalia was right; this wasn't an ordinary person. His clothes were curiously old-fashioned. The flared trousers and wide-collared, patterned shirt spoke of an era long gone. His tie was purple and had a large knot but was set askew. He walked heavily on his heels with the toes

pointing outwards. 'Hello!' called the young man, still with his
arms outstretched as if greeting long-awaited family or friends,
'and welcome!'

Natalia squeezed Michael's arm with the same strength as
when she was having a contraction. 'We must go!' she whispered. She needed to be somewhere safe, protected, to lie down.

'Hello—' answered Michael. He was about to explain their
predicament but the man interrupted,

'My name is Richard, welcome to my home . . .' he turned
slightly and drew one of his outstretched arms sideways to
encompass The Old Rectory and its lawns, '. . . and let me say
how much I am, er, looking forward to the events of today,
thank you very much.'

Now that he was closer Michael could see that his smile was
extravagant and frequent. His eyes were small, tight, crescents.
Michael couldn't think what to say. Richard carried on, 'Yes I
thank you – both! – enormously! Ah . . . for coming.'

'Please, come, please!' Natalia tried to drag Michael away.
The man frightened her. She craved safety, shelter. It was an
instinctive hunger to find her place, the right spot for this
birth.

'We're all right, hang on,' soothed Michael. He understood
what was happening now. He recognised the kindly disposi-
tion, the slightly enlarged lower jaw, the flat, straight hair, the
merry eyes, the small upturned mouth and thick neck of
someone who suffered from . . . what was it called . . . a condition of some sort. Was it Spina Bifida? No. But it was
harmless, he knew that much. 'Thank you,' he answered
loudly. He must plough on, keep Natalia safe, get to that
phone as soon as possible. 'But I'm afraid we have an emergency on our hands. This woman is in labour.' He would have
to keep it simple. 'She is about to have a baby. Can we use a
phone?'

Richard's smile grew larger at the news. 'My goodness,' he

exclaimed and clapped his hands together. 'Has it started already?'

'Yes it has,' said Michael.

Natalia tugged at Michael's arm and pleaded softly, 'Let's go.'

'It's all right, I promise. He's perfectly kind and helpful. All the best English houses have someone like this tucked away somewhere, hmmm? We need a phone.'

'Is it like the one in the village last year?' asked Richard loudly, looking Natalia up and down.

'I expect it's the same sort of thing,' said Michael. 'But first could we use a telephone, please?'

Natalia screamed and slumped to a kneeling position. All she could see was the gravel. 'Help,' she gasped.

'Wonderful!' Richard clapped.

'Inside. Please. Can we. Now!'

'Of course, this way!' Richard indicated – with the same dramatic sweep – the house behind him. 'You must tell me everything you need.' Natalia waited out the contraction, groaning and rocking from side to side. When she got to her feet her knees were weak. She couldn't go much further, every instinct told her.

Michael walked her along and headed for the front door, standing shadowy and half-open in the depths of the porch. Richard sort of walked sideways, as though ushering sheep into a fold. At the porch he stood and clapped formally. Then he followed them in. Michael glimpsed a library to his right, comfortably dishevelled and with a children's puzzle laid out on the floor. Ahead, at the other end of the spacious corridor, was a kitchen, brightly lit. 'The first room on your left!' announced Richard. Michael followed his directions and went into a large reception room panelled in dark wood. The heavy brocade curtains were drawn, which was odd on such a sunny day. A huge rug had been rolled back and a row of chairs had been set out. There was going to be some sort of talk or meeting thought Michael – the Women's Institute or suchlike.

Richard followed them in. 'Now!' he exclaimed in the manner of a genial host. 'You must tell me exactly what you need.'

'A telephone,' said Michael thankfully. 'We must call for an ambulance.'

'Certainly.' His hands folded and unfolded and he called to the ceiling, 'Anything else?'

'Somewhere . . . maybe a bed for her to lie down on. She's exhausted.'

'A whole bed might be difficult,' said Richard, 'we'd have to carry it down from upstairs. I'm not sure Mama would like *that!* But, we can carry in a sofa and pretend it's a bed. I will fetch pillows and a duvet! That will make it look more like the real thing.'

'Yes, yes,' Michael hurried on, 'but the phone, I need the phone now, man. Show me where it is.' He told himself not to be irritated at this fellow's extravagant, theatrical manner; after all he was doing everything he could to help and was in fact acting with great calmness and good humour and courtesy.

'Of course!' exclaimed Richard. 'Right away! A phone! I will bring it.' He clapped his hands and with his stiff-legged gait he trotted towards the door.

Michael was moved at the generosity and helpfulness of this . . . what was the right word? Nowadays, he should be sure to describe him as something challenged; that would be the right way of saying it. Or someone with something diffi-culties. Anyway, many a person of right mind wouldn't have answered the door, seeing the state they were in. Natalia in labour. He himself grubby and in no fit state . . . They were lucky to have happened on this kind-hearted man. Michael felt it was a sort of religious experience. No room at the Inn.

The two wayfarers, one of them heavily pregnant. And the meek shall inherit the earth, he thought.

At the door Richard gave his huge smile and said, 'I am almost taking part!' before disappearing. His words were drowned by Natalia, who dropped to the floor and started walking on her hands and knees, crying out. She rocked back and forth, and then walked some more. She reached the rolled-up rug and leaned over it. Awful noises which she didn't recognise came from her own throat but she couldn't help it. There was no time or space to feel embarrassed. She crawled around in a circle, coming back to the same position again, leaning over the rug, panting.

For a whole minute Michael waited for the phone. It felt like an age. He brought a chair over to her in case it was useful and was surprised to find she clambered on and sat astride it, facing the wrong way.

'Fucking hell,' she whispered over and over again until the repetition became a cry, a way of crawling through the contraction. Michael stood, useless, next to her, murmuring words of support and encouragement. She'd be grateful, he thought, for the gloomy atmosphere in here, with the curtains closed. He could see the slim beams of light standing at each side, where the sun from outside fought its way in. Dust motes swam in the air.

Natalia climbed off the chair and went back to leaning over the roll of carpet. She rocked forward and back and groaned. It looked like she was trying to push it along.

Michael stopped mumbling and went to shout down the empty corridor to Richard, 'Hurry man, the phone!' Then he came back and repeated, 'I'm here. We've got you. Good girl. You're doing fine.'

Natalia was homesick; she didn't want this strange man, her brother-in-law, anywhere near her. She looked around anxiously for the right spot. Somehow the pain was different because it was played out in a foreign language. She wanted her

own pain, her own people. Everything was wrong. She couldn't
find the right place. Before long she was off the carpet and swaying from side to side. Her moaning was louder.

'Let's unroll the carpet, make it a bit more comfortable,'
suggested Michael. 'Fuck off, off off!' shouted Natalia in her
own language and uttered a different type of scream and flung
herself down on her elbows; the noise had sounded worse, like
someone murdered, but maybe it signified progress. Nature
was having its way. He remembered something about towels
and hot water, but he wouldn't know what to do, what they
were for.

Richard came back at a trot. He was carrying a phone
wrapped in its cable as well as a small antique table. 'I brought
this' – he lifted the table – 'to put the phone on,' he explained,
'because I thought it might be more . . .' he paused at the sight
of the groaning Natalia. 'Oh my goodness,' he said.

Natalia drew breath and screamed loudly. Richard's eyes
popped out of his head. Quickly he set the table on its legs,
unwound the cable from the phone and placed it carefully. He
put the handset to rights and carried the end of the wire to the
wall. 'Is that all right?' he asked. His eyebrows rose nearly to his
hairline. He moved his lower lip over the top of his mouth,
again and again. Michael was inexpressibly touched by this
strange man. The fact that he'd brought a table for the telephone to sit on denoted such care and attention to detail, even
if it was misguided. 'Thank you,' he said vehemently and
snatched up the phone without delay. The buttons were in the
handset. He pressed 9 three times. It was the second time in his
life that he'd called the emergency services; the first time, he
remembered, was when his first wife had deliberately driven at
him, knocked him down and drove off without so much as . . .

Natalia noticed the phone but knew it was too late. She
squirmed round, panting, and leaned against the roll of carpet
and screamed.

Michael couldn't hear himself think. He pushed a finger in his other ear. Why wasn't the phone working? He should move it away from his deaf side, over to the other ear, but as he did so he fumbled, dropped it. He squatted on one knee and scooped it up. 'Hello? Hello?' he shouted into the receiver. He dabbed at the keypad. He was aware that Richard was sitting in the row of chairs. How strange it must be in the young man's head, thought Michael, but thank God for him. He listened, the handset against his ear. Natalia writhed on the rug. Nothing, no one on the phone. He started again. He wasn't sure there was even a dialling tone; it was difficult to tell with her making so much noise.

Natalia wanted privacy, a midwife, another woman, to be in her own country. The pain must go away. She swung round so her back was against the carpet. The zip on her elasticated leggings was open at the side. Her knees stood cocked up, wide apart. She panted, sweated, her shoulders heaving with each breath. 'Is coming,' she shouted.

'All right!' called Michael and hurried to her. He turned and bellowed at Richard, 'Duvet, blankets, anything to keep her warm, man! Sheets. A bowl of hot water!' Richard jumped to his feet, smiling broadly. 'Duvet,' he repeated. 'Coming up!' He trotted to the door again. 'Pickpockets!' he shouted as he went through.

Natalia's pain was continual now. She had an uncontrollable urge to tear off her clothes, every last garment. She couldn't help it. She kicked off her sandals and started to undo the buttons on her top but lost patience and tore it off. Her knickers and stretchy leggings were already at half mast; in seconds she'd pushed them down. She threw her bra across the room and scraped off her socks. Michael stared, overcome.

'Fucking idiot!' shouted Natalia. She didn't care about anyone. She only needed her baby to come out safe, pray God

safe. She wanted to be on the floor, right down at ground level.
Her legs must be wide open.

Michael tried to hold Natalia in a supportive way. She hit
him and cursed and flailed, turning on her hands and knees
again. He felt useless. She writhed naked against the rug. Her
belly was out, vulgar and hairy and round. 'The phone's not
working,' said Michael.

She threw a shoe at him. 'Fuck off!'

'There's no midwife, nobody who knows anything . . . can
you tell us what to do?'

'Aggghhh fucking bastard hell!!!!!'

Michael tried to remember what had happened when his
own daughter had been born – it was so long ago – while
Natalia closed her eyes and prayed, begged any and all forces
of nature to get her out of this, grant her what she wanted:
her baby in her arms, suckled, alive. The pressure across her
belly was a tight band of continuous agony. The urge to
push occluded every other instinct, took over all feeling.
Embarrassment didn't figure; the feelings of others didn't
impinge on her consciousness. Only those actions and reactions
which might help her body's current task reached her. She
rolled onto her hands and knees. She shouted, '*The baby comes,
now!*'

Michael knelt down, but by the time he'd done so Natalia
was moving away, heading further towards the back of the
room. He could only follow, walking on his knees.

Richard came back carrying the armful of pillows and trail-
ing the duvet; they partly obscured his face and muffled his
voice. 'D'you remember,' he said loudly, 'I had to say
"*Pickpockets!*" and I kept getting it wrong all during rehearsals?
I always said it at the wrong time, didn't I, it was awful wasn't
it.' He walked onto the stage. 'But then on the night itself they
had someone in the wings who waved at me and I said it at
exactly the right time, out it popped, "*Pickpockets!*" There we

are!' He dropped the pillows and the duvet on the floor and caught sight of Natalia who was sitting naked, knees wide open and her belly round and huge supporting the oversize, tight boulders of her breasts and her jaw bumping on her chest as she grimaced and hissed through her teeth and tried to feel for what was happening. Richard shouted, 'Oh my God!' and covered his face with both hands and turned away sharply. 'Help,' he moaned loudly and then made a low sound in his throat repeatedly, 'Urrr, urrrrr . . .'

Michael gathered up the two pillows and the duvet and set off. Natalia was gurgling and panting. When he caught up with her she grabbed the pillows and threw them, shouting in a language he didn't understand. He tried to drape the duvet over her; it was all he could think of. But her arms flailed; she didn't want it. The stream of foreign language continued. 'In English!' he urged her. She smacked him. The side of his face stung, reddened. She rose to her feet, carried her belly further off and squatted like an ape. He could only watch, helpless. Richard was walking in small circles, both hands still covering his face, repeating the first line of the Lord's Prayer. Natalia crouched in the furthest corner of the room. The world was shut off. She could only think of the enormous pressure, the rude crown of the baby's head protruding now. Michael watched, his mouth hanging open. The next push was like an enormous, virulent muscle which took every ounce of Natalia's strength. The pain was hateful; curses and screams tumbled from her mouth. She would never have another baby, this was the last impossible insult suffered by all women everywhere, and all men were hopeless, lazy imbeciles who didn't have a clue and she was dying of pain, without help, in a so-called first world country. 'That's my girl, good girl,' repeated Michael over and over. 'Just say if you want a hand. Brave thing. Good girl.' Natalia was being torn open. It was excruciating; her jaw ached with the length and volume of this screaming. Another surge of pressure visited – the wave picked her up and drove her with incredible force. She could look down and see the slick head of her baby daughter between her legs.

'Good girl!' shouted Michael.

Richard faced the wall and called, 'Hallowed be thy name.'

Natalia could feel the slippery lump, terrifyingly inert and lifeless it seemed, between her legs. More than anything, more than she wanted the life in her own body, she wanted her child to be alive and well. Another push arrived, virulent, it was like a kind of fury. She didn't recognise the sound of her own voice in this long, drawn out, deep, manly roar. Michael flinched, blinked. It went on and on, as, in her hands, the baby grew longer, more slippery, and in a rush of liquid and pain and relief from pain it slid through her grip, onto the floor. 'You've done it!' roared Michael. 'JOLLY WELL DONE!' He swayed in disbelief. Christ, was this how life started? No wonder, what awful magic, what strange sights! Natalia picked up her baby daughter and poked a finger in her mouth, cried for her, held her. She checked each limb, eye, ear of the new arrival. These were her baby's very first movements outside the womb. She kneeled and gathered her next to her skin, trying to cover every inch of the newborn body with her own warmth. Her ears rang with the baby's cry. She looked over and saw a blurred Michael squatting a short distance away, gathering the duvet. His mouth was moving but she couldn't hear him. He looked excited, tearful, alone. She nodded and gestured for him to hurry; she wanted that duvet. Further off, the madman cried childishly, walking in circles and tearing at his hair and in turns glancing at her and then batting away the sight, too much to bear, and now he ran from the room in his side-to-side, stiff-legged gait. All this Natalia saw in just a few seconds while she checked the environment was safe; then once again she only had eyes for the crying baby, trying to soothe her with a breast, shifting position to make it work. Michael arrived next to her; he'd brought the duvet and the pillows and she thanked him over and over. Clumsily she lay back, the baby against her breast. She wanted to tell him they must clamp the cord and cut it, but she couldn't find the English words. She was crying herself, exhausted and hoping the baby would suckle. She was surprised at the urge to answer the baby's cry with a breast – so visceral, immediate. She stared into Michael's face – how familiar it had become – and repeated, 'We must cut.' She jutted her chin downwards, to signify the cord.

Michael leaned slightly to one side, lifted a foot so he was on one knee. He pushed on it, leaned forward, keeping his back straight. He couldn't stand; the nerve had snagged. Natalia reached out and tried to help, but it was no good. Try as they might, he couldn't. He needed something to pull himself up with. He shuffled on his hands and knees and used a chair. Once on his feet he had to stay bent over for a while.

Having caught his breath he headed off to fetch scissors or a sharp knife. He'd glimpsed the kitchen at the end of the corridor. He walked as fast as his locked spine would allow and found the brightly lit room. At first he rummaged in drawers, but then found a pair of scissors in a giant clay pot by the cooker. He was about to go back when it occurred to him they should be sterile. An electric kettle was to hand. He stood there, grunting with each pulse of the nerve in his back, trying to keep in the dead right position, while the kettle boiled enthusiastically. It occurred to him that he might electrocute himself stuffing the scissors in there. He remembered to wash his own hands before returning, step by difficult step, to the scene of the birth. Natalia was propped up, wrapped in the duvet, her lank hair hanging over her face as she stared at the baby. Michael dragged a chair along with him to use as a prop. At her side he leaned on it and ponderously lowered himself to his knees again. He cut a strip of cloth from the clean tail of his shirt, at the front, where it had been tucked into his trousers.

They should have iodine, disinfectant? She peeled back the duvet and held the rubbery, purple cord while he used the strip of cloth to bind it tight, stop the blood flow. Then, with a glance at Natalia's face and following her instructions, he cut it. It was tough as old boots. It took some work.

When the scissors finally shut and the cord separated, Natalia burst into tears. As she tried to continue the baby's first breast feed she asked, over and over, crooning at her newborn, 'What is your name, my darling? Are you called . . . Emma? Are you?'

Meanwhile in the hallway Richard pressed two buttons on the cordless phone and held it to his ear, walking around, agitated. Then he suddenly stopped. His mannered, polite voice boomed, 'Mama? Yes it's me. How far away are you? Are you in costume yet? What? Well I'm afraid I've done something terribly stupid. Yes, I made a mistake. Listen Mama. There were two of them and they turned up at the front door. I thought they were the first actors in the play for my birthday.' His face creased. He shouted angrily. 'That's not true Mama, in the village last year we walked alongside the actors OUT-SIDE and ALL THE WAY from the scout hut to the church!' He listened to the handset. 'No they were not burglars.' Then he became agitated again. 'Mother, that is so like you, to be stupid. Don't be stupid. We need an ambulance straight away. Yes. You are not being quick enough, I've made a mistake but I've done the best I can. JUST A SIMPLE MISTAKE,' he shouted, 'THERE'S A BABY IN THE DRAWING ROOM.'

Mattie's baby, Michael Junior, was pink and large and hairless with plump limbs that looked like they didn't have any bones in them. He slept soundly during the day and woke at night to cry and beat his fists against the darkness, keeping Simon and Mattie awake for hours. Natalia's baby, Emma, was small and swarthy and wrinkled and red in the face and covered in dark hair that immediately began to fall out. She slept at night, waking only once to feed. She had an exaggerated panic response: lifting her or putting her down caused a sharp intake of breath and a reflex spasm of her arms. The friendship between the two women was put under strain because Mattie found her baby difficult but Natalia took hers in her stride.

In any case, all plans for the joint christening suddenly had to be brought forward, and the venue altered, when Granny Banana was admitted to the Bristol Royal Infirmary with an unstoppable nosebleed and it was feared she would not last the night. It was decided to hold the christening at her bedside that very afternoon. The chance to have all four generations of the family present had always been the most important element of the celebration.

Pinky was currently hosting Michael at his Wiltshire home so they could drive up together in Pinky's car, given the demise of Michael's Renault. The hospital agreed to allow Pinky to take the service instead of the hospital chaplain. Pinky had buried Michael's father, he'd married Mattie and Simon the previous year; now he would christen the two babies in the Churchill ward.

Patsy dug out the two christening dresses which had been so much discussed by Mattie and Natalia. She jumped into her Renault and drove like fury to be there in time.

For Mattie and Simon and their babe-in-arms, Michael Junior, it was easy; they lived in Bristol. Likewise it was no distance for Natalia and Philip and their daughter Emma.

Mattie was the first to arrive. It was, for her, a return to the scene of her six-week incarceration and the subsequent caesarean operation, and her baby's brief sojourn in the SCBU with a collapsed lung. She'd been woozy from the general anaesthetic, which had added to the crisis. She'd mobilised

well but her incision was still sore. Whoever had donated the
blood for her transfusions, she wished to thank them. It hadn't
been a happy time for Mattie since then, either. She'd fallen
prey to morbid thoughts. She hadn't been in love with her
baby as much as she'd have liked. Breast feeding was difficult
and tiresome. She'd been dragged down by the weight of the
wretched nappy bag. She'd watched Natalia's easy management
of her baby with envy. Altogether, she had been left with an
uncertain start to motherhood and she felt a chill dread on
entering the huge building in which she'd spent so long. In the
lift she was overcome with dizziness and chest pain and found
herself panting heavily. The lift gave that pronounced, stom-
ach-deadening tug downwards at the soles of her feet which
showed that it was coming to a halt. The doors opened.
Different sights and sounds suddenly entered the confined
space. Her head cleared; the wave lifted her back up. As soon
as she was out of the lift, the objects around her – walls, floors,
people – grew more solid. Strength seeped back into her
limbs. It had been a panic attack; she had never suffered one
before. The signs to the Churchill ward pointed to the right.
She made slow progress, carrying little Michael Junior in his
sling. The smell was utterly different from that of the maternity wards – up here it was of camphor, musk, aspirin. With a
shock she realised it was the same as in charity shops: the
scent of dead people's stuff. She adjusted the sling holding her
baby son and kept going.

She announced herself to the Sister and asked to be directed
to Lady Edith Gough's bed. She followed a nurse's stockinged
calves and sensible shoes.

'She hasn't regained consciousness, I'm afraid,' said the nurse,
'although we do manage to stop the bleeding from time to
time. She's all right at the moment.'

Mattie stood over her grandmother. How silent and still she
was. Her grey blue hair, usually so carefully arranged in waves,

lay in a distressed tangle around her head. Her skin was blood-less, wrinkled as paper which had been scrunched in a ball and then opened out again. The blue watery eyes were closed, the veins in the lids broken. A white dressing was taped over her nose. It looked like she'd been mugged or had fallen; in fact, the doctors had explained, it was the anti-coagulant that Granny took to help with her blood pressure that had made this ordinary nosebleed both inevitable and difficult to control. The cure for one condition had caused a different ailment. That's how it went with the elderly, the doctors had said.

She perched herself gingerly on the side of Banana's bed, un-hooked the sling from over her head, and put her baby down on the bed without his waking. The old lady remained motionless.

'Hello Banana,' Mattie murmured, and picked up the hand which lay there, starkly, against the white sheet. It was limp, deadweight. Her own fingers looked new and smooth and strong next to Granny's, which were wrinkled, discoloured by liver spots.

The blood from the older woman ran in her own veins, lit-erally.

The sight of the old lady's hands, papery and old, unmoving, entwined in her own, brought tears to her eyes. The fabric of life, passed from one person to another, with love and hope and promises . . . In the space once occupied on the old lady's wrist by the silver-and-copper wristband now lay the hospi-tal's identifying tag. Mattie caught sight of the handwritten name, 'Gough', blurred under the near-opaque plastic. Mattie continued to hold Granny's hand, trusting that the sensation might be carried into the old lady's unconsciousness. Only when she herself was as old as Granny would she take off the bracelet and give it to her own daughter, or grand-daughter, if she had one. Once again it would be warmed by youthful blood.

They'd been told that the sense of hearing was the last to be lost in unconsciousness, so she made an effort to start talking. 'It's me, Mattie, your granddaughter. And your great-grandson, Michael Junior.' She lay Granny's hand on her baby and watched her face for any sign of recognition. Banana's nose covered in its dressing was a bright, white beak against the cotton pillow. The eyes were shuttered, the wrinkled skin hanging in folds. 'Guess what,' carried on Mattie, 'we are having the christening here, did they tell you? Michael Junior and your granddaughter, Emma. So . . . please hang on. We want a photograph of you with them both in their christening gowns.' She squeezed Banana's hand. There was no response. A pulse beat tenderly in her neck.

'We've chosen the gowns from the ones Ma has in storage,' she went on. 'I've got the Edwardian one with the matching bonnet, but we don't know who wore them originally. Ma says you might, though. We need you to wake up and tell us.'

She waited.

Nothing. She couldn't even see breath escape from Banana's lips. She massaged her hand. The fingers were so cool and grey.

A spot of red appeared on the white dressing on Banana's nose. Mattie stared, entranced. The dot increased in size very slowly. Its flowering was a signal: danger. At the slightest chance the blood would run, and fall as far and as fast as it was allowed.

The stain on the dressing was the size of a penny piece. Mattie turned quickly, looked for a nurse. There was none. She told herself to be calm. Next to the bed was a call button. She pressed it and prayed hard.

The nurse came at a trot and checked Granny's pulse and blood pressure, and that the cannula was taped into position in the back of her wrist. 'Vital signs are all right. I'm afraid this is going to keep happening. Let me fetch the doctor.'

Blood – the flow of it, the release of it, the lack of it – for Mattie, during the six weeks she'd spent in here, had become the essence of the person in whom it ran. To look at anyone was to see not an object, but a coursing of blue and red, a pattern of flow beneath the skin. When the nurse stood checking Banana's pulse at the side of the bed, that person was revolving, slowly, a steady beat pushing the life-giving fluid around its circuit. Simon, her own husband, was aswirl, the red or blue always in motion under his skin. She marvelled at the amount of energy required to heat the blood and drive it around the body, every second of every day. No wonder people hungered for food, so. Meanwhile that white bandage on Granny's nose was a plug, stopping up her thinned, old, slow, blood.

Patsy was next to join her daughter at Banana's bedside, where she unpacked the christening dresses. Michael Junior's was deemed the more masculine of the two. Patsy lifted her baby grandson from where he lay in the sling on Banana's bed and began to change him. He was still undergoing phototherapy for jaundice and looked even yellower against the laundered white of the christening gown.

'I wish I hadn't cut my hair,' said Mattie.

'It will grow back darling.'

'I know, but.'

'Remember how I said it would be up and down? Well, you're in a down bit, but all you have to do is walk through it and you'll come out the other side.'

'Natalia hasn't cut her hair.'

'I know, it is annoying to watch someone else doing better with their baby, when you're not doing well with yours. In fact there's nothing more irritating. Do you wish she wasn't coming?'

'No! Of course not.'

'You're allowed to admit to the most murderous thoughts, as a young mother.'

'You are good to me, Ma. Sorry to be a bore.'

'Not at all. Your father and I are thrilled with our new grand-son, and thrilled with you. Remember that, Mattie, won't you?'

'Yes, yes I will.'

Covertly, Patsy checked the chart hanging from the end of the bed. 'Lady Edith Gough (aka Granny Banana)' was typed out, but there were lists of figures and a few indecipherable words in ink. How could anyone read that? A small anger grew in her at whichever doctor it was who had been so casual and hurried. It seemed important to have jolly good handwriting under the circumstances, she thought. She wondered if, behind those bruises, Granny Banana was dreaming.

Michael and Pinky arrived at the hospital, two quite large, bluff men. The automatic doors slid all the way back to let them in. Pinky went to see the hospital chaplain and change into his costume. Michael took the lift up. When he got out there were three different coloured strips set into the floor: red, blue and green, each one leading to a different ward. He was to follow the green one, to find Churchill ward. As he plod-ded along, wondering if his mother was alive or dead, he adopted the rule that he must not tread on any other bit of the floor except for this green line, as if it were a motorway taking him to his mother's bedside. The floor was so very glossy and polished and it sort of went up at the sides to become part of the walls for the first six inches – so it might be mopped, disinfected and polished effectively, he would suppose. He heard his name called out and stopped. Some way ahead was his ex-wife-number-three coming towards him. 'Hullo Pats,' he said. She approached and he stood his guard. 'How are you?' she asked.

'Trying not to step off the green,' he replied, 'otherwise might get eaten by tigers, you know.'

'That's a bit childish Michael.'

'I know. Is Granny all right?'

'As well as might be expected.'

'Good.'

'So I have to go around you, do I?'

'Would you, Pats? Thanks.'

'Where are you living Michael?'

'At Pinky's still.'

'Doesn't he mind? It's a tiny cottage.'

'On the contrary he is begging me to stay for longer.'

'You going to?'

'No, no. I shall get my own place soon.'

'Your own place? How come?'

'I shall buy somewhere.'

'What with, Michael?'

'It's called a mortgage. Utterly normal, you know?'

'I'm perfectly aware of mortgages, but you must have an income, and probably some security to put against it, in order to acquire one. Especially at your age.'

'Yes yes, I know that.'

'So you need a job.'

'Well, why not.'

'It's not particularly likely you'll find one, you know. Unless Gina hires you to stand guard in one of the rooms at Sitten Hall. Could you do that? Would you mind, darling?'

'Of course not. I'd do anything.'

'I'd bring you sandwiches and a flask.'

'Thank you. But, as it happens, Josephine Mclean has offered to stand as security for me.'

'Ah. Josephine Mclean. You should think very carefully before you accept that offer.'

'Why's that, Pats?'

'Because if she stands as security for your mortgage, she risks losing her own house if you can't keep up repayments. If the bank suffers any losses over you, they'll come after her. Not a very gallant position to find yourself in.'

'Hmmm.'

'And there's another thing that I wanted to say to you Michael, since I might not have the chance to speak to you in private.'

'What's that?' Michael was sticking to his guns: both feet were still on the green stripe. He and Patsy were toe-to-toe.

'You mustn't think that just because you're not married any more that some young woman will fall into your lap.'

'My charms not strong enough?'

'There must be something about you for a girl to be excited about, Michael, if you're going to attract a mate. It's not going to be youth and good looks is it? It's not going to be money or glory or power, either. So what's left? It's not enough to ask her to inhale your old socks.'

'I'd never make . . . the inhaling of my socks . . . a prerequisite of any relationship . . . Patsy, aren't we supposed to be attending a christening?'

'It's just that I know in my heart, Michael, that you saw Philip with Natalia and you thought the same might happen to you.'

'Well it might.'

'Philip has a bit of money and—'

'Less than before,' he interrupted.

'And,' went on Patsy, 'a roof over his head, and no ex-wives and children. You can't expect . . .'

'Patsy, I don't expect anything. I just wanted to be left in peace.'

'You were left in peace. God knows we knew better than to disturb you from your slumbers, Mattie and I. What new peace have you found at Pinky's, might I ask, that wasn't available to you at home?'

'He doesn't accost me in corridors and stare at me in that way you do, nor does he try and dent my fragile ego.'

'Michael you could hurl a cricket ball at your ego and not dent it.'

'What are you trying to say with that comment, that I'm . . .'

'I'm not going to tell you.'

'Why on earth not? Say what you think. What you want. Good or bad. We were married for heaven knows how long. There isn't going to be a surprise leaping out at us, here, now, is there?'

'The surprise is, Michael, that I am happier without you. No more of those disgusting noises you make in the shower inhaling hot water through your nose which you claim is a cure for the common cold. No more horrible coughing and spitting after you've cleaned your teeth. No more piles of fetid pants lying on the bedroom floor. No more snot on my nail scissors from your cutting the hairs in your nose.' She felt shame crawl all over her at that piece of cruelty.

'I'm pleased to have made you happy at last, Patsy. Now will you please step off my green line otherwise I will be eaten by tigers.'

'I'll just wait for a second while I think if there's anything else I wish to say to you.'

They stared at each other for a while. 'Anything?' asked Michael.

'Yes. Mattie needs help. She isn't too happy and we must do all that we can. I think she's suffering from mild post-natal depression.'

He nodded. 'All right. Very good. I will help in any way I can.'

'That means you should answer the phone. Call me back. We must keep talking Michael. You're not allowed to disappear.'

'I hear you.'

'And I promise it will only be about Mattie. I won't be cross
with you any more.'

'Very good.'

'I won't harangue you.'

'As you wish, darling.'

'Please don't go into this . . . condescending performance,
Michael, this "all right Patsy," and this "as you wish darling," I
can't bear it.'

'I thought you said you wouldn't harangue me.'

'I won't as long as you don't drive me bananas.'

'I shall try my hardest.'

'You don't have to stay on the green line Michael. There are
no tigers.'

'I've told myself that I do. That there are.' He felt a smile
coming, despite himself.

'Get out of my way Michael.' Patsy frowned.

'It's like being mown down by a . . .'

'Out of my way.'

Michael stepped aside and let her through.

Churchill ward's duty Sister organised a four-bedded bay to be
cleared to give the Gough family space and privacy; two geriatrics volunteered to be wheeled into the corridor for half an
hour.

Simon turned up, mired in the same cloud of depression as
his wife, although he was trying to dig them out. There was a
different atmosphere in geriatrics, he thought. The general
wards felt more temporary; people were reluctantly passing
through and they were fighting back against illness and injury
and getting out of hospital just as soon as they could, whereas
up here time passed slowly and everything seemed permanent.
He might almost believe the patients lived here. More of them
were asleep. They all looked half dead and many were close to

giving up. The staff looked a touch more impatient, defeated. Underneath there was a current of black humour – he could read the barely concealed smirks on the faces of the younger nurses. They were going to enjoy their work if it was humanly possible. He nearly stopped in his tracks when he saw Granny Banana, this frail creature with dark bruises under her eyes – the skin looked like it would drift away in your hands, as if sliding off an over-ripe pear, if you touched her . . .

Michael was sitting off to one side, face to face, knee to knee with a journalist who'd heard about the christening somehow. She was called Holly and was covering the story for the local paper but hoped to sell it to the nationals, given the fact it was four generations of a famous landed family. 'Can I ask you a few questions as we go along?' she asked Michael. A pair of small eyes blinked out from the face in front of her. Shambolic springs of brownish, greyish hair sprang from his scalp. His forehead buckled, then smoothed out. 'Yes, all right.'

'You said you were on your way to visit your brother?'

'I was . . .' Michael was cheered by this pretty young woman, her hair a blonde bell swinging fetchingly from one side of her head, and suddenly he made a promise: for the rest of his life he'd tell the truth, he would not give a damn and would say – utterly without fear – whatever came into his head as the first and most complete answer to any matter. Starting now. 'Or rather, I wasn't visiting my brother so much as leaving my wife,' he said. 'Or rather, leaving my ex-wife. We've been divorced for years.'

'Oh?'

'Yes. Not a hooray situation, more like bah humbug. I'd called my brother to ask if I might stay because it was the only place I could think of.'

'D'you mind if that goes in the paper? If everyone reads it?'

'I want it to go in the paper. I insist.'

'And what happened, in the accident? Your sister-in-law,

er . . . Natalia, said it was no one's fault, that she just came around a corner and . . .'

'Nonsense. It was my fault, as she well knows. She stopped perfectly satisfactorily. I sailed into her.'

'Were you going too fast?'

'No, but my car was rubbish and I wasn't concentrating.'

'Perhaps I ought not to print that. It might affect the insurance claim or—'

'Print it,' interrupted Michael.

Holly began to have a feeling that if this man weren't careful the TV cameras would be all over him. She felt a twinge of sympathy. A blustery old Lord so-and-so, in his dilapidated old car with his broken-down marriage, suddenly thrown to the tabloid wolves. She was sure there was more meat to be found, if she dug for it. 'And your wife . . . where is she?'

'Probably been recaptured. Dart gun you know. Taken back to the zoo.'

It was so unexpected and said in such a gloomy tone, Holly couldn't help laughing.

'No, I jest. She's around somewhere. She will be back soon,' said Michael. He glanced over at his mother, and was suddenly terribly saddened by her empty expression, the mouth crumpled and the eyes shuttered. The sight reminded him of Katherine's effigy in the chapel. The Black Death had swept out the population of Woodford as if with a broom – twice – and when it had visited Sitten Hall forty-four deaths had been recorded. When Michael had been a child he'd stuck his fingers in Katherine's stone ribcage; it had felt cool and dusty. He'd pulled his hand away as if it had been bitten.

Philip, Natalia and their newborn, Emma, were the last to arrive. Emma looked sweet and perfect when she was changed into her little gown. She had so much black hair, she was like a monkey.

The ward Sister stayed in the background. Pinky took charge: he arranged the new mothers with babes in arms to sit on either side of the bed, each with her spouse alongside, and then Patsy next to Simon, Michael sitting next to his brother Philip, and the journalist perched at the end. Between them lay Granny Banana. An ENT pack had been fed in through the back of her mouth and into her nose to try to stop the bleeding. She'd suffered a slight stroke and the immediate danger was that she might have another one. Electrical leads went from her chest to the heart monitor and the IV line ran to her wrist, delivering dextro-saline.

'Ladies and Gentlemen,' began Pinky, standing at the end of the bed and wiping a strand of blond hair from his forehead. His complexion glowed because he'd walked up the stairs, not believing in lifts. 'We all know why we're here, and that time is of the essence, so let us begin. I am advised that Granny is unconscious. I am also advised by her medical team that our sense of hearing is the last that we are deprived of, apparently. So, this joint christening service is conducted in the fervent hope that she can hear us. Granny Banana my dear, you are lying in a hospital bed with a nosebleed. The staff have kindly allowed us to hold the christening here. On your left sit your granddaughter Mattic and her husband Simon, and she's holding your new great-grandson in her arms. Michael Junior weighed eight pounds three ounces at birth, and he's got the most delightful little sausage fingers, and clear blue eyes which look right through you. On your right are Natalia and Philip, and in Natalia's arms is your new granddaughter Emma. She weighed six pounds and three ounces at birth, and she has lots of dark hair and the most perfect little scrunched-up face. Both babies are safe and well and growing fast. Both mothers are alert and beautiful. Also, here are Michael and Patsy, the proud grandparents of Michael Junior and proud uncle and aunt to Emma.'

Pinky organised the chalice on the table at the end of Granny's bed and then walked down the side of the bed to lift Michael Junior from Mattie's arms. 'First we shall christen Michael Junior,' he said, and settled the infant in the crook of his arm, but with the head in his palm. 'The scallop shell,' he went on, picking it up with his free hand, 'as you may or may not know, signifies pilgrimage. Because life itself is just such a journey, a travelling towards grace and beauty.' He dipped the scallop in the water. 'Michael William d'Angibau, I baptise you in the name of God the Father . . .' He trickled water onto the baby's forehead . . . 'And the Spirit . . .' He dipped the scallop again and poured a second trickle of water. Michael Junior's eyes bulged. He started to wail, his lips turning purple and juddering with distaste. 'And the Holy Ghost,' went on Pinky. He poured for a third time and then dabbed the baby's forehead with the purificator. Michael Junior was objecting loudly. Pinky walked the few steps to hand him back to Mattie. 'Granny, you should hear that, if you're going to hear anything,' he said and the family gave a murmured laugh of approval. Pinky crossed to the other side of the bed to take Emma from Natalia's arms. He arranged her in an identical way along his right arm, and then repeated the blessing, more loudly to lift the words above the sound of crying. 'Emma Jane Gough, I baptise you in the name of God the Father, the Spirit and the Holy Ghost.' Emma remained silent, awed. Pinky dabbed her forehead with the purificator. Michael Junior settled in his mother's arms; now there was quiet.

'And,' continued Pinky, 'let us all now pray for Granny Banana, for her recovery.' Everyone closed their eyes, heads down.

'And we thank thee, Lord,' said Pinky quietly, 'for Granny Banana's wholeness, and for the joyfulness of this occasion, when we have four generations of the same family gathered here. And we pray also for the support staff – the doctors and nurses, the porters and the cleaners – who have made this moment possible for us.' He paused for a while and then spoke out the Lord's prayer. 'Our Father, which art in heaven . . .'

The assembled family and the journalist murmured the prayer, following Pinky's lead. As they did so, Pinky decanted the water from the chalice into the aspergillum and walked it around the bed, sprinkling water on the floor and over the members of the family.

'. . . Amen,' finished everyone.

Michael felt a spray of water hit his hands, which lay folded in his lap. Good old Pinky, he thought, he always veered towards the Catholic, for an Anglican. It was comforting to have their own man doing this; it meant he, Michael, could summon in his mind's eye the chapel at Sitten Hall, the stonework, the effigies, the memorial plaque to the war dead, the altar, the ornately carved screens. Pinky's voice brought all that with him.

Pinky circled them with the aspergillum. 'And I also want to summon the baptism of Edith, of Granny Banana, long ago. I do this so that it might give her strength, and youth, in her fight for life. And I do it, also, so that the lives of these two lovely babies, of Emma, of Michael Junior, whom we have baptised today, will be informed by her life. So that they will be connected with her birth. So that her baptism will be linked to their baptism, across a gap of so many years.'

He paused. They could hear his breathing and the clink of metal against ceramic as he lifted the aspergillum into the chalice. 'Lord, in thy mercy, hear our prayers.'

Part Three

At first sight Sitten Hall might be thought a genuine mediaeval fortress. It had the keep, or gatehouse, plan with round towers at the corners and looked as if it might be impregnable. It was a fake, though, albeit an honourable one. The drawbridge wasn't a defence mechanism. There were no hinges; built of stone, it couldn't be lifted. The wall walk was a balcony, in effect. One side had a big section of wall missing where the boat house had been built into the moat. No self-respecting Knight would have tried to keep an army safe in there. None the less, it was old enough for anyone's tastes: building works had started in 1370, and its beauty held all who viewed it enthralled for ever. The gentle bowl of land in which it sat might have been scooped out for the purpose of hiding it, just so not too many people swooned all at once. It was a fairy tale, a magic kingdom in its own right.

At a few minutes before six p.m. on this April day, the castle was winding down, the day's work almost done. The National Trust's administrator, Gina Powell, cast the plastic cover over her computer and prepared to oversee security arrangements. In the gift shop the sales assistant signed the till roll and closed up. The two widows who ran the café covered the pastries with clingfilm and pulled on their coats. The small army of senior citizens – many of them ex-service men and women – ticked off the inventories of paintings, furniture and artefacts over which they'd stood guard for the last four hours. Raymond Luther, head gardener, stole a dozen saplings from his own garden shop while his apprentice, nicknamed Boy, went and stood next to his moped where it idled in the shadow of the beech trees. He pulled on his helmet and zipped up the leather jacket over his uniform. The last few visitors dawdled in the visitors' car park. One or two children ran about and kicked at the gravel. An elderly couple walked slowly, arm in arm.

Boy was startled suddenly by the noise of Sitten Hall's giant pair of front doors closing. He wandered for a step or two before starting up the moped's engine.

Then he, too, was gone.

Meanwhile, the iron bar was lowered into position and the bolts drawn on those enormous front doors. Over fifteen feet high, they were opened only during the day in good weather; at other times people used the opening which let into the bottom left-hand corner, resembling a catflap in scale, which was known as the monkey door.

This was the routine emptying of the house. Sitten Hall was left to itself.

That is to say, almost. Two faces appeared in the first-floor window of the gatehouse, blurred by the warped glass; one moment they were there, then not. A girl and a man – if it wasn't just a trick of the light – showed like ghosts, translucent through the reflection of the sky.

Mattie, aged twenty-five, smiled – and her dimples doubled up that smile – as she took Simon's hand and asked in a low voice, 'King's Chamber or Queen's?' She used to have the run of these rooms until the infamous '86 when her father had been forced to gift Sitten Hall to the nation in lieu of tax.

He smiled. 'King's, why not?'

She carried on up the newel staircase, her stockinged feet silent on the rough stone and on the tile mosaic floors, dragging him behind her. They climbed beyond the Queen's Chamber, one floor further.

Is life a staircase, wondered Mattie, a steady ascent from younger to older, from low in the food chain to higher, from carrying nothing to carrying everything?

Up, up the steps . . .

What *did* she carry at the moment? She had no job, no place of her own in which to live. Only Simon; she carried him. And she had the title 'Honourable' but never used it – rather, she wanted to slough it off, find her own way towards the notion of 'honourable' which for her, now, today, meant . . . Simon. Unknown to him.

The King's Chamber was a square block of a room with an open-timbered ceiling, restored as far as possible to how it must have looked in mediaeval times. The carpet had been pulled up, and the Slumberdown orthopaedic bed which Granny Banana used to sleep in had been sold by the Trust and replaced by a genuine fifteenth-century mahogany four-poster with a plain awning and a bolster against the headboard. The Trust's own range of coloured emulsions had replaced Banana's Laura Ashley wallpaper. The cheaply framed first-night posters she'd collected had been taken down and, instead, Mary Queen of Scots' embroidered map of England hung there, the great mediaeval houses important at the time stitched upon it: for each a stylised motif of the design of the house, its heraldic emblem and its surrounding park sewn into position. Included was Sitten Hall itself.

During opening hours a security guard would have prevented people touching anything in here but Simon and Mattie looked over it unchallenged.

Simon went to the window that gave onto the inner courtyard. She joined him and they silently took in the view. Peacefulness crept up and reigned undisturbed while they watched the sun drop behind the trees. 'Beautiful,' he murmured. A pair of damson flies – the first out this year – drifted outside the window, copulating. The male had a two-pronged

penis: one prong was for the normal job of insemination while
the other was shaped like a spoon and was used to remove any
competitor's leavings.

Together Mattie and Simon veered towards the bed but were
halted by the red velvet rope, looped through brass stanchions,
which prevented visitors from touching.

'Small,' commented Simon of the bed; he'd expected something of heroic proportions, not this matchbox which, although
grandly decorated and built of solid mahogany, was less than six
feet long. 'People were tiny, that many hundred years ago. To
them, we'd be like giants,' said Mattie, pulling her top over her
head. She unclipped her bra and stepped over the rope. 'Hey!'
he exclaimed, incredulous, 'that's not allowed . . .' She pulled at
him and he followed her, holding his breath and half expecting
alarms to sound, but none did. They were alone, safe. There was
the mole the size of a sultana on her left shoulder and her breasts,
which looked out optimistically to each side, waiting for him. He
unbuttoned his jacket, took it off. She pulled the shirt from his
belt and undid the buckle, flipped the shirt aside to sneak her
hands underneath and hold his ribcage. His skin was so much
whiter than hers. She murmured something; he held onto her
shoulders and stooped to kiss her, pushing her back onto the bed
so her legs fell open, the straps of her stockings suddenly loosen-
ing. His kisses moved from her mouth to her breasts to her belly.

In fact he'd never qualified as a diver – he'd been in the
Royal Navy but had opted out of his contract as soon as he
could. Mattie stopped him in his tracks and pulled him up by
his hair. She whispered, 'Just do it . . .' Simon reached into his
pocket to fetch a condom but she smacked his arm. 'No.' His
wallet dropped to the floor. 'No,' she repeated, and pulled at his
other arm. With her free hand she tugged at his cock and
wriggled her hips to line herself up. 'Come on.'

She'd run away from men before meeting Simon, but
marriage was one fence she wanted to crash through, knock

down, get the other side of now. With her fingers she moved
her panties to one side. She pulled him urgently, 'Go, go.'

Later, Mattie and Simon lay smoking cigarettes underneath the
antique coverlet. Simon's feet poked out of the bottom of the
bed and Mattie spilled over one side, holding her long hair in
a pile on the back of her neck to keep it out of the way. They
looked like Alice In Wonderland figures, they were so outsized.
Their arms lifted and fell with elaborate caution as they took
care not to drop cigarette ash.

'No?' repeated Simon, tapping at her wrist in the same way
as she had done earlier, when she was telling him to forget the
condom. 'Hmmm?'

She gave him a sideways look, which meant yes. Simon
looked at her for some moments. Then he leaned over and
kissed her on the forehead.

A moment later Mattie commented, 'Not a top-flight B&B.'
She drew on the cigarette. 'The sheets are a bit damp.'

'Unlived in.'

'Exactly.'

The sound of a car engine joined with the flutter of the
swans' wings as they settled on the moat. Mattie stepped from
the bed and trotted to the window as unselfconsciously as if she
were wearing clothes. The Renault 4 was pulling up in the private car park at the rear of the Hall. She confirmed, 'Dad.'

She climbed back into bed and listened to the sounds she
knew so well: the slam of the Renault's door, the crunch of
gravel beneath her father's shoes ending suddenly as he gained
the tarmac apron fronting Sitten Hall, the click of the monkey
door and then the distant rumble of his feet on the oak plank-
ing in the main hall.

They lay quietly and finished their cigarettes.

★

Sir Michael Gough, Lord Woodford, peer of the realm, aged fifty-nine, educated at Eton and Oxford, climbed the newel staircase in Sitten Hall's west range, running out of puff. He never used to glimpse a staircase until bedtime whereas, nowadays, just fetching the newspaper meant hours of up and down, plus twice on his knees to push the Renault's clutch pedal back on its stub . . . then having to stand again . . . His hips were going, he was sure of it. He wished his Grenson brogues, scraping against the stone, might carry him up by themselves – and magic shoes they might be indeed, lasting so long because of their formidable bulk and the metal Blakeys in the soles and heels. He fingered the pockets of the old jacket – bought from Hanley's of St James's in the 1950s – and those of the moleskin trousers, both of which had been handed down from his father; that was a measure of their quality. He was looking for pipe-making equipment. No. He'd left it somewhere. He'd catch up with it.

This staircase, and every object he could see, was familiar of course, but he was beginning to forget how and when everything had arrived. The enormous porcelain vase: was it the one given by the Tsar of Russia? Or not? He used to know. The collection of sculpture on the first floor was European but he'd have to stop and peer at the notices like a visitor to know if it was eighteenth or nineteenth century. Not long ago he could have rattled off the why and wherefore of every bit.

He rose further, step by step.

It was for others, now – the visitors – to learn about these objects; that was a relief. Yet it meant his old life was slowly eroding, he was becoming blind to the mixture of history and art which had been hoarded by his forebears over the centuries. He himself had added nothing to it, of course, rather the opposite: it had been his task to choose what to sell, in advance of handing over the entire property. He couldn't remember what it was he'd got rid of during those dark days of '85–'86. Mostly paintings; they'd been the most valuable.

However he did realise now – it rankled still – that the deal he'd done with the National Trust hadn't been much good. He'd only just paid off his second wife when his father had died and left him the estate. The tax bill had been so huge he'd never bothered to count how many zeros were tacked to the end of it. After two expensive divorces he was already skint. But he'd talked to his wife number three, Patsy, he was overheard by his young daughter Mattie, he'd telephoned his brother Philip, he'd consulted his mother Granny Banana and he'd faced up to the National Trust; in short he'd tried hard to make a proper job of it, not run away, but all the while the interest on the tax bill had gone up, day by day. It had been like chasing his own tail. He'd posted his Memorandum of Wishes but the Trust's Executive Committee had kept on refusing to sign. He'd suggested the place might be open to the public for a couple of months during summer but they wouldn't hear of anything other than seven days a week, plus they'd wanted a longer season. He'd proposed that visitors should be excluded from certain areas of the garden; they couldn't agree. He'd wanted a say in what happened to the cottages; wasn't allowed. The wrangling had taken over three years to settle and had cost him dearly. Now he looked at people like Lord Rothschild who ran Waddesdon more or less as he wanted, or Sir Francis and his like who'd managed to hang on to all the possessions in their houses, and he envied them because they had an illusion of ownership at least. All Michael had ended up with was a lifetime lease on an apartment tucked away under the parapets of Sitten Hall's west range. Those interest payments had boxed him in, he hadn't been able to move or take a breath; he'd had to settle. It came back to him – the disaster of it.

He stopped for a breather, leaned against the wall and considered his past life, the future years – not many – left to him, his condition, his fellow man, where he was now, what he amounted to: Sir Michael . . . what *was* his full name? Sir Michael Cedric . . . Bruce-Withering was in it somewhere . . . Wootton Gough, Cedric Gough? Something like that. Anyhow, aged fifty-nine, that he knew, and married to the Tall Woman.

At least, he wasn't sure he was married to her; maybe they *had* actually got divorced that time. He remembered the row – he'd homed in with his usual vigour on their little problem because he had a flair for singling out anything that might be wrong and ignoring what was good – and then he'd worried away at the situation. She'd suggested a divorce so he'd jumped in and demanded one. Then he'd redrafted the *decree nisi* three or four times, which he was well practised at, having been married twice before. Yet if he tried to think beyond that, to what had finally happened, he couldn't be sure if they'd completed the process. He'd continued to pay his solicitors' invoices without reading every letter they'd written. There'd been a series of court cases he'd had to attend anyway, concerning the prep school which he and Pinky had attempted to start up. The hotel idea had been in legal trouble also. So he couldn't be sure now if the divorce had been made absolute or not.

He was fed up with the pain in his hips, the sharp way it nagged him. He concentrated on numbers: how many stairs were left, which corners. Then he found himself, at last, unhooking the rope strung across the door marked 'Private', but before he went through this last indignity – climbing to what amounted to an *attic* – he stood, took a lungful of air and called into the open stairwell, 'Pour the tonic!'

It was a different story, on this side of the door. There was no more panelling, or tightly fitted oak or stone floors. These least favourable of quarters – formerly a rabbit warren for servants and visitors' servants to bump their heads on and squeeze in

their ablutions – had been converted into an apartment for
him and his family, the lease free of charge and lasting only for
his and his wife's lifetime. When they were both dead he supposed the National Trust would move staff in here.

The stairs were now carpeted, and the sides closed in. The
walls knocked at his elbows and the smell of emulsion paint
caught in his lungs. The student Crispin had stayed up here
when he was Michael and Philip's tutor; underneath this carpet
were the same dusty floorboards they'd scampered over when
they were children, invited to share another secret object before
it was locked in the rusty tin and put away again in its hiding
place behind the roof beam. A step or two further on used to
be the cook's bedroom, where they'd never been allowed to go
on account of her having an occasional visitor – a boyfriend
who could jiggle his almost womanly breasts up and down at
will. A parlour maid had lived at the far end. What had been
her name? He remembered the crowded side-table and her
pride in showing them various books and her father's pewter
retirement watch.

What would he and Philip have said – when they were two
small boys in short trousers and V-necked sweaters – if they'd
been told that this hidden space under the roof would be converted into an apartment into which Michael's life would have
to be shoe-horned in his declining years? They'd have laughed.

He could more easily see the attic as it was then. The memories crowded him as he passed blindly through, heading for
the sitting room.

Mattie and Simon were also on their way back to the apartment. The ancient corridor framed them, a set of mediaeval
arches they were walking through, the last of the daylight feint-
ing sideways from each window to fall in bright oblongs on the
floor.

They were holding hands. Neither was in a hurry. Her feet were silent, still shoeless; his sounded. Mattie was idly wondering if she was pregnant. She held her palm over her stomach. Swim, she urged the little tadpoles. She wished she was still lying down to make it easier for them. In her mind's eye they all had Simon's face, set in the same expression as when he swam the butterfly, their mouths 'o' shaped, determined, the sideways glance to see if they were being overtaken . . . she felt so fond of them; no wonder she hungered for more.

Inside her the sperm writhed powerfully enough through the mucus lining her uterus, but found no egg. They ended up in far-flung corners, dancing slower and slower. The timing was wrong, they'd been set against the rhythm.

'It must have been incredible . . .' murmured Simon. 'To *live* here.'

'What I remember most,' continued Mattie, 'is that Dad retreated completely. He had George fix a letter-box to the outside of his study and if you wanted to say anything to him you had to write it down and post it. Then, a few days later, you'd receive a written reply which you had to pick up from the same post box. So it was like checking for mail from someone a long way distant when it was in fact your father living in the same house.'

'Did you ever try and talk to him?'

'I did, once, when he was walking away from me and I remember noticing how slow he'd become. And smaller. His coat was sort of like an old sack stretched across his shoulders and the hem of it hung down. I suddenly saw him as a human being, you know, rather than Lord so-and-so, and I called out to him but he didn't turn around or slow down; it was like he was deaf.'

'He must have felt guilty.'

'Yes. Most of all he felt useless, I think. That melancholy he'd always had, that he was set apart from everyone else, different from his own family, even, because he was the heir, that just deepened by about a thousand per cent.'

'Has he got better, or worse?'

'Not sure.' She turned to him. 'Don't mention the words "property boom" or "the Chorley formula" or "leasehold apartment".'

Michael entered the sitting room, registering that the Tall Woman was there, doing what she always did – something useful. The computer was humming. He knew in theory what computers were for but hadn't tried one yet himself.

He took a quick peek in the mirror to check his eyebrows weren't out of control. There he was, same as ever, six feet tall, head unnaturally square as though he'd been kept too long in a box, face reddened by alcohol, the lower lip hanging open, the top lip covered by a crop of brown moustache, eyes small and dark, reflecting scenes from his past life, strewn as it was, yes, with divorces, and persistent refusal to achieve anything. Even his great-grandfather had had the bosky woods to his credit. What had he himself done? With such a family as his – every inch of their lives written down – it was like a powerful torch pointing back through the deepest shadows of the past, illuminating stories of success and triumph, as proven by the countless winning cups and gifts from home and abroad on display in the Hall below; prizes in sword-fighting, in cricket and in polo, honours and titles in politics and in administration of the empire; plus the usual eccentric acts and tall tales to spice up the whole history and add more glamour and make it less predictable. His own life had been minuscule in comparison. He'd pursued the smaller, more common pleasures – food in front of him, the telly, horse-racing, the hunt, a fine drink, the lie of the land around Sitten Hall and its wildlife, his pipe, Werther's Originals. He still relished hearing about other people's gardens. His only ambition was that his life would end peacefully and without further trouble.

His scalp moved a fraction over the top of his head, producing the characteristic wrinkling of his brow. He knew – his wife had told him often enough – that the same thing happened if he became angry, except then his ears moved up and down and filled with blood, in addition. He only lost his temper occasionally. He sometimes shouted in the Square after leaving the Whistle and Feather. He'd overturned a new litter bin commissioned by the parish council because he'd voted against it. In her flat in London Mattie had a photograph of him cut from the front page of the *Salisbury Times* in November 1988, in which he was pictured galloping alongside a Hunt saboteurs' Mini Metro, banging on its roof with a crop because they'd been broadcasting the sound of foxhounds from a loudspeaker poking out of the window. That had been his one and only attempt at upholding justice. He wished he'd done more of that kind of thing – too old now.

Luckily there was nothing to be cross about at the moment.

He threw down the car keys, approached the usual armchair and checked the prerequisites for a comfortable evening: vodka and tonic yes, newspaper yes. He took it from under his arm and unfolded it, sat down. He noted the TV was on Channel 4, burbling away quietly, the seven o'clock news imminent, and the remote control should be found on the arm of the chair. Yes. And when he stirred his hand around in the dragon bowl on the table at his elbow he felt not only his pipe, along with the pouch of Navy Cut, and not only the brittle wrappers encasing the Werther's Originals, but a half dozen Mini Mars bars as well. So – she'd filled up his treat bowl. Now, if he could hope for the phone not to ring, for life to pass by and leave him alone, then he was in clover. He stared resolutely at the television screen and emptied his head of thought, picked up his vodka and tonic.

Because these days, happiness was not what happened to him, but what didn't happen. He thought, 'Less is more,' and lifted the glass, said the usual 'Cheers!' to the Tall Woman and heard her call back, 'Cheers.' Then, before drinking, he gave a second lift of the glass, a silent toast to absent friends. He nudged the glass upwards a third time, murmured 'God Bless' to all those who'd died before him. A moment later his square face tilted, accepted the glass.

The ice-cubes bumped against his top lip – and his brow wrinkled in surprise. The drink was extra powerful. He took a second sip – it was at least equivalent to the Whistle and Feather's Monday night 'Double Trouble'. Had they won the lottery?

In fact, the whole early evening routine had gone surprisingly smoothly. And the Tall Woman, he noticed now, was seated at her table instead of trotting in and out. She was dressed nicely in a trouser suit. Any one of these things alone wouldn't be remarkable but together they were just that – an equivalent would be to drive through Salisbury's one-way system on green lights all the way. It was too lucky for something not to be wrong. Wryly he pointed it out. 'Fantastic drink. Treats in the bowl. Hundred per cent score.'

Patsy replied, 'Glad you're happy.'

'Who's coming?' asked Michael brutally.

'You know very well who.'

So – guests. That was it. He shook his head, tried to block out the prospect. So what? Just visitors. The task now was to squeeze in a bit of what he liked before they came. Eight p.m. was the usual kick-off. There wasn't long; he had to push ahead. The ads were on so he dabbed the 'mute' button to give himself some peace and quiet for a minute or two, which meant he could open the hard-won newspaper at page eighteen and suck a Werther and at least make a start on the crossword. He balanced the drink on the wing of his chair so that both

hands were free to scoop the tobacco out of the pouch and set
to work, build a pipe . . .

Patsy, five-foot-eleven-and-a-half inches tall, not including
the cliff of grey hair fronting her forehead, confident of her
abilities and station in life, dressed in the beige trouser suit in
readiness for this evening, watched her husband moving the
boiled sweet around his mouth and glancing at the TV with
that peculiarly intent look, even though he had the sound
turned down. The newspaper was open across his knees and
his pen and pencil were to hand as he fumbled at his pipe; she
had the sudden thought that when he was dead, this exact
picture would be her memory of him. That was her husband.

Michael was dimly aware of Patsy flying way above him.
What did she have on the cards, he wondered, his indefatigable
third wife – or ex-wife . . . His pencil scraped in the margin.
He enjoyed the way the vodka passed over the butterscotch
in his mouth; meanwhile he kept one eye on the TV. In a
moment, when it was the news headlines, he'd switch on the
sound and put a match to his pipe but he usually saved that as
a reward for having solved at least one cryptic clue. They were
impenetrable today, a confusion of meaningless words strung
together . . . he was distracted . . . no time . . . so he'd have to
light his pipe anyway . . . He hated having to cram all this in
rather than do things one at a time and in the right order. He
needed help with this clue if he was going to get anywhere. He
struck the Swan Vesta and planted the flame on the bowl, and
asked Patsy, 'Eight down, locked in a deathly place, beginning
with M. Mmm? Darling? Seven letters. Any idea?' He took a
lungful of smoke and a sip of the drink at the same time, plus
moved the sweet to the other cheek. 'Locked in a deathly
place,' he repeated.

There was silence. Patsy thought hard, it would be good politics if she could come up with the answer.

Michael had an idea what it was and wrote the word in the margin so he could count the letters. No, that was eight, think again. Patsy broke in and suggested, 'Mortise?'

'What?'

'Locked in a deathly place, seven letters beginning with M – Mortise. As in mortise lock.'

'Oh, yes. Of course.' Michael was satisfied and wrote the word in ink. Then he caught sight of what he'd written in the margin. 'Guess what I had?'

'What?'

'Locked in a deathly place, and I thought – marriage. Ha ha.'

'Marriage?'

'Yes.' Michael caught her eye, and – this might have been the effect of her G and T – but her smile grew into a smoky, husky laugh and there was that spark of fun leaping back and forth between them, like when they'd first met. He'd said something which had amused her and it twisted inside him pleasurably; he felt a smile crease his own cheeks which didn't happen often, and why not, he demanded as his eyes watered from holding on, seeing out the moment – utter pleasure, if small and low key. Good old Tall Woman.

'But – it's eight letters,' he said eventually, and took more drink. 'So it doesn't work. Marriage doesn't work. Ho ho.'

'For some people, Michael, marriage does work.'

That was an arrow in his eye all right. 'Yes. Indeed. For a few people . . .' He didn't carry on for fear of reprisals – and not just from Patsy. Memories of his two other ex-wives were always ready to haunt him, follow him about, beat about his ears.

Silence returned, only interrupted by a thud which could have been a muffled shotgun going off but which they knew was the sound of the door slamming downstairs at the entrance to the flat. Here come the guests, earlier than expected, thought Michael. Who'd let them in? Unless it was his brother Philip, who had a key . . . He'd have to get up. He folded the paper on his knees and, in preparing to rise, momentarily saw his lower half as if for the first time: a hump for a stomach, his trouser band describing the circular shape, his stockinged legs poking out at an angle, the trousers hitched at the knee, like something out of Dickens. The backs of his hands were purple. The cuffs of his jacket were ragged – threads escaped. He could feel a breeze on his elbow where the cloth had been rubbed away. He ought to change his clothes, and yes he'd look better standing up but . . . then he glanced at the television and the wrinkles on his brow retreated, his small eyes softened, because look, a lorry had crashed into the side of a house. The pictures held Michael transfixed. He dinged the sound on. Three people killed. Apparently inspectors were looking at the brakes and checking the paperwork of the runaway vehicle, which was said to have been in a poor state of repair . . .

'Michael, can we turn off?' asked his wife.

'Yup, right,' answered Michael; he waved his agreement. Bloody lorry! He felt a spasm of irritation flutter along his spine. For a moment he relived the Trust's half-hearted campaign to prevent the new A303 improvement coming as near as it did to Sitten Hall. They'd made a show of presenting some papers and signatures but there hadn't been a sniff of any high-up influence as you might have expected. An angry phone call direct from the Trust HQ at Queen Anne's Gate to the top desk at the Department of Transport was what had been needed. Michael had wanted to bang table tops, shout, argue that what was really inalienable about this place was the bloody view, the utter darkness at night, the quality of the silence here, just as much as the house itself . . .

'Dad . . .' His daughter was standing over him, smiling. Michael dropped his pipe, heaved himself to his feet, fumbled the 'off' button on the remote all at the same time. The paper slipped from his lap and his glass toppled off the arm of the chair. He took Mattie in his arms and it crossed his mind – so virulent, this thought – that she was lovely! Those dimples . . . something to be proud of . . .

It came back to him all in a rush: it wasn't a guest, it was Mattie and she was bringing a young man home. Thank God he'd remembered just in time. 'Where is he then?' he asked, covering up his forgetfulness with exaggerated enthusiasm, holding her by the shoulders and peering behind her.

'He's just using the facilities, he'll be along in a minute.'

'Ah, well. Can I set you up?'

'Please.'

'White wine? Cube of ice?'

'Perfect.' She liked the way he always remembered how she took her drink. There was a sulky swing to her hips as she drew up next to him at the sideboard and shifted her weight onto one leg. He was banging the ice with the tongs to break it into lumps. She glanced at her mum, who nodded, smiled and offered an exaggerated pair of crossed fingers. It was going to be like jumping into a cold bath so she did it quickly. 'Dad, I wanted you and Mum to be the first to know, Simon and I are going to be married.' She proffered her finger, showing her engagement ring.

Married? Disbelief crawled over Michael. Young people today lived together, didn't they? Had their babies any old how, just as they came along, which was quite right. As if from a long way off he heard his wife's voice and flinched. 'Great news, darling,' she was saying to Mattie, 'really splendid. Isn't it Michael?' He could tell from her tone that she'd known about it all along. He wasn't fooled one bit by her going over to give Mattie a hug. He sensed a plot and struggled with various confused feelings; uppermost was wanting the best for his daughter.

Then, he was irritated. Bang, bang, bang, this damn clump

of ice. Marriage – was that what she wanted – death by a thousand cuts? She'd know a touch more about marriage if only she'd been married before. A clot of worry stopped his breath. His daughter was in danger.

Maybe it was a *joke* . . . After all, she'd teased him about it before. As a teenager she'd told him she was engaged to a Pakistani cricketer. The twelfth Lord Woodford had been one of the best batsmen in England and cricket was inbred in the family; it was one of the ways the honour of the title was kept up, part and parcel of Eton and Oxford and the rest of it – Sitten Hall's sons were more than able to swipe a ball over a hedge. And so Mattie had come along with this joke that she was going to marry a foreign one. She'd kept up the pretence for long enough to fool him; she'd said it had been to test whether or not he was racist, because she was certain that she herself was.

On the contrary, Michael rather leaped at foreigners, he was over-keen if anything. The only breed of people he felt truly sorry for was the Royal Family.

So, hopefully it was a joke. 'Getting married?' he played along. 'Who is it this time, a *German*??! Ha ha ha!' He beamed.

'She really is getting married,' replied Patsy.

Both women watched him carefully.

He should stop banging this ice now, Michael thought, and simply play along. He carefully lifted a misshapen segment into Mattie's glass, poured white wine over it and handed it to her. 'Mattie,' he said.

'What?'

'Give me a kiss.' He ducked forward to her cheek. 'And another. Wonderful news, of course. Wonderful.' He held her by both shoulders and gave her a shake. Then he raised his own glass, freshly charged, and toasted her. 'Congratulations. To both of you.'

'You're pleased?'

'Delighted.'

'You haven't met him yet.'

'Well, show him to me, then. Where is he?'

'Hold on.' She put down her wine and went to fetch Simon from where she'd parked him in the corridor outside. His face was ringed by tight curls and his eyes bright with worry. He whispered, 'He sounds pleased?'

'He's pretending.'

'Oh.'

'But that's OK, it suits us. Could have been worse.'

'Hmmm, yes . . .'

Mattie towed him back into the room. 'Dad, can I introduce Simon d'Angibau, my fiancé.'

Simon had to screw his confidence to its highest level for this. His mum lived in a semi in Southampton. His ancestors had played no prominent roles in politics or commerce or society. The only thing he'd be able to say about his family – if Sir Michael asked about the odd surname – was that he came from French Huguenot stock on his mother's side. Mattie had coached him not to worry. She'd pointed out that he had a family tree as long as anyone's, as filled with character, that went as far back as Egypt and Solomon, Adam and Eve and all the rest, the same as everyone else's; it was just that it hadn't been written on a building, on one piece of ground, like theirs had. Besides, such a lack of historical baggage had advantages. He'd been free to cut his own path. It should make him more confident, stronger. Simon fed off her advice. It puffed him up.

Michael looked at this tall, thin youngster bobbing in front of him like a dragonfly, wearing a tie and with his jacket buttoned up, of all things. This was her fiancé already?

'Mattie says you're pleased, which is great news,' said Simon.

'Oh yes. Delighted. So I'm your father-in-law-to-be, good grief, poor you.' Had these clothes – the collar and tie and buttoned-up tweed jacket just like his own – come back into

fashion? It was like stepping back in time. Or were they worn
in an effort to impress him? But he registered Simon's strong
handshake, the plank-like shoulders and the long, agile legs, the
flexible neck. The yeoman farmer in Michael – the same one
that lurked never far from the surface of any member of the
aristocracy – saw that he'd make good breeding stock.

The four of them stood for a moment. Patsy mended her
hair. Simon stood at ease like a soldier, smiling hopefully.
Michael half leaned on the back of the chair he'd recently
vacated and jingled loose change in his pocket. Mattie made a
dive for the drinks tray. 'Simon, what d'you want?'

'Thank you, a Capri, if it's there.'

She worked the sideboard. 'Easy-peasy.'

'Is that a drink, a Capri?' asked Michael politely.

Mattie answered, 'Campari, Cognac, Vermouth. Stir and
strain to a chilled cocktail glass. Garnish with maraschino
cherry.'

'It's a holiday resort as well,' added Simon.

The awkward pause deepened further. Michael rode the discomfort, told himself not to mind, it would soon be gone.
Both women were fluttering now, looking for a way out of it.
He squared his shoulders. Good manners demanded he lead
them; he was the man of the house. 'So,' he began, 'what are
your prospects, isn't that what I'm meant to ask?'

'I've got a BSc in microbiology. I was in the Navy for a
while, and now I'm researching microbe flora in body tissue
under Doctor Angus Wist at the Bleuler Institute.'

'That sounds like terrific fun.'

'Yes it is.'

'Good lord, the Blooler institute.'

'You've heard of it?'

'No, no.'

Simon recovered fast, 'Oh . . . no, well, very few people
have,' and he began to explain his work. And so the angels flew

on; the conversation built comfortably. Everyone started to relax. Michael could join in and yet at the same time cut himself off; the chit-chat arrived in a fug of smoke now that he'd lit his pipe again. He became preoccupied with diverse thoughts. It was almost funny, wasn't it – marriage? Daft idea, nowadays, utterly unnecessary. The Blooler institute? Work so important. Men and women – chalk and cheese.

As the conversation burbled on, optimistic, fresh, the young people's love in the air, he found himself remembering a theory put forward by his friend, the late, great Master of the Quorn Hunt, Reggie Cayman, still riding to hounds in his seventies despite breaking his back twice, who'd pronounced the difference between men and women to be one sole ingredient – shame. Men had it; women didn't. Reggie's wife just as often claimed the opposite. She'd light another cigarette off the tip of the old one, and her face by that time had gone to pot – the powder was always caked unevenly in the wrinkles – and her lipsticked mouth would twist comically and the bangles would rattle on her wrist and she'd say, 'Look for the *shame* in a man, and *all* you'll find, if you're lucky, is the unmarked grave . . .' and her eyes would bulge, 'where he's *buried* it.'

He often remembered his dead friends. And, what with feeling the weight of his own shame now, mixed up with perceiving none of it in this young man's frank and handsome face, plus the effect of the drink of course, tears sprang to his eyes. Michael felt sorry for Simon. It wasn't the youth's fault, but this wedding would never happen. Not in a million years. It was going to hurt when Mattie cut him off.

From May through to August the brambles crept underneath Sitten Hall's rhododendrons, their tentacles growing a calm two inches a day and securing themselves every now and again by putting down clusters of rootlets, like base camps, in their

aggressive exploration of the area. Silverweed crept surreptitiously through last year's vegetation. Delighted by the cool
dampness, ferns unrolled their croziers and set to work – pho-
tosynthesis – until the summer heat passed, and now, in
September, they could look forward to shrinking, performing
their yearly death.

Throughout these summer months Michael watched as his
wife's list of wedding chores grew to cover three sides of A4
paper. The computer whined, printing out new versions. Each
item on the list cost them dearly in time and money. Yet, inex-
orably, things were crossed off. He watched closely, kept his
counsel, waited for the signal that his daughter's love affair was
going to fall apart, because she hadn't known Simon long, or
he'd disappointed her, or she'd fallen in love with someone else,
at which point he'd be allowed to step in and mend her broken
heart. And he would have to be on good terms with his daughter in order to help her recover. There would be a week or two
of family hoo-ha and he'd be at the centre of it, saying the wise
and kind things . . . Mattie hanging off his neck, thanking him
for his experience, his sympathy, inviting him to a party to
meet her young friends . . .

Unbelievably, Patsy's list shrank to just one page. August had
gone in a blinding, hot flash. Michael started to batten down
the hatches. His last two marriages began seriously to haunt
him: the scratches on his face, that blood stain on his collar, the
bulging veins in wife number one's forehead, a tuft of wife
number two's hair unaccountably in his fist; wife number one's
lawyer like some awful goblin, the car crash, the legal expenses,
court appearances, the mothers and fathers-in-law sobbing and
shouting; the lists of unreasonable behaviours, that scuffle in the
narrow corridor, the toilet door bolted, the sound of running
feet, his thumb caught in the car door and swelling to the size
and colour of a plum, the dragging out and public flogging of
every inch of private emotion coiled inside him, the sudden

haemorrhage of vast sums of money . . . It was exhausting even to think about. And now he was forced to contemplate the idea that all this might be about to happen to his beloved daughter.

The invitations were long gone. The replies had all been logged.

One week to go.

Three days.

One more day – and that day passed.

By six o'clock on the evening of 6 September the last rope had been tightened on the purple and grey-striped wedding tent and its flag was hoisted. It was L-shaped, positioned on Sitten Hall's west lawns to catch the afternoon and evening sun. The sides facing the park were rolled up so guests might enjoy the view. The tent stood silent and empty, waiting for its work tomorrow, while the light faded. A grey veil was drawn over the stonework of Sitten Hall and the surface of the moat no longer glistened with reflections. The water revealed more of its own dark character and in places you could see the sandy bottom through the floating tracery of weed. The same dusky greyness enhanced the mystical aspect of the chapel and crypt, which stood just a few hundred yards from the castle itself, as the flower delivery man parked his van and unloaded flowers, a waistcoated and aproned figure moving back and forth in the gathering dusk.

Patsy shuffled once more through the lists, searching for anything that hadn't been done. It was gratifying to see almost all the items were crossed out, except for the one glaring exception: the words 'wedding dress' were typed in bold capitals and then overwritten a dozen times, with four or five boxes and several inches of doodling around them. She heard a familiar, distinctive engine noise and glanced from the kitchen window to see – exactly as she'd expected – a wooden-framed Morris Minor estate bumbling down the drive. It was Pinky, rector of this parish and old friend of Michael's, the first to arrive. She went to the corridor and called Mattie and Simon. 'Pinky's here, I'm going on down.'

'OK!' came the faint reply.

Then she called her husband, 'Michael?' She waited for the answer.

'What?'

'Your mother's arrived. Time to put on your tie. We're in the dining room.'

Patsy trotted downstairs. By the time she stepped out of the monkey door Pinky had already unpacked the wheelchair and loaded Granny Banana into it. Patsy hurried over to kiss her mother-in-law's cheek. How frail she was, thought Patsy, with her grey-blue hair glued into those waves, her face long, the skin scored by age and plastered with make-up. 'Banana my dear, you look fabulous.'

'Thanks . . . awfully. Am I staying the night?'

'You're staying exactly where you'll most like to be,' replied Patsy tactfully. She didn't want to confuse her. She moved on, gave Pinky a hug and a kiss. 'Thank you, Pinky.'

'My bag . . .' began Granny Banana.

'She's been no trouble.' Pinky stopped for a moment to dab his brow with a handkerchief while Patsy settled the travel rug over Banana's knees – she needed it whatever the weather – and then took the helm. As she wheeled Granny inside, from the corner of her eye she saw Philip's Rover saloon turning into the car park, but Mattie and Simon now stepped through the monkey door, so help had arrived. 'Mattie, could you see in Granny, while I . . .'

For the next quarter of an hour Patsy, Mattie and Simon ferried their dinner guests from the car park through the Hall to the dining room. Patsy had hired it for the occasion – although she'd negotiated a discount on the rate usually paid by groups of Japanese businessmen and so on – but the irony was, it was where they'd always taken their meals prior to '86.

With pre-dinner drinks in their hands it was Pinky and
Philip who attended Granny Banana; they stood on either side
of her wheelchair, responding to her various bizarre questions.

'Is this the electric tablecloth?' she asked.

'Hmmm?'

'There used to be an electric tablecloth. It had wires in it. So
you could put the lamps on the table without having unsightly
cables' – she stirred the air with a finger – 'all over the place.'

'What a good idea. But no, I don't think this is an electric
tablecloth.'

Out of the sun and no longer driving, Pinky wasn't as hot,
and his bright complexion eased a shade; the last beads of sweat
had been dried off by the handkerchief. He was dressed in
'mufti' as he called it, but the dog collar none the less made its
presence felt, a strip of white beneath the pink of his face and
neck as he talked on, keeping things light and cheerful.

Philip was better at listening than talking. He was slim, and
his side parting was a razor-sharp straight line as if cut with an
axe, and he was immaculately shaved. He wore a Gieves &
Hawkes suit and, at five-foot-ten, was short in the leg next to
Michael's six foot. He managed to keep Pinky happy just by
lobbing in another question or two, and hoped that he himself
wouldn't be asked anything; it always made him uncomfortable.
Philip had followed a traditional journey from the army to a
career in financial services, making use of a well-thumbed
address book – all the great and the good he'd been to school
with – but his working life and his social life had depended on
just this: keeping other people talking while he waited for
financial gain. He dangled the vicar's favourite subject in front
of him so all he had to do was listen to the latter's familiar, dramatic voice explaining the various different versions of religious
services, dates of prayer books, changes to the scripture.
Meanwhile, he let it wash over him and instead watched the
newcomers, Simon's side of the family. The mother was dressed

in a printed floral dress, quite graceful and smiling; she was a
widow, apparently. There was his sister, as pretty as Simon was
handsome, wearing a short skirt and black tights and enormous clodhopper boots, ridiculous but setting off a nice pair of
legs, and that was the cousin . . . so who was the older man? An
uncle, or boyfriend of the mother? Pinky's voice drifted past –
all this fuss about gay clergy, he was saying, the whole point of
it was, it was a job that gay men did well, and in Pinky's opinion they should be encouraged, he hoped the Anglican
movement could mend itself . . .

Meanwhile, Simon's mother, sister, uncle and cousin were
taken on a tour around the oblong, cavernous dining room.
They went first to peer into the chimney. Mattie read out from
the square of card adjacent, 'Twenty feet of carved alabaster
towering over an inglenook lined with pink marble, constructed subsequent to the eighteenth-century Palladian
window.'

They craned their necks to look at the arched ceiling, dated
1623. The strapwork enclosed figures symbolising the vices
and virtues, heaven and hell, war and peace, feast and famine.
A skylight was built into the top of the arch for almost the
entire length of the room. The panelling had been fitted in the
nineteenth century. Chandeliers hung overhead, the light
reflected in hundreds of pinpoints from the glass skylight falling
primarily on the table and feathering outwards to the panelled
walls but leaving the paintings – in the evening – in moody
obscurity. The family group wandered from picture to picture,
stopping politely at each, taking in this series of fourteen still
lifes of food and drink painted by Sir Robert Barker which nar-
rated the course of a typical eighteenth-century dinner, from
salmon broth to cheese and port. In the background of some
pictures could be seen a musical quartet. 'Sir Robert took two
hundred and thirty-eight dinners here himself while complet-
ing his artistic commission,' read Simon from the information

cards. 'Wow. Greedy so and so. Probably had to be carried out.'

The table was of seventeenth-century English oak, long enough for thirty covers, the unused chairs this evening standing, backs to the wall, waiting until the full complement of guests from Nabisco Cereals arrived on the following day. 'Beautifully set,' said Simon's mother emphatically, touching the cloth. '*Yes*,' replied Patsy, 'good, isn't it? Gina's idea – Gina is the boss here, National Trust through to the bone, terribly committed to the place – anyway she had the brainwave, that if you're jolly well hiring out this facility, you should try and make it like it used to be, like an actual dinner one might have taken when these pictures were painted, in the late eighteenth century, and she's even gone so far as to provide the exact linen and glasses and plateware; just the same, it's really quite spooky.' She didn't tell them, because she didn't want to appear cheap, that live classical music was usually included in the price – four members of the Salisbury orchestral society played for two hours – if you could afford it. The wedding was costing a lot of money and Michael couldn't bear it. The only money well spent as far as he was concerned was earmarked for the licence fee, Sky Plus and the Tote. This reminded Patsy – where *was* Michael? He'd better arrive soon; it was rude of him.

For the sake of making conversation, Patsy alerted Simon's mother to the decrepit fan heater on the floor, and the long extension cable leading from it. 'Whenever we have Granny over,' whispered Patsy, hoping the other woman would be drawn into the conspiracy, 'we have to dig out this fan heater and aim it at the back of her chair. Even if we don't switch it on. It's like a comfort blanket I suppose, it makes her feel at home. And that's all right, too.' Patsy looked into this woman's strangely bright-eyed expression and hoped she was comfortable but somehow knew she wasn't; something odd was happening, the other woman looked as if about to burst into tears. Patsy didn't know if it would help but she took her hand, placed it on her arm and worked harder: she poured out a torrent of polite conversation. 'There was a fire in here, a jolly raging fire it must have been, because it virtually destroyed the room, 1750 something. So after that, came the make-over, of course. Everything different. Originally it was quite like a monastic style of refectory, I believe. You know, stern, simple. I like it how it is now though. A touch more glamour, a bit more show-offy. Makes it easier to dress up oneself doesn't it and there's . . .'

Some minutes later, as if they were psychically connected, Mattie and Patsy asked each other the same question, 'Where's Dad?'

'I did tell him.'

'We both did. Shall we wait, or . . .'

Pinky, standing stiff as a board next to Granny Banana, overheard. 'Let's not wait for him. Michael's always late. I should know. I wasted my teenage years loitering at the end of the driveway.'

'I'll fetch him,' said Mattie. She squeezed Simon's hand and was gone.

Mattie hurried back through the Hall. She was furious at her father's behaviour: not bothering to come and meet Simon's family on the very eve of her wedding, at a dinner which he himself was meant to be hosting. At the top of the west range she passed through the door marked 'Private' and went up the stairs that led to the apartment. She heard the loud blare of the television and her anger went up a notch. Then came a crash and a swear word from the kitchen, so she swerved and hurried in there instead. All her accusations were lined up but she was left speechless because Michael was wearing an apron and holding a broken egg shell, the egg white dripping from his fingers, his other hand cradling the mixing bowl. She couldn't understand what he was up to. 'Dad . . .'

Michael looked up sharply, surprised. When he saw her, he relaxed fractionally and peered into the mixing bowl. He was wondering how he was going to fish out the bits of broken shell.

'Dad,' she repeated, more emphatically. 'What are you doing?'

'I couldn't hold on for ever, I thought I'd better feed myself. If you're all going to run off and leave me, don't be surprised when I have a stab at scrambling an egg.'

'What are you talking about?'

'Well, I can't be expected to starve. Where is everyone?'

'We're all in the dining room.'

Michael looked up; he was certain of his ground on this one. 'There's no one in the dining room. I checked, several times.' Mattie stepped closer and pointed to the floor beneath her feet. 'Dad, the *dining* room dining room – *downstairs*.' Michael paused, but then realised, 'Downstairs? In the Hall?'

'Yes. *Mum* told you. *I* told you.'

'Oh Gawdd. I *am* sorry. How stupid of me.'

'We're all waiting for you. Granny's here, Uncle Philip, the whole of Simon's family . . .'

'I am *sorry*.' He'd hoped that by some miracle the wedding had been cancelled at the last minute but instead here he was, being herded back into the fray.

'So you should be!' Mattie stamped her foot. A rush of anger mixed with affection for him, and frustration.

Michael dropped the bowl onto the draining board and wiped his hands on the towel. He'd have to find his coat and tie, put them back on. He couldn't help being mean and thinking about the money. 'We hired it?'

'Yes.'

He shook his head at the irony of actually paying to use his own dining room. He added, 'Hope we got a discount.'

'We did as a matter of fact,' said Mattie tightly. Michael untied his apron. 'Oh . . . All right. I see. Does anyone ever tell me anything.' He wiped a drop of milk from his shoe. 'OK, hurry hurry hurry. Has eating started?'

'Probably. Mum's cross with you as well.'

'Cross,' repeated Michael as he looked for his jacket. A sadness blossomed in his chest. He was expected to walk Mattie down the aisle, hand her straight into the lion's mouth. 'Darling Mattie, any second thoughts about the wedding?'

She followed him into the living room. 'Dad, come on, turn off the bloody television and come downstairs for dinner.'

'Can't find the remote.'

'Just switch it off.'

'Are you sure you *want* me to walk you down the aisle? I'm hardly the best advert. Three marriages, three divorces, one hundred per cent fuckup.'

'Three divorces?'

'You know what I mean. Not exactly the soul of romance, am I?'

'I don't care, you're my dad. It's all right, isn't it?'

'Hope so,' he mumbled.

'Hope so? What d'you mean hope so? What's the matter?'

'Well, what time do we kick off?'

'You know what time. The service starts at midday. Buffet lunch afterwards, so it's not long until you're onto the champagne and the food. It can't be that bad. It's not much to ask.'

Michael interrupted, 'I know, I know. It's fine.'

Mattie was in the clutches of a familiar dread. Warning bells sounded at his tone of voice. 'What? Switch off the damn TV, I can't hear myself think. What are you trying to say?'

He found the remote control and dinged the off button.

In the silence Mattie repeated her question, 'What is it?'

Michael hefted the black, heavy instrument of the remote, as if he could control his daughter with it, change the track she was on. He rolled it out, there was no other way of doing this. 'Does it make any difference if we delay by fifteen minutes?'

She slumped on one leg. 'Why d'you want to, what's the point?'

He jumped in blindly. 'There's racing at Cheltenham. The Vodafone Handicap. Twelve o'clock. And I've got thirty quid on By Desire to win, no half measures, Gibby tipped him so it's as good as from the horse's mouth. I thought we could watch it together.'

Mattie was speechless.

'It's only ten minutes, isn't it,' went on Michael, 'and no one will notice. The bride's meant to be late, isn't that so? What do you say? Might be great fun. We watch it here and then trot down . . .' He could see this wasn't going down well. That stare of hers was killing. 'I'll put the winnings in the honeymoon kitty.' He blushed, not in anger this time, instead with shame. Surprisingly, the symptoms were very similar – the rush of heat to the brain, an intense desire to kill whoever was causing it, the sense of injustice. He pointed at the television with the remote control. 'Could be a bloody good race.' Mattie stamped her foot, gave a short bark of annoyance. 'For God's sake! How can you even suggest that?' She snatched the remote from his hand, strode to the door and in an uncontrollable gesture she turned and *hurled* it.

Patsy knocked a fork against her wine glass. 'Can I interrupt for a moment?' Silence fell. She folded one hand into the other and gripped hard, it was a trick she'd learned to stop herself from talking too quickly. She addressed the table, trying to ignore the two conspicuously empty settings. 'There's a tradition in this family,' she began, 'that dates back to a particular occasion when the Honourable Mrs Ronald Greville, the notorious Edwardian society hostess, stayed here. She took it on herself one evening to say Grace, which was an unheard of thing for a woman to do, causing, at that time, a terrific stir. And we've always tried to keep up with her.' Then as usual she deferred to Pinky, 'If that's all right with you, Pinky.'

'Of course.'

'Thank you.' She bowed her head, waited a moment. 'For what we are about to receive, may the Lord make us truly thankful.' The party joined in with, 'Amen,' and the spell broke. Conversations started around the table. Pinky launched into a description of his favourite haunts in Morocco. The two frocked attendants who'd been hovering by the sideboard moved forwards to pour wine and serve soup and bread.

Granny Banana was reminded by Patsy to take her medication. The little circular blue tin had been formerly used for her fishing flies and now she asked Pinky to open it for her. Then she poked and stirred with her finger at the quite beautiful colours and shapes – they did make pills so much more attractive now, she thought. As conversations grew around the table, she concentrated on the glass of water, the placing of the pills on her tongue, the swallowing. She felt a bit like the mechanised monkey in the window of the village pub, lifting a glass quite so often, but she must take all of them. At last there was only the little white one left. She picked it up, lay it in the palm of her hand. Such a tiny thing. Last one. She clumsily tried to chuck it towards her mouth but the pill missed its target and flew behind her, skittering unseen and unheard across the oak floor. Granny Banana lifted the glass of water, ready to help the pill down, yet she couldn't find its little, helpful presence in her mouth. With her tongue she searched – no, nothing. She took a sip of water none the less. Presumably it had gone down by itself. After a little rest she picked up her soup spoon, to catch up.

Pinky had been asked about himself: who was he, how had
he met the family, and now he pinned down the whole table
with his loud voice. 'Before I joined the clergy I was a Renault
salesman. And I still like anything to do with cars. I am probably Michael's oldest school friend and owe my job to him,
because in those days the family still had a say in who got the
living. You know,' he went on, 'there was a time, not so long
ago, when the actual Gough family used to advertise for their
vicars in *The Field* magazine. Apparently they got a better type
of chap, not too much God, someone with muscles, you know,
help with the harvest and so on, keep the ladies occupied.
Whereas I am dramatically opposite to this "better type of
chap" – and I have been in the post here for fifteen years.' As
abruptly as this declaration had started it ended. His audience
felt abandoned. No one could come up with anything to
follow it.

Mattie came in suddenly. A strand of her hair had come
loose; colour burned on both her cheeks. Her eyes glistened as
she crossed the room.

'Darling, everything all right?' asked Patsy.

'He's coming,' said Mattie, of her father.

'You found him?'

'Yup. Sorry everyone.'

There was only the sound of Granny eating – a rapid click-
ing as she brought her teeth together even though it was only
soup.

Mattie wiped the strand of hair from her face. Too much was
going wrong. Her father was doing everything he could to
belittle the wedding. The dress was a disaster. She scraped back
her chair and sat, smiled tightly at everyone. She didn't want to
get married, not like this. She wanted a perfect dress, a perfect
father. Which meant she was a hopelessly bourgeois, prissy,
goody-goody perfectionist, she realised.

She lifted the spoon to her mouth but her throat was too

strangled to swallow. Beneath the table, Simon's hand moved to her thigh to comfort her. Mattie's hand covered it, quickly lifting it higher. She took his index finger and pressed it on the clip holding up her stocking. Simon felt a surge of excitement.

No sooner had the conversation in the dining room returned to normal than it was broken again by the sound of approaching footsteps. They were heavy and metallic.

Pinky looked towards the door; he was annoyed at Michael blundering his way through yet another social occasion. His dog collar was too tight so he had to twist his whole frame in the chair to watch for Michael's entrance. His jowl wobbled.

Philip looked at Patsy to see if he should read a signal from her as to how to handle this. As Michael's brother – and someone who had made money as steadily as Michael had lost it – he was often called on for advice, but never presumed to deal with anything or get involved.

Granny Banana shoved her empty bowl away from her; she didn't know what was going on – something though.

Simon's mother, his uncle, sister and cousin watched the door, wondering whose were those voices they could hear, while Simon watched them, hoping they were all right. He'd prepared them to expect eccentric behaviour but this place was daunting.

There was a pause, the sound of more footsteps, increasing in volume. Michael came in carrying a plate in front of him like a schoolboy returning from the dinner queue. 'Sorry I'm late,' he offered. It was the rack of lamb he'd got hold of – he'd jumped a course and had ignored all advice to the contrary. He never could be bothered with soup. He was too upset to listen to anybody – when Mattie had thrown the remote control it had gone out of the open window. And how could life be expected to carry on as normal without it?

He was followed by a waitress who signalled an apology to Patsy before scurrying back.

Michael sailed over to his position at the head of the table, replying to various greetings. Simon's family waited to be introduced; Patsy did the honours. Michael went through the motions while he sat down, shook out his napkin and picked up his knife and fork. 'Sorry, I'm on the main course, aren't I? Came at this skew-whiff, I'm afraid. I'll crack on, though, if no one minds.' Simon's family were quick to forgive him; yes, they all agreed, do. Patsy held back; she could see it was best to leave well alone.

Granny Banana cottoned on to her eldest son's arrival. She turned towards him and said, 'Michael, there's a black . . . um . . . plastic bag thing . . . in the back of the car. With Sprocket in it.'

'Sprocket?' The little terrier was his mother's only companion, and a hefty extra cost on the bill from The Sharland House Accommodation for the Elderly.

'Yes. He died – very unfortunately. I put his body in one of those – bin bags. I want you to bury him for me, under my tree.'

'Ma, I am sorry. That is bad news. Poor Sprocket.' He was sad, in theory, but the dog surcharge would presumably disappear. He should remember to check.

'The tree I like, you know. Old Quercus.'

'Yes, I know. Quercus.'

'Thanks awfully.' Without a pause Granny Banana changed the subject. 'You're making too much noise in your mouth Michael. I take my false teeth out during the main course. You should try it.' She made a face, dropped her teeth into her hand. Her cheeks and lips shrank into the empty space of her mouth.

'Well done Mother,' said Michael grimly.

Her voice became muffled, 'I tuck them in here, in my sleeve – you see?' She tugged at her right cuff and deftly inserted them. 'Like a hanky.'

'Good for you, for organising your teeth.' He stood up,

poured more red wine into his own glass. He took two strides around the side of the table to reach the mint sauce. The fact that he tore through all normal good manners made everyone else feel that he was the one who was doing all right and they themselves were slow and boorish.

Patsy tried to overturn the wrong atmosphere. She addressed everyone, 'Doesn't the *garden* look in good shape for tomorrow, though?'

Before anyone could answer Granny leaned dangerously far forward in her chair and asked Michael, 'Was it at Cheltenham?'

'Granny, we've already spoken about it. There was a Steward's enquiry.'

'I thought it was Cheltenham.'

'Claire lives in Cheltenham if that's what you're talking about.'

'I see darling.'

Michael put his mother out of his mind and concentrated on the lamb and mint sauce. He hated being dragged into her confused world. Mattie had lost the remote control and he should focus on the immediate challenge: to find it. He'd briefly gone out to look, but nothing doing. Infuriating. And he hated having so many people around the table, it made all his thoughts come at him jumbled up. Every one of his actions seemed disconnected. He wanted to put his head down and run through this evening.

Would the remote control float if it had fallen in the water? It was quite heavy, solid . . . maddening that she'd thrown it. He gobbled his food, carelessly massacring the lamb. *Was* he making too much noise?

There was a loud *clang* as Mattie dropped her soup spoon in her empty plate.

'Philip?' said Michael, changing the subject suddenly.

'Yes, Michael?'

'That housekeeper of yours.'

'Natalia?'

'Yes. Would you mind if I phoned and talked to her? I wanted to ask if she'd be willing to take on some extra chores, over here, on her day off?'

'Extra chores?'

'Spring cleaning. That sort of thing.'

'Michael we have a cleaner,' Patsy put in. 'Mrs Burrell will do however many extra hours. If you want her to.'

'Oh. All right. Just thought someone with a bit of go about them. What d'you think, Philip?

'I'm not sure she's got the time. And she doesn't yet have a UK driving licence.'

'Will you ask her? Or shall I ring?'

'I'll ask her, if you like.'

'Many thanks.'

Simon's mother had rescued Patsy, meanwhile, by asking her about the garden and how much preparation had had to be done for tomorrow. Pinky touched his napkin against his brow as he watched his friend's bad manners. His complexion glowed like a light bulb again now he'd had two glasses of wine. He asked, exasperated, 'Michael maybe you could wait for the rest of us to catch up, now?' Michael was mopping up his gravy with a potato just as the soup plates were being taken away. Didn't he see the effect he was having?

While the others were brought their main course, Michael put his knife and fork together, pushed back his chair and went to scoop a bowl of gooseberry crumble from the sideboard, taking his wine glass with him. He stood eating his pudding and gave a verdict. 'Delicious. First class. Are these our own gooseberries?' He tossed back the last of his wine and refilled with tawny port from the decanter. 'Cheers.' He dumped his pudding bowl with a clatter and called, 'Right. A million thanks. Very good grub. Bravo.'

Patsy rose from her chair, 'Michael, it's very disconcert- ing . . .' Michael took an extra fingerful of pudding before heading for the door. 'Does anyone mind if I head off . . .' Then he remembered his port and turned back to pick it up before finally leaving the room. 'Lots to do. Many thanks.'

He left them in silence.

The dining room cooled down. The pictures stood unmoved, the ceiling remained intact. They'd seen much worse after all. Michael's own father had thrown the brandy decanter against the chimney-piece before seizing a cane and beating Michael, enraged by the latter's refusal to stop riding the old lawnmower around the house.

Here, this evening, Philip leaned sideways to allow the wait- ress to serve the mint sauce in the proper way. Mattie stared at her place mat, inwardly cursing her father for being rude to Simon's family, for turning this meal to nothing . . .

Everyone wanted to repair the damage; the goodwill was shared by everyone around the table but they were stuck. They swallowed wine. Simon cleared his throat, wondering what to say. His relatives looked ashen. It struck him that he didn't know them very well, not as human beings in their own right. Suddenly his mother seemed old and invisible. His heart went out to her. He wanted her to enjoy herself. A step sideways or backwards was required – a distraction – or maybe he should just face up to what had happened, talk about it? He'd once read a story by Goethe called *Elective Affinities*. It had compared people to chemicals, and when chemicals were mixed together under certain conditions mol- ecules could either attract or repel one another. Mattie's father couldn't sit down with them for very long; it was a shame but it was no one's fault. He squeezed Mattie's hand under the table. She squeezed back. 'Has anyone read a book by Goethe,' he began . . .

        ★

Outside, the darkness thickened perceptibly. The middle distance disappeared as if by magic and the coming night stealthily
closed over any object which might or might not be the TV
remote control. It deepened the shadows and made pockets
of dark between clumps of grass, and blackened the underside of
the drawbridge. The lights from the castle's narrow, upright
windows sparked reflections on the surface of the moat and the
stillness of that surface might lead one to believe there were
lamps glowing beneath the water. Foxes always avoided the
lights and the smell of human kind; they only now dared cross
the metal fence between the castle and the motte.

Michael was standing over his television set, which was blar-
ing away. It looked as though he was massaging or stroking it.
In fact he was pressing the plastic casing in various places in
order to find the panel which would open to reveal the manual
controls. He wanted to catch the ten o'clock news and the late-
night satirical thing on Channel 4.

Patsy appeared, hesitant. 'Michael,' she began.

Michael straightened up, pointed at the television and looked
at her. He asked, 'D'you know how to find the knobs on this
thing?'

Patsy was deflated by his carelessness. 'What's wrong with it?'

'Mattie snatched the remote from me and hurled it, in an
absolute fit, out of the window. I went and had a look but
couldn't find it. I'm sure there's a way of pushing the buttons by
hand, if one could find them.'

Patsy walked over and helped him prod and poke the set.
'Here – no.'

'Otherwise it's stuck for ever on three,' explained Michael.

Patsy tried another spot. 'Here, what about this?'

'The on-off button, is all that is.'

There was a brief lull while they both searched. Michael was
talking to himself, 'There should be a panel that opens up,
but . . .'

Patsy interrupted, 'And you went down and looked, where it fell?'

'Yes. Nothing doing. It probably went in the moat, I would guess. In which case, not worth worrying about, time for a new one.'

She went to the window and looked out, half-listening as Michael rambled on, 'I could ring Currys for advice, tomorrow morning. Are they open on a Saturday I wonder. Of course they are, probably on a Sunday too, nowadays.'

'Michael . . .'

'Mmmmm?'

'We're in the billiard room, for coffee. Philip and Pinky would like you to come down for a game of billiards and a brandy. D'you care to?'

He took no notice. 'I suppose I should have another look, take a torch this time, there's always a chance it's lying there and I didn't find it.' He was on his way out again. 'Just in case.'

Patsy pressed her fingers to her forehead.

'I didn't actually hear a splash,' finished Michael.

Downstairs, everyone made the long trek to the billiard room. Simon and Mattie followed Simon's mother, uncle, his cousin and sister, who were in turn being led by Philip. Some way behind came Granny Banana, wheeled by Pinky.

Granny lifted her head and asked, 'Where's everyone gone?' Pinky leaned forward and spoke into her hearing aid, 'We're going to the billiard room.'

'Where's Mattie?' demanded Granny.

Pinky walked her chair forward. 'They're just a step or two ahead of us.' He repeated, 'We're going to the billiard room.'

Granny persisted, waving the knife that she'd somehow kept hold of. 'Why've we all got down from the table?'

'It's time for coffee, Granny, so there's been an exodus.'

'Is it my fault?'

'No, absolutely not at all. Nothing's wrong. Everything's going according to plan.'

They crossed the Great Hall on the ground floor of the gatehouse, over to the west range and along. Mattie wished that her mother and father would come back, make everything sweet. Her dark eyebrows were drawn in a frown and she held her hair loosely to one side. Simon trailed along beside her. Windows passed by; outside it was dark except for where the floodlights bathed the ground. Sitting low in the sky the moon showed three-quarters full.

Mattie was criticising her own behaviour – why couldn't she *not* worry about the dress? Someone else – a different Mattie, a better Mattie – would carelessly throw something together from their own wardrobe and look brilliant, meandering down the aisle. This mythical, romantic, carefree Mattie wouldn't mind about her father watching the race; in fact she'd insist that everyone watch it. Her fiancé would be a desperately poor foreigner, a refugee who didn't speak a word of English and who worked in the grounds, but somehow . . . Mattie stopped herself, it was fruitless to go down this track. Yet she did wonder if she was so conventional and straight-laced because she'd been brought up in an eccentric environment. She released her hair and it tilted from side to side, as she slapped her hip and nodded to emphasise, 'I suppose I should let him watch his stupid race.'

'I don't mind,' said Simon. 'It doesn't make it any less of a wedding, for me, if we delay it a bit.'

'It's just . . .'

'Hold on,' interrupted Simon, because through one of the windows, illuminated by the floodlights trained on the draw-bridge, he'd caught sight of torchlight: a figure was walking on the other side of the moat, staring at the ground. He touched Mattie's arm. 'Is that him?'

She cupped her hands against the glass. 'Yes.'

They watched as a shadowy Michael followed the torch beam, painfully slowly, towards the drawbridge. Then he knelt quickly, picked up something, looked at it, tossed it aside. He turned the other way, walked back.

'What on earth's he up to?' asked Simon.

'Will you do me a favour?' Mattie clutched his hand.

Michael patrolled the banks of the moat, eyes fixed on the circle of light thrown by the torch – but nothing doing, so far. His face was blank, serious. Every now and again his scalp tilted forwards and the creases in his brow deepened momentarily. A slight breeze lifted his hair.

He made a thorough search, but eventually couldn't be bothered to go on with what was probably a wild goose chase. He started to head back.

On the drawbridge, he picked up the glass of whisky which he'd left on the stone parapet.

Yet, he didn't want to go indoors and join the others, either.

The whisky tilted dangerously in his hand. He hitched his trousers and parked his rear on the side of the bridge, put down the torch, placed the glass carefully so he could reach into his jacket pocket for tobacco and pipe. He filled the bowl, tamped it with his thumb and then set the match on it, sucked at the stem quickly. Smoke filled his mouth. He sipped at the whisky for that famous smoking-and-drinking satisfaction, and looked out over the darkened, moonlit garden and parkland of his family home. This place – so beautiful. He let the tranquillity and mystery of it cloak him; it entered, sat in his heart. He held it there.

The enormous grey and purple-striped marquee stood quietly; there was no wind. Ready for its duties tomorrow, thought Michael. It was a beautiful sight, he had to admit. Made for revelry and excitement. He sighed.

The stone was uncomfortable for his old hips. He eased himself off the bridge; he was better off standing with his legs decently apart. He fumbled his whisky, his pipe, got a bit more of both.

A bat silently scurried past and disappeared in an instant against the blackness of the moat. He heard an owl call – a sinister warning. He wanted to go backwards in time, have all of this land and castle to himself. Put everything to use. Employ a hundred people and set them to work . . . Not that he disapproved of the National Trust's motives, or its existence – God save it for doing something to keep land and houses inalienable. Yet he was with Octavia Hill and the others involved in setting it up: couldn't they do something more alive, more current, than turn these places into museums? Shouldn't they be schools, hotels, old people's homes? Michael's square face was beset with frustration. He and Pinky had had a stab at turning Sitten Hall into a boys' school but had fallen foul of the local authority who'd deemed them unqualified and unsuitable, which was probably only right, but he could picture himself as the chairman of the National Trust, standing up at the board meeting or whatever they have at Queen Anne's Gate, and pounding his fist on the table, his brow crinkled and his ears bright with passion, saying no more tourism, we don't want these people wandering around wasting their dull, ever expanding leisure time. We want some life, some work, we want boys playing rugby football in the park, girls playing netball, we want smoking in the rhododendrons, or war veterans soothed until their dying day, or hotel staff running about carrying baggage. Michael's fist hammered down again and again on the polished table. The seasoned, grey-haired aristocrats looked astonished. Michael ordered them to clear out the pretentious bric-a-brac, shut out the meaningless, idiotic visitors, choose life, not death. 'The National Trust no longer sanctions the "mortmain" of tourism!' he thundered and took his seat to resounding applause.

Yes, this castle had always been under attack of one sort or another. Most especially, the year 1894 ought to be engraved above the portal of every stately in the country. It was the year death duties had been ushered in by Act of Parliament. They'd torn into Sitten Hall's jugular, all right. Just three large bites, taken at precisely the junctions between successive generations, had left the place bleeding to death. Just a year later, in 1895, Octavia Hill and the others had inaugurated the National Trust. Precisely as death duties took the life-blood from his ancestral home, so the National Trust was able to take advantage: they stepped in and saved the core of it. One parasite had fed off the other, and both fed off the building itself and for ever changed the use and upkeep of Sitten Hall.

He came back to earth, wishing that he'd done something useful after all – work etc. – yet not once had he lifted a finger, done one jot. He'd just played the cards as they'd been dealt to him and taken the easiest possible way out. A line of Wordsworth, remembered from school, came back to him – 'The good die first' – in which case he'd reach a ripe old age.

Maybe he should visit the House of Lords once in a while. Did they do anything useful? Were they still there? He had an idea they'd been booted out.

Michael was brought out of his reverie by the click of the latch, and turned to see a pair of trousered, male legs pick their way through the monkey door. He recognised Mattie's fiancé, Simon. Such curly hair he had. Michael had become quite fond of him. He enjoyed his company, but wasn't sure if now was the right moment for a *tête-à-tête*. He didn't know if he could trust himself not to give the lad all the sorry tales of his own divorces, the losses involved, and how it had led to him being here, utterly alone, drinking too much . . .

'Hi,' called Simon.

Michael rode out the spasm of pure grief: the boy really did not deserve such bad luck. God, marriage would knock the shine off him! Poor creature – he couldn't see the coming terrors . . .

'How's things?' asked Simon.

'Not good.' Michael started off like he was in a court of law. 'Mattie and I had a fight and she threw the remote control out of the window.' He watched as this went in; any normal, sentient being would spot the danger signs – girl who picks fights and throws things – but Simon turned it around into something positive. 'I always wished I could have had rows with my parents, it was something we never did, but—'

'It fell from the window,' interrupted Michael, 'and landed somewhere over there.' He waved in the general direction. 'Probably in the moat. If you spot it let me know, otherwise we'll have to drive into town tomorrow and get a new one.'

Simon took a step or two, looked into the water. Michael took a sip of whisky and the question fell from his lips almost at the same time as he swallowed – a sign of drunkenness. He managed to choke out, 'What about you? Taking a breath of fresh air?'

'Not exactly.' Simon took his chance then. 'Mattie asked me to come out here and give you a message.'

'What message?' Michael coughed; his eyes watered.

'She wanted to say that she doesn't mind if you want to watch that horse race, tomorrow.'

There was a pause while Michael remembered the scene, clicked as to what was being said – the whip had been called off, he'd get to see the Vodafone Handicap after all. 'Is she sure?'

'Yes. Patsy's agreed to walk her down the aisle instead.'

The warmth increased in Michael's breast. This was a turnaround. 'Oh, that is so very good, so very kind of her.'

'And when the race finishes,' added Simon, 'I'm to tell you, you could still come along, but you don't have to.'

Not turn up at all? The words had the perfect flair and pitch of a good popular song to Michael's ears. He sucked at his pipe. Tomorrow – his small pleasures were intact, after all. He could duck out. Suddenly he was blindingly, tearfully overcome by Mattie's generosity. She was a wonderful daughter. The heat of his emotion, fuelled by drink, turned on Simon himself. He pointed. 'Maybe she could do the same for you.'

'What's that?'

'Let you off the hook.'

Simon laughed. 'I *want* to be there.'

'Well, that's your business,' replied Michael, stung with pleasure, with the weight of meaning. 'We're all a bunch of animals and we live in a farmyard. That's all I know. Let each creature get on with its own ways, if possible.'

'Yes, indeed,' Simon agreed.

There was a long pause.

'If I had a guinea,' mumbled Michael, waving at the moat, 'for every damn picnic glass and pair of cutting shears that we've lost in there, over the years. Hmm?'

The bulk of the wedding party prepared to enter Sitten Hall's billiard room. Philip pushed and pulled at the double doors, but only one swung open. It was enough for everyone to walk through, but Granny had to be left behind momentarily because the wheelchair wouldn't fit. There were gasps at the enormous granite fireplace, the huge comfort of the arm-chairs, the prize billiard table bathed in light in its own enclave hung with enormous tapestries. There were murmurs of approval and excitement; meanwhile Philip could go back for Granny.

He tried hard but the wheelchair wouldn't fit through the

one half of the door they'd managed to open. Everyone's attention turned to solving the problem. The bolt was jammed, it wouldn't be drawn. Philip failed. Pinky had a try, so did Mattie, who had her mother's height and strong bones. Patsy returned, the Tall Woman herself, but she couldn't do it.

Simon now caught up with them and volunteered, and he managed to pull the bolt partly out of its housing, but still it refused to be drawn the last quarter inch.

As a final stab at answering the crisis Philip took a turn behind Granny's chair and pushed her forward, negotiating the tight space carefully to see if there was any way they could wangle her through.

'Ouch,' called Granny as the wheel of her chair snagged the side of the locked door. Her head nodded forward with the collision.

'Impasse,' said Philip, drawing her back again. 'Pinky, shall you and I carry her?' Simon undid his hand from Mattie's and was about to volunteer but Pinky got there first and everyone watched, concerned, as the two men stood one on each side of the chair and lifted Granny out. She draped her frail arms over their shoulders; they carried her with their arms locked together under her knees and around her back.

She asked, 'Is it bed time?'

'No, Granny – we're just lifting you to your chair for coffee.'

'I have to go to the toilet before bed.'

'I know, but this isn't bed time, I'll tell you when.'

'All right darling.' She wasn't sure everyone had got it right. Now she was in her usual chair close against the log fire, but it wasn't alight. She asked, 'Am I staying here tonight?'

'No, I think you've got your usual room at the hotel,' cut in Philip.

'No, I think I'm staying here.'

'Well that's all right then.' It was probably true. 'Let me light the fire, shall I?' He took the handle of the gas-fired poker and laid it in the grate, carrying the miniature gas cylinder with him on its flexible hose. He took the box of matches from the mantel and struck one while at the same time turning the knurled tap on the cylinder. He touched the flame against the baffled end of the poker, which ignited with a '*whumph!*' He thrust it underneath the logs to set them going.

Michael was alone again on the drawbridge; the young man had gone. He tapped out the extinct remains of his pipe and lifted his glass to his lips – but it was empty. He turned to go indoors and refuel.

Then he paused. He didn't want to fight it out in the billiard room with the others. A possibility occurred to him: the Whistle and Feather was only a short distance away. He checked his watch – ten-fifteen, still time to get in a couple before last orders on a Friday night. The landlord was never one to stick to the letter of the law, anyway. He turned towards the car park where the Renault 4 was waiting, but he hadn't got his car keys with him and the thought of the clutch pedal put him off; it was easy enough to peg it back on its stump in daylight but in the dark it was a fiddle. He'd rather go on foot and thereby save himself from being arrested again for drunk driving.

He set off at a brisk pace, a solid figure walking along the driveway leading out of Sitten Hall. The beech trees were giant markers, looming out of the dark one by one. He admired the unbroken length of dark, malleable tarmac, unlike the white concrete of his era, punctuated as it had been by holes which had grown in size with each tyre that had flopped into them.

At the end of the drive he saluted the giant oak as usual, 'Hello Quercus!' It reminded him – Sprocket was dead; it would be his job to bury the poor dog underneath this tree. Tomorrow's work. More sadness.

He turned right to head for the village. Fifteen minutes later he was under the pub sign, depicting a whistle and a feather, and pushing his way through the double doors into the fug and warmth. The noise was bracing; suddenly there was a burst of applause and cries of hurrah, as if greeting him. The place smelled of beer and cigarettes and ladies' perfume. On his left was the public bar which he could see was crowded on this Friday night with pool players and those gathered around the darts board. A wall of stout, muscled backs leaning over a circular table told him the arm-wrestling league was in action. The public bar wasn't the place for him, not on a Friday.

Instead he turned into the saloon. He nodded at faces he knew but didn't stop to talk; he was anxious to get to the bar. His scalp twitched and brought out the wrinkles on his brow in heavier relief. He ordered a whisky and a cigar.

As he went to fish out his pocket-book the realisation hit him: he'd forgotten to bring it. He wasn't wearing the same jacket. And the drink was standing poured and ready to be paid for. Embarrassment swept over him.

He continued to search, relying on a stroke of good luck – maybe there'd be a few coins stuck in the lining of his jacket or a note forgotten in the little used top pocket . . . The barman walked away to serve someone else, at least allowing him some privacy to gather his wits and think what to do. As he knew all too well a sign above the till proclaimed, 'Do not ask for credit as a refusal often offends.' He'd have to phone Patsy. Human dignity ebbed from him.

Then he saw one, two, three coins slide over the polished surface of the bar, pushed by a slim, elegant hand, although the fingernails were seamed with dirt. He turned and saw the austere, white-bearded figure of Sitten Hall's head gardener, Raymond Luther.

The latter's calmness, his steady gaze and upright bearing,

and especially the measured glide of the coins across the counter, dispelled Michael's panic. He was saved.

'Sir Michael,' Raymond greeted him.

'Mr Luther . . .'

'I'd be pleased if you'd let me buy you a drink.'

'Thank you, that's civil of you. I've forgotten my pocket-book.' Michael blushed.

'I saw that to be the case,' replied Raymond. 'Not to worry.'

The barman picked up the coins and returned with change which Raymond pocketed.

Now they were obliged to speak to each other. It might be OK, thought Michael – after all they shared several interests. He sipped the whisky and felt it nip at his tongue. 'How's everything in the garden. Lovely as usual?'

'The *garden* . . . is *fine*,' replied Raymond. Michael waited. That tone had implied something else wasn't fine, and sure enough it came out. 'But my own growth – has been stunted,' added Raymond, smiling wanly.

'Why's that?' asked Michael.

The head gardener lifted his chin. The white beard dropped from the end of it like a lady's glove. 'Because of a sudden and unexpected dislike with which I find myself afflicted,' he admitted, eyeing Sir Michael steadily to gauge his reaction.

Michael was sympathetic. He visited his own dislikes often and he knew how time-consuming they could be. 'A dislike of what?'

'My employers.' Michael felt a start of guilt before he remembered that although Raymond worked at Sitten Hall he wasn't his, Michael's, employee; he wasn't running the place any more. This was about the National Trust. 'The NT?' he asked, feeling a stir of interest. Raymond Luther nodded slowly. 'Afraid so. Or rather, the Enterprises part of it.'

There was a pause in the conversation then; and another

cheer exploded from the public bar, followed by loud clapping. Michael took a bite out of his whisky and tilted it quickly to the back of his throat. He asked, 'What on earth have they done now?' His words came out in a ponderous, overly constructed fashion, in imitation of Raymond Luther.

The other man paused for a moment then replied with certainty, 'They have forgotten my importance.' Michael's scalp moved in surprise. He himself could have spoken those exact words. Raymond went on, 'I'm a vain man and they have chosen to pretend I don't, or shouldn't, exist.' He wagged the handle of his glass from side to side. Michael felt sympathy. Sitten Hall's head gardener might as well have been describing his own predicament. He, Michael, also had the feeling the NT would prefer him not to exist. 'How odd you say that,' he said. 'How very odd.'

Raymond described how, when he'd first arrived in '86, he'd put his shoulder to the wheel, he'd worked around the clock to advance the charm and beauty of the place. Every inch of the light angling around those gardens, where its heat landed, the places it avoided or left early – morning, noon and evening – he knew. And he still loved Sitten Hall, there was no doubt. He admired the building's mute power, its heavy permanence. And he was proud of what he personally had done here; his life's work could be seen, measured, judged, enjoyed. Lately, in the last ten years, his delight had been to oversee the design and planting of games pitches – croquet, badminton, boules. He'd treated each as a place for lovers, incorporating seclusion, intimacy and beauty into the design, but with the function of the game at the centre.

Raymond's steady gaze, a gleam in it daring anyone to contradict, was trained on Michael. 'I've worked for the Trust for thirty-six years. Not all of them here at Sitten Hall, mark you,' added Raymond, 'but still, always for the National *Trust*.' He emphasised the last word to hammer home its double meaning.

Then he continued, 'The money was poor, but such work was
not to be found anywhere else on God's earth. For me, it was
a bonus to live here, on site, and to receive any money and to
be given so many long hours of my own, in paradise.'

Michael nodded. Yes. Paradise, it was.

'I live in a tied cottage on the estate, as you know,' said
Raymond. 'The Trust looked after us in fine style. They gave
me the happiest years of my life. I reared four sons, fit and
healthy. I often thought of myself and my wife and my children
as the same as any other animals on the estate: we had our
burrow, our set, our earth, whatever you like to call it. We were
untroubled by predators, just like at the beginning of *Watership
Down*. Thank God for those times. But then, along come
National Trust *Enterprises*.'

'Boo,' said Michael automatically.

'This chap came to the cottage and suggested we should pay
a little bit of rent, because it was in our own interests. He
explained that if we paid a token sum each week to the *Trust*,
a token sum mind you, we'd enjoy statutory rights as tenants.
And this would be to our advantage because when I retired, the
wife and I would be legally entitled to carry on living here.
Great, I answered. Sounds worth it, hmmm?'

'It does.'

'So the rent agent was the next gentleman with a briefcase
who visited us – two in as many months. Amazing. This rent
agent knocked on my door and mentioned a figure. X pounds
a week, I forget exactly how much. I later found out it was
the most, the *upper* limit which the Trust, technically, could
have charged for the property. There was neither sight nor
sound of the so-called "token sum".' He paused, and his
resentment showed in his taking a deeper breath. 'What they
wanted, was to bounce me out of the cottage. So they could
rent it out for holidays. But I wasn't going to let them have it.
At the same time, I mentioned my retirement which is

coming up pretty fast. Only five years away. D'you know what they said? Mm?'

'No.'

'They suggested I should contact the local council and put my name down on their housing list.' After a pause, Raymond repeated, '*The local council*? I told them to stuff it. D'you know what, there's an old horse in the Park that's retired and they're treating that horse better than me, the horse has got the run of the place while I'm shown the door.'

Raymond swallowed from his pint and shook his head. His eyes stared in disbelief. He curled a fist and brought it down slowly, repeatedly, hammering his enemies into the ground. 'I felt like burning that fucking cottage to the ground and poisoning every tree and shrub I'd ever planted. And you know what I hated most? I hated the name National Trust Enterprises.'

'Boo, *hiss*,' said Michael emphatically. He was enjoying himself enormously.

Half an hour later Raymond Luther and Sir Michael were poised over a small, round table near the window. The Whistle and Feather's Friday night custom, stretching the envelope of opening time, pressed around; as people carried drinks back and forth they often caught at the chair legs and jogged the elbows of the two men but it didn't affect them. They'd fallen into a place of their own, because on everything they touched they found agreement. It had been Michael's turn next and he'd described the negotiations with the National Trust over Sitten Hall. His family had owned the place for hundreds of years and he'd been unceremoniously dumped in the attic like an unwanted piece of furniture. He had nothing to leave to his heirs. Mattie and her future children would have to fend for themselves. He went into some detail concerning his Memorandum of Wishes. For instance, if he could have kept ownership of the contents of the house,

Sir Michael argued, he'd have been left with something to hang on to.

'Are you saying there might have been a case for your keeping ownership of the goods and chattels, gifting the house alone?' asked Raymond Luther.

'It's what others have managed to do, but with me they wouldn't allow it.'

Raymond swirled the last third of his pint of bitter in the bottom of his glass. 'Bastards.'

They'd approached from opposite directions, but had met in the middle. Each man respected the other's position. There was no hint of jealousy or reverse snobbery from Raymond Luther nor any condescension on Michael's part. Something chimed – recognition.

Their interests coincided on other dislikes, also. Michael gave his usual aggrieved account of the National Trust's weak defence against the A303 improvement. Raymond Luther surprised him by announcing, 'I was a member of Road Action.'

Michael's eyes popped; he nodded forwards in admiration. Road Action was the militant group involved in the hand-to-hand fighting against the bulldozers and security guards employed by the A303 contractors. As Raymond told him his war stories, the white hair fell from his chin in a groomed curtain, the fork at the end like the devil's own beard, and Michael felt intense, loving respect.

The volume of their voices rose to compete with the crush of people. Their eyes became glassy. They were oblivious to their surroundings as they faced each other over their neat circle of a table with heavy iron legs. The rings marked the spots from which they lifted a third round of drinks – all of them bought by Raymond Luther but that didn't matter; they had become comrades.

The last bell for chucking-out time had already rung but they ignored it. Raymond's hand touched his own chest and then moved out to grasp Michael's shoulder. Squeezing gently and indicating them both, the other man said hoarsely, 'The dispossessed!'

The dispossessed – under this title it might be the first time in his life that Michael had had a sense of belonging. Tears sprang to his eyes. He felt his loss, only the more magnified by Raymond's own.

The connections piled up between them; it made Michael dizzy. They both smoked their pipes and shook their heads. Then Raymond asked, 'How old are you?'

'Fifty-nine.'

Raymond nodded his head slowly. It seemed obvious. 'I too am fifty-nine.'

'When's your birthday?'

'The twentieth of December.'

Sir Michael frowned, straightened his back, stared in shock. He rolled once in his chair. He offered his hand and the other man, with a tentative action and a quizzical look, asking to be told, clasped it. 'Me too,' said Michael. 'We were born on the same day.'

The pub's curtains were closed, the doors locked, the die-hard few carried on drinking. Michael listened to the head gardener admit to certain small-scale criminal activities. Apparently, Raymond took plants intended for sale in Sitten Hall's garden shop to his own home, from where he ran a clandestine garden centre. Every now and again he and the warden topped up their freezers with fish poached from Sitten Hall's reach of the Avon. 'You?' asked Raymond, 'Ever . . .?' Michael shook his head.

'Maybe you ought to.' Raymond grinned. 'Why not?' Then, merry-eyed, his words slurring and interrupted by laughter, Raymond Luther proposed the wholesale sacking of Sitten Hall. 'Your contents!' he shouted. 'Let's reverse a . . . a fucking . . . great big truck . . . right up to the entrance and . . .

clear them out.' Raymond's finger drew a line several times between themselves and the door to the pub. 'Out! Completely! There won't be a stick left in the place. We'll do it together. You will be our man on the inside.'

They smiled, but moments later they began actually to discuss the details of how it could be achieved. The alarms. Night watchmen. A plan grew. Somehow it was no longer fantastic, it hardened into reality – the head gardener wanted to do it; Michael also. A nagging voice in his head advised him: it's the drink that's spawned this. In the morning the pair of them would be left feeling foolish and regretful. Don't, the voice said.

Philip, Pinky and Patsy, glasses in hand, together led Simon's mother, uncle, his sister and his cousin on an expedition down the corridor to show them the Compton Library which was never open to the public for fear precious manuscripts would be lost to thieves. Simon and Mattie in their turn started a game of billiards.

Sitting by the fire, unattended for a minute or two, Granny Banana became lonely. She picked up a magazine but couldn't make head nor tail of it. She glanced over to where her only grandchild was playing billiards. Mattie looked rather beautiful in that separate part of the room, like she was on a stage set.

Granny decided to wheel herself over and watch the game. She looked down – and found she wasn't in a wheelchair after all. Could she walk then? Or not? Whichever was the case she currently was seated in a perfectly normal armchair. She drew a breath to call to Mattie for help but stopped when she saw her embracing a stranger. Not only embracing, but kissing now. She frowned, watching the man's hands searching Mattie's body . . . it had been such fun when her own body had had the power to command that sort of attention. She was too old now, more was the pity, and it was unnerving to sit here playing gooseberry, of all things, to her own granddaughter.

The man had his hand right on Mattie's bottom – amazing cheek – and they were kissing passionately, but he didn't look very good at it. She could advise him not to treat a girl like an ice-cream cornet. This was more than she ought to have seen already; she had to get out of here. How invisible old ladies became – she'd always marvelled at that. Such a difference from when they were young, when everyone stared at them all the time. She frowned and pegged both thumbs and forefingers on the upholstered arms of the chair. She wriggled forward another few inches until she was right on the edge. She pushed hard, swayed from side to side, then leaned further forwards, her weight on her ankles. Firelight flickered on her face as she pushed, hard . . . but she couldn't stand. She sank back. Oh Gawwd, she thought, look at them, the man was lifting Mattie up in the air, she could see their tongues. They were getting carried away. Mattie's legs were wrapped around his waist and he carried her to a more private location over by the window where the moon stood in the upper quarter of the darkened sheet of glass; it looked, yes, even more like a stage set. His mouth moved to her neck, which in Granny's experience was usually the last straw. Some sort of murmuring could be heard. It was awful; a serious tryst was going on. She didn't want to spoil Mattie's chances of attracting a mate. He looked a good one. She was reminded rather of a young Captain Isles of the 11th Foot, back in . . . whenever it was . . . wartime romance of course . . . doomed . . .

She tried again – and this time she rose to her feet and stood there, swaying. Bravo! She gave herself a metaphorical clap on the back. Well done. Quite amazing. She had the idea that it might have been some time since she'd last actually done this. Obviously the cocktail of tablets prescribed for her by the Sharland House Accommodation for the Elderly was having a beneficial effect.

Next, walking? She tried one step: that went OK. The other foot . . . yes, bloody hell, now she could leave Mattie in peace. She was off.

By eleven-thirty that same evening the party had broken up and all had gone their separate ways.

Mattie reluctantly let go of Simon; she had to stay at the Hall because the wedding dress had yet to arrive and besides, it was the last meagre remnant of the tradition of virginity, that the groom shouldn't sleep with the bride on the night before the wedding. Simon went with Philip; they climbed into the Rover saloon and drove to the hotel where they had rooms waiting. Simon's mother, uncle, his sister and his cousin returned to the house of a friend where they were staying for two nights.

Mattie and her mother went upstairs to the apartment to wait for the wedding dress. Mattie was parked against the edge of the kitchen table, her arms folded, while Patsy couldn't keep still: she busied herself with changing the batteries in the old Hallmark radio set. The fluorescent lights hummed steadily. Outside was invisible; the windows showed only reflections of the kitchen. The debris from Michael's earlier attempt at scrambled egg had been cleared so the table was ready for their last ditch try at a fitting. On a corner of the table stood Patsy's sewing basket.

The dress – two or three versions of it so far – had been a disaster. Mattie had chosen to use a college friend of hers, Janine, who'd switched from Politics and Philosophy to fashion design. They'd been through the mill. If the dress were no good tonight then it would be the straw that broke the camel's back; she'd prefer to call it off. What was the point if she couldn't look her best, and her father was watching the racing? No one would go ahead under those circumstances, surely. She considered embracing her mother just to have someone hold her, but didn't. She'd seen friends hugged by their parents but it wasn't the done thing with hers.

Patsy continued pressing the batteries into the slot in the back of the radio. Each of them had to fit in a particular way.

Mattie stirred uneasily. She felt a pang of desire for Simon. She wanted his touch again – they hadn't gone all the way, down in the billiard room. She was ovulating; she was sure of it. Her desire had had a certain insistence. There was a point to it beyond entertainment. She felt it again, like a page turning in her middle.

'Car?' Mattie saw a flash of light cross the window.

They both went and cupped their hands against the glass to see, yes, a car coming down the drive. The beech trees interrupted the headlights, they switched on and off like morse code.

'Must be her.'

Mother and daughter headed for the door. They passed out of the apartment and down the west range staircase.

Mattie thought how everything – the wedding, her whole future with Simon – depended on this dress being right. She touched one hand against the central nub of the stairs and kept to the innermost path; her feet dabbed lightly, fast, finding only an inch or two of triangular stone as she expertly tripped down the precipitous slope like she'd being doing since she was a child, giddier and giddier . . .

Janine drove fast up Sitten Hall's driveway; her headlights swept the tarmac and picked out the figure of Michael who was walking home from the Whistle and Feather.

She skidded to a halt beside him and rolled down the electric window. 'Sir Michael!'

He squinted into the car, trying to identify the face cast in the light from the instrument panel. 'Janine?' He was fond of this friend of Mattie's who always treated him as if he were a teenager.

'Yes. Hop in.'

Michael's hand scrabbled for the door handle but he found nothing. The door popped open anyway and in the flood of light he caught sight of Janine straightening, having leaned across to open it for him. He was grateful to have won a peek at her cleavage. She was a favourite among his daughter's friends.

'Thank you,' he said, arriving heavily in his seat. 'A lift down the drive. More good news.' He tucked his legs in and slammed the door shut, surprised at how easy it was after the Renault 4. Janine set off with a squeak of complaint from the tyres. Her hair was cropped short and she wore tight black jeans and a T-shirt cut short to show her midriff and a glossy leather jacket. She asked, 'So what good news have you had already?'

'I suppose,' said Michael carefully, 'I've had a bloody good time in the pub.'

'What doing?'

'I formed a new secret society with my head gardener.' Strictly speaking he shouldn't have said 'my' head gardener, but old habits died hard.

'A secret society,' exclaimed Janine. 'To what end?'

'That shall remain secret,' said Michael, 'but suffice to say that blood promises were exchanged. Resolutions passed. An agenda was drawn up. A plan of action was engaged.'

Janine changed subject. 'I see. And – all well with bride and groom?'

'How would I know?'

'Well, I've brought the dress, which might help things. At last, I hear you say.'

'Not at all. More like, oh dear, how much.'

'Not nearly enough. I've lost buckets on it.'

'So have we, no doubt,' finished Michael.

They drove straight onto the apron in front of Sitten Hall;

Michael admired her lack of respect for the car park. He started to itch at the side of the door to find the handle. No luck.

Janine stepped from the car, opened the boot and took out the wedding dress which was wrapped in plastic bin-liners to keep it clean. Michael was still trying to claw his way out. 'Janine?' he called, but she'd gone; she was walking towards the drawbridge. She shouted a greeting, 'Lady Patsy, the Honourable Mattie!' The wedding dress trailed behind her like a banner. Mattie and Patsy hurried to meet her. The three women stood in a group, with the dress like an enormous insect pod, shiny in the light cast by Janine's car headlamps, as it was handed over.

'Are you going?' Patsy asked in disbelief, when it became clear that Janine was sauntering off.

'Yes,' she replied, 'Can you believe it, got to go to some bloody awful *ball* . . .'

Patsy watched in dismay as their dress designer headed back to her car, leaving them in the lurch yet again.

When Janine was behind the wheel she found Michael still in the passenger seat. 'I can't find the handle,' he complained.

'A likely excuse.' She leaned across him to pull the lever. 'You're not coming home with me, Michael, and that's that.'

Her body left an impression of strength and energy. Clambering out of the small, modern vehicle, swaying from the drink, these qualities were what Michael wished for. Maybe he could have them, if he made some effort. He remembered Patsy had bought a keep-fit bicycle some years ago; it was gathering dust somewhere. He should look it out, work himself up to peak condition. He might have to fight hand to hand with security guards, lift heavy objects, drive a container lorry.

Was this wedding dress any bloody good now or not, wondered Mattie. In the brightly lit kitchen she laid it across the table and picked at the sellotape holding the bin-liners together. Patsy waved a kitchen knife. 'Let the dog see the rabbit.' She cut it open and inside was a concoction of polyester and feathers unlike anything they'd seen before. Patsy fumbled at both ends before finding a set of four straps which might have been the top of the garment. She gathered them and lifted, holding it up for inspection. How short it was, and there seemed to be virtually no top to it – just a spider's web of these pencil-thin straps and a bit of netting. She looked at Mattie. 'Is this anything better than we saw before?'

'I'll look like a mermaid.' Mattie touched the fabric, it felt brittle and electric. Did she hate it? Not quite . . . she unzipped and stepped out of the dress she was wearing.

'Maybe it works when it's on,' said Patsy.

Mattie shrugged, and started threading her legs into it. 'It's not very like the drawings she gave us,' she commented.

'Thank the Lord.'

Mattie wriggled into the bottom half of the dress. It had a self-contained bodice, so she unclipped her bra, dropped it off the ends of her arms. She told herself to give Janine a chance. Then she lifted her breasts into the thing and tried to work out the straps.

At that point they heard the dull thud of the door into the apartment closing followed by Michael's footsteps.

Mother and daughter looked at each other. Patsy went to the door, taking a kitchen chair with her as she went. She opened the door a fraction and called out, 'We're in here, Michael, but Mattie's not decent!' and then shut it again. She propped the chair under the handle.

'What?' came his voice, and more footsteps. The door handle turned. Both women stopped dead, watching the chair effectively stopping him. 'I'm not decent!' repeated Mattie. She folded her arms across her chest.

There was a pause. They could hear him breathing. 'Just wanted to thank my daughter,' he said.

'Thank me what for?'

'For letting me off the aisle thing. Your man told me. Many thanks.'

The women could see the door handle twitching as he held onto it – he was probably trying to stay upright, thought Patsy. 'Are you drunk Michael?' she asked.

'I do need another bottle of whisky,' came Michael's voice. 'The decanter's leaked.'

'You've had enough.'

'Go away Dad!' called Mattie. 'I'm trying my dress on.'

'Best give him what he wants,' Patsy said, half to herself and half to Mattie. She ducked to the cupboard and pulled a fresh bottle of Bells from a box intended for tomorrow. 'I'll just park him in his spot, then he won't bother us.' She moved the chair out of the way. 'You see if you can fit into that thing.'

Michael's voice came again, muffled. 'Anyone else want a nightcap?'

'Dad,' groaned Mattie.

Patsy squeezed through the door, shutting it behind her. She took her husband and walked him to the sitting room. He mumbled, 'Very kind, much appreciated,' and followed the whisky like a dog follows its dish.

'You've made your daughter unhappy, Michael. She thinks none of this means anything to you. She's getting married for heaven's sake. It won't happen again.'

'Won't happen again? Someone should tell her the statistics.'

'What?'

'Two out of three marriages end in divorce . . .'

'Divorce isn't always a bad thing,' interrupted Patsy. 'Sometimes marriage can end gracefully and just because love sometimes – often – doesn't last for ever is no reason to scrap it altogether.' She pushed him into his chair, took a glass from the sideboard and poured him a finger.

'Look at my own record,' went on Michael. 'Three wives, three divorces, one hundred per cent ballsup. That's her inheritance.' He made the sound of an explosion and sent his hands up like fireworks.

'Could drink have anything to do with this . . . this tirade, d'you think?'

Michael waved in annoyance. 'Boo hoo, I've had some alcohol.'

'What did you say?'

He looked at her blankly. 'Hmmm?'

'What did you say just then?'

'You mean, boo hoo I've had some alcohol?'

Suddenly her mad old husband with his square, blustery face, the springy hair on the crown that moved as though it had a life of its own, his old-fashioned clothes and his dishevelled attitude, was funny. Patsy couldn't help it – and hearing herself laugh made it worse, it was difficult to stop.

Michael stared in consternation. 'What?' His wife number three looked awful, her false teeth so obviously made out of white plastic, tall as anything, ankles thicker than when they were first married, wrinkly old eyes . . .

Patsy blinked away tears and another two, three moments passed when – vague and out of practice as they were – they loved each other like in the old days. It seemed miraculous.

The spell broke. She'd be an old woman before another moment came along like the one they'd just enjoyed. He struggled to his feet, leaned over to press the on/off button. 'Stuck on the one damn channel, still,' he said, half to himself.

Wretched man, she thought. What could he possibly want to watch at this hour?

Normality returned; Patsy recovered her frustration. She was suddenly *bored* with Michael. That was *it*, she agreed with herself – bored – except that implied a slow, dull pain whereas her boredom with him, at this moment, was a virulent and fierce thing, so intense as to have her heart beating hard enough to burst. She'd spent twenty-seven years with this man and all she felt like doing now was boxing his ears, out of sheer, utter, excruciating . . .

Well, there was no point in hanging around. She had important things to do.

She went back to the kitchen. What sight would greet her eyes?

Mattie was standing there, looking ghastly, her torso barely constrained in the net-and-feather assembly. The hem at the front didn't reach as far as the knee and had a fur trim. It was a wrap-around skirt, ready to separate at the slightest provocation. On the kittenish Janine it would probably have looked devastating; on big-boned Mattie it looked ridiculous. Mattie's expression didn't help – abject misery. Patsy would have been ready to say she liked it – except Mattie's boobs were going to jump out when there was dancing – but she could only take her cue from Mattie herself, who looked beaten, depressed. 'Oh dear, I am sorry Mattie. You don't like it.'

Mattie saw herself in the reflection of the kitchen window – it looked like a clothes hanger had been dipped in glue and dragged through a dressing-up box. She couldn't trust herself to speak; she could only shake her head, mute.

Patsy agreed. 'I know. Don't say *anything*. The thought of actual people, staring. Men et cetera. Simon . . .'

'I hate it!' The misery was drawn heavily on Mattie's face. This was her punishment for being bourgeois, for wanting a hand-made dress. 'All this . . . is *telling* me not to get married.'

'We could go into town tomorrow, early, and just buy something . . .'

'It's no good. I don't want to get married any more, I just want to die.'

'Darling, everyone's coming, it's too late.'

'It doesn't bloody matter! We can just say it's my funeral.'

'Mattie – you'd spend the whole day talking about why you'd changed your mind.'

'*I* won't be there. I'll be slitting my wrists in the bloody bath! Mum, I'm not getting married.'

'Sweetheart . . .'

'Don't you see,' went on Mattie in a strangled whisper, 'I'm not getting married, am I, really? I can't.' She stared madly, her face was twisted. 'The dress won't let me.'

The Garden House Hotel was two miles from Sitten Hall – its proximity meant that all tonight's bookings were those of guests attending the wedding. Although it was small it was run as a proper, grown-up establishment, with a reception desk, a lounge for visitors, an honesty bar, and room service during civilised hours.

Philip and Simon walked into the foyer just fifteen minutes before the eleven-thirty deadline. Philip dingled the bell which stood on the reception desk. 'I always stay here since Michael sold up, it's a good place.'

'Yes, seems so.'

'Seen your room?'

'Yes, I have,' replied Simon.

'Is it all right?'

'It's in the modern extension bit at the back, but it's fine, it's comfortable.'

There was no response to the bell so they had to continue in one another's company. Philip stood as he had been taught at prep school – knees locked, one hand dug in his trouser pocket. Simon leaned against the counter. Philip wasn't unduly worried at the silence. He had plenty of self-confidence to tide him over. There was money in his bank accounts, his share portfolio was right as rain. Arm Holdings had given him three hundred per cent last year, internet companies were like a firework display lighting up the market. SMG had just bought Ginger Evans – his stock was rising. The new millennium was just around the corner; he could throw away these few moments and not even have to think about it. Finally he said, 'I like climbing into a strange bed.'

Simon didn't know if there was any innuendo attached to this. 'Well, um . . .'

'No no,' interrupted Philip, and chuckled, 'I mean, because it reminds me of school, peeling back the clean sheets. Everything spick and span. Rather like being in a dorm, but on your own.'

'Ah. I was a day boy.'

'A day bug?'

'Afraid so.'

The proprietor of the hotel appeared, tying his dressing gown, shaking water from his long curly hair. 'Sorry, I was in the shower.'

'No, we're sorry.'

'Don't be, part of the job, absolutely cool and happy about it.' He looked at the two guests – one tall and young and with a halo of tight brown curls, the other shorter, old and grey haired. It was easy to guess which of them was the more likely to be married tomorrow. He unlocked the glass-fronted cabinet, unhooked their keys. 'Anyway, that's nice to hear.' Simon and Philip looked at each other, uncomprehending. Philip asked, 'What is?'

'Your describing this as a good place.' The proprietor gave them their keys and fastened the cabinet shut.

'Oh, I see, yes.'

'Day bug eh?' said the proprietor, winking at Simon. 'Not sure we should be letting you in.' He grinned and flipped up the counter, ready to walk through.

Simon laughed, 'Fair enough.'

'D'you need to bolster your nerves for tomorrow? If so, you

can have an after-hours whisky or something, in the lounge? Help yourself from the honesty bar if you want a cheaper brand, or I can fetch you a malt if you want.'

Philip and Simon agreed that two malt whiskies were a good idea. They liked the proprietor, wanted to please him, and they both felt they ought to get to know one another better – Philip's farm wasn't far from where Simon and Mattie lived in Bristol, and he didn't have children of his own.

The proprietor reached behind him into his cubby hole and took out two plastic-covered morning suits. 'Delivery.' He walked them through the hatch and into the lounge where he draped them over the back of an armchair

'Ah yes,' said Philip, following him. The proprietor went back to fetch two matching hat boxes, resting them on the cushion of the same armchair. 'Back shortly with the malts.'

'Thank you,' said Philip. He leaned over to read a label attached to one of the suits. 'Simon d'Ange . . .' – he struggled with the pronunciation. Simon helped him, 'D'Angibau. It comes from my Huguenot ancestors.'

'OK, this is yours.' Philip lifted the suit and laid it down separately. 'D'Angibau. A very romantic name. Like a musketeer.'

'Thank you.'

'That's you as well,' added Philip, holding out a hat box.

A minute later the proprietor came back carrying the malt whiskies on a tray. Then he produced a key on an oversized, triangular fob. 'Can I give you the key for Lady Edith?'

'Granny?' asked Philip.

'Only I'm off to bed soon. Can you see her in safely?'

'She's staying up at the Hall.'

The proprietor was careful not to appear to know better. 'Oh. Well, there's a reservation in her name, is the only thing. Someone thinks she's staying here.'

'I see.'

All three men looked at each other. The proprietor saw the

quick answer. 'Shall I make a call, to check? Will someone be up, still?'

'Would you mind?' asked Philip.

'Not at all. I've got the number. Back in a tick.'

Simon and Philip were left with this new anxiety about Granny. They had to say or do something while they were waiting so they sipped their whiskies and Philip took the lid off his hat box, peeled back the tissue paper. He lifted out his hat. It slid easily over his crown and sat too low, almost on his ears. At the same time, Simon followed suit and tried his but it was too small: it perched on his tight curls. He slanted it back, then forwards.

'Oh,' said Philip, 'd'you think — is it going to stay on?'

Simon took it off and consulted the label inside. 'It's not the right size.' He tried again but the hat looked daft; it sat on his head like an apple.

'Too small,' said Philip.

'Perhaps I've got yours and you've got mine.'

'Oh, d'you think?' Philip lifted off his own hat. 'What's your head size?'

'Seven and a half.'

'You're right,' confirmed Philip. They swapped hats.

'Better,' said Simon.

The proprietor clipped his hands to the doorframe and leaned in. 'Lady Gough says that Granny should be here, and you say she should be there. Which begs a question.' His eyebrows rose.

Patsy banged the phone down hard on the receiver. She'd been a trifle curt with the hotel, and hoped she hadn't caused offence. Too much wine had made her cross. Of course Granny was there. The chair had been empty. Philip had taken her.

As she walked back to the kitchen she paused for a moment outside Mattie's bedroom. She could hear her cursing and sniffing, rummaging – looking through her old frocks maybe? She might as well not bother, just admit they'd have to take an early morning trip into Salisbury to find something. Monsoon had lovely dresses. More expense. She had a good mind to give Janine the bill. The sound of Mattie's voice came through the door: she was talking to someone on the mobile. Patsy didn't want to eavesdrop so she tapped lightly on Mattie's door. 'Mats?'

'Come in.'

Patsy pushed the door open. 'You OK darling?'

'I'm going to drive over and see Simon.'

'Shouldn't the bride *not* see . . .'

Mattie interrupted, 'Normally, I know, but this isn't normal. I have to see him.'

'Well, then take my car.'

'I'm not insured.'

'You can't take the Renault.'

'I'll be all right.'

'Can't Simon come here?'

'We want to be private. It's fine Ma, don't fuss.'

'All right. Darling, be careful.'

'I will.'

'See you tomorrow bright and early, and we'll go into Salisbury.'

'Yes. Thanks for everything, Ma.'

Patsy shut the door and moved on down the corridor. In the kitchen Michael donned his apron and announced he was going to do the washing-up – it was his nightly contribution to the household chores. Patsy tried to stop him. She wanted to go to bed. He persisted – he was going to do it, the same as always, which meant that Patsy felt she had to stay and dry. While she waited for the first dishes to reach the draining board she cleared up the plastic and paper from the earlier dress fitting. They could hope never to see this dress again. She was tempted to throw it away but probably she ought to return it to Janine and, what's more, tell her about Mattie crying and rampaging in her bedroom – ugly, unhappy events threatening the entire wedding . . . Patsy flitted in and out of the terror that it actually, really might *not* happen if Mattie was unhappy. Maybe if she went to bed she might wake up and find everything all right. If only Michael wasn't . . . 'Michael?' she asked sharply.

'Mmm?'

'Is there any point in doing these measly few dishes?'

'There is indeed. It means they'll be done.'

Self-righteous prig, she thought. Aggressive thoughts bubbled to the surface; she hadn't the power to quell them. She wished she hadn't had quite so much to drink. Her annoyance with him went back to an earlier comment he'd made; it had rankled with her. 'And Michael?'

'Mmm?'

'D'you remember, you said three marriages and three divorces, one hundred per cent fuckup?'

'Did I? Ballsup, I think I said.'

'Whatever. But I thought it was careless.'

'Ahh.'

'What if Mattie had been listening.'

'Mmm.'

'Michael, can I ask a favour?'

'Is there something I have in my gift?'

'Yes, there is.'

'What?' He steadily pushed the brush in and out of the cut-glass tumbler he'd earlier drunk from – the whisky, the laugh with Patsy, seemed a distant memory.

Patsy said tightly, 'I don't mind, in principle, if we tell Mattie that we are actually, technically divorced – that is, I don't mind if we tell her sometime within the next year or two. But I do mind, very much, if it slips out now, on the day she's getting married herself.'

Michael finished the glass and turned on the hot tap, adding more washing-up liquid and starting on the saucepan. The sudsy water blurred in front of him, then cleared back into focus. Would it be another of those times when he'd drunk so much, and talked so much, that he wouldn't be able to sleep? Still, he could lie down in a stupor and watch the ceiling spin around.

'Right you are,' said Michael. His wife number three was banging on; he recognised that insistent, repetitive tone. It meant bad weather in the marital climate. He wished she'd go to bed and leave him in peace. But Patsy was irritated. Michael was deliberately not taking any notice of what she was saying. Didn't he realise that she was dying to go to bed? She snatched up the cloth and began drying the few plates which had appeared on the draining board.

'Of course, darling.'

'So let's not allow it to slip out, if that's all right?'

For a moment he didn't follow, then he realised she was back to talking about their divorce. 'Darling, whatever you say. We can tell Mattie we're divorced . . . now . . . or in the future . . . or never at all. Just say when. I leave it to you. I'll be the villain shall I, or is it your turn?'

Patsy grew angry. Their divorce had hurt her badly yet he was inferring it was like a set-piece in a tired old stage play – plus the cloth was damp and she couldn't make a good job of drying. 'Michael, can't you sort of decide either way what you think about the whole thing? This pretence at not caring, I mean, it's maddening . . .'

'What d'you mean, what should I think?' asked Michael, but Patsy rolled over the top of his question. 'At least then,' she said, 'our relationship would be something you either believed in, or not, and we'd have a more or less clear idea of the *right* reason for it all having gone wrong.'

Michael couldn't make head nor tail of that. He said, in the same resigned tone, 'I agree.'

He wasn't listening again; it made Patsy furious. 'What?'

'Whatever you suggest.'

Patsy stopped drying-up. Her husband was dribbling out the same condescending little phrases as he had done countless times before and in precisely the same tone.

'As you like darling,' soothed Michael.

She was motionless, holding the plate in her hands. She couldn't say if she was more angry with the plate for not being properly dry or with her husband for not listening or with Janine's useless dress . . .

Michael continued his ironical list of platitudes. 'Exactly as you wish.'

Abruptly Patsy lifted the plate and threw it down – crash – on the floor. Michael flinched and uttered a brief, quiet exclamation, 'Bloody hell Pats.' He leaned against the edge of the sink, wondering if she was going to hit him.

A moment later he braced his shoulders, stood straight and carried on. Best to say nothing; he didn't want to prod the beast further. He rinsed the saucepan with clean water and placed it on the draining board.

'Michael!' demanded Patsy.

'Yes darling, all right darling.' A throbbing started in his head. Her voice was too loud.

'What's all right? Nothing's all right!'

'Whatever you say.'

Patsy fumbled for a second plate, grasped it and threw that one down as well. Michael, just as determinedly, carried on. There was no washing-up left so he cleaned the sides of the sink. He was damned if he was going to be driven away. Patsy picked up the saucepan. It was made of cast iron. 'Why can't you . . .' Michael eyed the saucepan. His voice broke. 'I'm not sure I remember, even, if we actually did get divorced or not,' he said hoarsely, 'but you seem sure about it, so let's say we did, and that I'm very, very sorry.' Patsy waited . . . she hefted the saucepan, won a better grip on the handle. But his admission had been so full of despair. A wave of guilt overtook her; she wilted visibly and started trembling. 'Is that really true, you can't remember . . .' She put the saucepan down.

'Did we go all the way?' asked Michael. Patsy sat in a chair, weary. It was too much up and down altogether. She must have drunk a lot more than she'd thought. What on earth was going on?

At that moment they heard a voice call, 'Hello?'

Philip was the only one who had a key. What could he want? She swallowed her sobs and dabbed the drying-up cloth against her eyes. 'Philip, is that you?' Her voice was cracked.

'Yes, it's all right, it's only me,' came the reply. 'I would have called first but your phone was off the hook.'

'Come on up,' called Patsy. She fought hard to put on a cheerful face but anyone could see there'd been a row; she couldn't pretend.

Philip stood in the doorway. 'Ah . . .'

Facing away from him, Patsy made as if to mend her hair so it looked like she had a reason not to turn around . . . this damn hair, it was ridiculous. Plus she had to pick up the broken pieces of crockery. She said, 'Philip, if you can force Michael to behave like an ordinary human being then please try, because I can't seem to make any headway.'

It was obviously a bad moment but Philip couldn't leave them to it. This was urgent. 'It looks like there's been . . .'

Michael walked out, his feet crunching on the fragments of china. 'Going to start a new life!' he said as he went past.

Philip ignored his brother's exit. He carried on, 'Sorry, but have you got Granny, is why I came back.'

Patsy replied, 'Granny? No. You have, at the hotel, I said on the phone.'

'She's not there. And I thought she was meant to be with you, here in the Hall.'

'She's *not* at the hotel? You didn't take her with you?'

'No. She said she was staying here.'

They heard the door to the apartment slam – Michael had run off, which was the least of their concerns. There was a moment's silence. 'I assumed you'd got her,' said Patsy.

Unknown to either of them, Mattie had crossed with Philip on the road between Sitten Hall and the hotel: she was on her way to join Simon.

She had got used to driving her father's Renault. She'd twisted the key in the door lock: there was no sense it was doing any work but it had opened after a determined tug. She'd ducked into the footwell to make sure the clutch pedal was properly on, then climbed in. A pair of cushions was lost in the split front seats and she'd squirmed from side to side to try and find a comfortable position.

Two of the car's cylinders stuttered into life; after some moments the other two joined in and she could move off. She pulled the dash-mounted gear into second and revved the engine, letting the clutch in slowly and keeping the plates slipping for some distance. To avoid using first gear was a necessary tactic: if she could navigate Sitten Hall's driveway in third, drop to second to pull onto the main road, and up to third again to reach the village then she wouldn't have to stop the car en route.

It occurred to Mattie, as she drove along, that a marriage would be like this car journey, wouldn't it, break down, stop, mend it, carry on, maybe a swoop downhill and a thrilling corner, then a slow uphill, then break down, stop, fix it . . . Regular servicing was the key. She smiled at the thought.

It was midnight, she saw by the diode on the Renault's dash. The car droned along easily; the beech trees flashed by. The broken seat quickly set up a disabling cramp in her right hip and the gear stick vibrated in her hand. She upped to third and determined to stay there.

An oncoming vehicle caught Mattie in its glare. She lifted a hand to shade her eyes and cried anxiously, 'Dip, you fucker, dip!' She had no clue where the road ahead lay; all she could do was aim a touch to the left of the dazzling white circles coming towards her and hope for the best. She slowed dramatically, moving her foot across to the brake and pumping it twice. The tone of the Renault's engine plummeted. There was a noise from the front right-hand damper like a row of rabbits being run over.

The danger was past and she was left, blinking, as her foot moved back to the accelerator pedal and pushed it flat to the floor. The carburettor gave a hollow sigh, gasped for air. The transmission dragged on the underpowered engine. Her whole marriage was at stake! A deeper, more resounding vibration shook the vehicle. She'd lost too much speed to sail up the slight incline and was forced to drop back to second gear. With mournful reliability the clutch pedal disappeared from under her foot – *twang*! – and became a useless elbow of metal adrift on the floor.

Stop and mend.

Now she would be killed in a road accident. Angrily she punished the brake pedal, pumping hard. The outer rim of her shoe caught the accelerator so she was fighting a confusing, stop-go battle while wrestling to pull out of gear. Finally she stalled.

A light summer rain sounded like a plastic bag rustling against the roof of the car. Mattie switched on the emergency flashers and doused the headlights to save the battery. She bashed the steering wheel three times. This wedding was driving her insane! Why couldn't she and Simon just fuck each other and have children? A flush of blood suffused her face and she struck out with her elbows, hurting only herself.

Quickly she got out, looked carefully in each direction and took a minute to listen hard; nothing was coming. She kneeled at the sill, scrabbled on the floor of the vehicle and tried to fix the pedal as quickly as she could. She prayed that no drunken driver would swipe the Renault's door off and crush her . . . urgency numbed her fingers and the feeble glow from the Renault's interior light hardly reached. Nevertheless, because she'd done it often before, she completed the task.

'Now,' she shouted, admonishing the car, 'stay fucking on!' She kicked the rear panel and followed up with her knee, felt the car's skin pop inwards. 'Make it all the way to the hotel,' she commanded.

She restarted the engine and drove on.

The Garden House Hotel was in pitch darkness, as was the pub next door. On the other side of the road the river slid by, a mature trout stream crossed by a hump-backed bridge. Half of the hotel's land was on this far side of the road, next to the river, while the other half – and the car park – was next to the building itself.

Mattie guiltily coasted into the car park and pulled up next to Simon's red MG, a welcome friend.

She switched on the interior light and leaned across to flip down the vanity mirror. She looked dreadful – the smeared eye make-up had turned her into a ghoul. Never mind. Everything tonight was tinged with an extravagant colour. She texted Simon to say she'd arrived, please to let her in.

Patsy and Philip walked smartly along, cutting through the top floor of the deserted mediaeval castle, heading for the east

range. Their path was illuminated only by the yellow 'Exit'
signs. The colours were leached from the walls and the narrow
strip of crimson carpet showed up as grey-green. It gave their
features a sickly pallor. Patsy was scared of the mixture of
darkness cut with moonlight because at this time of night the
ghosts of Sitten Hall could be felt in the static-laden air. How
many haunted this house – countless dead, there must be.
Maybe Banana had joined them.

Patsy said cheerfully, 'It's a blip, Granny's just slipped between
pillar and post . . .' Wisps of hair had escaped; it gave her a
bedraggled look. She dabbed a wrist against her forehead. That
was an awful row she'd just had with her husband, but private
concerns had to be put aside. She tried to soothe Philip's guilt.
'Not to worry too much, she can't fly, after all.'

They went to the billiard room first; it was the obvious place
to start. Both the armchair and the wheelchair remained obstinately empty.

'She must have either walked off or we're dealing with . . .'

'Walked?' interrupted Patsy. 'She hasn't walked for months.'

'Must have, unless persons unknown took her away.'

The embers of the fire were dying slowly behind the fire
guard. Patsy flipped the big old bakelite switch and the billiard
table came to life, an oblong of bright green set in the obscurity of that part of the room. Philip moved here and there,
checking the spots where his mother might have fallen. Patsy
waited.

No joy.

They stared at the armchair as if it might give up some clue
as to her whereabouts. Philip remembered the question she'd
asked when they'd lifted her over here; she'd asked if it was bed
time. 'D'you think she's gone to her room upstairs, here at the
Hall?'

'Would she really have managed that all by herself?'

'She wouldn't have made it up the stairs.'

'We should check the route, though, shouldn't we?'

There were two possible ways to reach the King's Chamber. She might have headed for the gatehouse, or maybe she thought she was able to climb the newel here in the east range and make her way across, two floors up. Either way, they had to reckon on finding her in a crumpled heap somewhere.

They decided to split up and cover both routes. They'd meet at the bedroom door and if one of them didn't turn up, that person would have found her, obviously, whereupon the other should return that way and together they'd deal with whatever medical situation confronted them. Patsy remembered her nurse's training. Was it five pushes on the chest for every two breaths in the mouth, or five breaths in the mouth for two pushes on the chest? Either way . . . she traipsed up the stairs in the gatehouse, expecting at every turn to find the old lady sprawled in front of her.

As it turned out she was the first to arrive outside the King's Chamber, where she waited, out of breath, for a moment. She was about to follow Philip's route back when he suddenly appeared.

'Find anything?'

'No.'

All that was left, then, was to believe that Granny had actually made it, in which case she would be right here, in her old bedroom.

Patsy pushed the door and it drifted open. Philip went in first; it was dark. Behind him Patsy called, 'Granny?' Her voice sounded unnaturally loud. There came the answer, 'I can't find my overnight bag.' Patsy's heart beat wildly. 'Granny, you're there!' She asked Philip, 'D'you remember where the switch is?'

'Hold on,' came Philip's voice; she waited for the click.

The light came on to reveal Granny Banana perched on the side of the bed, knees vulgarly set apart, perfectly all right. The red velvet rope was on the ground, the stanchions knocked awry. She looked Patsy in the eye and said, 'I need my toothbrush.'

Michael's head throbbed in exact time with each thud of his heel on the hard tarmac drive, but he wasn't going to stop walking, not ever. Who cared where he would end up?

He left the safety of the floodlit castle walls and took to the driveway – for the third time this evening he was going to walk its fresh, even surface in the dark. Yet now he did it with some purpose and a sense of vengeance. He'd turn left or right. He'd brazenly walk on roundabouts like a lunatic and blindly take any exit. He'd end up in Penzance or in London, Southampton or John O' Groats, or dead in a ditch beside the A303. Any of these eventualities would do as long he was far, far away from wife number three! He held his hand to his head. He'd had too much to drink. Stupid man. He swore. Patsy, also, had had too much. He imagined hiring a team of men to remove her and all her effects forthwith. Only then might he return.

He reached the end of the drive. 'Quercus!' he greeted the old oak automatically but with a touch of bitterness. He envied the tree its calm, self-contained life. No one ever moved Quercus from *his* armchair, so to speak. The giant oak was never shouted at, nor expected to perform duties it didn't care to. It was only ever admired, and occasionally patted and stroked. He remembered again – Sprocket, dead in a bag in the back of Pinky's car.

Left or right? He wished he had a coin to toss. He turned right towards the village, mostly out of habit but also a thought prompted him: would the lock-in at the Whistle and Feather still be going on?

He walked steadfastly, with hardly a wobble. A car or two passed him and he knew he would be almost invisible in such dark clothes in the middle of the night. He steeled his nerves and kept going all the way to Woodford, to the pub. It looked closed, of course. The windows, previously so cheery and warm, the glass polished and the little orange lights inviting custom, were now as dark as night. The curtains were drawn. The pub wore the face of someone fast asleep. However, it could be deceptive: they used the tap room if it got late. He was about to knock but then thought first to peer through the windows. He stepped across the border, trying hard not to damage any plants. He leaned on the sill and looked for a crack in the seam between the curtains. There was no glimmer of light that he could see. He stepped back again. Everyone's gone home, he thought, he shouldn't disturb the landlord.

He stood in the road, all alone, in the village which his ancestors had once owned every stick of. They used to wind up this place and set it going as if it were a clockwork toy.

What should he do next? He refused to go home or even call by phone. Let Patsy really *worry* about what had happened to him! He'd be the new Lord Lucan – just disappear. She would be arrested for his murder. Good. He turned around a couple of times, staring hard into the darkness. Someone ought to start up a battered husband's refuge somewhere.

Should he knock up Pinky? No. He started walking towards Amesbury just for the sake of keeping warm. One foot went in front of the other. The throbbing returned. He would keep going, to London even; he'd head into the West End. He'd wind up in a vice den in the arms of a young exotic dancer. She'd take him back to her cramped room and . . .

For some reason, he noticed, he'd given the young woman a face very similar to Philip's housekeeper, Natalia.

Granny Banana was perfectly upright and alert. She hadn't been out of a wheelchair for months, yet now she walked easily between Philip and Patsy as they found their way down through the Hall. They applauded the drugs regime at Sharland House: undoubtedly it was the medication which had caused such a dramatic improvement. She was able to walk with barely a guiding hand on the stairs; she went down as gracefully as in former years, pointing each delicate, stick-thin ankle while she listed her old boyfriends. 'Johnny Lightfoot used to carry a whip, you know. He didn't distinguish much between one type of riding and another.'

Downstairs, Patsy waited with Granny on the drawbridge while Philip trotted to the car park to fetch the Rover. They helped Banana into the front seat and Philip headed off, slowly.

'Where's my bag? In the boot?' she asked her younger son.

'It's waiting for you at the hotel, Mother.' Philip followed Mattie's route exactly but covered the ground faster; his vehicle was only two years old. The light rain which had fallen earlier had left him with a smeared windscreen and he fiddled with the stalk to eject the cleaning fluid. In the passenger seat Granny flinched when the alcohol-and-water mix hit the glass as though it were aimed at her personally.

He tried to avoid looking at the white lines reflected in the glare of his headlights; they looped towards him in the middle of the road and, despite his attempt to avoid their hypnotic effect, they blurred and separated into two lines. One more corner and they were there . . .

Granny was being increasingly vulgar. 'D'you know he had a nickname? Black Balls. Because his balls really were black, not just the hair but the skin, for some reason, a touch of the tar brush maybe.'

'Really Mother, is that true?' He coasted into the village, on tickover almost, and dipped his headlights to cause the least disturbance. He inched the Rover into the Garden House's car park and killed the engine. 'Are we here?' asked Granny.

'We are, exactly that. Here.' Philip went around to the passenger side and helped Banana out of her seat. He guided her through the wooden gate and across the paved area to the glass front door.

'We called him Johnny Lightfoot,' said Granny, 'because of the way he creepy-weepied around the corridors.'

'I see.' Philip let them in and double locked the front door as he'd been instructed to do. They crossed the darkened lobby. 'Nearly there. Last leg,' he said. They turned right into the hotel's downstairs back extension and stopped outside Granny's customary quarters at the hotel, room number four, chosen for its ground floor location to allow for wheelchair access. He opened the door and ushered her in.

'The thing about Captain Isles of course,' she said, 'was that he never settled down, ever. All that talk about marriage and he died a bachelor.' She chuckled and began to murmur a little song. Philip switched on the bedside light and showed Granny her overnight bag. 'There it is, Banana old thing, d'you see?' He knelt to help her out of her shoes. He considered for a moment undressing her but with all the excitements he decided just to put her straight to bed. He folded back the covers while she went to the bathroom. He waited patiently, listening to the noise of the cistern. 'Come on Mother. In you get. Well past bed time. Well done for walking so far. It really is incredible.'

'The doctors at Sharland House,' said Banana proudly, 'have done wonders.'

'We'll soon have you dancing again.'

'Remember Doctor McTaggart? He was too quick to reach for the bottle to be much use in bed, you know.' Granny organised herself and lay down. Philip was only half listening. 'And with doctors,' went on Granny, 'of course you never know quite where their hands have been . . .'

Philip kissed her forehead and tucked the summer-weight duvet around her, then took the spare pillow from the other side of the double bed to bolster the edge and prevent her from inadvertently rolling out.

'Dennis Jowell,' said Granny, 'you know, the son of the grocery magnate who bought Chester House – he tried to lick my bottom.' She scowled. 'Imagine! I don't know if he knew what he was doing, or not, but Captain Isles . . .' She held up her fingers, spread out. 'Six out of ten, no, eight out of ten for Captain Isles.'

'Jolly good,' said Philip. 'I'll come and find you in the morning, Mother. You know what number to ring if you need me in the middle of the night.'

'Eight, as usual.'

'That's it.'

'Thank you Philip. You're a good son to me.'

Philip went to his room and slowly performed the usual ablutions, while half expecting to be summoned for more help. It was extraordinary how alert his mother was, suddenly.

He knotted and buttoned his pyjamas and climbed into bed. He lay on his back and pictured his mother's death, which would happen eventually. And then his own, also inevitable demise. He wondered what the vicar would say, how would he himself be described, on being consigned by Pinky, or whomever, to the cold earth? Pinky would draw breath and announce, 'Philip Gough . . . was the proud owner of a Rover motor car.'

His morale shrank. His life was made up of precious little. He'd managed to fasten his shirt cuffs and tie his shoelaces day after day, that was all. It had been a purposeless existence. What effect had he had on anyone? He was a member of the Wiltonian Club, though, and few managed to join. The conversations he'd had with other members – that had been a privilege – and the meals he'd enjoyed there. The colleagues he'd worked with. Perhaps there could be a memorial service organised by the club, when it came to his time to go. He imagined his own grave with him lying in it, just like this, on his back looking up, the mouth of the grave surrounded by other sturdy, established club members, plus his Polish house-keeper Natalia looking down on him. He could picture her easily, that timid glance she gave, the soft pad of her flat shoes, the crescent shape of her calf muscles. He imagined her on the phone. His brother Michael was calling to offer her extra chores. She came to ask him, could she go and stay at Sitten Hall for a week . . .

Who was he kidding? The church would be empty at his funeral except for Patsy and Michael, should he outlive them. The service would echo in the cavernous space. He saw his coffin lying on the trestles. No flowers. Pinky, bravely carrying on . . .

Michael reached the Millstream Cross roundabout on the A303. Here was exactly what he needed – the twenty-four hour Little Chef. It would provide a coffee and a bite to eat, keep him going. As he pushed through the doors he was harshly lit by the fluorescents – in this unkind light every thread of his jacket could be seen unravelling; his skin looked corrugated with age and blistered by alcohol. He took a seat and waited for service. Immediately the pain in his hips eased. His blister became less hot and insistent.

From his table he could see the sodium glow hanging over the roundabout. At this time of night – around one-thirty – there were mostly lorries using the road. The orange streetlights cast them all in a similar khaki colour and their engine tones made an identical pattern of noise: the over-run as they slowed for the roundabout, the surge of confidence as the drivers took their cue, followed by the acceleration and, finally, the bite of the hill on the other side. Occasionally a car followed the same pattern but more nimbly.

The headache beat in Michael's crown. Should he leave home for real, no joke? He must – right now – add up all the

pros and cons. The waitress came; he ordered coffee and mini-
doughnuts and also asked her if she might bring a pen and
some paper. She only had the stuff they gave to children so
Michael found himself with a red wax crayon and the back of
a printed cartoon.

He made two columns, 'for' and 'against'.

He wrote down 'no more Patsy' under the 'for' column.
'Live somewhere new,' he added. Then, 'Freedom.' A minute
later he wrote, 'New young wife?' Then he crossed out 'wife'
and put 'girl friend'. If he didn't actually reach London he
might answer one of those adverts for Polish women in the
back of *Private Eye*.

Under the 'against' column he wrote, 'Loneliness. Homeless.
Bad food.' And what about money, he wondered. He wasn't
sure how much they spent every week, or where their income
came from, but he did know that Patsy found most of it. He'd
be left with nothing. Did he have a state pension? Christ, his
great, big, long-winded family, cutting a swathe through the
empire, bringing home untold riches and so on, reduced to this
poor specimen, himself, in a late-night Little Chef, contemplating the few coins available from government handouts . . .
history swept its heavy cloak around his shoulders. So he added
next, 'Poverty' and then, because he'd be reduced to stealing in
order to survive, he wrote in capital letters, 'PRISON'. He was
burning up with grief and self-pity.

His snack arrived. He dipped the doughnuts and carried on.
He drew boxes around the word 'poverty' in red crayon. Not
necessarily, he thought, not if he teamed up with Raymond
Luther and emptied Sitten Hall of its contents. There was
enough money in those knick-knacks to allow him to move to
a foreign climate, start a new life in Spain or the Bahamas, yet
he knew the conversation with the head gardener had been just
a distraction. He would never have the courage to pull that
off . . . They'd both been drunk. All the bravado and vigour

they'd felt had been just the alcohol talking. He was hardly a man of action after all; he had proof enough of that.

He swallowed. The doughnut stuck in his throat.

The columns listing 'pros' and 'cons' stared up at him. Should he or shouldn't he actually leave Patsy – given they'd been divorced for such an age?

There might be glory – a new life, young Polish girl on his arm, driving him around in a fast little car. Or there might be misery, debt, humiliation, his family against him for ever. There might be all of the above, mixed up together. Or, if he went back home with his tail between his legs, there could be life-as-before, with no difference. His time was nearly up after all. What was the point in changing anything? The red crayon and the children's cartoon paper put the whole enter-prise into perspective – it was childish to leave one's wife at his age.

He asked for a third cup of coffee, and then a fourth. He idly wondered if caffeine was any kind of pain killer and with his fifth cup found it wasn't. He doubted he could manage the walk home, a distance of over two miles, which was all very well once in an evening, but quite a different prospect to do twice – especially as he might be sober on the way back. His calf muscles ached and the heel of his right foot was sprouting that painful sore. Perhaps he would call the Woodford mini-cab to come and collect him . . . He rose to his feet. Go home, old man. He picked up his list of pros and cons; he didn't want anyone else to read them. He took the bill from the fork of plastic in which it sat among the menus and sauce bottles and looked it over – six coffees he'd had, as it happened, and twelve mini-doughnuts in chocolate sauce. He walked to the cash desk. The cheerful middle-aged woman who'd served him fished for a key at the end of a length of chain hanging from her waist and unlocked the cash register. She took the slip of paper and read from it, dabbing at the keypad twice. The drawer opened and, simultaneously, she mentioned the sum required, smiling at him expectantly.

He put down the list of pros and cons. For the second time tonight he'd come somewhere without money. He patted his pockets. They were empty of course, he already knew that.

The woman's face was still friendly but the blood filled his ear lobes as he searched more pockets, dug everywhere. Time stretched to elastic proportions. Everything became ridiculously meaningful. The whole of his life was contained within this red-and-yellow plastic interior. Sir Michael Gough – alone and penniless in an all-night Little Chef on a much hated stretch of the A303.

The woman's face wasn't quite so pleasant now. The cap perched on her head began to take on the look of a policeman's helmet. She sensed his predicament, no doubt, and was deciding on a way of handling it. She'd noticed his frayed cuffs. She'd seen the word 'PRISON' written in big red letters on the list of pros and cons which rested between them.

Michael's repeated searching through his clothes had, in his own mind, taken on a symbolic status – this is my distress; this is how I show it to you . . .

Finally, he stopped; his hands came to rest on his chest. The woman wore a steady frown. There was the hum of the extractor sucking at the barbecue-style cooking surfaces. The white-coated figure of the chef moved in the background. The forest of tables waited emptily.

'I'm sorry,' began Michael.

'We take debit cards or cheques,' began the woman in a low voice, 'if you have one of those?'

He moved towards the doors, but she stepped from behind her desk and barred his way. He could see the lines sketched around her mouth as she pursed her lips. 'If you haven't the means to pay I must ask you to wait here while . . .' He pressed on. His legs tangled with hers as he walked through. Her hands were against his chest: she was struggling to push him back and complete her warning, '. . . while the police can be called to verify your name and address . . .' He pushed through, made it to the swing doors, and then he was outside, in the car park. He managed to break into a trot for a few yards. He didn't look back.

The brook which gurgled behind Sitten Hall continued on its way, a noisy, twisting thread of water until it was soothed, diluted and lost in the river Avon, marshalled into a steady, orderly sequence, part of this much larger whole. The surface of the Avon was almost dead flat on top and only slightly turbulent beneath where it dragged against the bed; and now this same volume of water sailed past the riverside acreages owned by the loftier residents of Woodford. Many of them had installed miniature jetties from where they could fish, or launch their grandchildren in dinghies which ended up trapped among the native weeping willows. It was a romantic river, not so big that you couldn't see the hungry expressions of the fishermen on the opposite bank, who'd had to pay to be there, yet wide enough to form an enchanting barrier against the outside world.

The river passed by the feet of the Honourable Mattie Gough and her fiancé Simon d'Angibau as they lay on its bank, flat on their backs on the canvas tarpaulin borrowed from its usual place protecting the hotel's croquet set.

They were looking at the stars. Dew condensed out of the night air. Simon smoked a cigarette. Mattie blew her nose.

'I think it translates across any type of egg,' said Simon.

'How d'you mean?'

'Well, I like boiled eggs soft but on the point of going hard. I like my fried eggs the same way, soft but going hard. I like my omelettes exactly the same, my poached eggs, scrambled eggs. Therefore . . .'

'You like chocolate mousse which has *raw* eggs.'

'That doesn't count. It's a chocolate dish rather than a proper, bona fide egg dish.'

'Meringues are made of eggs, and cooked hard. You like meringues.'

'Ditto. It's a pudding. I'm talking about main courses.'

'I suppose.'

Under the stars, feeling small and insignificant and yet inflated with cosmic importance, Mattie took Simon's face in her hands and squeezed her lips against his. 'I was asking how you like your eggs, because I'm ovulating.'

'Oh.'

'You must fuck me, today.'

'Of course. We're getting married. It's the tradition.'

'It must be after we're married though.'

'All right.'

'I'm superstitious.'

'That's fine. We can wait until after we're married.'

'Shall we head back?' she asked.

'OK.'

She tugged at her clothing, pulled the zip higher on her borrowed coat. The night air had crept in and she gave a brief shiver, then got to her feet, flapped her arms and hopped from foot to foot. He stood, picked up the tarpaulin by a corner and dragged it back to its duty as a cover for the croquet set. Then they joined hands and trekked across the road, past the misted-up cars and through the wooden gate to the hotel.

They arrived at the porch, where Simon put his Yale key in and pushed the by-now-familiar glass door. However, it didn't give. He tried again, repositioning his hand closer to the latch. Still, it didn't budge. He ducked to examine the handle, pulled and pushed several times. So did she.

'Double-locked,' he whispered. 'We're stuck.' They stared at each other. Simon pointed to the bell marked 'Night porter, emergencies only' and raised his eyebrows. Mattie shrugged.

'Maybe we should just drive back to the Hall? We can sleep in my room.'

Simon walked a small circle, frowning. He was a romantic figure in his overcoat with plain chino trousers emerging from underneath. Mattie pointed at the bell. 'Or wake him up?' Then she moved her finger closer; she was about to push it when she felt his hand on her arm.

'Hang on a minute.' Simon pulled her after him, heading around the side of the building. 'The room's on the ground floor, I might be able to get through a window.'

Granny Banana woke to hear something – or someone. What was it? There were more noises – unmistakable, she wasn't dreaming. A thief? Someone was breaking in. Her heart thumped wildly. She pulled herself up in the bed, given extra strength because adrenalin had shot into her system and bucked her up. She tried to call out and ask what was going on, but her voice had become frozen – she was frightened.

There was no doubt: someone was coming through the bathroom window. She heard cursing and laughing. Was it a yob from the village?

Now her legs were over the side of the bed and she sat there trembling like a leaf but very determined. She should wake up the helpful, nice man who worked here; he would drive this lout away. She rose to her feet and took a first step, but there was a thump from the bathroom and a second later the light switched on. She stopped, squinted – ready for whoever it was to appear. She'd utterly shame him, the brute . . . That was her weapon. A few choice words, a rebuke. An old lady such as herself, and with the silver-backed, monogrammed hairbrush set so long in her family's possession. She blinked – a naked man, of all things, was now standing in the lighted doorway. This wasn't really happening, surely . . .

She realised – yes – she recognised him. Without question, this was someone she knew. He wasn't looking at her but facing sideways. He stood to attention and gave a faultless salute. She heard him say, 'At your service, madam.'

It must be. It looked just like Johnny Lightfoot. What else could explain this? Was she dead already? A plumb dread opened in her middle. This was a ghost.

All strength left her; her legs had gone. She must sit down. She reached for the bed but missed, so she ended up kneeling on the floor.

Johnny Lightfoot had come to take her over the other side. So this was what dying was like – banal, yet extraordinary at the same time. What was required of her, now? She wanted to form some words, ask a question, but she couldn't speak.

Then he disappeared from the lighted frame of the doorway and she heard a girl's voice.

The smile fell from Granny Banana's face. He was about to bring a girl in here, into her own bedroom. He'd always been such a bastard! She felt her mouth dry with anxiety; was she going mad? She could hear more noise and talking in the bathroom. The sound of the girl's voice was full of fun, laughter. Banana should tick him off – this was a terrible cruelty, a malicious haunting. Once again, for her, there was going to be a high price to pay for being involved with Johnny Lightfoot . . . Suddenly she thought this might be Hell. He was trying to take her down there, instead of . . . up to Heaven.

She thought she might make it to the door and escape, but a further burst of noise told her she never would. She looked underneath the bed but it was solid, there was only a gap of an inch or so. No good. On hands and knees she turned around, then reached up and clung to the handles on the wardrobe and hauled herself to her feet. She pulled open the heavy, mirrored door. She clutched both sides, lifted one foot in, pushed her weight forwards, felt her forehead knock against the back wall.

But – she was in. She turned around. By the time she'd finished untangling herself it was too late to close the door because she could hear – he was in the room.

Mattie applauded Simon's naked salute. She noticed the red marks down the front of his torso and pride leaped in her. What injuries he'd suffered in the course of his mission! She picked up his clothes and pushed them through. 'What about the bench?' she asked.

'Leave it 'til morning.'

They agreed she'd make her way around to the front door and he'd let her in.

Simon pulled on his trousers for decency's sake and hurried through the empty bedroom, recognising the curtains, the bedside tables, the dishevelled bedding, the comforting presence of the hotel room where he and Mattie were going to . . . well, whatever. He hurried out, leaving the door propped ajar, and trotted to the reception area to let in Mattie who was smiling broadly.

A thin gleam from the streetlights outside filtered into the hotel. She touched his injuries, winced in sympathy.

Together they returned to the bedroom. The wing of the door guided them into the darkened interior. They were safe and sound. Simon shut the wardrobe door which had mysteriously opened of its own accord – it was so heavy, he noticed, because there were mirrors hung in the shaped panels.

They stood facing each other in the space between the bed and the wardrobe.

'D'Angibau,' Mattie exclaimed, 'my clever Knight, my musketeer . . .' She placed her hands gently on his chest, covering the raw patches with a gentle touch.

He took her bulky figure in his arms and for a moment enjoyed the cold, rough sensation of her coat against his raw, smarting chest. He pulled her closer; she felt his tongue slide into her mouth, their kiss was fluent, practised. Mattie was expecting to be turned towards the bed, but instead he pushed her up against the wardrobe and pulled the coat from her shoulders. 'Ahh,' she said.

'Ahh what?'

'You're so predictable.'

'What?'

'The mirror.'

In the half-dark, she could make out the smile cross his face. His teeth nipped at her neck, as he peeled off her top half. She felt the chill of the glass against her naked back. He pushed her harder against the wardrobe – he knew she liked to be roughly handled when she was a bit drunk. He spared a forearm to keep her pinned there, while the other hand circled her breast and lifted it to his mouth. He held the nipple between his top teeth and his bottom lip, squeezing hard enough to send a sharp, light signal to her groin. Then with a click of saliva as his mouth separated, more of her breast disappeared and his sucking pulled threads of sensation from her . . .

A short while later he relaxed his forearm and his mouth grazed more softly at her neck, then up to her mouth. She took his hair in her hands and held him at a few inches' distance. She could make out his face in the gloom – there was an ardent glimmer in his eyes. She loved his excitement; it became her excitement. The breath snagged in her throat, lust growing deliciously in the dark. She could make out the two or three freckles which traversed the bridge of his nose. 'I'll start you off,' she said. 'As long as you promise not to come. You have to wait, to give it to me properly, after we are married.'

'Is that my wedding gift?'

'One of them.'

He planted both hands against the wardrobe, took a step back to give her some room. 'Ready?'

'Yes. Tell me what to do.'

'Sit.'

She slid her back down the wardrobe door, sank to the ground and looked up at him. 'Yes master.'

He could see everything, shadowy and indistinct, in the mirror. 'Take my cock in your hand.'

She smiled. 'Like this?'

'Perfect. Stroke my balls with your other hand.'

'Is that all right?'

'Yes . . .' His voice tightened. 'Now pull it down, pretend it's a gear stick, pull it into second, pointing down to your mouth.'

Granny Banana pursed her lips, frowned. How typical of bloody, bloody Johnny Lightfoot, cruel and arrogant as he was. She floated in darkness – when she blinked there was no dif-ference – and cursed these ghosts or poltergeists or whatever they were. The wardrobe lurched backwards; she lost her bal-ance. She crouched, braced herself against the sides, breathing heavily. What was going on, the whole thing was on the tilt, it was like she'd taken off. She'd only just recovered her balance when she was tipped forwards again. She fell, bumped her nose. The girl had gone quiet of course; it was only Johnny Lightfoot talking now, bossy as ever . . . 'Open wider. Stroke the shaft with your wet hand.'

Horrid man. Granny Banana was embarrassed. It really was beyond the pale. He was assaulting this other woman knowing that she, Granny Banana, was in here. The wardrobe began to rock back and forth.

Michael called into Jamie's Mini-cab Service which was located in premises converted from a redundant fish-and-chip shop in Amesbury. He was pleased to see two or three people lounging about – there must be someone willing to take him home.

Jamie and his wife and another driver whom Michael didn't
know were watching satellite television in the lounge area. A
football team was in action. Jamie struggled to his feet, his
belly like an overnight bag stuffed under his T-shirt. 'Sir
Michael,' he said.

'Jamie.'

'The usual is it, sir?' Jamie's breath came loudly, steadily, as if
he were asleep.

'Thank you, yes, if you can.'

Jamie moved automatically to the glass display cabinet
which they hadn't bothered to dismantle; it had been the fish
counter but now it held the general detritus of the drivers'
lives – hats, gloves, a motorcycle helmet, magazines and old
newspapers already yellowing. A logbook lay on top of the
cabinet and Jamie swivelled the book to sign himself out, writing his destination. Then he led Michael outside to where his
Peugeot waited at the kerb. He held the car door open and
Michael sank gratefully into the interior. Bliss, he thought.
Thank God.

As the diesel engine started its familiar rattle Michael bent
down and eased his shoelaces; his feet had swollen up. Then he
leaned back in his seat and felt the tiredness sweep over him.
Luckily, Jamie never talked to his customers. Amesbury
dropped behind them and Woodford went by in three seconds. Past the hotel. Granny Banana in there somewhere. And
Philip. And the bridegroom. All were asleep no doubt.

The headlights picked out the hedges on the road to Sitten
Hall. Jamie always drove to save on wear and tear: he set an
appropriate speed for the terrain and maintained it. The
odometer never topped three thousand revs and his foot rarely
touched the brake pedal. It was like driving in a tractor, an illusion helped by the sound of the diesel engine. The muted
drone was soporific. The car rolled from side to side as gently
as a cradle. The darkness in the back seat was comforting.

There was every chance he'd reach home. He fended off tiredness and took his pipe from his pocket, filled it with the soft, pungent strands of tobacco and pressed it down with his thumb. He remembered the Giving Up Smoking book his wife had given him after his lumpectomy. 'Nicotine should be regarded not as a stimulant, but as an anaesthetic.' The first thing anyone contemplating leaving their wife needed was an anaesthetic. A supply should be made available free on the NHS.

His hand strayed to the handle for winding down the window, but he didn't find it. Then he realised it was electric. Finding the tit, he pushed it and the glass zoomed down. The night air streamed in, caressed him. He closed his eyes and inhaled. His ex-wives came to him: their faces appeared like Halloween lanterns. Snakes dropped from their hair. In their armpits lived creatures. They all suffered from enormous, deafening flatulence. He remembered Mattie hurling the remote control at him and felt a plummeting, dizzy panic. Poor Simon.

Michael's eyes flickered open – Christ! – and he tilted forward sharply. Through the open window he recognised the sharp right-hander with the old iron railing leaning askew, brilliantly lit in the Peugeot's headlights, and there was dear old Quercus, guardian of the entrance to his ancestral home. He raised a salute as they turned past the lodge into the driveway and tracked along between the lines of beech trees.

They came to a halt in front of the drawbridge. As always, Michael fell in love with his big, fat, thick-walled, ancient castle. It looked unimpeachable. He loved the fact that it had *defences*, even if they had been designed for cosmetic effect. He wanted to man the wall-walk himself. The floodlights gave it a clean, modern appearance, as though it were freshly built. If only he could conjure up a small gang of servants to come and carry him to his bed. With a last ditch effort he climbed out of the taxi, on his way home now, thank the Lord.

The driver's window slid down, Jamie's head swivelled, and his mouth – because there was a piece of gum in it – chewed out the amount required for the journey.

Michael stopped. He automatically lifted a hand to his pocket. His scalp tilted forwards and the blood heated his ears. Why was *everyone* tonight deliberately and unkindly and continuously asking for money?

A robin sang a wistful tune to herald the dawn of Mattie's wedding day, as the earth slid fast but imperceptibly around its axis, bringing Woodford its turn in the sun, the latter strong and bright as any bride could wish for, silently heating a sky devoid of early mist, even, and therefore as blue as a child might colour it with a pencil. A host of butterflies – peacocks, commas, red admirals – rose and flitted silently. A lick of dew was spread on Sitten Hall's lawns and glittered on a cobweb strung from the arm of a wheelbarrow left out overnight. The ground-dwelling members of the insect world continued their automatic lives, bizarrely efficient, the quirkiest of life forms and incapable of being interrupted. Rabbits nibbled on the edges of the pasture while their enemies, foxes, took one or two and sought out their own dens to lie down, sated. In the wooded valley a fallow deer threw out a foreleg and levered herself up nimbly to follow her stag. In a sulky, slow-moving part of the river, a trout altered holding position, solemnly moving one length upstream. On the A303 a lone Morris Minor made slow headway on a road that was too wide and fast for its old fashioned design, surfboards lashed to the roof, the girl's hand on the boy's thigh.

There were other, more heartless creatures mating on this early Saturday morning. Bedbugs lived out their rowdy, aggressive lives in one or two of the mattresses at the Garden House Hotel, and one particular male was energised by the heat given

off by Simon and Mattie's bodies. He set to work in his miniature world. He extended his penis – it looked like a double
bladed saw with hammer drill and scissor attachments – and
approached the nearest female. Any would do. She'd have done
well to run away – she was already much scarred by previous
traumatic inseminations. None the less he got hold of her,
sawed into her body any old how, any old place, and left his
seed in her body cavity. That was their romance. One could
only imagine any tiny squirt of pleasure there might have been
on either side. In a flash more bedbugs were made. By rights
this extraordinary event deserved a puff of smoke, a flash of
light and an exclamation, 'Abracadabra!' but there was no ceremony.

Simon and Mattie had gone through a certain amount of the
usual repertoire; this night before the wedding had almost
turned into their honeymoon tryst but with one important
exception: Simon had kept his promise not to ejaculate. They'd
found all the excitement anyone could want, but this final
release was left in him like a coiled spring. They'd pushed the
heavy old lug of a bed up against the wardrobe doors so they
could play and see themselves in the mirror at the same time
and they'd just carried on and on but, heroically, almost comically, he'd abstained in this one respect.

Tired out, they'd embraced with more tenderness than ever
before. The new daylight painted them in an unearthly glow,
softened their responses. Everything slowed down. The wedding would place them at the centre of the universe today.
Others could only look forward to the daily grind – going to
work, buying the daily paper, shopping at the supermarket –
whereas they, Mattie and Simon d'Angibau, would be stars in
the firmament on a day arranged especially for them. Their
skin was silken to the touch, their hair glistened with youth,
they barely needed to wash or brush their teeth. Together
they watched the pink sheet of dawn painted thicker and the

sun rise higher in the sky. A core of happiness would remain untouched within her, Mattie realised, whatever happened now.

When Simon went to have a shave and she took a moment to look around, Mattie noticed Granny's overnight bag. Its extraordinary presence held her spellbound. She was just puzzling it out when Simon appeared, his astonished face dripping wet. He said, 'This isn't my room,' and pointed behind him, into the bathroom. 'I put my shaving things out on the glass shelf and they're nowhere to be found.'

They stared at each other.

'We climbed into the wrong room,' said Mattie. 'And guess whose? Look.' She pointed at the bag. 'Granny's!'

Simon strode towards the door. He pulled it open and read the brass number screwed on the outside. 'This is room 4!' he exclaimed, 'I was in 3. So where is she?'

Mattie's hand flew to her mouth. A moment later she dropped it. 'Up at the Hall, it must be. Thank God – Christ! Imagine!'

They pushed the bed away from the wardrobe and back into position. They fetched the various sheets and blankets from where they'd ended up and made the bed. Simon straightened the pictures on the wall and tried to mend the broken wall light. Mattie tidied the bathroom. When everything was neat and in order they gathered up their stuff and took the two steps down the corridor, Simon fishing the room key out of his coat pocket.

When they were in their own room it was as if a spell had been broken. The night before had happened in a parallel world. Now it was time to get ready. Simon found his shaving gear and leaned over the basin, splashed cold water on his face, dragged his chin from side to side in the bathroom mirror. His first appointment was the earliest time given on the back of the door against 'Full English Breakfast'. The night's activities seemed to have given strength to Mattie whereas he felt weaker, in need of fuel. The unassuaged lust made itself felt in the bottom of his groin.

He thought of his friends and relatives preparing to make the journey or already in transit. There was a feeling of satisfaction at their coming, all aimed at him. It was precisely this attention on himself and Mattie that would make it a ceremonial occasion. He saw the proof of this in what had happened with Mattie and her father – however unaffected she pretended to be, she did in fact want Michael to be there – it would mean the wedding was really happening.

Mattie stood in front of the window. She could make out the ghost of her reflection and as usual took the roll of fat around her middle in both hands and tugged at it. She tilted her head; the dark hair fell to one side. Men looked sheepish when they were naked, she thought, whereas women looked just plain naked, or like they were starring in a film. Two slim lines were drawn vertically between her eyes; she must take care that unhappy thoughts didn't engrave them any deeper. After she'd zipped up her jeans she pressed her forefinger hard into the flesh of her upper arm and took it away to watch the white circle slowly fade back to the colour of her skin. Her blood was that close to the surface. Only a few millimetres of membrane held it in. She lifted her hands to gather her hair and as she did so she was conscious of her breasts fronting the window. She wanted a man to see them, an old man who might get most pleasure – she was reminded of a tramp who she saw masturbating on a tube train in London. She restrained an impulse to run naked on the lawn of the hotel, instead turning inside, disappointed at the empty room. She heard the gurgle of the tap in the bathroom and thought, I love Simon d'Angibau. And she did, truly. She found his very ordinariness, his scientific job, his sensible and steady nature, adorable, unusual. He was her man. She wanted him.

She shrugged on the borrowed Barbour, put together a proper good-bye with Simon and left the hotel. She drove the Renault back to the Hall.

Sir Michael Gough's few hours of sleep were filled to the edges with a dream about Mattie. She was a five-year-old girl, walking towards him. He waited to applaud and lift her in his arms. She was wearing a grey cardigan and a striped blue dress and that dark hair was tied to one side with a flower. She smiled at him; she was carefree. He slowly found his gaze dropping from her face, down her body, to her legs, and he could tell from the knee joints and the way they moved that they were fixed on the wrong way round and so she was actually walking backwards. If he concentrated hard on the legs – with their little socks and buckled shoes – then he could force them to turn round the right way so they walked forwards, but then her top half was facing away from him. That was a worse terror. He woke with a jerk, trying to sit upright in the bed. Patsy was shaking his shoulder. His head throbbed. She was calling him, 'Michael, Michael?'

'Hmmm?'

'Don't go back to sleep. There's a foul smell and it's that dog in the plastic bag. I'm not having that in here when the bridesmaids arrive. You are to take it out and bury it at once.'

The first vehicle to turn into Sitten Hall that morning was the Trust's bottle-green Land Rover containing head gardener Raymond Luther and warden Griffith Jones, who both nodded over the speed bumps. As he topped the rise Raymond caught sight of the castle and, as with others who loved it, the beauty of the place soaked into him. He and Griffith had put the grounds and the garden at their best for Mattie's wedding. She was a favourite, and Raymond had known her since arriving with the Trust, in '86. They'd excelled themselves; it had been like going back to the old days, before their current disaffection. The place looked immaculate.

They drove on, and pulled into the yard around the back. Their apprentice, Boy, appeared and toiled back and forth carrying fencing tools, rolls of 2mm wire, the ratchet device used to pull the wire taut, a heavy rubber mallet and dozens of stakes. Their first task this Saturday was to re-hang part of the fence on the pasture to the west of Sitten Hall where the neighbour's sheep had broken through.

Raymond pointed a long thumb behind him to the youngster. 'The strain is showing, Griffith.'

'It is,' agreed the warden, shuffling his boots in the gravel.

'Land Management Trainee . . .' announced Raymond.

'That's what he is, all right.'

'Does that mean that he manages to train things, or that he's trained to manage something?'

'It's gobbledegook, isn't it.'

'Meaning diddly-squat.'

'Exactly.'

There was a moment of hiatus. Raymond disappeared somewhere and Griffith and Boy lounged in the sun, waiting. When Raymond returned he was smoking his pipe and carrying something.

'Boy!' called Raymond. Boy stood up straight, wondering what was coming next. Raymond held out a long, black object. 'D'you know what this is?' he asked. Boy peered closer to make sure.

'It's . . . a television remote control.'

'Correct. And I happen to know it was thrown by Sir Michael Gough's daughter Mattie, from the window. In a fit of rage. He looked for it last night but didn't find it, but I . . . I've been lucky. The cold light of day showed it to me, like an offering. We shall have to return it to him at the appropriate time and we can make this a task for you, hmm?'

Boy nodded warily. He smelled a rat, something that was going to be bad news for him. He waited to be sent on his mission but Raymond said, 'Let's carry on then, shall we?' They climbed into the Land Rover and pointed it in the direction of Sitten Hall's outer perimeter. It was going to be a long, hot day but they'd have a bird's eye view of the wedding.

At nine o'clock the choir arrived to hold a rehearsal in the chapel. Twelve-year-old Jim Staines from the village felt his voice break, then climb back. He held his throat, alarmed.

The car park attendants – a couple of teenage brothers hired from the local scout troop – arrived hours early because their mother had to work. They lounged in the area designated for the wedding guests' cars, wearing their armbands on their heads. They stood to attention smartly, practising salutes and royal waves. Gina herself – wearing a well-cut suit because she'd been invited to the wedding – hooked a chain across the pathway to the chapel and hung the sign on it saying 'Closed to the public.'

Two members of the catering team struggled across the lawn with a hot-water urn, heading towards the marquee.

Pinky appeared in his white and purple skirts, carrying a block of service sheets. His gown swept the ground as he headed for the chapel. Neither his legs nor feet could be seen and he took such small steps that it made him look like he was on roller skates.

Patsy shepherded Mattie inside. 'We shouldn't just forget breakfast, should we?'

'No.'

'And Monsoon will be open, we can dash off and buy a dress.' She steered her daughter to the kitchen and made boiled eggs and marmite soldiers. She could hardly bring herself to sit down and cleared the egg cups the minute the last spoonful had passed Mattie's lips.

'Where's Dad?' asked Mattie.

'Don't know and don't care.' She chucked the eggshells into the bin. 'Next job for us is fetching out all the bridesmaids' nonsense, for when they arrive. After that, open up the Green Room downstairs . . .'

'And Granny's all right?' asked Mattie.

'I presume so. I've entirely left Philip to deal with her this morning. He's at the hotel after all.'

'But Granny is here, isn't she? I thought?'

'No. At the hotel. Philip drove her back.'

'Oh.' Mattie had been on the point of telling her mother what had happened last night but now she held off, listening instead to Patsy's account of finding Granny in her old bedroom.

'And then Philip drove her to the hotel?' she repeated.

'Yes. Walking and talking. Amazing.'

Which room had Granny been in, Mattie wondered?

At nine-fifteen, Granny Banana was found standing uncertainly in the foyer of the Garden House Hotel, dressed in yesterday's clothes and dishevelled in appearance. 'I was trapped by the ghost of Captain Lightfoot,' she announced, 'in the wardrobe.' The proprietor of the hotel called Philip from his room immediately.

'He behaved disgracefully,' said Banana.

'Who did, Mother?' Philip steered her towards the breakfast lounge.

'The Captain. He had another girl with him. Deliberately flouting all the common rules of decency.'

'Mother have you had anything to eat?'

'No.'

'Would you like your orange as usual? Cut into quarters?'

'I would like that, thank you.'

'Sit yourself down here and we'll look after you.'

'Do you know I think I fell asleep in there.'

'Did you.'

'They wouldn't let me out. They deliberately shut me in. Poltergeists? I don't know the technical term.'

'Wait there, let me get you a cup of tea et cetera,' said Philip. She sat quietly while he went to the buffet.

'I think that was one of the oddest things that's ever happened to me,' she declared on his return. They talked in a civilised way about her extraordinary fantasy, or dream it must be, thought Philip. He excused himself and went to her room, and all was as it should be; there was no sign of the poltergeists. He unpacked her bag. With his usual care he counted out the prescription from the various bottles of pills and loaded up with a day's supply the little blue tin marked 'fishing flies'. He went back and sat with her and watched as she talked away, holding up to her mouth pill after pill, and after each one lifting the glass of water to her lips briefly, taking the medication without complaining.

Michael headed straight for the shower. While he'd been out burying Sprocket the apartment had become a different place. Patsy, Mattie and her three teenage consorts and their mothers were milling around. He took a walk up and down in his dressing gown in the vague hope he could somehow say something to impress a bridesmaid. He inadvertently stumbled on Mattie having a proper laughing jag with the Tall Woman. Mattie was wearing a preposterously short skirt and her mother was trying to tug it down an inch. The mirror showed him everything: the Tall Woman's smiling face, his daughter's mane of glossy hair, her long legs. The laughter rang in his ears. He felt terrible jealousy. Such easy happiness.

He quickly withdrew and headed in the other direction. He knew better than to interfere. Ribbons, dresses, hats, trains, veils and posies were being carried everywhere; squeals of laughter intermingled with arguments. It was like walking through a girls' school. From outside came the sound of the chapel bell, sounding its hourly toll. He was going to have to fight very hard to stay in his chair. He side-stepped countless boxes and other wedding paraphernalia. No one seemed to want to make him a cup of tea or fry him a breakfast. He peered out of the window for a while and watched it all happen under the painfully bright sun; no doubt he should be helping. There were unlikely vehicles parked in odd places, including on the lawns. He carried on – business as usual. The Tall Woman did everything, it was one of the advantages of that type of wife. Besides, he had enough on his plate with the television problem. No remote control. Channel 4 not available.

After he'd washed and brushed his teeth he returned to the bedroom and cast yesterday's clothes aside, distasteful reminders. He rooted in the drawers for a fresh shirt. Today – the midday at Cheltenham, thirty quid on By Desire at 16 to 1 . . . winnings to be spent on himself and Raymond at the Whistle and Feather, plus give Jamie his fare from last night.

Just then he heard a thump from overhead. That was unusual because this apartment was at the very top of the building already. He looked up, half expecting to see the roof caving in. Then he remembered there was a bit of roof space up there where they kept various old boxes of stuff. Who was it, messing about? Never mind, carry on.

Freshly clothed, Michael took his square, painful head to the kitchen to put together a cup of coffee and a glass of orange juice – or at least he would have if he could have fought past the girls and their mothers, all of whom he recognised but whose names slipped his mind. He just gave out a constant stream of hellos.

Coffee – he fiddled with the plunger and put the kettle on; it would help him concentrate. The race was at twelve o'clock, and he heard Simon's words again from the previous evening, on the bridge, 'Mattie's agreed to let you off aisle duty . . .' It seemed like a long time ago. He went to the fridge and found a carton of orange juice. He fumbled with the screw-top and drank it straight away, not troubling with a glass. The cold liquid chilled his stomach and made the roof of his mouth ache. Hopefully the kettle would boil soon.

While he was waiting he went to stare at the television. How might he sort this machine out? Maybe he should skulk into the bookies, in town. Or he could telephone Pickering and invite himself over. He'd undoubtedly watch the racing. He was a terrible bore, but what option was there?

Mattie told her mother, 'It was a full moon last night. Simon and I saw it. Which might explain everything.'

The photos were due to be taken in an hour's time. Her mother reminded her, 'Come on, keep going. Slip that hand-kerchief off.'

Mattie stepped out of the Lycra mini-skirt which was no bigger than a pair of knickers. It was a shame in a way – it would have been an outrageously sexy garment to be married in. The passion yet the restraint of last night would live with her for ever, she thought. It had wound up the tension of the ceremony today to a delicious breaking point. She shut her eyes and cast around for a way of engraving each moment in her memory, to make them, always and for ever, as potent and as meaningful as they should be. The knowledge chimed in her, like the church bell, that there would be no few hours more valuable, not in her whole life, than those she was going to pass with Simon today.

'Will it fit, Ma?'

'I hope so. Come on. Step in. Let's hope I remember how on earth it all does up.'

'Cobwebs!'

'I know. Sorry.'

'I like them. After all, it is a Miss Haversham dress.'

Raymond and Griffith took three paces uphill from the scene of their endeavours and sat down on the grass, lighting up a pipe and a cigarette respectively.

Griffith had already taken his shirt off, it was so hot.

They admired Boy's youth as he carried on hammering in the post. Beyond, in the distance, they could see the proceedings down at the Hall. The first cars were arriving, waved in by the two young scouts. The doors opened like flies' wings and women dressed in bright colours and pinning hats to their heads were accompanied by the black, white and grey menfolk. The bells rolled in the valley while guests milled around, filtering towards the chapel. Sitten Hall's ordinary Saturday visitors felt privileged to be caught up in the celebration; there was a sense of frivolity sponsored by the unfolding pageant.

When his pipe was burning steadily Raymond Luther pegged it in the corner of his mouth and they watched Boy sweating in the sun, bringing the rubber mallet down repeatedly on to the head of the stake. They waited long enough to see it split in half and so now he had to lever it back and forth, pull it out and put in a new one. A moment later Raymond called, 'Boy?' and the lad stopped and asked, 'What?'

'Break time.'

'We only just had one.'

Raymond sucked at his pipe. 'First there's a fag break. Then there's coffee. Then there's a breather and a fag break, then lunch. Then another fag break, followed by a second breather. After that there's tea, then we go home early because it's Saturday.' He turned to his colleague. 'Which one are we on now?'

Griffith answered, 'This is our breather.'

Boy smiled, let the handle of the mallet drop to the ground. He knew he was expected to work hard; they'd soon have something to say if he didn't.

Raymond took the Twix from his lunch box and handed it to Boy. 'Since you don't smoke,' he explained. 'All yours.'

'Ah – thank you.' Boy took it uneasily, looking at his boss, how his beard lifted in the breeze. He'd grown to like and admire Raymond during the summer but he knew he ought to wait for the catch, with this gift. When he'd bitten halfway through the Twix, it came.

'Now then, have you got the energy for a trot back to the Hall?'

Boy's heart sank – there it was. The payment was melting in his fingers. 'Sure. Yes.' Raymond tossed the television remote control in Boy's lap. Boy picked it up and turned it in his hands.

'It's a simple quest.' Raymond pointed at the Hall. Boy squinted into the sun. Raymond went on, 'But an important one. D'you know – would you recognise – Sir Michael, Lord Woodford?' Boy nodded. 'You know where he lives, where the apartment is? OK. You'll find him there. He won't be at the wedding, he's been let off, so don't get yourself mixed up in all that nonsense. He'll be up in his living room, watching the television. Or rather, hoping to. He's due to watch the midday at Cheltenham, and he won't be able to do so happily without the remote control, apparently.' Raymond waved at the people and the vehicles moving like ants beneath them. 'So take it down there and give it to him. But more importantly, as you do so, I want you to ask him a question. Make sure he knows it's me who's asking.' Raymond pointed at the remote. 'Ask him, should we press the Stop button, or the Play button?'

'OK,' said Boy, uneasy.

'Repeat that for me,' said Raymond, 'pretend I'm Lord Woodford. Hand me the remote control and let's hear it. A rehearsal.'

Boy frowned, uncertain.

'Go on then.'

Boy tried to fathom the steady look of Raymond Luther but gave up and decided simply to obey. He pushed the remote control forward and said all in one breath, 'Here you are sir, from Raymond Luther, and he asks a question, should he press the Stop button or the Play button?'

'Perfect,' said Raymond. 'And don't come back without an answer.'

Around the east range of Sitten Hall, Mattie and her train of bridesmaids walked across the lawn and stood in the sun with nothing behind them but parkland studded with trees. The photographer ducked, aimed his lens: this would be the last photograph of Mattie as an unmarried woman. The dress had been her mother's, a fall of cream silk with a simple empire line bust, as fluid as if poured from a jug, the veil a light spray over her head, albeit a bit moth-eaten. She held a posy of wild flowers. He just had to duck over and remove that spider that was crawling across her chest. He caught it on his finger and there was laughter — he put it back on her shoulder and took a quick snap. It was deemed to be a sign of good luck.

In the chapel, Miss Mason unscrewed her thermos and poured hot water into a plastic bowl which stood on a ledge to one side of her organ keyboard. She rolled up the cuffs of her dress and immersed her hands in the hot water to loosen the sinews in her fingers.

The pews filled up; guests were ushered to their seats by Simon's cousin and his sister on their side while the Gough branch of the family were meant to be ushered in by Philip. He did turn up, but late, pushing his mother in her wheelchair and looking flustered.

Granny Banana had a hunted look. She seemed unaware of the young women on either side who were helping to pin on her hat. Then Philip wheeled her carefully, as if she were a royal personage, to the front. At the altar he steered left. Then he had to pull back and turn around and reverse back in because there wasn't room. Eventually she was parked off to one side, from where she might see everything and yet not be in the way. She gazed steadily at the floor about a yard in front of her wheelchair, like a cat waiting for a mouse to come out of its hole.

Bridegroom Simon d'Angibau and his Best Man waited at the back of the chapel, greeting people as they came in. Simon was hoping for Michael to turn up after all; he knew it would complete Mattie's happiness. All his own family were here. She should have the same. Suddenly he was angry with Michael. He checked his watch – fifteen minutes to go. He conferred with his Best Man.

Was there time? He decided yes, and headed off. The Best Man tried to stop him but could only accompany him to the porch and watch him go.

Outside, Simon broke into a trot. He passed the sign positioned earlier by Gina to prevent visitors from wandering down to the chapel. He crossed the drawbridge and entered Sitten Hall, threading past the visitors slowly moving in and out of the ancient building. Two at a time he took the stairs which coiled upwards in the west range. He climbed to the apartment, sidestepping the debris from the wedding. The sound of the

television led him towards the room in which he'd first met Sir
Michael all those months ago. He rested his knuckles on the
door, ready to knock, but under his touch the door opened.
He pressed it further and caught Michael just leaning back in
his chair. In front of him were two television screens – one
blank, switched off, while the smaller, portable one was busy
with the race meeting at Cheltenham. Simon interrupted,
'Hullo . . .'

Michael sat forward, startled at the interruption. 'Ahh –
Mmm?!' He recovered, stood up. 'Changed your mind?' he
asked. 'Come to watch the race?' He'd gone to considerable
trouble to get this television here – the Whistle and Feather had
out-voted him and Mrs Pickering wouldn't have him in the
house but they'd lent him their portable. He'd dragged it all the
way back here only to find it was black and white, which was
a disappointment when you were looking out for a set of gaily
coloured silks in a field of horses at full gallop; thank goodness
for the numbers on their flanks.

'Sorry to trouble you, sir.'

'Not at all,' replied Michael. 'If you don't want to go through
with it, much better to say now rather than later. She'll forgive
you, you know. Pull up a pew. You've just got time to call the
Tote. Use my account.'

'It's not for . . . why . . . I've come . . .'

'Oh,' said Michael. 'What's happened, Mattie not turned
up?' he asked hopefully.

'No, she's there, she's fine.'

'Oh. All right.' For a moment Michael had thought it was
going to fall his way and Mattie be saved.

'I just thought I'd ask you . . . with all respect . . . if you
would walk her down the aisle, after all. She does want you to.'

'Walk her down the aisle? I thought it was all sorted out, to
everyone's satisfaction? With Patsy doing it.'

'She pretends she doesn't mind, but . . . I think she does.

Even if, maybe, you weren't to walk her down the aisle, it would be good if you at least turned up.' He waited. When there was no reply he pressed on, fumbled for a convincing argument. 'The perception of the event *is* the event itself, I think, anyway, so . . . people attending – or not attending – either proves or disproves the marriage.' Simon stopped, put off by Michael's blank stare. Then he glanced at his watch. 'We're almost ready to go.'

'And she . . . asked for me?'

Simon found himself rambling on. 'No, I can't lie, she didn't ask, not as such, but I thought I ought to, on her behalf, because I know she'd like it if you were there.'

'I see.' He was ashamed of himself. She wanted him there; he was turning her down.

'I'd better go back.' Simon again looked at his watch, although it wasn't to check the time – he knew he hadn't any left – but to signal to the other man his urgency.

'Right,' said Michael.

'We're using the 1662 service, it's still very beautiful, and relevant, which is surprising, and we've got some half-decent music. Everyone's ready and waiting.'

'Very good,' replied Michael.

Simon had to go. He'd tried his best. 'See you there if you can make it,' he called before he turned and fled.

Michael leaned back in his chair. The young man's unexpected visit had unnerved him; it had put a note of panic in the room. He didn't like it. His dream came back to him – Mattie's legs on the wrong way round. He'd been powerless to help. He shivered.

Automatically, he turned his attention once more to the portable TV, hoping for a win. He consulted the paper to find that By Desire was carrying number 9. Now he could search for his horse in the enclosure. John McCririck, Channel 4's famous presenter with the side-whiskers and the waving arms, was describing the scene, '. . . and she had this great, great ride offered to her on the three-year-old—'

She? Michael shook his head and blinked, not believing the news. 'Christ, female jockey,' he swore. Was this a lady's race, then? No.

McCririck burbled on, '. . . really cheering up the race course here at Cheltenham, everyone willing her to win of course, she's a great favourite and I wouldn't be surprised if they simply allowed her through on the rails; the applause as you can hear . . .'

Michael stood. He was nonplussed. There was a girl jockey riding his horse. Women were taking over the whole bloody world.

Simon scatted down the stairs, out of the Hall, full pelt. Visitors barely managed to part for him. Among those whom he passed was Boy, who'd reached the drawbridge at the same time. He ducked sideways and then maintained progress in the opposite direction, heading into Sitten Hall. Simon meanwhile ran back to the chapel, tipping headlong. Outside he tangled with Mattie and Patsy and the bridesmaids who'd been stalled there by the Best Man. He could be seen explaining something, waving his arm in the direction of the Hall; it was a good-tempered exchange. Mattie shooed at him; as he slid past she gave him a light-hearted kick.

Inside he was greeted by the Best Man and marched briskly up the aisle. The congregation gave a brief, ironic applause as he took up position. Simon blushed and waved, acknowledging their reaction.

Pinky nodded to the organist. Miss Mason craned her neck to see that Patsy and Mattie and the train were in order and, having caught the bride's eye, she nodded and gave them their cue. Freshly dried from the bowl of hot water her fingers executed a

florid, ornate introduction and then segued to the traditional
'Here Comes the Bride'.

Covered by this torrent of music, Patsy took Mattie's arm
and they walked through the porch and into the chapel and
made steady progress down the carpeted aisle. Everyone turned
to watch; the dress gathered long, admiring looks from friends
and family which were none the less tinged with sadness in the
hearts of those who didn't have quite whom they wanted
beside them.

The bride and her mother arrived in line with Simon and his
Best Man just as the music came to a final point. Patsy squeezed
her daughter's arm and stepped aside. Bride and bridegroom
stood alone.

Pinky waited a second or two for the reverberations to leak
from the stonework and then began. 'Ladies and gentlemen, as
you see from the sheets of paper in front of you we'll be sticking
to the 1662 service, because none of us involved in the preparation of this ceremony could imagine using the modern version.
To give you an example of the poetic verve and style of the
revised text, I'd be required to say at one point, "In marriage
husband and wife belong to one another and they begin a new
life together in the community." I ask you, what kind of pro-
nouncement is that? Are we a gang of social workers? I don't
think so.'

A smattering of laughter greeted Pinky's criticism. He waited
two or three seconds longer than it took for it to die down and
then he sucked all the self-importance out of the address; he
spoke as if it were one side of a conversation he was sharing
with one other person, in private. 'Dearly beloved, we are
gathered together here in the sight of God . . .'

Pursued by thoughts of his own wives, of his daughter Mattie,
of the girl jockey and the Little Chef waitress, of Janine and the

bridesmaids, Michael strode through the apartment. He shook his head to clear it of an awful premonition of disaster: to have thirty quid on By Desire and not actually *see* how the money was taken off him, by however many lengths the horse lost . . . that was true, grown-up grief . . . He escaped; he was in Sitten Hall proper. More stairs opened beneath him.

On the ground floor he had to force a path through a batch of visitors who'd signed up for the guided tour and who were listening to an account — he gathered as he slid by — of his great-great-grandfather, Sir Thomas, who was so keen on hunting that he'd gone out with the earth-stoppers. He was tempted to delay a moment and tell them that just next to where they were all standing, right there, was the electrical point where he — Michael — had plugged in three extension leads strung together to feed the single bar heater they used to huddle around in the winter of '85, sitting in armchairs valued at five or six winters' worth of fuel, making toast with rugs over their knees, pressing the sliced white against the orange glow of the element.

He pressed on towards the main entrance, checking his watch. The race was about to start. Momentarily he was confronted by a young man, vaguely familiar, who was attempting to give him something, but Michael brushed past; he couldn't stop now.

Boy took the knock-back manfully. He held onto the remote control, made an about-turn, and followed Michael. So the younger man pursued the older; they passed over the drawbridge and towards the chapel, skirting the sign on the path.

Boy understood that Michael was about to go inside the chapel and he accelerated in order to catch him before he disappeared — otherwise he'd have to wait for an hour. However, he was wrong-footed: Lord Woodford cut sideways over the grass — not going into the main door at all but heading towards the spire. Boy's pace dropped back for a second, to judge what to do.

Michael tugged at the miniature doorway. As he'd hoped it was unlocked; he went through. The cut of studded oak swung shut behind him. He struggled up the narrow spiral staircase. His breathing, the scraping of his heels and the scuffing of his elbows against the stonework were amplified by this vertical tunnel as he worked his way up. A snatch of Pinky's address – like a whispering echo – reached him via the openings set in the wall each time he came round, '. . . to satisfy men's carnal lusts and appetites . . .' Yes, he could tell Mattie something about carnal lusts and appetites. It brought to mind the extraordinary insult issued by his first wife towards the end of their marriage: she'd looked over her shoulder at him while he was taking her, he thought rather valiantly, from behind; and she'd frowned and said, 'Is it in?' He blushed with shame at the memory. Christ! The gruesome nonsense of sexual behaviour!

He made another circuit of the tower. He could hear Pinky again, 'like brute beasts that have no understanding . . .' Exactly, yes. He remembered how brutish, how furious, had been his hurt. It had taken him a week to think up a suitable reply. He'd managed to start another row on purpose just so he could shout at her that she had a fanny as loose as a broken rucksack. Yes, that had been his first marriage – or the second? He couldn't remember.

Mattie getting married? Poor angel!

It was a long ascent and looking out of the loopholes stationed at regular intervals made him dizzy. He had to pause and wipe his brow. 'First, it was ordained for the procreation of children . . .' He pushed himself up the increasingly narrow staircase. '. . . secondly, it was ordained for a remedy against sin . . . to avoid fornication . . . keep themselves undefiled . . .' The effort of the climb was etched on Michael's face.

'. . . help, and comfort, that the one ought to have of the other, both in prosperity and adversity . . .'

Quite right. Who could he go and stay with, if he decided

actually to leave Patsy? Who would have him? Someone like
Janine might need to hire out a spare room in her place; she'd
be grateful for the money.

Michael reached the two-foot high gothic arch which let
onto the interior of the main body of the chapel directly above
the central aisle. He could stop climbing now. This was it: a
bird's eye view. He would send this claim to Mattie – he was,
sort of, here. He rested his knuckles on the sill and caught his
breath, surveyed the scene below. His old friend Pinky, ex-
Renault salesman, fronted the congregation which was divided
into two halves by the central aisle. Mattie, his own daughter,
stood there, her back to him, next to Simon, with Patsy and the
Best Man attending on either side. From here the ladies' hats
looked like so many eccentric flowers blooming among the
plainer, grey or black-and-white menfolk.

His gaze stuck fast on his daughter. He should have given her
away – yes. He could see the shine on her dark hair which was
tied up with flowers and decorated with a veil. She was almost
as tall as her young man. Her back was straight as it always had
been in Wiltshire's various dressage arenas. She was a bit horse-
like herself, in fact; that thick hair might have been borrowed
from a pony's tail . . . his lovely daughter. He remembered
how, when she was a child, she'd been let loose in the show-
jumping ring on her pony Fillet, but there were no numbers on
the fences and so she'd buzzed hopelessly around without a clue
as to which to jump first, what direction she should take, while
everyone else had done it neatly and got a rosette.

Her dress had a large, cream-coloured bow tied to the
rump – he frowned. Patsy had had the same thing, he remembered, when they were married.

Pinky was saying, '. . . into which Holy estate these two
persons present come now to be joined.' At that moment –
whether by accident or because, as far below as he was, Pinky
could hear Michael's stertorous breathing – he looked up and

caught his friend's eye. Nothing in his demeanour betrayed that he'd seen him, and for his part Michael also remained motionless, watching.

Pinky realised well enough why Michael was perched like a model soldier in the opening high up in the back wall of the chapel and he predicted there'd be trouble, but there was only one thing for it – to carry on. He gazed over the congregation, and offered the usual chance for anyone to interfere. 'Therefore if any man can show any just cause why they may not lawfully be joined together let him now speak or else hereafter for ever hold his peace.'

The rustling and coughing died down. Pinky glanced up at Michael. He steeled himself.

The silence was broken only by a baby's impatient mew.

Michael looked down and saw the offending infant twisting and bucking in its mother's arms, a small patch of movement in an otherwise still congregation. Watching this struggle, Michael found he was reddening, and frowning . . .

Mattie, his only daughter, now turned and found him out. She smiled, waved. In an instant tears sprang from him. He caught her gesture, waved back. His breath hissed, spluttered; he coughed. He had to give another wave to Simon, her husband.

Pinky continued with the marriage service. Michael cried as little, and as quietly, as humanly possible.

Then he heard a whisper, 'Sir . . .' Startled, he turned around and saw, through a watery blur of tears, on the step below him, the same youth, the one whom he'd nearly bumped into just now as he'd come through Sitten Hall. He recognised him this time – it was the lad who'd been working in the grounds this summer. He looked anxious and was holding out something in his hand. Michael registered that it was – could it be? – the television remote control which he'd lost the previous evening. Here it was, returned to him like magic. 'And I have to ask you a question, sir,' whispered Boy, 'from Raymond Luther.'

On Sitten Hall's west-facing expanse of lawn the purple and grey-striped marquee filled with a light breeze. Its sides ballooned slightly, as if struggling to contain the chatter of a hundred-and-fifty-odd people and the sound of 1920s dance music played by the four-piece band. The sun had passed the apex of its September track but was uninterrupted by cloud, so the whole county of Wiltshire, it seemed, was laid out in its late-summer finery, the fields worked on for centuries but showing the twenty-first-century pattern of agricultural care: treeless, hedgeless rolls of land fitted together, easy on the eye and impeccably looked after, the crops harvested by now, shorn close, the earth to be drilled, fertilised, weedkilled, harvested again.

Children ran about in their best clothes, eating sausages; two dogs followed hopefully.

Boy stood at a respectful distance, uninvited, waiting his turn with Michael. He'd repeated Raymond Luther's question every now and again – stop or play? – but hadn't received an answer yet, beyond a 'Hmm, what?' or a 'Let me think about that' and a 'Hang on a moment', which wasn't enough. Michael was holding a third glass of champagne and a paper plate with the remains of a meal on it, sitting on a shooting stick, in the very thick of it, with Pinky; they were having to talk loudly to hear themselves.

Pinky stood uncomfortably, trying to balance his drink and the paper plate in the same hand so he could pick at the food. He leaned over and shouted, 'She looked very good, I thought.'

Michael was watching Granny in her extraordinary hat, a glass of champagne tilting dangerously in her lap. She wore an absent expression on her face, he thought. He answered, 'Yes, not bad for a woman of eighty-five.'

'No, I meant Mattie.'

'Oh,' said Michael, wrong-footed, 'yes, Mattie looked very good. Well, guess what,' Michael complained, 'it was her mother's dress, my own wife's dress, as it turned out.' He lifted his champagne glass. 'The last time I saw it, I was getting married to it myself. That's what really, bloody well shut me up, Pinks.'

An usher came outside and made an announcement. Something was going on. At the same time, inside the tent, someone flapped an arm in front of the band – which wound down, comically. Speeches were about to start. Simon and Mattie and the Best Man were lining up on the stage. Glasses were topped up ready for the toast. Those who were outside made their way into the marquee to listen.

Patsy ducked out of her conversation and made her way to where Granny was parked in her chair. She dropped to one knee beside her. The people in front separated to allow them a clear view. The speeches, Patsy was saying. Granny Banana looked only at the ground.

Michael didn't trust himself to get off his shooting stick; he felt a bit woozy. Besides, he didn't want to listen to a whole list of thank-yous and so on, followed by an account of Simon's misdeeds when he was younger. He would stay where he was, outside, and let the whole event flow past him . . . breathe in and out . . . wait . . .

He became aware, then, of a little girl with hair tied in bunches, wearing a pretty blue dress to match her eyes, which were also painted blue. She had glitter sprinkled on her face like fairy dust, and her sandals were gold. She was asking Michael something.

'Hmmm?'

'Aren't you going to listen to the speeches?'

'Oh . . . well, no, I think not.'

'Everyone else is.'

Michael swayed on his stick. 'I sort of know what they're going to say anyway.'

'Oh.'

'Maybe I'll do my own speech, from here.' He tapped his glass with his fingernail. 'Silence please.'

She smiled. 'I like weddings.'

'Well, I think for the parents, you know, they are a bit like being in those relay races, when a man runs around the track with a stick, and then he passes it on to the next man.'

'We have relay races on sports day.'

'They're fun aren't they? Well,' he touched his chest, 'I remember when the bride was your age, and it was not so long ago.'

'Are you sad?'

'Good question. Yes. No. I just wonder what's going to happen next. Whether I like it or not, I'm handing over the baton and it's her turn . . . you know, hmm?' The little girl's eyes widened. He didn't want to frighten her. 'And I haven't quite earned my place on the team. I haven't run very quickly, you know . . . nor in a straight line . . . instead I've wandered around. Gone backwards even. Sat down for long periods. Left the arena on occasion . . .' He squared his shoulders, ground to a halt. 'It's your turn now,' he said to her.

She watched him for a while to make sure he'd finished, then she gave a clap. Her hands were so small they hardly made any sound. 'And now you have to lift your glass and give a toast,' she said.

'Oh yes . . . can I make a toast . . .' He pointed at the house and chapel. 'Ummm . . .' He couldn't think of anything.

'Go on.'

'Er, raise your glasses to . . . this lovely house, this valley . . .

this old country of ours, this . . . and . . .' He glanced at her to
see if she was still listening and she was, gravely. 'Mattie and
Simon.' He lifted his glass. 'The bride and groom!'

'You're not really the bride's father at all, are you,' said the
mystery girl.

'I am,' he protested.

The girl shook her head slowly. 'No you're not.'

She ran off. Michael blinked. He had rather fallen in love
with her in a fatherly way. It only meant he was a bit drunk. He
leaned forward, swayed on his stick and was lucky not to fall
off. The solid wall of applause from inside the tent rung in
his ears.

He launched himself into a standing position and folded the
shooting stick. If he walked around for a bit he'd be all right.
He filled and emptied his lungs several times. In the background the speeches continued but he had no inclination to go
in. He wished for his pipe but he'd left it somewhere.

This boy who'd been following him around for the last hour
or two was still there. Michael greeted him, shook his hand, even
took his shoulder. 'Now, d'you have a cigarette, young man?'

'Er . . . no.'

'Can you go into that tent and find me one, d'you think?
And a light for it.'

Michael waited for several minutes while the cigarette was
brought back for him. He took it and tapped the end against
the back of his hand. 'The warnings don't work, do they.'

'No,' agreed Boy, operating the lighter, but it was difficult
when Michael was swaying so; he had to follow the cigarette
with the flame but couldn't catch it. He needed to repeat his
question for Raymond. 'Um . . .'

Michael gave up trying. He ignored the moving flame for a
moment and interrupted, 'Buy a packet of tobacco, and there's
a warning as big as you like, yet I've been killing myself for
years with the stuff.' He leaned the shooting stick against his

hip, took the lighter and concentrated on doing it for himself, afterwards inadvertently pocketing the lighter and offering his thanks before turning away.

Boy followed, lurking at a distance; he had to stay with him, keep up his courage.

A while later, after the speeches had finished and people were circulating outside again, Michael cornered a glamorous young friend of Mattie's with golden hair and a long crimson dress. 'The bloody motorway lights are getting closer and closer,' said Michael. He wanted to poke his shooting stick through her shoe to stop her from running off.

The girl gave a bemused smile and asked, 'Motorway lights?'

Michael gestured in the direction of the A303. 'Is it my imagination or is the traffic getting louder – that darn road is moving towards us.'

'I don't know,' said the girl, 'we come from Cheshire and—'

Michael interrupted. His voice was sinister, 'But we're all travelling on motorways now aren't we. No turning off allowed.'

'Oh I see, you mean metaphorical motorways.'

'All herded together, closer and closer. Roped off. Packed like sardines.'

'I know,' said the girl, 'it's crazy.'

'Make a break for it and you trip and fall and you're not meant to be there anyway . . . and all the cars speeding past . . . brummmm . . .'

The girl had disappeared, as if it was one of those magic shows. Disconsolate, he cast around for another victim but couldn't find one.

Children ran back and forth, their cries a faint background to his melancholy. All that was needed now was to know for sure that some couple or other – not necessarily the bride and groom – was going to make love in the bushes. A good wedding needed that to happen before it could be called a success.

★

Mattie was called on to say goodbye to Granny Banana. Patsy
wheeled her over and joked, 'Banana's got another party to go
to, haven't you Granny?'

Mattie leaned over Banana's wheelchair and kissed her on
both cheeks. 'Thank you so much for coming and for staying
so long,' said Mattie loudly. 'It meant everything that you were
here. Everything.'

It took several goes and Banana had to open her mouth and
close it again three times before anything came out, but she
pointed and mumbled a few incomprehensible phrases and
eventually Patsy understood and her handbag was unhooked
from the back of the chair and she had it on her lap. Mattie had
to help her with the clasp and then Banana ferreted inside it
until she brought out something loosely wrapped in tissue. She
pushed at the paper clumsily to make sure the gift was covered,
then took Mattie's hand and planted the whole thing in her
palm, folding her fingers over it. She tried to say something,
but lost her way. She held on tight to Mattie's hand. 'Promise?'
she asked.

'Promise what?' Mattie was heartbroken at the old lady's
deterioration. She caught her mother's eye and they smiled at
each other.

'Always have breakfast,' mumbled Banana, 'together.
Hmmm?'

'That's *such* good advice,' said Patsy.

Mattie leaned over and kissed her grandmother's cheek
again. 'Is this for me?' She pointed at the gift. Granny Banana
made a motion with her hand and pointed. 'Wait,' she managed. 'When I'm gone. Open it.'

Patsy turned her mother-in-law around and wheeled her
towards the Hall. She nodded and mouthed at Mattie – yes, it's
for you.

When Banana was a safe distance away Mattie unfolded the
tissue paper and lying there was the wristband made of silver

and copper which had always been worn by Granny Banana. It was oval in shape and hinged at one end – and still warm. Mattie opened it to find the ornate lettering she knew was there, on panels of silver set into the copper. It read on one, 'In memory of many acts of kindness.' On the other was engraved, 'Christmas 1972'.

Later Mattie showed it to Simon, who put it on her wrist and closed the catch. Mattie looped her arms around his neck and the bracelet was in front of her eyes, an inch away. She would never, ever take it off.

Dusk fell. The jazz band packed up their gear; they were replaced by a rock group called Phantasma. Forty guests left but a hundred more arrived. The balance between friends and family swung in favour of friends and the average age of the partygoers dropped by fifteen years. Darkness closed in. Simon and Mattie were torn apart by their guests, snatching bits of conversation everywhere, happiness a cloud around them. A true depth of romance and passion had been inaugurated last night, and both the chapel ceremony and this party afterwards were like their being carried aloft by the crowd so to speak; and now there was just the first hint of the sexual glory awaiting them – the shine in Mattie's eye, his purposeful holding of her. They led the dancing. The tide of alcohol rose again swiftly, the volume was turned up.

Patsy headed outside for a breather; and after she'd finished a brace of 'hullos' and 'how are yous' to various of Mattie's friends her eye was caught by a pair of figures walking towards her from the direction of the car park, and her curiosity was piqued. She made out, then, that it was Uncle Philip, with what she thought was a school child on his arm, but as he came closer she saw it wasn't a girl but a fully grown woman, shorter than him, slender, and moving with the shy, self-conscious gait of a child. The woman, dressed in a green housecoat that looked like a school uniform, was dark-haired but with the whitest skin, and she looked painfully shy – could hardly meet her eye. Philip had his hand firmly clamped on hers, holding it in position on his arm. 'Patsy,' said Philip as they drew close, 'this is Natalia, my housekeeper.'

'My goodness, all right, yes. How d'you do?'

'She doesn't speak English very well, but I did want to invite her to the party, if that's all right.'

'Perfectly all right. Marvellous that you've made it!' Patsy's head spun with what Philip was obviously telling her. 'Where does she come from, what language does she speak?'

'Um . . . God. I don't know. Poland? Or is it Russia . . .'

'Never mind,' said Patsy hurriedly. 'She's here now Philip. Well done.'

'I sent a car for her.'

'Sent a car?'

'I mean, I drove back. It was the only thing I could think of. A lot of driving, but I thought why not?'

'Well, that is . . . wonderful. Welcome, Natalia, please make yourself utterly at home, and I hope you enjoy yourself very much. Philip, can you translate?'

'Er . . . no, I'm afraid I can't.' He was ashamed of himself. 'But she'll understand, I hope, more or less. Just gestures, you know,' he added lamely.

'All right, jolly good.' Pasty performed the first gesture that came to mind – she shook Natalia's hand. And then gave a bow and a curtsy as well, just to make sure. 'Natalia, welcome.' Natalia smiled and nodded so she must have got the message. 'I'm delighted, truly delighted, that Philip has invited you to the party.' Patsy was aware she was committing her usual crime of talking to foreigners as if they were children. She tried to think of a joke to make up for it but failed. Instead she went on her way, murmuring his name 'Philip, Philip,' as she went, shaking her head in astonishment – a two-hour round trip, it was, to Frome and back . . . She laughed; couldn't help herself. It was a mind-boggling scandal. Just wait until Michael found out. Patsy reached full speed across the grass, moving like a colourful boat in her frock, through the gathering darkness, as always on some important errand, to the very last.

Philip and Natalia went into the tent arm in arm, Philip almost speechless at such a volume of music and excess of physical contact all at once. Natalia was crushed against him. The band was revving up, beads of sweat broke out on the drummer's forehead, the din was punishing – and Natalia was happier, he could tell, now that conversation was impossible; it was dancing that was going on, everyone jerking and moving . . . if only he knew how. Instead he and Natalia stood by the bar and he got her a drink. Natalia looked at her shoes and at the roof of the tent and at the dancers and at the man working behind the bar and back at her feet again while Philip looked at her, and away, and at her again. An hour later they embraced clumsily. Both were flushed and slightly drunk. He leaned down to her ear but realised there was no point in saying anything. He clutched her, harder. They stood there. All eyes were on them; the scandal had by now run like wildfire through the wedding. They were famous.

Simon and Mattie, meanwhile, took a break from dancing and ran about on the lawn. The noise, the flashing lights and the vibration of the music dropped away as the night claimed them. The lawn swooped, tilted them to its edge. They became detached from the other youths who were playing the same game. They had gone further out and there was an unspoken agreement to allow them the space to disappear and find one another, alone. Simon could only see a white dress moving in the dark like a wayward, headless puppet, dancing. The youth and strength of Mattie's body gave power and movement to the ephemeral sight. He ran after her and gained ground and the very fact of her figure – face, hair, ankles, hands, the physical being – became evident, emerged into reality. He caught and held her. His breath sent a shiver down her spine. Her hand tightened on his arm and she led him towards undergrowth. They found a pathway through the rhododendrons and kept going, stepping through a greater darkness. She sneaked her hand in his. They turned corners and more corners. Minutes later they were standing in an embrace. She drew him to her, reaching a hand to the back of his neck and standing on tiptoe against him so they might kiss. His hands were gathering the great volume of her skirts, lifting them and feeling the usual pleasant shock of her stockinged legs. She unbuttoned his wedding clothes, pulled undone the bow tie, unclipped his trouser band. When he was standing in just an unfastened shirt and his socks he lifted her off the ground and she cried out, 'Ah . . .' as he entered her, but off they went, hard and fast and careless. As they made love an unspoken agreement arose between them: they wouldn't break eye contact not even as he lay her down on the bare earth. They were ready to love as never before. He knew enough of her by now to help her climb so they might tip over the edge together; and so they did . . . eye to eye they worked out the last inch of feeling between them.

Above them, in the half dark, a squall of midges danced; their orgy was a thin cloud, busily moving. The successful males had this trick of snapping off their penises and leaving them inside the females to stop anyone else getting in.

Spermatozoa leapt from Simon and swam inside Mattie, resting in a pool below her cervix. She trembled, a wrist draped over her eyes, her mouth slightly open. Her cervix ululated and sipped at the pool of sperm, which swam through. This time everything was set, they'd hit the rhythm: Mattie conceived. For all the signing of registers, the orders of service, the glasses of champagne, this secret, invisible happening, microscopic in scale, was everything.

Sir Michael Gough weaved over to where his younger brother Philip and Natalia stood. The music was too loud to be able to hear easily but none the less Michael demanded to be introduced.

'Natalia this is Michael, my older brother,' shouted Philip. 'Michael this is Natalia, my housekeeper.'

'Natalia!' exclaimed Michael. 'I've heard so much about you.' She hardly looked at him even though they shook hands. Shy little thing, wouldn't say boo to a goose, thought Michael. And she seemed to be a bit mentally retarded; she wasn't answering but instead looked to Philip to answer for her.

'She doesn't speak much English,' explained Philip. Michael nodded vigorously, made several gestures. 'Of course *I* realised, Natalia, very early on, that I'm no damn good at love. Absolutely no bloody good,' he swore. He directed his forefinger at his own chest and swayed gently. 'Instinct told me, *don't fall in love Michael*, because you can't look in enough directions at once.' He pointed up, down, to the left and right. 'Hmm? Ha ha.' He shook her hand again, then peeled off, feeling terrible jealousy. He reeled outside, to escape. The night air was soft, kind. Out there, in the parkland, silence waited, just out of reach. This beautiful place!

He became aware of someone at his elbow. He turned and had a good look. It was the young fellow who'd found the remote control, who'd popped out of nowhere. Had he been following him all this time? He was sure not. He must have come back. 'Hmmm? Ahh?' he asked vaguely, aware there was unfinished business between them. He looked Boy square in the face.

'Raymond Luther . . .' began Boy, taking his chance.

Michael tilted back the other way, brought up short. 'Is a brilliant man,' he said. Boy struggled on, 'He said that I can't go back until I have the answer to the question.'

'What question?'

'Should he press the Stop button, or the Play button? He said you'd know what it meant.'

'Oh yes, I remember.' Michael frowned, waited for a moment while his thoughts unrolled in this new direction – Raymond Luther. The coins sliding across the bar. Their conversation in the pub.

Stop or Play? All those valuable objects in the Hall, gathered by his family, bought and paid for, were quite rightfully his, surely? Why not sell them to the four corners of the world? No one would notice the difference, it was just a whole load of dead people's stuff, the same as you could buy in the junk shop in Amesbury, except it was worth more. It would be enough to fund his separation from Patsy and win a young girl's hand. Progress – it couldn't be stopped. And standing here was the young lad that he had to give the answer to, a queer-faced type . . . something lurked behind his heavily lidded eyes, thought Michael, a creaturely something which elicited an unsettling response. It made Michael want to stamp on him, before he himself were eaten. Yes, there was something predatory about him, maybe it was just his youth, that was always the threat, youth . . . and yet, the Hall standing there was so beautiful and harmless and eloquent, lit up, yes, on display.

'Tell him . . . thank you for the remote control. And . . .' He waited.

'I'm not allowed back without an answer,' Boy repeated.

'Tell him . . . tell Raymond . . . Stop. Tell him I'm too old. Stop.' Boy nodded, began to turn away. 'Hold on,' said Michael, 'no, wait,' and tears blinked from his eyes; it was definitely the alcohol. And Mattie's wedding of course. She loved that man. Everything, he thought vehemently, every bit of it, the whole social geography and the history of this old country of theirs, was all about who had loved whom, and what children had come of it. And he'd written on the land in exactly the same way, spiritually and physically. After all, how many of his forefathers had walked this exact spot? Their life was in his own veins; he had passed it on. And with all his heart Michael wanted Sitten Hall to stay exactly the same, nay, he wanted even to dial time backwards, make this place what it once had been, the whole nonsense and grandeur of it . . .

'Tell him, Rewind,' he said.